FYODOR SOLOGUB

The Little Demon

Translated by RONALD WILKS

D1258794

PENGUIN BOOKS

PENGUIN BOOKS

Published by the Penguin Group
Penguin Books Ltd, 27 Wrights Lane, London w8 5tz, England
Penguin Books USA Inc., 375 Hudson Street, New York, New York 10014, USA
Penguin Books Australia Ltd, Ringwood, Victoria, Australia
Penguin Books Canada Ltd, 10 Alcorn Avenue, Toronto, Ontario, Canada m4v 3b2
Penguin Books (NZ) Ltd, 182–190 Wairau Road, Auckland 10, New Zealand

Penguin Books Ltd, Registered Offices: Harmondsworth, Middlesex, England

The Little Demon was first published in Russian as *Melkii bes* in 1907.

Published in Penguin Books 1994
1 3 5 7 9 10 8 6 4 2

Set in 9.75/12 pt Monotype Baskerville
Typeset by Datix International Limited, Bungay, Suffolk
Printed in England by Clays Ltd, St Ives plc

THE LITTLE DEMON

FYODOR SOLOGUB (1863–1927) is the pen name of Fyodor Kuzmich Teternikov who was born in St Petersburg of humble parents. After his father's death, his mother became a domestic servant and with the help of her employer Sologub received a good education at a teachers' college and obtained a post as schoolmaster in a remote provincial town. His first two novels *Bad Dreams* (1896) and *The Little Demon* (1907), which he wrote between 1892 and 1902, are drawn from his experiences as a schoolmaster facing provincial stagnation and petty bureaucracy. For many years Sologub could not find a publisher for *The Little Demon* and it wasn't until 1905 that the novel appeared in magazine instalments. When in 1907 the novel was at last published in book form – to immediate and resounding success – he was able to leave his restricting career and devote himself to literature. His later novels, however, were less successful; *The Created Legend* (1908–12), a trilogy of novels in which Satanism, politics and fantasy are curiously interwoven and *The Snake Charmer* (1921) had indifferent receptions. Superior to these later novels are his many short stories, particularly the collections *Shadows* (1896), *The Sting of Death* (1907) and *Decaying Masks* (1909). In addition to being novelist, short-story writer and the author of several lyric dramas, Sologub was one of the leading poets of the Symbolist movement of the end of the century and wrote many volumes of highly polished poetry. The collections *The Fiery Circle* (1908) and *Pearly Stars* (1913) epitomize his dualistic, Manichean view of the universe as essentially evil, where in love, truth and beauty lurks the diabolical. Like most of the Symbolist writers, Sologub had little interest in politics and remained 'coldly aloof' after the 1917 revolution. His life in the following years was difficult and he was seldom published. He scraped a living mainly from translations. In 1921 his wife committed suicide and Sologub died a few years later in 1927.

RONALD WILKS studied Russian and Spanish language and literature at Trinity College, Cambridge after training as an interpreter, and later Russian literature at London University where he received his Ph.D in 1972. Among his other translations for Penguin Classics are *My Childhood*, *My Apprenticeship* and *My Universities* by Gorky, *Diary of a Madman* by Gogol, filmed for Irish Television, *The Golovlyov Family* by Saltykov-Shchedrin, *How Much Land Does a Man Need?* by Tolstoy and four volumes of stories by Chekhov, *The Party and Other Stories*, *The Kiss and Other Stories*, *The Duel and Other Stories* and *The Fiancée and Other Stories*.

CONTENTS

INTRODUCTION

THE LITTLE DEMON: HARSH LESSONS

All of Sologub's prose represents a sharp turn away from the highways of
naturalism, away from its methods of portraying everyday life, its language and its psychology. If one looks carefully at the stylistic experimentation of the most recent Russian prose, at its struggle with the traditions
of naturalism and at its attempts to build some sort of bridge to the
West, one can see Sologub's shadow. A new chapter in Russian prose
begins with Sologub.[1]

Thus wrote in 1924 Fyodor Sologub's younger contemporary Yevgeny Zamyatin, the author of the novel *We*, and concluded: 'Cruel
time will erase many, but Sologub's place in Russian literature is
assured.'

Now, as the century draws to a close, it is clear that Zamyatin's
prophecy has come true. Sologub has indeed earned a permanent
place in Russian literature, even though the time, which turned
out to be more than cruel, did everything it could to erase him.

Sologub, who was one of the most significant writers of the early
years of the twentieth century, died in 1927, and since then his
books have been published extremely rarely and reluctantly in
Russia. His undoubted masterpiece, the novel *The Little Demon*
(*Melkii bes*), was published unexpectedly in 1958 after an interval
of many years (in Siberia, by the Kemerovo publishing house).
This caused an almighty rumpus, a real scandal. There then
followed another awkward pause until the age of perestroïka. It
seems therefore that Sologub must have made too sharp a turn
away from the beaten track, that the route was too terrifying.

Before becoming a celebrated writer Sologub, who was born in
1863 and whose real name was Fyodor Kuz'mich Teternikov, had
to endure the unhappy years of a childhood of semi-poverty and to
experience floggings and humiliations. On graduation from the
Teachers' Institute he went to teach for ten years in the wild world
that was the Russian provinces in the 1880s. He had good reason

therefore to write in the Preface to *The Little Demon*: 'All the events in the novel, everything that concerns everyday life and the psychology of the characters, is based on the most precise observations – and I had plenty of models on my doorstep.'

Sologub started to write poetry early, and he wrote a lot, pouring his wounded soul into his verse. What he wrote was frequently mediocre, not only at the beginning of his career, but later, indeed always: in both his prose and verse there are masses of flat, workmanlike pieces. At the very beginning of the 1890s he was welcomed by the first generation Symbolists, moved to St Petersburg, and gradually joined their circle. As a young poet of 'poverty and labour', as a stubborn epigone of melancholy civic lyric poetry, Sologub, unhurriedly, explains himself to himself:

> The more harshly I observe myself,
> The easier I find it is to recognize others.

Such immersion in one's own self leads to the discovery of a rich world of human evil, which is portrayed by the poet in the unique, aromatic spirit of *fin de siècle*, sometimes despairingly, sometimes cynically, sometimes with a provocative sympathy. Sologub introduces into his verses themes previously forbidden in Russian culture – the themes of erotic and sadistic desires. The 'cook's son'[2] turns into a fashionable decadent refined by sinful passions, an 'underground Schopenhauer' who, nevertheless, dreams of a 'blessed land of eternal beauty'.

In 1905, at the height of the First Russian Revolution, *The Little Demon* was published in the journal *Questions of Life* (Nos. 6–11) (though the first complete publication of the work was an edition that appeared in 1907, the journal having ceased publication before the novel could be published in its entirety). Sologub, who had begun the novel in 1892 and completed it in 1902, became a national celebrity; the work itself in many respects sets the tone for literary experimentation in the 1910s, in the post-revolutionary period. In the heat of polemic Gorky christened these years a 'disgraceful decade', but with the passage of time it becomes ever clearer that it was precisely then that the Silver Age of Russian literature began. In the space of a few years such a wide variety of literary talents flourished, from Sologub to Gorky himself, from Blok to Khlebnikov, that the list of major names alone would fill a whole page. It is as if Russian culture before its dramatic *finale* had decided to produce a rich harvest of every possible type of talent, with the result that a whole century of study would be required just in order first to begin to understand, and then to investigate, *what* exactly had happened and *what* exactly was the essence of the new literature. No one has seriously doubted that many canons of nineteenth century literature were destroyed and overcome in the Silver Age, but the evaluations of this period have varied considerably. They range from the monstrous and absurd sentences pronounced on the Silver Age in the denunciatory articles written by many Soviet critics from the 1930s to the 1950s, to the rapturous praise (exaggerated at times) one finds in the works of Western scholars of Russian literature.

Only now has the time arrived for a more sober examination and evaluation of the art and literature of the beginning of the century. The fact that we were forcibly estranged from this culture not only impoverished but also weakened us Russians, for we were deprived of the opportunity to reflect freely on the cardinal problems of life and death, on human nature. The myth that portrays Sologub as a pessimist overcome by *The Sting of Death* (the title of one of his collections of short stories) is a threadbare and trivial myth, for ever since the days of Ancient Greece it has been traditional to look upon philosophy as the form of knowledge able to teach man the art of dying. If literature can do this too, so much the better. True, in his writings Sologub was much possessed by death: in the majority of his short stories death (not infrequently, the heart-rending death of children: 'In the Crowd', 'The Worm' and others) is the pivot of the story.[3] Sometimes this does indeed look obsessive, especially to members of a society in which, for many decades, people have been weaned away from thoughts about death in order to encourage their enthusiasm for reforming society: there is no death! Just as, similarly, there is no shadowy side to human nature: all evil comes from the imperfections of society with its antagonistic relations. This humanistic thought was inculcated over decades, though part of the blame also lies with the historical optimism of the nineteenth century. Sologub looked at things differently:

I have never belonged to Russia's ruling class and do not have the slightest personal reason for lamenting the passing of the old way of life. But I don't believe that it has passed away. Not because I like what we had before, but simply because in our present ways I can sense our past ways. I would believe that the old world had breathed its last, if not only the social structures, the external features of life had changed, but also the make-up of the soul. But it is precisely this latter change which can't be found in anyone, anywhere.

The 'old man' was allowed to die in his own bed, but a few years before his death his wife, Anastasiya Nikolayevna Chebotarevskaya, was subjected to interrogations, and she couldn't stand the strain: she threw herself into the river Neva.

I regard *The Little Demon* as a borderline work. This relatively short novel contains elements of an inner drama caused by the novel's own contradictory relationship to the powerful and universally significant tradition, created by truly outstanding individual talents, which is nineteenth-century Russian prose. Incidentally, one should say straight away that the author was not fully aware of any estrangement or conflict. On the contrary, it would appear that Sologub felt that he was protected by, and was himself continuing, the great tradition.

To bring out the artistic originality of *The Little Demon*, I shall recall some of the fundamental features of Russian classical realism. On the whole I select those features that not only form the collective image of the truth of the Golden Age of Russian prose, but that are reformulated, parodied or polemicized with in Sologub's novel. *The Little Demon* is a tense dialogue with the realist tradition.

Russian classical literature professes a *philosophy of hope*. This is one of the most important categories. There is no truth without hope. Russian literature is united in its certainty that the future must be and will be better than the present. In other words, it is directed towards a better future.

If there is to be a new life, there has to be a suitable new hero. The search for the *new man* ranges far and wide – from Chernyshevsky's *What is to be Done?* (Rakhmetov) to Dostoyevsky's *The Brothers Karamazov* (Alyosha Karamazov).

Russian realist literature is a literature not only of questions, but of answers too. One can even say that for the Russian tradition there are no unanswerable questions. In the spirit of the philosophy of hope, in which there is no place for despair or a lack of faith in 'a beautiful time', any question can be solved: either by means of a radical transformation of the institutions of society, or – if one takes the metaphysical route (Dostoyevsky, Tolstoy) – by means of discovering a universal meaning.

The philosophy of hope is intertwined with the idea of social progress. The *social* character of the tradition has been stressed, and with justice. Inherent in Russian literature is not only a critical attitude towards the crying shame that is social reality (*critical realism*), but also a search for the social ideal of universal justice.

In this way the truth, which is part of the tradition, is the same for all. Russian literature has always asserted the monism of truth and the pluralism merely of deviations from the truth. Rephrasing Dostoyevsky, who would have preferred to remain with Christ rather than with the truth,[4] one may say that if it had been found that the truth lay *outside* (or *without*) the people, Russian literature would have preferred to remain with the people rather than with the truth.

The philosophical–aesthetic principle that the Truth, the Good and Beauty form a trinity is not confined to the Russian tradition, but when it is complemented by the equating of truth and justice (in Russian the very word *istina*, 'truth', connotes justice), it acquires within that tradition a special logic and meaning. A whole series of conclusions follows from this trinity.

Truth *without* the good is inconceivable. The Russian tradition is distinguished by its enthusiastic advocacy of the good. In its model of the world evil never triumphs, and even if it does win some temporary victories, in the final analysis these victories turn out to be insignificant and illusory. The basic weakness of evil is that it has no independence, it isn't primordial. Instead it has some cause or other, and it is possible to remove these causes. In contrast to evil, good is independent and *has no cause*. As a result evil is ontologically powerless before good.

Truth *without* beauty is inconceivable. But beauty is also inconceivable *without* truth, that is, beauty cannot be self-sufficient. Beauty is directed at aims which are outside the realm of aesthetics (Dostoyevsky's 'beauty will save the world'). The link of beauty with evil gives birth to a terrible, demonic beauty. Elements of demonic beauty can be seen in Pechorin, the hero of Lermontov's *A Hero of Our Time*, but they find fullest expression in the form of Stavrogin in Dostoyevsky's *The Devils*. However, this is not a genuine beauty, but merely an alluring mask, a deception and, in the last analysis, a deformity, an ugliness.

In the Russian tradition the notion of beauty is indissolubly linked with chasteness. Preference is given to spiritual, platonic love rather than to sensuality, or carnal, physical passion. The latter is frequently exposed, discredited, parodied. I won't even mention Tolstoy's *The Kreutzer Sonata*. The erotic is placed beyond the pale of literature, but even beyond the pale it is more ironic than erotic (Barkov's poems, Pushkin's 'The Gavriliad', Lermontov's poems written when he was in the Guards). Within such a tradition Artsybashev's completely innocuous novel *Sanin* (1907), denounced as pornography, caused a genuine scandal.

Finally, and arguably this is one of the most important things of all, the truth is inconceivable *without* meaning. In other words, the absurdity, chaos and disorder of life are evaluated in Russian literature as chance, temporary, inauthentic phenomena, conditioned by concrete circumstances of a social or psychological nature. These circumstances can and should be removed, and with their removal life will regain its lost meaning. The idea that human life is full of an eternal meaning informs all Russian literature and returns us once more to the philosophy of hope.

And so, all the parts of the artistic model of the world created by Russian literature are in accord with one another and form a *harmonious* whole. Very important is the projection into the future, which is literally tangible in every line, the dissatisfaction with the present, the demand for change. This dissatisfaction, this refusal to be reconciled with vice, is a source of energy of a revolutionary kind. Russian literature was frequently not only the ally of the Russian movement for liberation, but also its ideological underpinning. For precisely this reason this literature had the right to talk about the negative, nihilistic tendencies that were appearing ominously in this broad movement (Dostoyevsky's *The Devils*). It also needs to be said that Russian literature facilitated the formation of a particular cast of mind, a special type of national consciousness, a way of thinking directed towards ideal models, a way of thinking whose influence can be felt even today.

The artistic model of the world that the realist tradition created embraced the most varied levels of existence and gave answers to the most pressing problems on the social, national, individual and metaphysical planes. In this model, which in contrast to other models is sometimes interpreted as a mirror held up to or a window on to the world (in doing so the interpreters neglect the fact of its selectivity and forget that it possesses its own special structural and typological characteristics), we find the most varied and at times diametrically opposed points of view. We find arguments that to this day arouse the passions and excite the intellects of millions of readers. One can say without fear of contradiction that nineteenth-century Russian literature is one of the richest and most important cultural phenomena of human culture as a whole.

Nevertheless, towards the end of the nineteenth century, at the beginning of the 1890s, a literary trend arises and starts to form a particular literary movement, a movement that calls into doubt certain beliefs which had been developed by the tradition. Let us leave to one side the question of the genesis of Russian Symbolism and its links with the French literature and German philosophy of the time. It is, however, important to determine where the dividing line signalling the break with the tradition lies, where the watershed of different literary directions is to be found. In this regard one should say that the move away from the tradition is signalled above all by the division of the tradition into live and dead elements (the dead elements being those which have, in the eyes of the supporters of the new art, outlived their usefulness). This division cannot occur within the system: a view from outside is required.

Dmitry Merezhkovsky's programmatic article 'On the Causes for the Decline and on the New Currents in Contemporary Russian Literature' (1893) is just such a view of the tradition from the outside. In it the author picked out three main elements of the new art: its 'mystical content, symbols and the broadening of artistic impressionability'. Russian artistic practice of that time answered to this manifesto only in part, however, in Symbolist poetry; the novel remained under the influence of the tradition right up to the 1907 book publication of *The Little Demon*. Although Sologub's first major prose work, *Bad Dreams*, which he wrote in the 1880s and 1890s, also contained extra-realistic elements (in it naturalistic features are fantastically interwoven with features of the Symbolism that was in the making), it did not become an important turning point in the move away from the tradition, largely because it did not come together artistically. It was precisely in *The Little Demon* that the dismemberment of the tradition into live and dead elements took place, and it was the correlation of these elements that turned the novel on its head.

At the same time, *The Little Demon* in a certain sense relies on a realist aesthetics. Its link with the artistic systems of Gogol, Dostoyevsky and Chekhov is beyond doubt. Tolstoy's influence can be felt in the novel's very exposition. Sologub opposes outward appearances to the essence. In the town described by Sologub 'all was perfect peace and harmony'. But Sologub goes on to warn that 'appearances, however, are deceptive', and it *appears* to the reader that hard upon this will follow an exposure of these outward appearances, analogous to a Tolstoyan exposure, 'the tearing away of all and sundry masks'.

A brief characterization of the novel's content would probably say that it gives the impression, if read in the tradition of realist literature, of being a work about the absurdity of Russian provincial life at the close of the last century. Such a résumé puts *The Little Demon* in line with other realistic works, and with many of Chekhov's short stories in particular. But if one analyses the novel more attentively, one notices that such a résumé is too verbose: some of the words are clearly optional and are just asking to be put in brackets. Therefore a novel about the absurdity of (Russian) (provincial) life (at the end of the last century) becomes a novel about the absurdity of life in general, if one understands 'life' as meaning everyday, social, *earthly* reality. In line with this change of emphasis the myth about the main hero, Peredonov, whom critics have at times been happy to rank alongside Gogol's Chichikov from *Dead Souls*, Goncharov's Oblomov, Chekhov's 'Man in a Case', and so on, is transformed too.

Let us examine how this peculiar reduction takes place. I should point out that the demonstration of the absurdity and idiotic nature of any concrete form of life is in keeping with the tradition and even represents one of its fundamental socio-critical principles. If *such* a life is absurd, then it follows that one has to live differently, one has to transform life – thus preaches the tradition. To a certain extent Sologub is in agreement with this sermon. But he cannot accept it in its entirety.

The author of the novel is unwilling to be reconciled with the life he describes. Sologub's contemporaries, writers with revolutionary inclinations (in particular, Gorky and Blok, both of whom pointed out the social importance of both the novel and the figure of Peredonov), insisted on this point. It is particularly obvious that this is the case in those chapters that in compositional terms are an almost exact replica of the device in Gogol's *Dead Souls*: the hero's visiting of various people in the furtherance of his single aim. Peredonov does the rounds of the most influential people in town, and in the description of these visits, in the discussions and manners of the city fathers, are gathered together many details that point to local time (the 1890s). Conversations take place concerning the beneficial effect of the death penalty, a book by a certain Madame Shteven, the role of the nobility in society, and so on. If one summarizes the narrator's appraisals and takes his sarcastic and ironic tone into account, he emerges as a fairly progressive figure. At the same time though this is, in essence, a hopeless progressivism, one which lacks any future prospects.

Social changes of which the author would approve take on a utopian appearance, a development that stems from the thought that base human nature is unchangeable. Peredonov's words about a future life parody Chekhov's dreams: '"Do you think that people will still have to work two or three hundred years from now? . . . people themselves wouldn't have to work. Machines would do everything. You would only have to turn a handle, like a barrel-organ, and there you are . . . But it would be boring to turn it for long."' Peredonov's interlocutor, Volodin, happily picks up these words, but feels sad at the fact that '"we shan't be here"'. '"You mean *you* won't be here, but I shall,"' argues Peredonov. '"God grant you,"' Volodin gaily replied, '"live two hundred years and crawl around on all fours for three hundred."' This whole scene is a profanation of the philosophy of hope. A shroud of absurdity eclipses the bright, optimistic dreams.

Although the backdrop of the provincial town, this hotbed of gossip, rumours, slander and barbarity, is of some importance, it is not of central significance. There is no other form of life with which life in 'our town' is contrasted in the novel. In particular, there is no juxtaposition of life in the town with life in St Petersburg or Moscow, the sort of comparison that is so vivid in Chekhov's *Three Sisters* (*three* of Sologub's sisters are potential brides for Peredonov). In Chekhov's play the province is horrified by its own absurdity, but at least the distant metropolitan life takes on a certain enigmatic meaning. It is not a question of Chekhov's sharing his heroines' opinion concerning the big city. It is simply that Chekhov's sisters maintain an opposition of 'genuine' existence (taking the form of metropolitan life) to 'inauthentic' existence, of 'ideal', to which all thoughts are directed, to 'reality', an opposition that indeed may be illusory, but which is nevertheless sufficiently well defined and which is able to express metaphorically the philosophy of hope. Sologub maintains no such tension for his heroes. The world of the capital, where the mythical princess lives on whom depend Peredonov's prospects for receiving the post of inspector of schools (Peredonov himself travels to St Petersburg hoping to meet with her), does not act as a counterweight. (One may contrast this also with *Madame Bovary*, where Emma's trip, not to Paris even but just to Rouen, is a real occasion for celebration!) The capital turns out to be a spectral, unreal city, lacking all qualities. It makes no difference whether it exists or not. Lyudmila orders perfume from St Petersburg by post, but she too is indifferent to the capital. Thus the town is not contrasted with anything, and therefore everything that goes on in it comes to symbolize the *norm*. It is true that Volodin and Peredonov start to talk about their 'home town', but this conversation quickly degenerates into a senseless quarrel. Lacking a 'home town', lacking, what is more, a biography (the reader merely finds out in passing a few facts about Peredonov's family and past), the hero, along with all the other characters, lives in a town which embodies a generalized social setting for life, that is, a town which has come to symbolize the real world. In this way the novel banishes any hope not just for another time – the future – but for another place too.

There is another dashing of hopes that should be mentioned. In a certain respect *The Little Demon* can be seen as a novel about Peredonov's hope that, with a little help from Varvara, he will receive the post of inspector of schools. Although all Peredonov's thoughts revolve around this desired position, his hopes are non-existent from the very start. It is clear that Varvara is incapable of obtaining a position for Peredonov, but she does all she can to marry him, playing on his hopes by means of forged letters from the princess. As a result a novel about hope turns into a novel about a foul deception. Hope becomes synonymous with deceit.

In contrast to the meaning possessed by the provincial setting, the meaning of the national aspect of the novel has many layers. The novel is rich in specifically Russian features. Events unfold in an atmosphere that is the product of centuries of national history. The mutual relations between the different segments of society, between the different estates, but also people's habits, customs, rites, superstitions and their language, are all marked by a local colouring. The peculiarly 'Russian Spirit' and 'Russian smell' of the novel is unmistakable. In *The Little Demon* Sologub has created his own image of Russia, and it is not a flattering one. It is a picture of a heavy, immobile country set in its old Russian ways. To a certain degree one would be justified in calling it a caricature. The image of Russia Sologub has created is that of a country which has no future, because it does not possess any forces capable of constructive activity. The author himself referred in his Preface to the novel to the concept of Peredonovism, which by analogy with Oblomovism has the potential to take on the significance of a national myth. But this myth is far darker than not only the sweet myth of Oblomovism, so dear to the national mind, but also the brood of Gogol's dead souls, for Gogol's epic offers a bright image ('the bird-troika') of a Russia overcoming the diabolic nightmare. Once again, Sologub has no contrast of 'given' to 'ideal'. His image of Russia is what it is. And if in Gogol's novel the souls are dead and immobile, Sologub has, instead of a necropolis, a kingdom of madness. This kingdom is ruled by the little demon. It can not be overthrown.

In this sense local time is not of decisive significance. The novel bears the features not of any clearly defined time, but of a period of *achronism*, a period of *without time*, of stagnation, a time out of joint; this concept characterizes various periods of Russian history. In the novel, *achronism* triumphs over time. One can even say that, according to the conception contained in the novel, *achronism* is a constant of Russian history.

Any discussion of the social sources of Peredonovism should also point out that Sologub's answer as to the causes of this problem differs from traditional criticism of reactionary obscurantism. A useful contrast is provided by the main character of Chekhov's short story 'Man in a Case'.[5] Chekhov's Belikov is the child of his society's lack of freedom. All that is needed for Belikov to vanish of his own accord, to disappear into thin air, is for the fear in that society to be dispersed and for its bureaucratic ways and authoritarian tendencies to be done away with. Not for nothing does the story end with the listener's call to arms: '"No, I can't live this kind of life any more!"' As is well known, Chekhov's story is discussed in Sologub's novel. In actual fact, though, it is a conversation that fails to get off the ground. If in Dostoyevsky's *Poor Folk* Devushkin has read Gogol's 'The Overcoat' and feels personally affronted by it, then Peredonov (just like Volodin) not only has not read 'Man in a Case', but he hasn't even heard of 'a Mr Chekhov'. Chekhov's story appeared while Sologub was working on his novel. He could not avoid responding to this story, whose hero had turned out to be one of Peredonov's colleagues. To have passed over the story in silence would have been to acknowledge the thematic influence of Chekhov. Sologub chooses another path: he absorbs the story, he includes it in his own story in order to overcome any real or imagined anxiety of influence, to overcome any dependence on it. He even points out in the exchange between the characters the edition of the journal *Russian Thought* in which the story appeared (incidentally, and interestingly, the wrong number is given); but he does not go on to discuss it. The only opinion about the story belongs to the emancipated young lady Adamenko: '"It's very well written and observed, isn't it?"' In this way it is hinted that, in the eyes of Adamenko and her younger brother, Peredonov is Belikov's double.

It is however an extremely questionable likeness. Peredonov is far more rooted in real life than is Belikov, who is a social and not an ontological being. Peredonov can't be *abolished* by a decree or by reforming the state educational system. Just like Belikov, he stands fairly and squarely on the side of order, and he is just as obsessed by the question 'But what if something should come of it?'; yet all this is but one side of his conceit. At bottom, his delirious, arrogant and ambitious plans, his thirst for power are not shared by Belikov. Belikov frightens others, is himself frightened and in the end dies a *victim* of an all-embracing fear. He is more of an instrument of arbitrary power, the agent of someone else's will, than he is a deliberate tyrant and despot. In contrast to him Peredonov is a cruel sensualist, and his sadistic passions are subordinate to a Karamazovian force (I have in mind old man Karamazov), and not to any social forces.

The social roots of Peredonovism are two-fold. They are conditioned not only by the reactionary régime, but also by Peredonov's own liberal past. By representing Peredonov as an unbeliever for whom the rites and sacraments of the church are 'evil witchcraft' aimed at 'enslaving and stupefying the masses', Sologub is at one with Dostoyevsky. He shares Dostoyevsky's criticism of liberal consciousness: when it lacks a metaphysical dimension, liberal consciousness takes on a destructive, nihilistic character, as Dostoyevsky shows in *The Devils*. Indeed, the echo of Dostoyevsky's novel in Sologub's title (Dostoyevsky's *Besy* should perhaps be translated as *The Demons* and not *The Devils* or *The Possessed*) acquires an ideological significance. Peredonov has taken in the utilitarian ideas of the radical writers and critics, the *shestidesyatniki* ('men of the 1860s'): 'He preferred the smell of freshly manured fields to any perfume – in his opinion it was very healthy.' But this utilitarianism decayed after a while because it did not have any firm ground under it. The result is that 'any thought of hard work depressed and frightened Peredonov'. Peredonov is the repository of the myths of the liberal intelligentsia, myths which are the subject of Sologub's irony. '"In every town,"' claims Peredonov, '"there's an officer from the secret police. During the day he doesn't wear uniform and he works in the civil service, or does business deals or something. But at night, when everyone's asleep, he puts on a blue uniform and in two seconds he's a police officer."' Peredonov considers himself to be a 'deadly enemy of the State', and imagines that 'he had been under police surveillance from his student days'. On the other hand, and in defiance of the liberal tradition, the image of the police officer, Lieutenant-Colonel Rubovsky, has been fashioned without any particular antipathy. Rubovsky 'knew everything about everyone in the town and loved listening to gossip, but he himself was a model of tact and discretion'. Sologub even stresses that Rubovsky is 'charming and therefore well liked in local society', although he also notes the fact that the Lieutenant-Colonel keeps some of Peredonov's wild denunciations 'just in case he should need them later'.

Sologub therefore divides the social responsibility for Peredonov's madness (although this madness cannot be explained away by social factors alone) between, on the one hand, the obscurantist régime, and the liberal–nihilistic ideology on the other. Such a sharing out of the responsibility leads, in essence, to the conclusion that everyone is to blame, and that, accordingly, a whole layer of life in society in general is corrupt and corrupting. The thing to do is not to change it, but to overcome it, to run away from its inauthenticity. The falsity and inconsistency of progressive aspirations are incarnated in the figure of the emancipated Adamenko. She welcomes 'Man in a Case' and is indignant at Belikov, yet at the same time she is thinking up refined, enlightened punishments for her younger brother.

The theme of the absurdity of the world is expressed particularly vividly by the all-embracing motif of human stupidity. Sologub creates his own town of fools, paralleling the town of Glupov (Stupidville) in Saltykov-Shchedrin's *A History of a Town*. The word *glupy*, 'stupid', is one of the words most frequently met in the novel. It characterizes a considerable number of the personages and phenomena in the work. I shall give a few examples: the 'stupid-looking landowner' Murin; the inspector of national schools, Sergei Potapovich Bogdanov, 'an old man with a stupid dark face'; Volodin is a 'stupid young man'; Grushina's children are 'stupid and evil'; the mayor Skuchayev seemed 'simply a tottering, stupid old man'; the face of the district police chief Minchukov is 'eager, sensuous and stupid'; during an attempt to marry Volodin off, Peredonov and Volodin 'looked more solemn and stupid than usual'; the Rutilov sisters bawl 'stupid words from ditties', and so on and so forth. In relation to Peredonov himself the narrator constantly uses the more specific epithets 'dull' and 'gloomy'. Sologub's town is indeed gloriously, famously idiotic; what is more, against this background of idiotism its inhabitants grow even more stupid by believing each and every cock-and-bull story, because they are frightened of being thought stupid. The piling up of stupidity creates the impression that this stupidity can't be eradicated.

It is not surprising that in this bacchanalia of stupidity people are very slow and reluctant to recognize that Peredonov is a madman. His insanity is tangible even on the very first pages of the novel, but despite this a climactic crime is needed for it to be recognized as such. In a world where ignorance is king, madness becomes the *norm*. This is precisely how the novel's heroes treat Peredonov: as a normal member of society. People make friends with him, visit him, drink with him, play billiards with him. What is more, he is a very eligible bachelor, and various women are engaged in a secret battle to marry him. The grotesque scene in which Peredonov asks for the hand of each of the three Rutilov sisters in turn provides evidence that Peredonov is thought of as a good catch. Even Lyudmila, whose role it is in the novel to act as Peredonov's most obvious antagonist, and who responds to his offer of marriage with a guffaw, nevertheless is quite willing to take it seriously, as a natural and reasonable proposition. Sometimes those surrounding Peredonov can see that there is something the matter with him, but they regard his behaviour as part of his eccentricity. Peredonov's normality is the grotesque basis on which the novel is built. To divine that Peredonov is suffering from mental illness, to individualize his case and isolate him, would be to put an end to the diabolical delusion, the hallucination, to dam the novel in mid-stream; but the delusion continues, and the novel keeps on flowing.

The influence of the Gogolian and Chekhovian traditions can be felt in *The Little Demon*. The very approach to, and treatment of, the heroes splits into two, taking on Gogolian features one moment, Chekhovian features (marked also by Dostoyevsky's practice) the next. To a certain extent the duality and instability of the world in the novel are achieved due to the fact that the characters are neither the dead souls of Gogol's novel (where the only *live* soul is the narrator), nor the living souls of Chekhov's short stories, where the subtle psychological manner of writing facilitates the creation of images of perfectly adequate, real flesh-and-blood individuals. In Chekhov's stories the possibility of far-fetched, strained interpretations is almost totally excluded, since they would contradict the psychological basis of the narrative. The story-line of the prospective romance between Varenka ('Aphrodite') and Belikov ('Judas') in 'Man in a Case', which struck some of Chekhov's contemporaries as lacking in verisimilitude, is perhaps therefore one of the few exceptions proving the Chekhovian rule. On the other hand, we are not at all disturbed by the fact that Chichikov is confused with Napoleon. Within the system of Gogol's fantastic prose such a grotesque incident is totally in order, though to what extent a Gogolian hero can be called a human being is of course a problem. The second volume of *Dead Souls* was doomed to fail from its outset, as a consequence of the poetics of the first volume: in a kingdom of masks living people would have destroyed the very texture of Gogol's masked epic 'poem'.

Sologub however aims for just such a rupture, and achieves it by bringing into his novel the completely lifelike (psychological) images of Lyudmila, Sasha Pylnikov, Sasha's aunt, Sasha's landlady and others. The other heroes, the various officials, Volodin and Peredonov himself, lie somewhere in between Chekhovian and Gogolian personages. They are half-alive, half-dead souls, a kind of not-fully-human people lacking a well-defined outline (like the elusive 'little demon'[6] itself). Their consciousness is obscure, dark, as is true of Gogol's characters, but they have a certain capacity for intelligent behaviour, as is the case with Chekhov's. This intermediate position, which gives birth to mediocrities who are neither one thing nor the other, qualitatively changes the novel's semantics, so that it is no longer straightforward or monosemous, but becomes two-faced. There is an internal discrepancy in the characters in *The Little Demon*. They remind me of centaurs, and their Janus-nature is blatantly underlined in the image of Varvara in particular: the body of a nymph and the wanton face of a drunkard and voluptuary.

The joining together of that which cannot be joined together (in the eyes of the realist tradition, at any rate) creates an impression of absurdity and nonsense. Gogol's heroes do not create such an impression, since they are the product of the satirical hyperboliza-tion of one particular aspect or another of the human character. They are what they are. There can be no tragedy in their world. When the public prosecutor dies of fright because he fears he is going to be exposed, his death is only relative: he is *already* dead, from the very beginning, and his death scene is if anything comic. A diametrically opposite example is the death of Tolstoy's Ivan Ilyich. *The death of Ivan Ilyich* describes the death of a *human being*. As far as Sologub is concerned, Volodin's violent death is some-where in between: he is primordially a sacrificial victim (a ram, a sheep, a lamb), but at the same time this centaur also has some human features. Again, the result is that one sees double.

The spectral, half-alive, half-dead world of Sologub's novel corresponds to the philosophical and aesthetic principles of the Symbolist prose which was then coming into being, and which expressed itself most fully in Andrey Bely's novel *Petersburg*. It is impossible to change life in such a world of ghosts. The only option is to escape from it on to another plane of reality.

In Sologub's novel the amorous liaison between Lyudmila and the schoolboy Pylnikov provides such an escape. In analysing this layer of the novel it helps to recall that traditionally Russian literature has stressed that all people are equal before the truth. The escape that Sologub proposes, however, is intended for the chosen few and is in essence forbidden. Moreover, the fact that it is forbidden fruit, that it is illicit, is the very thing that, according to Sologub, constitutes its sweetness. This is an élitist solution of the problem, and as such it is alien to the democratic principles of the tradition in general, and to Dostoyevsky with his critique of the idea of Man-godhood in particular.

One should make special note of the role of the narrator in the story of the relationship between Lyudmila and Sasha. He is clearly someone with a stake in the proceedings. In the scenes of erotic pranks the narrator almost seems to become a character in the novel as he takes on the role of a voyeur, greedily spying on the scenes where 'darling Lyudmilochka', the seducer, undresses Sasha and dresses him up in women's clothes. He even seems to assert, through Lyudmila, that 'The best age for boys is between fourteen and fifteen.'

Let us now imagine a traditional narrator. How would he have responded? He would have found angry words of condemnation for Lyudmila and would have wept for the poor, corrupted victim. But Sologub's narrator is different. One moment he's touched by it all, the next he seems to be ashamed that he's touched by it, and tries to hide behind words about how these are just innocent, joyful amusements; but he gets himself tied up in knots and ends up by giving away his true feelings. The narrator gets so carried away by the corrupting of the young 'transvestite' that he literally loses his head: Lyudmila turns out to be merely a female screen, a way of disguising his homosexual passions. Russian literature had never before known such an unchaste narrator, and indeed had always had a completely straightforward, one-sided attitude towards 'un-natural vices' (in fact it totally avoided describing them, with the exception of Dostoyevsky ('Stavrogin's Confession' in *The Devils*).

Thus not only are the laws of decency broken, but the very literary rules themselves. The failure to keep one's distance means that the erotic situation ceases to be an extended metaphor (a metaphor about escaping a vulgar life), and takes on instead the features of an unambiguously expressed passion.

The forbidden nature of the passion is stressed, as is the notion that only a forbidden passion is capable of bestowing real pleasure. At the same time eroticism in *The Little Demon* possesses a liberating function. It urges one to seek pleasure and reflects an idea similar to Dmitry Merezhkovsky's idea concerning the 'sanctification of the flesh', the 'Third Testament' whose purpose it is to unite Christian morality with paganism (the pagan Lyudmila shamefully confesses her love for 'Him . . . who was crucified'). This gospel of eroticism has a certain propagandistic element, although it is addressed not to the general public, but to like-minded spirits, to the initiated. But liberation is impossible, and in the scene with the director of the high school, Khripach, Lyudmila is forced to conceal the true nature of her relationship with Sasha. Neither Khripach nor Sasha's aunt, who has been worried by the rumours, would be able to understand her. The gulf between Lyudmila's pagan moral-ity, with which the narrator is in sympathy, and the generally accepted norms of behaviour (Khripach's position) is too wide for one to try to reduce it by means of frank admissions. One just has to fall back on lies.

Such an atmosphere of falsehood is fatal, and it exists in many novels for the initiated. One can find it in the novels of André Gide and D.H. Lawrence, and also in Nabokov's notorious novel, whose hero enters into a marriage of convenience with Lolita's mother in order to conceal his wanton passion for the twelve-year-old girl. In this sense one can see in *The Little Demon* and *Lolita* a mirror symmetry: the grown-up Lyudmila and the schoolboy Pylnikov, the experienced sensualist Humbert Humbert and the American schoolgirl.

True, in *Lolita* the erotic element consistently takes on the function of a metaphor, the explicitness of a number of scenes notwithstand-ing. Rejecting moralistic interpretations of the novel, Nabokov takes his stand on a position of aesthetic, not erotic, pleasure-seeking. In his Afterword to *Lolita* he writes that 'For me a work of fiction exists only in so far as it affords me what I shall bluntly call aesthetic bliss.'

But the very propounding of pleasure-seeking (erotic or aesthetic) puts one at odds with the Russian literary tradition. Although the tradition has been prepared to allow epicurean, hedonistic elements (above all thanks to Pushkin's influence), it has however always shunned them and made them peripheral. It has chosen instead (Gogol, Dostoyevsky and particularly the later Tolstoy) to preach a gospel of no mercy to the pleasure principle, and to argue for the ideal of sacrifice and the serving of supra-individualistic (social and metaphysical) values.

The erotic subject-matter of *The Little Demon* is thus a rather unusual phenomenon for the Russian reader, and is a measure of the shift in direction away from the tradition. Moreover the erotic themes form a ramifying system which is by no means exhausted by the Lyudmila–Sasha relationship. Indeed, on the novel's very first page, the motif of incest appears, in relation to Peredonov and Varvara ('"How can you possibly marry Varvara?" asked the red-faced Falastov. "After all, she's your cousin! What gave you the idea it's legal to marry blood relatives?"'). (The Russian, more ambiguously, uses the word *sestra*, the primary meaning of which is 'sister'.) This is a note that continues to sound in the work: not confirmed, but not refuted either.

Peredonov's thoughts about the princess are tinged with geron-tophilia: 'She's barely warm and smells like a corpse, Peredonov imagined, and a feeling of wild lust made him feel quite faint.' The letter Peredonov sends to the princess is of interest. Gerontophilia is used as the pretext for a parody, the target of which is not the tradition that was being overcome, but the Symbolism that was then in the process of coming into being. Sologub ironizes at the expense of Symbolist love: 'I love you because you are cold and remote ... I want a cold, distant mistress. Come then, and let us share our love.' In this repetition of the favourite Symbolist attributes 'cold and distant', and in the unexpected juxtaposition of the princess to Varvara, who 'sweats', one can see the author's attitude to the newfangled stock phrases of Symbolism.

The relationship between Lyudmila and Sasha is permeated by sadistic complexes: 'He wanted to do something to her, be it pleasant or painful, tender or shameful — but what? Should he kiss her feet or beat her long and hard with supple birch twigs?' One finds a suitable answer in Lyudmila's dreams: 'She was seated on a throne and was watching the naked boys whip each other. They laid Sasha on the floor ... and beat him. He laughed and cried and she laughed too ...' Before Sologub, sadism in Russian literature had a socio-psychological motivation. Exploiting their power and virtual immunity from any punishment, the 'strong' mocked and offended 'the humiliated and the wronged'. Sologub converted sadism from a social vice into a human passion. There are many shades in this dark passion. In his discussion of the reasons why Peredonov is attracted to Varvara Sologub notes that: 'Perhaps it was because he enjoyed making fun of and being cruel to her.' There are numerous scenes of mockery, humiliation and offences in the novel, but the wife of the public notary Gudayevsky emerges as a particularly loathsome individual, since she gains sensual pleasure from watching her own son being flogged.

In general it should be said that Sologub has shown no mercy to his heroines. He has created a 'rouged' gallery of the most repulsive female images: Varvara, Grushina (the intriguer and forger of letters, whose body is covered in flea-bites), the Peredonovs' drunken landlady Yershova, with whom Peredonov dances a wild dance in the courtyard, Adamenko, Mrs Gudayevsky, the procuress Vershina, Mrs Prepolovensky. Instead of worshipping the Russian woman, as is normal for the tradition, Sologub portrays his women as drunken, shameless, lascivious, lying, malicious, coquettish *fools*. In the context of the tradition it would be possible to call Sologub a misogynist, were it not for the fact that his male characters are just as vile.

Amid all the images of the 'evil spirit' created by Russian literature, Sologub's *nedotykomka*, the 'little demon', occupies a special place. A Russian reader can't be surprised by witches and werewolves, changelings and ghosts. From Pushkin's story 'The Undertaker' and his fairy tales in verse to the devil in *The Brothers Karamazov*, from Gogol's 'Viy' to Chekhov's 'The Black Monk', Russian literature has more than its fair share of foul evil spirits.

However the evil spirit is either of a folkloric nature ('Viy') or forms a part of a grotesque satire (Dostoyevsky's 'Bobok'). Even more widespread is the evil spirit that is treated as a hallucination which provides an *explanation* for certain aspects of a work. Both Ivan Karamazov's devil and Kovrin's black monk help the respective authors to illuminate their heroes from inside, to force the unconscious to reveal itself. In this way the evil spirit is a device which gives the writer the opportunity to speak the whole truth about his hero, but the actual existence of the evil spirit does not possess any objective meaning. Through the black monk we get to learn more about Kovrin (about the extent of his vanity in particular), but Kovrin doesn't make the black monk any more visible. The little demon is a far more objective image. Peredonov is perhaps more of a *medium*, who is able to see it as a result of his sickness; but this does not mean that Peredonov's mental sickness gave birth to the little demon. The little demon provides more evidence about the chaotic condition of the world of things than it does about Peredonov's madness. It is a symbol of this chaos and as such belongs to the world, and not to Peredonov. The little demon threatens everybody without exception, and it is significant that its existence continues beyond the bounds not only of Peredonov's mental state but also of the novel itself. We find its double in a famous poem by Sologub, where it torments the author himself. It is this objectivization of the little demon that makes it a unique figure in Russian literature.

In *The Little Demon* Sologub does not transubstantiate life into a 'sweet legend', but manages to create something which is its artistic equivalent largely by means of a crude and impoverished linguistic texture that lacks a metaphorical dimension. The deliberate monotony of the descriptions of nature and characters alike also helps in this process of creating something that corresponds to life. The parsimoniousness and laconicity of *The Little Demon* allowed Andrey Bely to make a most intriguing observation to the effect that in this novel Sologub's 'Gogolism' reinvents itself as 'Pushkinism'. Bely found the self-possession of a 'quasi-Pushkinian prose style' in the style of *The Little Demon*.

The novel is built around several frequently repeated key words and concepts. I have already pointed out the role of the word 'stupid'. The heaping up of stupidity in the novel has its counterpart in the abundance of jollity. People laugh, guffaw and giggle in *The Little Demon*, in short, they enjoy themselves in whatever ways they can. Even the police officer Lieutenant-Colonel Rubovsky has 'jolly' eyes. But the impression created by this jollity is an oppressive one, and the jollity reaches a climax in the scene of the fancy-dress ball, the masquerade that almost costs Pylnikov his life. This senseless and absurd jollity has within it a catastrophe just waiting to happen.

But perhaps the narrator is the figure who is able to overcome the chaos he himself describes? Let us note that the narrator is *many-faced*, moreover his faces can't be combined very easily or indeed can't be combined at all. He is rudely ironic and blunt in his evaluation of town society, and at times he is witty and sarcastic ('one of the assistant masters, who was so liberal a young man that he would say "Mr Thomas Cat" instead of "Tom"'), at times gloomy and morose. His comparisons sometimes go to extremes: 'One only had to compare the demented, coarse, filthy Peredonov with that happy, radiant, sweet-smelling, prettily dressed Lyudmila.' Mention has already been made of the narrator's pleasure-seeking role, but it is curious that in his evaluation of Peredonov as a 'walking corpse' and in his statement 'how absurd that he felt he could reconcile his belief in Christ and a living God with his belief in witchcraft!' the narrator is close to the position of an orthodox Christian. In his lyrical digressions and commentaries, particularly in the second half of the novel, the narrator expresses himself as an ideologist of Symbolism. In such instances his speech frequently becomes so bombastic that it's difficult to keep the rather cruel thought at bay that perhaps it wasn't only Sasha Pylnikov who had Nadson as his favourite poet. 'Indeed,' exclaims the narrator with great feeling, 'as is so often the case in our day and age, beauty is debased, abused.' With no less bombast does he write about children as 'those eternal tireless vessels of divine joy'. However, the real images of children in the novel hardly answer to the description 'tireless vessels': 'but they were already showing signs of being afflicted with inertia. Some faceless and invisible monster seemed to be perched on their shoulders, peering every now and then into their blank faces with eyes full of menace'.

A narrator made up of various fragments is himself therefore the embodiment of chaos, and to a certain extent is an appropriate figure for a novel about the world of things as a world of chaos. In this lies his difference from a narrator in the realist tradition, who, however neutral he may be (Chekhov's narrator), nevertheless always represents some kind of integral figure, someone whose consciousness resists chaos and opens up a path to hope. The category of *hope* in *The Little Demon* is replaced by the category of unending *yearning*.

Sologub's composition is of course in marked contrast to Chekhov's short stories, for example, which within the limits of the classical tradition are models of artistic perfection. But from the point of view of the aesthetic that is immanent in *The Little Demon*, a novel about the imperfection of the world really has to be *imperfect*. I am not saying that this was a fully conscious decision on Sologub's part. However, the link with the aesthetics of late Modernism is very clear. Far from being coincidental, this link has, when viewed from a historical perspective, a symbolic character: not only does it place the novel at the edge of the break with a rich tradition, which had generously and fully expressed itself, but it also foreshadows the new features of the literature of the twentieth century.

Victor Erofeyev

Translated by Andrew Reynolds.

TRANSLATOR'S NOTES

1. From Yevgeny Zamyatin's 1924 essay, 'Fyodor Sologub'. There is a translation in *A Soviet Heretic: Essays* by Yevgeny Zamyatin, edited and translated by Mirra Ginsburg (Chicago and London, 1970), pp. 217–23.
2. See footnote 2, p. 80.
3. These and other stories may be found in: *The Kiss of the Unborn and Other Stories* by Fyodor Sologub, translated and with an Introduction by Murl G. Barker (Knoxville, 1977). Recent translations of other works by Sologub include the following: *Bad Dreams*, translated by Vassar W. Smith (Ann Arbor, 1978); *The Created Legend*, translated and with an Introduction by Samuel D. Cioran

(Ann Arbor, 1979), 3 vols.: *Volume I: Drops of Blood*; *Volume II: Queen Ortruda*; *Volume III: Smoke and Ashes*.

4. The reference is to a famous passage in a letter of 1854 to Natalya Fonvizina:

That credo is very simple, here it is: to believe that there is nothing more beautiful, more profound, more attractive, more wise, more courageous and more perfect than Christ, and what's more, I tell myself with jealous love, there cannot be. Moreover, if someone proved to me that Christ were outside the truth, and it *really* were that the truth lay outside Christ, I would prefer to remain with Christ rather than with the truth.

The whole letter may be found in: *Fyodor Dostoyevsky: Complete Letters*, edited and translated by David Lowe (Ann Arbor, 1988–91), 5 vols.: *Volume I: 1832–1859*, edited and translated by David Lowe and Ronald Meyer, pp. 193–6.

5. *The Kiss and Other Stories* by Anton Chekhov, translated with an Introduction by Ronald Wilks (Penguin Books, 1982), pp. 121–33.

6. The words that appear in the title of Sologub's novel, *Melkii bes* (*The Petty Demon*/*The Little Demon*) are not the words used in the text to describe the evil spirit. In the text Sologub uses the single word *nedotykomka* to refer to this creature. The title of the novel refers first and foremost to Peredonov, but because the word *nedotykomka* is to all intents and purposes untranslatable, the translator of the novel has chosen to use the words 'little demon' where Sologub has *nedotykomka*. *Nedotykomka* has the connotations of a person who is over-sensitive, sullen and touchy, but also of someone or something that can't be touched or grasped. Perhaps 'will-o'-the-wisp' best conveys the feel of Sologub's rare, 'touch-me-not' word.

THE LITTLE DEMON

AUTHOR'S PREFACES

SECOND EDITION

The novel *The Little Demon* was begun in 1892 and completed in 1902. It first appeared in the journal *Questions of Life*, 1905 (nos. 6–11), but without the final chapters. The novel was first published in its entirety in the Shipovnik edition in March 1907.

I have noticed two contrary opinions in the printed reviews and in the verbal judgements I have happened to hear.

There are those who think that, since the author is a very depraved person, his aim was to provide a self-portrait and thus he depicted himself in the character of Peredonov. Being an honest person, the author had no desire to justify or idealize himself in any way, therefore he smeared his image with the blackest colours. He completed this astonishing undertaking so that he could ascend some kind of Calvary, there to suffer for some reason. This resulted in an interesting and harmless novel.

Interesting, because it shows what evil people there are in this world; harmless because the reader can say, 'This wasn't written about *me*.'

Other people, who are not so hard on the author, think that the state of Peredonovism as depicted in the novel is a fairly widespread phenomenon. And some people even think that if any one of us cares to take a close, careful look inside himself, he will find unmistakably Peredonovian characteristics.

Of these two opinions I prefer that which is more agreeable to me, namely the latter. I was under no obligation to create or invent anything with myself in mind. All the events in the novel, everything that concerns everyday life and the psychology of the characters, is based on the most precise observations – and I had plenty of models on my doorstep. And if my work on the novel has been so protracted, this was merely to elevate the contingent to the realms of necessity, so that inexorable Ananke[1] should be enthroned

1. Greek goddess of necessity.

where once reigned Aisa,[1] the scatterer of stories.

It is true that people love to be loved. They are pleased if the loftier, nobler aspects of their souls are portrayed. Even in villains they wish to see some signs of goodness, the so-called 'divine spark' as it was called in days of old. That is why they cannot believe it when confronted with a picture that is true, accurate, gloomy and evil. They want to say, 'He's writing about *himself*.'

No, my dear contemporaries, it is of you that I have written my novel about the little demon, about Ardalyon and Varvara Peredonov, Pavel Volodin, Darya, Lyudmila and Valeriya Rutilov, Aleksandr Pylnikov and the others. About *you*.

This novel is like a skilfully fashioned mirror. I have polished it meticulously, laboured over it diligently.

Smooth is the surface of my mirror and pure its construction. Repeatedly measured and painstakingly checked, it has not a single blemish.

The monstrous and the beautiful are reflected in it equally faithfully.

January 1908

FIFTH EDITION

Once I thought that Peredonov's career was finished and that he would never leave the psychiatric hospital to which he was sent after cutting Volodin's throat. Recently, though, rumours have started reaching me that Peredonov's mental derangement was only temporary and that after a short while he was discharged. These rumours, of course, are highly improbable. I mention them only because, in our days, the improbable does happen. I have even read in one newspaper that I intend writing a sequel to *The Little Demon*.

I have heard that Varvara apparently succeeded in convincing someone that Peredonov was justified in behaving as he did, and that on numerous occasions Volodin had said something quite outrageous, had betrayed shocking intentions, and that before his death he had made an unbelievably impertinent remark that had

1. Greek goddess of chance.

4

brought about the final catastrophe. Varvara has interested the princess in this story, so I'm told, and the princess, who had previously never said one word on Peredonov's behalf, is now taking a lively interest in his fate, so it seems.

As to what happened to Peredonov after he left the hospital, the information I have is vague and contradictory. Some people have told me that Peredonov joined the police, as Skuchayev had advised, and has worked as a councillor in provincial administration. In some way he distinguished himself in this position and is now enjoying a fine career. On the other hand, others have told me that it was not Ardalyon Borisovich Peredonov who served with the police, but a relative of the same surname. Our Ardalyon Borisovich, in fact, wasn't successful in entering the force, or perhaps he didn't want to, and took up literary criticism. His articles reveal the same characteristics that had distinguished him before.

This latest rumour strikes me as even more implausible than the first. However, should I succeed in obtaining accurate information about Peredonov's latest activities, I shall provide a sufficiently detailed account of them.

August 1909

SEVENTH EDITION

Attentive readers of my novel *Smoke and Ashes* (part four of *The Created Legend*) already know, of course, what path Ardalyon Borisovich is now pursuing.

May 1913

Dialogue for the Seventh Edition

'My soul, why are you so troubled?'

'Because of all the hatred surrounding the name of the author of *The Little Demon*. Many people who disagree about so much else are agreed upon this.'

'Accept their malice and abuse with humility.'

'Surely it cannot be that this labour of ours is unworthy of gratitude. What is the reason for such hatred?'

'This hatred is like fear. You awaken people's consciences too loudly, you are far too frank.'

'But won't some good come from my truthfulness?'

'You're fishing for compliments! This isn't Paris, you know.'

'Oh no, it's not Paris.'

'You, my soul, are a true Parisienne, a child of European civilization. You've come in your elegant dress and dainty sandals to a place where peasant blouses and greased boots are worn. Don't be surprised if a greased boot sometimes rudely stamps on your tender foot. Its owner is really quite a decent fellow.'

'But he's so morose. And so clumsy.'

May 1913

I

The service was at last over and everyone was leaving the church. Some of the parishioners stayed behind to chat by the white stone wall, under the old lime trees and maples. Everyone was in festive attire and gave each other friendly looks. A stranger to this town, looking upon this idyllic scene, would have thought all was perfect peace and harmony. Appearances, however, are deceptive.

Peredonov, who taught in the local high school, gloomily surveyed with small swollen eyes the circle of friends around him from behind gold-rimmed spectacles and said, 'But Princess Volchansky promised Varvara personally. "As soon as you marry Peredonov," she said, "I'll do all I can to get him made inspector." Those were her very words.'

'How can you possibly marry Varvara?' asked the red-faced Falastov. 'After all, she's your cousin! What gave you the idea it's legal to marry blood relatives?'

Everyone burst into laughter. Peredonov's red, usually impassive, almost somnolent face became angry. 'She's only my second cousin,' he said with great irritation. He looked furiously beyond his audience.

'Did this princess of yours promise you *personally*?' said Rutilov, a tall pale-faced young man in a loud, vulgar suit.

'No, she promised Varvara,' replied Peredonov.

'And yet you can still trust both of them!' said Rutilov excitedly. 'Anyone can make up stories like that. Why didn't you go and see the princess yourself?'

'I went to her house with Varvara, but we missed her by five minutes. She'd gone to the country and left word she would be back in three weeks. Of course, we didn't have time to wait, as I had to be back for the exams.'

'It all sounds very fishy to me,' said Rutilov. As he laughed he displayed two rows of rotten teeth.

7

Peredonov stood deep in thought. Everyone left for home, except Rutilov.

'Of course,' began Peredonov, 'I can please myself whom I marry. There're plenty of others besides Varvara.'

'Of course, Ardalyon. Any girl would rush at the chance of marrying you, my dear fellow.' Rutilov's words reassured Peredonov.

They left the churchyard and slowly crossed the dusty unpaved square. Peredonov said, 'But what about the princess? She'd be furious if I gave up Varvara.'

'Why worry about the princess? Let her get you the job first – it's no good pussyfooting around with her. There's plenty of time to become involved later. Don't be an idiot and rush into it blindly!'

'Yes, quite right . . .' Peredonov said without much conviction.

Rutilov continued, 'Just tell Varvara, "The job first, and then I'll marry you." As soon as you have it safely in your grasp you can think seriously about marriage. And you can choose whom you like. Have you ever considered my three sisters, for example? They're all cultured girls and excellent company. I'm not flattering them unduly if I say Varvara's not a patch on them. She's not fit to clean their shoes!'

'Go on,' mumbled Peredonov.

'I know what I'm talking about. I could tell you some things about Varvara . . . Have a sniff of this.'

Rutilov bent down and broke off a furry stalk of henbane. He crushed the leaves and flowers into one dirty white mass and stuck it under Peredonov's nose. The sharp, unpleasant smell made him screw up his face and frown. Rutilov said, 'Crush and then throw away. That's Varvara for you in a nutshell. She doesn't even bear comparison with any of my sisters. They're lovely girls. Believe me, you wouldn't have a dull moment with any of them. What's more, they're all young – the eldest is a third Varvara's age.'

Rutilov always smiled as he spoke, briskly and cheerfully. But that tall weak-chested man had the frail, unhealthy look of a consumptive and his short straw-coloured hair stuck out pathetically from under his fashionable new hat.

'Not even a third her age?' Peredonov said limply, taking off his spectacles and wiping them.

'It's true!' exclaimed Rutilov. 'And if you really fancy any of

8

them you'd better be quick about it. They've no illusions about themselves and can pick and choose. So you'd better make up your mind before it's too late. On the other hand, any one of them would be only too glad of the chance of marrying you, my dear fellow.'

'Yes, all the girls fall in love with me here,' said Peredonov, boasting solemnly.

'So you must take the chance while you can,' urged Rutilov.

'But I just can't stand the thin sort,' said Peredonov anxiously. 'A nice plump girl for me every time!'

'You can rest assured that you won't be disappointed if you marry one of my sisters. They've all developed well, and if they're not yet fully mature they can't be very far off. Once married they'll fill out like my eldest sister, Larisa. As you know, she's a tasty little dumpling!'

'I'd like to marry one of them, but I'm afraid that Varvara will make a dreadful scene.'

'If it's that you're afraid of, then I'll tell you just what to do,' said Rutilov with a cunning smile. 'You should get married either today or tomorrow and then suddenly appear at home – with a young wife. That's all there is to it. Can I arrange it for you? Would tomorrow evening suit you? Which of my sisters do you fancy?'

Peredonov suddenly burst into loud fits of laughter.

'All right? It's a deal then?' asked Rutilov.

Peredonov stopped laughing as suddenly as he had begun and said in a morose, quiet voice, almost in a whisper, 'She'll report me, the filthy slut.'

'Of course she won't. Report what?'

'She'll poison me then,' whispered Peredonov in a voice full of fear.

'Don't worry, and leave everything to me,' said the excited Rutilov. 'I'll fix you up so nicely –'

'I refuse to marry without a dowry,' Peredonov said angrily.

This sudden demand from his gloomy companion didn't surprise Rutilov in the least. He continued in the same animated and persuasive tone, 'You *are* a strange one! Of course my sisters have dowries. Well? What do you say? I'll dash off now and start making arrangements. Only don't breathe a word to a soul!'

He shook Peredonov's hand and ran off. Peredonov watched him in silence. He thought of the three cheerful sisters and his lips twisted into a lewd, fleeting semblance of a smile. Then, all of a sudden, he felt agitated. But what will the princess say? he wondered. Those sisters don't have a copeck between them and they can't pull any strings. If I marry Varvara I'll become an inspector and even end up as a headmaster, no doubt about that. He watched the wretched Rutilov scurrying off and thought maliciously, let him run.

And this last thought gave him a dull, languid pleasure. But only for a moment. It was depressing to be alone. He pulled his hat down over his forehead, knitted his blond eyebrows together and hurried home along the unpaved deserted streets which were overgrown with white-flowered pearl grass, watercress and various weeds that had been trampled into the mud.

Someone called out in a soft, hurried voice, 'Ardalyon Peredonov! How nice to see you, do come in.'

Peredonov raised his mournful eyes and peered crossly over a hedge. Natalya Afanasyevna Vershina, a small, thin, swarthy woman, with black eyes, black eyebrows and dressed completely in the same colour, was standing by the garden gate. She was smoking a cigarette in a dark cherry-wood holder and gave a faint, inscrutable smile. She urged Peredonov into the garden, not so much by verbal invitation as by her swift, delicate movements. She opened the gate, stood to one side, smiled reassuringly and made a gesture as if to say, 'Do come in. What are you standing there like that for?'

And Peredonov did go in, unable to resist her enchanting silent movements. But suddenly he stopped dead on the sandy path, where a few dry broken twigs caught his eye. Then he looked at his watch. 'It's time for lunch,' he said gruffly.

Although he had had the watch for a long time he still looked with childlike pleasure at its golden case, something he always did in the presence of others. It was twenty to twelve. He decided to stay a short while and glumly followed Vershina along the garden paths, past neglected redcurrant, raspberry and gooseberry bushes.

The late flowers and fruits had turned the garden to yellow. There was a great variety of fruit trees and shrubs, including low-spreading apple trees, round-leaved pear trees, lime trees, cherry trees with smooth, shining leaves, plum trees and honeysuckle. The berries on the elder bushes were a bright red and near the fence was a profusion of Siberian geraniums; whole tiny pale pink flowers were veined with purple. Thistles thrust their prickly purple heads from beneath the bushes. To one side of the garden stood a small grey one-storeyed house with a summer kitchen opening on to the garden. It had a welcoming, cosy look. Beyond was part of the kitchen garden. There dry poppy heads rocked to and fro, together with the large pale yellow camomile caps. The yellow sunflowers were beginning to droop before withering, while among the edible herbs rose the white umbels of hemlock and the pale purple ones of water hemlock. Bright yellow buttercups and small spurges were in flower too.

'Did you go to Mass?' asked Vershina.

'Yes, I did,' said Peredonov morosely.

'Marta has only just returned. She often goes to our church instead of the Polish one. She really makes me laugh. "Tell me, Marta," I ask her, "why do you go to our church?" All she does is blush and not say a word. Let's go and sit in the summer-house,' she said, suddenly changing the subject.

In the middle of the garden, shaded by maples, stood an old grey summer-house, very small, with three little steps. Its floor was overgrown with moss and its curious hexagonal roof was supported by six rough-hewn pot-bellied posts. Marta was sitting there, still in her Sunday best. Her bright dress was decorated with bows, which didn't suit her, what with those short sleeves, sharp red elbows and large, strong hands. Apart from these defects Marta was quite pretty. At least her face was not marred by her freckles. She was even considered a beauty by her fellow Poles, of whom there were a fair number in the neighbourhood.

Marta was rolling cigarettes for Vershina. She was anxious for Peredonov to see her and to fall into raptures. As a result her innocent welcoming face was strained and nervous. The reason for this desire to please was not that Marta was exactly in love with Peredonov, but that Vershina wanted to see her married and settled as she was one of a large family. Marta had been living with her since Vershina's husband had died a few months ago. She very much wanted to please Vershina both for her own good and for the sake of her young brother who went to the local high school and was living in the same house.

Vershina and Peredonov entered the summer-house. Peredonov greeted Marta somewhat gloomily and sat down. He was careful to choose a place where one of the supporting posts kept the wind from his back and the draughts away from his ears. He glanced at Marta's yellow slippers with their pink pom-poms and at once suspected that he was being trapped into marrying her. He always thought this with girls who were friendly and pleasant towards him. But he could see only faults in Marta – a great number of freckles, large hands and a rough skin. He was well aware that her father, a Polish nobleman, had a small estate on lease not far from the town. The income was small, and the children many. Marta had left her preparatory school, one brother was still at the high school and the others were even younger.

'Can I offer you some beer?' said Vershina quickly.

On the table were some glasses, two bottles of beer and a tin box full of fine sugar. Beside them lay a silver teaspoon that had been dipped in beer.

'Thank you,' said Peredonov abruptly.

Vershina looked at Marta, who filled a glass and handed it to the guest, smiling as she did this with a strange smile, half glad and half afraid.

'Have some sugar in your beer,' said Vershina as rapidly as before.

Marta gave Peredonov the box. Peredonov said with great irritation, 'What a revolting idea! With sugar!'

'But it's delicious with sugar,' said Vershina.

'I tell you, it's revolting sweetened,' snorted Peredonov.

Vershina replied with a curt, 'Please yourself' and decided to change the subject. 'Cherepnin bores me to distraction,' she said, laughing. Marta giggled. Peredonov was not amused, however. Other people's affairs had no interest for him. He was not fond of his fellow men and only valued them in so far as they affected his own well-being and happiness. Vershina smiled in self-satisfaction and said, 'He really thinks I'm going to marry him.'

'He's got a nerve,' said Marta, not because she really thought this for one moment, but to please and flatter Vershina.

'Last night he climbed up to our window,' related Vershina, 'while we were eating and tried to spy on us. The rain-tub by the window was full to the brim and we'd covered it with a board, so the water was completely hidden. He climbed up and looked at us through the window. As the lamp was alight he could see us without being seen himself. Suddenly there was a loud splash. At first we were frightened and rushed outside. He'd fallen right in but he managed to get out before we arrived and ran off down the garden path, soaking wet, leaving pools of water. We knew it was him from his back.'

Marta laughed with the high-pitched happy laugh of a well-behaved child. Vershina told the story in her usual rapid and monotonous way, as if she were just pouring out her words, and then suddenly she was quiet. A smile appeared at the corner of her mouth, which creased her swarthy dry face. Her smoke-blackened teeth parted slightly. Peredonov pondered for a moment and then burst out laughing. He did not always immediately react to what was funny as his brain worked slowly, sluggishly.

Vershina smoked one cigarette after the other. To exist without perpetual clouds of tobacco smoke under her nose was inconceivable.

'So we shall soon be neighbours,' announced Peredonov.

Vershina glanced swiftly at Marta, who blushed slightly, looked at Peredonov timidly and expectantly and then quickly looked out into the garden again.

'I didn't know you were moving. Why?' asked Vershina.

'Where I live now is a long way from school,' explained Peredonov.

Vershina smiled, not believing this. It's more likely he wants to be nearer Marta, she thought.

'But you've lived in your present flat quite a while – several years in fact,' she said.

'The landlady's an absolute bitch!' Peredonov said angrily.

'Why do you say that?' exclaimed Vershina incredulously and with a sly smile.

Peredonov livened up somewhat. 'She's repapered the rooms in the worst possible taste,' he said. 'None of the pieces match. For example, the part above the door has a pattern of stripes and carnations, while the rest of the room is done in arabesques of flowers. And the colours don't match. We wouldn't have noticed if Falastov hadn't drawn our attention to it. Now everyone thinks it's a scream.'

'I can't imagine anything more hideous,' agreed Vershina.

'Of course, we shan't tell her we're going,' said Peredonov, lowering his voice. 'First we'll find somewhere and then just leave without saying anything.'

'That's the best way,' said Vershina.

'She might kick up a fuss otherwise,' said Peredonov, his eyes full of fear. 'We'd be out of our minds to pay a month's rent for that dump.'

The thought of leaving the flat without paying made Peredonov laugh with joy.

'But she's bound to ask for the money,' said Vershina.

'I don't care what she does, she won't get anything out of me,' said Peredonov crossly. 'Anyway, most of the time we were in St Petersburg, so the flat wasn't occupied.'

'But it was still in your name,' said Vershina.

'Much I care! She had to have the flat redecorated anyway. How can she charge us for the time we weren't even there? But worst of all – she's terribly impertinent.'

'Well, you really can't blame her when your . . . hm, cousin is so difficult,' said Vershina, hesitating slightly at the word 'cousin'.

Peredonov frowned and peered vaguely in front of him with half-somnolent eyes. Vershina started to talk about something else. Peredonov took a caramel from his pocket and started chewing it. His eyes chanced to fall on Marta and he thought she looked jealous and would like one. Shall I give her one or not? he asked himself. She's not really worth it. But if I don't they might think I'm mean. And I've a whole pocketful of them. And he pulled out a handful of caramels. 'Have one,' he said, offering the sweets first to Vershina and then to Marta. 'They're very good bonbons, cost me a lot of money – thirty copecks a pound.' They each took one and Peredonov said, 'Have some more. I've plenty. And all of the best quality. You wouldn't catch me buying rubbish.'

'Thank you very much, but no more for me,' Vershina said in her quick toneless voice.

Marta said exactly the same, but with less assurance. Peredonov looked at Marta in disbelief and said, 'What! You don't want any more? Here, help yourself.'

He took one for himself and put the rest in front of Marta. She smiled and leaned forward to take one, without saying a word. The ignorant slut, Peredonov thought. She's never been taught how to say thank you.

He didn't know what to talk about with her. He was no more interested in her than in anybody else, except those with whom he'd had a long relationship, whether pleasant or not. The rest of the beer was poured into his glass. Vershina looked at Marta.

'I'll fetch some more,' Marta said. She always guessed what Vershina wanted without having to be told.

'Tell Vladya to get it, he's only playing in the garden,' Vershina said.

'Vladislav!' cried Marta.

'Yes?' replied the boy, from so close that he must have been hiding and listening to the conversation.

'Bring two bottles of beer,' said Marta. 'They're in the box in the hall.'

Vladya soon brought the beer and handed it through the window of the summer-house to Marta, greeting Peredonov at the same time.

'How are you, Vladya?' said Peredonov. 'And how many bottles have you swigged on the quiet today?'

Vladya forced a smile and said, 'I don't like beer.' He was about fourteen, freckled like his sister and with the same heavy, clumsy movements. He was wearing a coarse linen blouse.

Marta whispered something to him and they both laughed. Peredonov eyed them with suspicion. As always, if people laughed in his presence and he didn't get the joke, he concluded that they must be laughing at him. Vershina was worried and tried to attract Marta's attention. But Peredonov himself suddenly exclaimed in a malevolent voice, 'What's funny?'

Marta shuddered and turned towards him, not knowing what to say. Vladya just smiled at Peredonov and blushed slightly.

'This is most impolite, in front of a guest!' said Peredonov. 'Is it me you find funny?'

Marta blushed and Vladya trembled.

'I'm terribly sorry,' said Marta. 'We weren't laughing at you at all. It's a purely private joke.'

'Aha! A secret, then!' said Peredonov irately. 'Don't you know it's impolite to discuss secrets in front of guests?'

'It's not exactly a . . . secret. We were laughing because Vladya isn't wearing shoes or socks and he feels shy about coming in.'

Peredonov was placated by this piece of information and started to think of some jokes he could play on Vladya. Then he offered him a caramel.

'Marta, bring me my black shawl,' Vershina said, 'and while you're about it have a look and see how the pie is getting on.'

Marta obeyed, realizing that Vershina wanted to be alone with Peredonov. The lazy girl was glad that there was no hurry.

'And you go and play in the garden, Vladya,' said Vershina. 'You don't want to be here with us.'

Vladya ran off, the sand crunching under his feet. Vershina gave Peredonov a cautious sidelong glance, peering through the perpetual haze of cigarette smoke. Peredonov said nothing, looked straight ahead with a torpid expression and chewed his caramel. He was glad that Marta and Vladya had gone – he was frightened they might laugh again. Although he was sure that they weren't laughing at him the annoyance still rankled in him, like the pain left by a stinging-nettle, which remains for a long time and grows worse, even though the cause is no longer there.

'Why don't you get married?' Vershina said suddenly. 'What are you waiting for, Ardalyon Borisovich? If you don't mind my saying so, Varvara isn't good enough for you.'

Peredonov ran his hand through his slightly ruffled chestnut-coloured hair and said with mournful solemnity, '*No one* in this town is good enough.'

'Nonsense,' said Vershina with a wry smile. 'There are plenty much better than Varvara. And anyone would quite willingly marry you.' She flicked the ash from her cigarette with a swift, decisive movement, as if to add an exclamation mark to what she had just said.

'But I wouldn't marry just anyone,' answered Peredonov.

'We aren't talking about just *anyone*,' said Vershina quickly.' I know a dowry doesn't interest you if the girl is good enough. I mean to say, you have a good salary, thank God.'

'No,' replied Peredonov, 'I couldn't do better than marry Varvara. The princess promised to take me under her wing if I marry Varvara. And with her help I'll get a very good job,' Peredonov added in grave excitement.

Vershina forced a weak smile. Her entire wrinkled face, so swarthy it might have been cured in tobacco smoke, showed a grudging disbelief. 'The princess herself said that to *you*?' she asked, emphasizing the 'you'.

'Not me personally. She told Varvara,' admitted Peredonov. 'But that makes no difference.'

'If you ask me, you're putting too much trust in your cousin. Isn't she much older than you? Fifteen years older, would it be? Or perhaps more? I suppose she must still be under fifty?'

'What are you talking about?' said Peredonov angrily. 'She's not even thirty.'

Vershina burst out laughing. 'Really!' she said, not attempting to hide her derision. 'She seems much older than you. Of course, it's a great pity that such a fine, clever, good-looking young man shouldn't find a wife worthy of him.'

Peredonov was filled with self-satisfaction. However, no smile was visible on his highly coloured face and he seemed annoyed that Vershina was the only person who really appreciated him.

Vershina went on, 'Even without someone to use influence for you, you'll go far. The school board must surely know what a good man they've got. Why hang on to Varvara? And as for those Rutilov girls! They're not your type at all. Far too flighty, in my opinion. What you need is a nice steady wife. Have you ever considered Marta?'

Peredonov glanced at his watch. 'It's time I was going,' he said, getting up.

Vershina was certain that Peredonov was only leaving because she had touched a tender spot and that it was only his inability to make up his mind that made him unwilling to discuss the matter there and then.

II

Varvara Dmitriyevna Maloshin, Peredonov's mistress, was waiting for him at home. She was sloppily dressed, but had taken care to paint and powder her face.

She was baking some jam tarts for lunch – Peredonov loved them – and bustled about the kitchen on her high heels, hurrying to have them ready by the time he returned. Afraid that her fat pock-marked maid Natalya might steal some of them, she didn't dare leave the kitchen. As usual, she was giving Natalya a good telling-off. Her face, though wrinkled, had preserved some of its former charms, but she looked perpetually spiteful and frustrated.[1]

As he always did on coming home, Peredonov felt discontented and exceedingly bored. He made a loud noise as he entered the dining-room, threw his hat on the window-sill, sat at the table and bellowed, 'Varya! Where's my lunch?'

Varvara hobbled out of the kitchen with the food, deftly manoeuvring in her smart shoes that were far too narrow for comfort, and waited on Peredonov herself. When the coffee came Peredonov bent down and sniffed the steam. This strange behaviour worried Varvara and she asked him in a trembling voice, 'What's wrong, Ardalyon? Doesn't it smell right?'

Peredonov looked at her mournfully and crossly said, 'I'm just trying to see if you've poisoned it or not.'

'You're out of your mind! God, where did you get that idea from?'

'I think it's hemlock!' Peredonov growled.

'And why should I want to poison you, just tell me!' said Varvara. 'Don't be such a fool!'

Peredonov sniffed away. Then, satisfied that it hadn't been poisoned, said, 'You can always tell from the strong smell. But you have to put your nose right into the steam.' He said nothing for a while and then exclaimed in a spiteful, sarcastic voice, 'The princess!'

Varvara looked worried. 'What about her? What do you mean?' she asked.

'Write and tell her that I want the job first. Then I'll think about getting married.'

'But you know very well,' implored Varvara, 'she made this promise on condition we get married. And it's not right for me to ask her about the job.'

1. See variant 1, p. 268.

'Write and tell her that we're already married,' said Peredonov, congratulating himself on this sudden burst of inspiration.

Varvara was dumbfounded for a moment but, recovering herself, said, 'How can you lie like that? Besides, she might find out. Anyway, you'd better think of a wedding date and I must start making a dress.'

'What dress?' said Peredonov.

'You don't really suppose I could get married in this, do you? Please give me some money for the material, Ardalyon.'

'Is it a shroud you have in mind?' Peredonov asked viciously.

'You beast!'

Peredonov suddenly felt the urge to tease Varvara and asked, 'Varvara, do you know where I've just been?'

'Where?' she anxiously asked.

'At Vershina's,' he replied and burst out laughing.

'That must have been very pleasant for you, I don't think!' Varvara exclaimed.

'I saw Marta,' Peredonov continued.

'She's covered with freckles,' said Varvara, getting angrier and angrier. 'And her mouth stretches from one ear to the other – you could pin it on a frog.'

'But she's still much more to look at than you. I think my mind's made up.'

'Just you dare and I'll burn her eyes out with acid!' Varvara shouted, flushed and trembling with anger.

'I feel like spitting in your face,' Peredonov calmly said.

'Go ahead!' Varvara cried. 'I bet you can't reach me from where you are!'

'Oh yes I can!' Peredonov replied. He stood up and with an expression of complete indifference spat right in her face.

'You pig!' Varvara said quietly, but apparently refreshed by the spray. And she started wiping it off with a napkin. Peredonov said nothing. Lately he had been rougher with her than usual. And even before that he'd been treating her badly enough. Encouraged by his silence she said in a louder voice, 'Yes, you're a pig. It was a direct hit.'

Suddenly a loud bleating came from the hall.

'Be quiet,' said Peredonov, 'we've a visitor.'

'It sounds like Pavlusha,' Varvara sniggered.

In came Pavel Vasilyevich Volodin, cheerfully laughing. He was a young man who resembled a sheep in every respect. He had dull protruding eyes and curly hair – everything about him suggested a playful young sheep. A stupid young man, he was a joiner, had trained at technical college and was now teaching carpentry at the town school.

'How are you, my dear Ardalyon!' he said in a gay voice. 'I seem to be in time for coffee!'

'Natasha, bring another spoon!' said Varvara.

Natalya could be heard rattling the only remaining teaspoon in the kitchen; all the others were hidden away.

'Help yourself, Pavlusha,' said Peredonov, playing the cordial host. 'Did you know that I'm going to be made an inspector soon? The princess promised Varvara.'

Volodin was delighted and burst out laughing. 'And our new inspector is drinking coffee!' he cried, giving Peredonov a hard slap on the shoulder.

'Do you think it's easy to get a position like that? One false step and you're out.'

'And what could they report you for?' Varvara asked, grinning.

'Lots of things. They could say I've been reading Pisarev[1] – that would be curtains!'

'Well, Ardalyon, you'd better put your Pisarev on the back shelf,' advised Volodin, tittering.

Peredonov glanced warily at him and said, 'Perhaps I never even had a copy. Fancy a drink, Pavlusha?'

Volodin stuck out his lower lip and assumed an expression of self-importance, nodding like a sheep. 'If it's to be sociable, then all right. But never on my own!'

Peredonov was also always ready for a drop and they both had some vodka and then started on the jam tarts.

Suddenly Peredonov turned and spattered the wall with his coffee dregs. Volodin opened his sheeplike eyes wide in amazement. The wallpaper was already covered with stains, and torn as well.

'That's a fine way to treat wallpaper,' Volodin said.

Peredonov and Varvara burst out laughing.

'It's to spite the landlady,' Varvara said. 'We're moving soon, so not a word to anyone.'

1. Dmitry I. Pisarev (1840–68), leading nihilist and radical critic.

'Splendid!' exclaimed Volodin and broke into a loud joyous cackle.

Peredonov went up to the wall and gave it a vigorous kick with his boot-soles. Volodin followed suit. Peredonov said, 'We always do this to the wallpaper when we leave a flat, just so they'll remember us!'

'You've really landed some good ones there!' Volodin rapturously exclaimed.

'Irishka will go out of her mind,' Varvara said with a dry, spiteful laugh. And all three of them spat on the wall, tore the paper and rubbed their shoes against it. Then, exhausted and contented, they turned away.

Peredonov bent down and picked up the ugly white fat cat and began to pull its ears and tail and shake it by the neck. Volodin was highly amused and suggested more subtle torments. 'Blow in its eyes, Ardalyon. Brush its fur the wrong way!'

The unfortunate animal hissed and made a vain attempt to escape. It did not dare show its claws, fully aware of the cruel beating it would get for scratching. When at last Peredonov grew tired of this sport he threw the cat to one side.

'Listen, Ardalyon, there's something I've got to tell you,' Volodin began. 'All the way here I was wondering how not to forget – and I almost did!'

'Well?' Peredonov said morosely.

'I know your liking for sweet things,' Volodin said cheerfully. 'Well, I've found a recipe that will make you lick your lips.'

'You can't tell me anything about recipes for sweets. I know them all.'

Volodin was offended and said, 'You might know everything that's made in this place. But how can you know what's made where *I* come from, if you've never even been there?' Satisfied with his logic Volodin produced a sheeplike laugh.

'In your part of the world they guzzle dead cats,' said Peredonov irately.

'Excuse me, Ardalyon,' Volodin said in a shrill laughing voice, 'it's possible that they eat dead cats where you come from, but we won't go into that now. So you've never had erli?'[1]

1. Dish from the Tula district, made chiefly from millet and raisins; a kind of wheaten gruel.

'No, I can't say I have,' replied Peredonov.

'What is it?' asked Varvara.

'I'll tell you. Well, you know what kutya[1] is?'

'Of course I do,' Varvara replied, smirking.

'Well, erli is ground kutya, only with sugar and almonds.'

Volodin then described in great detail how erli was made where he came from. Peredonov listened restlessly and thought, they serve kutya after funerals. Does he want to kill me off?

Volodin said, 'If you want the real thing, give me the ingredients and I'll make it for you.'

'And that would suit you down to the ground, wouldn't it?' Peredonov gloomily remarked. He might poison it, he thought.

Volodin took offence again. 'If you think that all I want is to filch your sugar you're mistaken. I don't need any.'

'Now stop this clowning!' Varvara interrupted. 'Surely you know how fussy he is. You'd better come here and make it.'

'And you can eat it yourself,' Peredonov said.

'But why?' asked Volodin, his voice trembling from the insult.

'Because it's horrible muck. Fit only for pigs like you.'

'Please yourself, Ardalyon,' Volodin said, shrugging his shoulders. 'I only wanted to please you. But if you don't want any, then do as you like.'

'I hear the general's had his knife into you,' said Peredonov.

'What general?' Volodin asked, going red in the face and indignantly sticking out his lower lip.

'We know all about it,' said Peredonov.

Varvara grinned.

'Well, Ardalyon, if you've heard about it you didn't hear the whole story. I'll tell you exactly what happened.'

'Go on,' Peredonov said.

'It really happened like this. The day before yesterday I was taking my carpentry class in the back room of the school because of the repairs in the workshop. In came General Veriga with our inspector. We wondered what Veriga was doing in the school, but that's not my affair. We went on working without taking any notice. But when they came over to talk to us I saw that Veriga hadn't taken his hat off.'

1. Rice pudding with honey and raisins, eaten at funerals or at Christmas.

22

'So he showed no respect,' Peredonov said glumly.

'I should say not! I mean to say, there was an icon in the room and we'd all taken our hats off. Suddenly in he comes like some Mameluke. Up I went to him and said, as politely as I could, so he couldn't take offence, "If you don't mind, sir, would you kindly take your hat off? Out of respect for the icon, sir." Do you think I was wrong to say this?' asked Volodin, his eyes almost popping out of his head.

'Of course you weren't,' said Peredonov, 'you had every right to speak to him like that.'

'Quite right,' said Varvara. 'Someone had to say something. Well done, Pavel!'

With the look of an innocent man unjustly insulted Volodin went on, 'And then he had the nerve to say, "Every cobbler should stick to his last." Then he turned his back on me and left. That's the whole story.'

Nevertheless, Volodin felt quite heroic and Peredonov gave him a caramel by way of consolation.

Another guest arrived. This time it was Mrs Sofya Yefimovna Prepolovensky, a forester's wife. She was a plump woman, with a good-natured but cunning face and smooth movements. Invited to eat, she sat down and slyly told Volodin, 'You seem to come here a lot!'

'But it's Ardalyon I came to see, not Varvara,' he meekly replied.

'So you're not in love with anyone at the moment?' Mrs Prepolovensky laughed.

Everyone knew that Volodin was after a wife with plenty of money, that he'd chased quite a few women but had always been turned down. He didn't like the joke at all and in a plaintive voice that sounded just like a bleating sheep said, 'If I fall in love, it's a matter that concerns only me and the lady and it's nothing at all to do with *you*.'

Mrs Prepolovensky, determined to have her fun, said, 'What would happen if you fell in love with Varvara? There'd be no one to make jam tarts for Ardalyon!'

Volodin puffed out his lips, raised his eyebrows and was at a loss for an answer.

'It's no good being shy, Mr Volodin,' Mrs Prepolovensky went on. 'It's high time you found yourself a wife. You're young – and handsome.'

'Supposing Varvara won't have me?' Volodin chuckled.

'And why not? The trouble with you is that you're much too modest.'

'And what if I don't want to marry her?' asked Volodin, preening himself. 'Perhaps I don't want to marry other people's cousins. Perhaps I've a nice young niece of my own back home.'

By now he really believed that Varvara would be only too pleased to marry him. Varvara was furious – she thought Volodin a complete fool. Besides, he earned a quarter of Peredonov's salary. But Mrs Prepolovensky wanted Peredonov to marry her own sister, a priest's buxom daughter, and for this reason she was trying to cause a rift between Peredonov and Varvara.

'Why are you always trying to marry me off?' Varvara said, highly annoyed. 'You'd do better to marry your stupid fat sister to Pavel Volodin.'

'Why should I want to take him away from you?' said Mrs Prepolovensky, revelling in the situation.

And now Mrs Prepolovensky's jokes set Peredonov's sluggish brain working in a new direction; those erli had become firmly lodged in his mind. What was Volodin up to with his erli? Never inclined towards rational thought, Peredonov was exceedingly gullible. He really did believe that Volodin was in love with Varvara. Once Varvara and he were married, he would be poisoned with erli whilst travelling to take up his inspectorship. Volodin would take his place and he'd be buried under the name of Volodin, who would then become inspector. Very clever!

Suddenly there was a noise in the hall which made Peredonov and Varvara start. Peredonov blinked at the door, while Varvara crept up to the parlour door, opened it and silently tiptoed back, balancing herself with her arms. She gave a perplexed smile and sat down again. From the hall came shrieks and shouts and it sounded as if a fight was going on. Varvara whispered, 'It's Irishka Yershova, dead drunk again. Natasha won't let her in, but she's still trying to get into the parlour.'

Peredonov was terrified and muttered, 'What shall we do?'

'We'll have to go into the parlour so she can't sneak in here,' Varvara decided.

They went in and shut the doors tight behind them. Varvara rushed into the hall in the faint hope of stopping the landlady from coming any further, or making her sit down in the kitchen. But she was too late. That brazen woman was already at the door, hands on hips and cursing everyone indiscriminately. Peredonov and Varvara fussed around her, trying to make her sit down as far away from the dining-room as possible, and then brought her some vodka, beer and tarts from the kitchen on a tray. But the landlady wasn't at all tempted and would have burst into the dining-room – had she been able to find the door. She was very red in the face, filthy and dishevelled, and one could smell the vodka a mile off.

'I want to sit at your table!' she shouted. 'And I won't eat off a tray. I want a tablecloth. I'm the landlady 'ere and expect to be treated like one! And stop gawking at me like that. What if I am drunk. At least I'm faithful to my husband!'

Varvara sniggered half-heartedly and said, 'You don't have to tell us!'

Yershova winked at Varvara, gave a hoarse laugh and then smartly snapped her fingers. She was becoming even more audacious. 'Cousins!' she shouted. 'We know what kind of cousins you are! Why does the headmaster's wife never come to see you, eh? Why?'

'Shut up!' said Varvara.

But this only made the woman shout all the louder. 'I won't be ordered around by the likes of you! It's my house and I can do what I like in it. If I wanted to I could make you clear out here and now, lock, stock and barrel, so even your smell wouldn't be left behind! But seeing as I've a soft heart I'm letting you stay – if you don't make no more trouble.'

While she was ranting away Volodin and Mrs Prepolovensky sat by the window in humble silence. Mrs Prepolovensky smiled weakly and kept glancing out of the corner of her eye at that virago whilst pretending she was looking into the street. Volodin tried to look insulted.

For a few moments Yershova calmed down somewhat and, with a cheerful drunken smile, she patted Varvara on the shoulder and told her in a friendly voice, 'Now listen to me. I want to sit at your table and to be spoken to like a lady. And I fancy some of those nice cream gateaux that the master has. Please have a bit of respect for the lady of the house, dearie!'

'Tarts is all you'll get,' said Varvara.

'You can keep your tarts! I want some gateaux, nice creamy ones, the kind gentlefolk eat!' screeched Yershova, waving her arms and blissfully smiling. 'Ooh, they're ever so tasty!'

'I don't have any for you,' Varvara replied, growing bolder as the landlady was rather more cheerful now. 'It's tarts or nothing.'

Suddenly Yershova made out the dining-room door and let out a wild shriek. 'Out of my way, you viper!'

She brushed Varvara to one side and rushed to the door, too fast for the rest. With head lowered, fists clenched, she crashed it open and charged into the dining-room. She stopped in the doorway and when she saw the wallpaper she gave a piercing scream. Then she put her hands on her hips, jauntily planted one foot on the floor and shouted, 'It looks like you really are leaving!'

Varvara trembled and said, 'Whoever told you that, Mrs Yershova? We've no intention of leaving. Don't be so silly.'

'We're not going anywhere,' confirmed Peredonov. 'We're quite satisfied staying put.'

The landlady turned a deaf ear, went over to the terror-stricken Varvara and shook her fists in her face. Peredonov sought refuge behind Varvara. He wanted to beat a hasty retreat but was curious to see the landlady and Varvara fight it out.

'For two pins I'd tear you limb from limb!' raved Yershova.

'Why don't you behave yourself?' said Varvara. 'You're forgetting we have visitors.'

'And they'll get the same treatment!' Yershova shouted. 'What the hell do I want with your visitors!'

She lurched into the parlour and then, with a sudden change of tactics, bowed so low to Mrs Prepolovensky that she almost fell on to the floor.

'Don't take any notice of a drunken old woman, dear. But there's something I'd like to get off my chest. You ought to know what she says about your sister when you're not here! And why does she tell *me*, a cobbler's drunken wife? Because she wants the whole world to know, that's why!'

Varvara went purple and said, 'I didn't tell you anything.'

'You didn't? You're a dirty liar,' Yershova shouted, rushing at Varvara with clenched fists.

'Now shut up!' Varvara muttered in confusion.

'No I won't,' Yershova said spitefully and turned to Mrs Prepolovensky once more. 'That bitch told me your sister is sleeping with your husband, that's what!'

Sofya Prepolovensky flashed her angry, cunning eyes at Varvara, stood up and said, with a weak attempt at a laugh, 'Delighted to hear it, I didn't expect that!'

'You're lying!' Varvara screamed at Yershova.

Yershova made an angry gurgling noise, stamped her feet and shook her fist at Varvara. Then she turned to Mrs Prepolovensky and said, 'If you only knew what the gentleman's been saying about you. That you were sleeping around before you got married! They're scum, that's what. Spit in their faces, lady, that's the only way with trash like that.'

Mrs Prepolovensky turned a deep red and went out into the hall without saying a word. Peredonov scurried after her and tried to explain.

'She's lying, don't believe a word she says. Only once did I tell her that I thought you were a bit silly and that was because I was angry. I swear to God that was all. She made up the rest.'

Mrs Prepolovensky calmly replied, 'Don't worry yourself, Mr Peredonov! Do you think I can't see that she's drunk? She doesn't know what she's saying. But what I cannot understand is why you allow all this in your own house.'

'Well, you tell me what to do with her,' replied Peredonov.

Angry and upset, Mrs Prepolovensky started putting her coat on. Peredonov didn't think of helping her but went on muttering. His words fell on deaf ears and he went back into the parlour, where Yershova gave him another taste of her tongue. Varvara ran out on to the porch to console Mrs Prepolovensky.

'Well, you know what a fool he is, he doesn't know what he's saying half the time.'

'Now don't you worry yourself,' Mrs Prepolovensky replied. 'A drunken woman is liable to say anything.'

A thick clump of tall nettles grew outside, just where the porch jutted out. Mrs Prepolovensky smiled and the last trace of displeasure faded from her large white face. Once more she became polite and friendly towards Varvara. She would take her revenge for that insult and there wouldn't be the need for any dramatics either. They walked around the garden waiting until the landlady sobered up.

Mrs Prepolovensky didn't take her eyes off the nettles, which grew in profusion along the garden fence too. After a while she said, 'You've so many nettles! Do you think you could spare some?'

Varvara laughed and replied, 'Take some, they're no use to me.'

'Well, if you don't mind, I'd like to. We don't have any.'

'But what do you need them for?' Varvara asked in amazement.

'Oh, I'll find something,' Mrs Prepolovensky laughed.

'Please tell me for what, dear,' begged the inquisitive Varvara.

Mrs Prepolovensky leaned over to Varvara and whispered in her ear, 'A good way of putting on weight is rubbing yourself with nettles. That's why my sister Genichka's so nice and plump.'

Peredonov's predilection for fat women and distaste for skinny ones was well known. Varvara was very worried that she was so thin and getting even thinner by the day. How to put on weight – that was one of her main preoccupations. She kept asking everyone if they knew of something that would do the trick. Mrs Prepolovensky was now convinced that Varvara would give the nettles a good try: in this way she would be her own scourge.

III

Peredonov and Yershova came out into the garden.

'Come on!' he was muttering.

Yershova was very merry and shouting at the top of her voice. The two of them were about to dance. Mrs Prepolovensky and Varvara had gone through the kitchen into the main living-room, where they sat by the window to see what was going on.

Peredonov and the landlady, locked in a close embrace, danced on the grass around the pear tree. Peredonov's face was, as usual, quite blank and his short-cropped hair and gold-rimmed spectacles bobbed up and down in lifeless rhythm. Yershova kept letting out little squeals and shouts, waving her arms and staggering all over the place.

'Hey you, Lady Muck, come and join us!' she shouted through the window to Varvara. 'Or are you being snooty again?'

Varvara said nothing and turned away.

'You can go to hell! Ooh, I'm on my last legs!' Yershova shouted and sank on to the grass, taking Peredonov with her.

They sat for a while, closely interlocked, and then got up to dance again. The routine was repeated several times: first they would dance, then rest under the pear tree, on the bench or on the grass. Volodin enjoyed the performance immensely, watching the dancers from the window. He roared with laughter, pulled funny faces, bent his knees and shouted, 'They're crazy! What fun!'

'She's a filthy slut,' Varvara said angrily.

'Yes, a slut,' agreed Volodin, laughing out loud. 'Just you wait, my dear landlady, I'm going to do you a nice little favour. Let's mess up the parlour too. It's all right, she won't come back today. She'll tire herself out over there on the grass and then go and sleep it off.'

He broke into peals of bleating laughter and leaped about like a young sheep. Mrs Prepolovensky egged him on, 'Yes, let's, Pavel – why give a damn for *her*! If she comes back we could say she did it herself when she was drunk!'

Leaping about and laughing his head off, Volodin rushed into the parlour. After he had wiped the soles of his boots on the wallpaper he cried, 'Varvara! Do you have some rope?'

Varvara waddled like a duck across the parlour into the bedroom and returned with some threadbare knotty rope. Volodin made a noose, stood a chair in the middle of the room and hung the rope from a lamp-hook.

'That's for the landlady! She'll find it very handy when you've gone!'

Both women squealed with laughter.

'And now a pencil and some paper!' shouted Volodin.

Varvara ferreted around in the bedroom again and emerged with a small piece of paper and a pencil. Volodin wrote on it *For the landlady* and pinned it to the noose, making the most hilarious faces. Then he furiously attacked the wallpaper once again, wiping his boot-soles on it in convulsions of laughter – his bleating laugh could be heard all over the house. The white cat, its ears pinned back in terror, peered out of the bedroom and apparently didn't know where to run. Peredonov managed at last to detach himself from Yershova and came back on his own, while the completely exhausted landlady went home to sleep. As he came in, he was met by Volodin who told him, 'We've decorated the parlour as well! Three cheers!'

'Three cheers!' shouted Peredonov and he discharged short loud salvoes of laughter, as if he were firing from a cannon.

The ladies shouted 'Three cheers!' too and a general jollification commenced.

'Pavlusha, let's dance!' Peredonov shouted.

'Yes, let's, my dear Ardalyon,' Volodin replied with an inane giggle. They danced under the noose and kicked out wildly. The floor shook under Peredonov's heavy stamping.

'Ardalyon's really letting himself go,' observed Mrs Prepolovensky with a faint smile.

'There's no telling what he'll do next, he gets the craziest ideas,' grumbled Varvara, admiring Peredonov all the same.

She really thought he was handsome and a fine young man and found nothing exceptionable about his wildest behaviour. In her eyes he was neither ridiculous nor repugnant.

'How about a dirge for the landlady?' said Volodin. 'Give me a cushion.'

'Whatever will he think of next!' Varvara laughed.

She brought a cushion in a dirty calico case from the bedroom. Then they put it on the floor to represent the landlady and read the funeral service over it in wild, shrill voices. Natalya the maid was called to turn the handle of the musical-box, while all four of them danced a quadrille, making absurd faces and kicking their legs high in the air.

For some reason the dancing put Peredonov in a generous mood and his bloated face shone with a strange vigour. He was suddenly filled with an almost mechanical determination, perhaps induced by his previous exertions. He pulled out his wallet, counted some notes and, with a proud, self-satisfied expression, threw them to Varvara.

'Catch these, Varvara!' he shouted. 'You can get yourself some material for the wedding dress.'

The notes fluttered over the floor and Varvara wasted no time in picking them up, far too pleased with the present to take offence at Peredonov's rudeness. Mrs Prepolovensky thought, It's anybody's guess who'll marry *him*, and smiled wickedly. Volodin, of course, did not dream of helping Varvara pick up the money.

Mrs Prepolovensky made her farewell and on her way out she met a new visitor, Grushina.

Marya Osipovna Grushina was a young widow of prematurely decayed appearance. She was very thin and her dry skin was covered with fine wrinkles seemingly filled with dust. Though her face was not unpleasant, her teeth were black and neglected. Her hands were small, her fingers long and clawlike, with filthy nails. At first glance she did not so much appear filthy as give the impression that she never washed herself but merely shook off the dust. One imagined that a few strokes with a carpet-beater would send a column of dust to the very heavens from her clothes, which had never seen an iron and hung on her in crumpled folds as if they had been tied up in a bundle for many years. She existed on a scant pension, supplemented by income from small business commissions and interest on mortgages. For the most part her conversation was quite indecent and she was always pursuing all the men in the district in the hope of finding another husband. There was nearly always an unmarried clerk or minor official renting a room in her house.

Varvara was delighted to see Grushina as there was something that she very much wanted to tell her. They whispered to each other about their maids and the inquisitive Volodin moved his chair closer and tried to hear what they were saying. Peredonov sat alone at the table and dejectedly crumpled up the corner of the cloth.

Varvara grumbled about her maid Natalya. Grushina recommended Claudia, a real treasure, and they decided to go at once to see her at Samorodina, where she was working for the time being in the house of an excise officer who had just been given a transfer. All that worried Varvara was the name. She asked in a quandary, 'Claudia? So what can I call her then – Clashka?'

Grushina advised, 'Call her Claudyushka.'

Varvara liked that. She repeated, 'Claudyushka, dyushka.' And she gave a rasping laugh.

It should be pointed out that in our town pigs are called dyushkas. Volodin produced a grunt. Everyone laughed. 'Dyushka, dyushenka,' Volodin babbled between fits of laughter, screwing up his stupid face and puffing his lips out.

And he carried on grunting and clowning until they told him

that he was getting on everyone's nerves, whereupon he walked away with a hurt look, sat down beside Peredonov, lowered his sharp forehead like a ram and stared at the tablecloth, which was covered with stains.

Varvara decided to buy the material for the wedding dress on the way to Samorodina. She always went shopping with Grushina, who was a great help when it came to making up her mind and getting the best price. Unnoticed by Peredonov, Varvara had stuffed Grushina's pockets full of sweets and tartlets and other gifts and Grushina guessed that Varvara was going to ask her a big favour that day.

Varvara found walking very tiring in her tight high-heeled shoes, so she usually took a cab, even though it didn't take long to get very far in such a small town. Recently she had been visiting Grushina a lot and the cab-drivers, of whom there were about a score, had taken note of this. When they seated her, they didn't even have to ask for the address.

They drove off in a drozhky[1] to the house where Claudia was working, to make inquiries. There was mud almost everywhere, even though it had rained only the previous evening. The drozhky clattered along the stone pavement for a while, only to get bogged down again in the sticky mud in the unpaved road. By way of contrast, Vershina's voice twanged incessantly, to the frequent accompaniment of Grushina's sympathetic chatter.

'That goose of mine has been to Marta's again,' Varvara said.

Grushina answered spitefully, 'She'll get him in the end, mark my words. He'd make a wonderful husband, especially for Marta. She wouldn't find anyone like him again in a hurry.'

'I don't know what to do for the best,' Varvara complained. 'He's been so touchy lately it's simply terrible. Believe me, it makes my head go round. He'll marry someone else and I'll be out on my ear.'

'You're worrying yourself for nothing. He won't marry anyone else because he's too used to you,' Grushina said consolingly.

'He's been going off on his own in the evenings and then I just can't sleep. For all I know he might be getting married. Sometimes I toss and turn all night. Everyone's after him – those three fat

1. Low four-wheeled open carriage.

32

Rutilov cows who hang around everyone's necks, and that fat-faced Zhenka.'

Varvara went on complaining for a long time. Grushina could tell that she wanted a big favour from her – and she looked forward to a large reward.

Claudia proved satisfactory. The excise officer's wife sang her praises. They hired her and told her to start work that evening, since the officer was due to leave the same day.

Finally they drove to Grushina's. She lived a slovenly life in her own dingy little house with her three dirty, scruffy, stupid brats who were as vicious as scalded puppies. Only now did the women get down to serious business.

'Would you believe it, that idiot of mine wants me to write to the princess again. But it's a sheer waste of time writing to her. Either she doesn't reply at all or she writes some stupid nonsense. We hardly know one another.'

Princess Volchansky, for whom Varvara had once worked as a dressmaker, doing simple little jobs, could very easily help Peredonov. Her daughter was married to Privy Councillor Shchepkin, who was very high up in the Ministry of Education. She had already written a year ago, refusing to have anything to do with the matter unless Varvara was married to Peredonov. Peredonov was piqued by this reply, which offered only a vague hope and gave no firm promise that she would ensure he got the job once they were married. So they went to St Petersburg to make everything clear to the princess. Varvara made certain she saw the princess first, on her own, and then deliberately delayed going there with Peredonov, so that they didn't catch the princess when she was home. Varvara knew very well that the best they could expect was for her to advise them to marry as soon as possible and then make some vague promises, which would certainly not satisfy Peredonov. So Varvara decided it was best for Peredonov not to see her at all.

'I'm counting on your rock-solid support,' Varvara said. 'Please help me, dear.'

'But what can I do?' asked Grushina. 'You know I'd do anything for you. Would you like your fortune read?'

'I know all about your fortune-telling,' Varvara laughed. 'No, there's something else you can do for me.'

Grushina trembled with pleasure. 'What's that?'

'It's very simple. I want you to write a letter to Peredonov in the princess's handwriting and I'll show it to him.'

'But how can I do a thing like that, my dear?' Grushina said, pretending to be scared. 'What would happen to me if anyone found out?'

Varvara was quite unperturbed and took a crumpled letter from her pocket. 'This is one of the princess's. All you have to do is copy the handwriting.'

Grushina took a long time to be persuaded. Varvara realized that she was merely hedging and wanted as much from her in return as she could get. Varvara, however, was prepared to give her very little. She carefully increased her offer, promising her an old silk dress and various small gifts. A stream of entreaties poured off her tongue. When Grushina saw that she would get no more, she took the letter, pretending she was agreeing out of softness of heart and nothing more.[1]

IV[2]

The billiard-room at the club was stuffy and full of smoke. Peredonov, Rutilov, Falastov, Volodin and Murin – an extremely tall stupid-looking landowner with a small estate, shrewd and well-off – had just finished their game and were preparing to leave.

It was getting late and the dirty rough table was covered with empty beer bottles. The club members had been drinking a great deal while they played – their faces were flushed and they filled the whole place with their drunken racket – with the exception of the pale, sickly Rutilov. He had drunk less beer than the others but a lot of wine, and wine only made him even paler. Obscenities and insults flew around. No one took offence: it was all among friends.

1. See variant 2, p. 269.
2. See variant 3, p. 272.

Peredonov had lost as usual. He was a poor player, but he maintained an expression of imperturbable gloom and paid up with bad grace. Suddenly Murin shouted, 'Fire!' and aimed his cue at Peredonov, who jumped back in horror. The ridiculous idea that Murin wanted to shoot him flashed through his mind. Everyone else laughed.

Peredonov growled, 'I don't think that's funny.'

Murin was sorry he had frightened Peredonov, for the simple reason that his son was in Peredonov's class and he therefore felt it was his duty to please the teacher as much as he could. He apologized profusely and bought him wine and seltzer.

Peredonov said glumly, 'My nerves are a bit on edge. I'm not at all happy with the present headmaster.'

'The future inspector's lost all his money again,' bleated Volodin. 'What's more, he's a bad loser.'

'Unlucky at billiards, lucky in love,' Rutilov said, chuckling and showing his rotten teeth.

Peredonov was already in a temper because of his loss and the scare with the cue, and now they were teasing him about Varvara. 'I'll get married to someone else and Varvara can clear out!' he said.

Everyone laughed and provoked him even more. 'You wouldn't dare,' they said.

'Wouldn't I? I'll do it tomorrow!'

'It's a bet! Ten roubles?' suggested Falastov.

Peredonov was in no mood for taking risks – if he lost, he'd have to pay up. He turned away without a word. At the gate the others went off in various directions, leaving Peredonov and Rutilov together. Rutilov tried again to persuade him to marry one of his sisters without further ado.

'I've arranged everything, you don't have to worry about a thing,' Rutilov assured him.

'But the banns haven't even been read,' said Peredonov.

'I'm telling you, everything's arranged. And I've found a priest who knows you're not related to the bride.'

'There're no men on the bride's side,' said Peredonov.

'True. But I can easily get hold of some. I only have to send for them and they'll come straight to the church. Or I'll bring them myself. You understand, I couldn't arrange anything earlier as your cousin would have found out and interfered.'

Peredonov didn't reply and looked around despairingly at the dark outlines of a few silent little houses with their sleepy front gardens and ramshackle fences.

'If you wait here by the gate,' Rutilov said persuasively, 'I'll bring out whichever one you fancy. Listen, and I'll prove something. Now, twice two is four – right or wrong?'

'Right,' Peredonov replied.

'Well, as sure as twice two is four you should marry one of my sisters.'

Peredonov was really taken aback. Yes, he's right, he thought. Of course twice two is four. And he looked at the sober-minded Rutilov with respect. Yes, I'll have to marry one of them. There's no arguing with *him*.

Just then the two friends reached the house and stopped at the gate.

'But you just can't force them to come out,' Peredonov said angrily.

'Don't be so silly! They're not going to wait for ever for someone to come to them, you know.'

'Well, suppose I don't want to marry any of them?'

'Have you gone off your head? Do you want to stay a bachelor all your life? Or end up in a monastery? Or are you still hankering after Varvara? Think of her face when you bring a pretty young wife home!'

Peredonov gave a short cackling laugh but then became serious again and said with a frowning face, 'Suppose *they* don't want to marry me?'

'But why shouldn't they, you silly man!' Rutilov replied. 'I give you my word!'

'They think too much of themselves,' objected Peredonov.

'All the better – for someone in your position.'

'They like to mock other people,' Peredonov objected.

'But never you,' said Rutilov persuasively.

'How can I be sure?'

'You must believe what I say. I won't trick you. They respect you. You're not some sort of Pavlushka, always making yourself a laughing-stock.'

'Well, I shall take your word for it,' Peredonov said sceptically. 'All the same, I want to make sure for myself.'

Rutilov said in amazement, 'You *are* a strange fellow! How would they dare laugh at you? Anyway, how do you want to convince yourself?'

Peredonov thought for a moment and said, 'I want to see them here in the street, right away.'

'You have but to say –'

'All three of them,' continued Peredonov.

'All right.'

'And I want each one to tell me what she has to offer.'

'Why on earth –?' Rutilov asked in amazement.

'I want to see for myself what they want. I don't want to be led up the garden path.'

'No one's going to do that.'

'Perhaps they'll want to laugh at me,' Peredonov reasoned. 'Well, let them come out. If they want to laugh at me, I'll laugh at them!'

Rutilov pushed his hat to the back of his head, then over his brow, and reflected. At last he said, 'Right. Wait here a moment and I'll go in and tell them. You really are a queer fish, I must say! But stay inside the gate – you never know who might come down the street and see you.'

'I don't give a damn who sees,' said Peredonov, following Rutilov all the same.

All the sisters were sitting in the room that looked on to the front garden. All had the same features as their brother; all were attractive, rosy-cheeked and high-spirited. Larisa, the married sister, was quiet, pleasant and rather plump; Darya, the tallest and slimmest, was flighty and lively; then there was Lyudmila, so easily amused; and Valeriya, small, delicate and frail-looking. They were all eating nuts and raisins and, judging from the fact that they were excited and laughing more than usual, were clearly expecting something to happen. Close friends and people they had never even met came in for ridicule as they discussed the latest town gossip. Since early that morning they had been ready for the altar and needed only to put on a suitable dress, veil themselves and pin flowers to their hair. The sisters made no mention of Varvara in their conversation, as if she didn't exist. But the fact that those merciless scoffers made no mention of her, when they picked everyone else to pieces, proved that she was firmly entrenched in their minds, an ever-present menace.

'He's here. At the gate,' Rutilov announced as he entered the drawing-room.

The sisters stirred themselves at this news and began talking and laughing in chorus.

'There's only one snag,' laughed Rutilov.

'What's that?' asked Darya.

Valeriya knitted her beautiful dark eyebrows together in annoyance.

'I don't know whether I should tell you,' Rutilov said.

'Don't keep us in suspense!' Darya urged.

With some embarrassment Rutilov told them what Peredonov wanted. The young ladies shrieked and vied with one another in showering Peredonov with abuse.

Gradually, however, their indignation gave way to laughter and jokes. Darya assumed a grimly expectant expression and said, 'This is how he's standing at the gate!'

It was a very good imitation.

The girls looked out of the window towards the gate. Darya opened the window a little and cried out, 'Mr Peredonov! Can we speak to you like this?'

Back came the gruff reply, 'No, you can't.'

Darya quickly shut the window. The room was instantly filled with unbridled laughter as the sisters ran from the drawing-room into the dining-room so that Peredonov couldn't hear them. In that happy household they could pass in a flash from the angriest of moods to laughter and jokes, one cheerful word usually being enough to tip the scales.

Peredonov stood by the gate and waited. He felt miserable, even frightened. He thought of running away, but did not have the courage. Somewhere, far off, he could hear someone playing the piano – most likely the marshal's daughter. Those faint, delicate sounds flowed into the quiet hazy air of evening, awakening sadness in the heart and inducing sweet day-dreams.

At first these day-dreams took an erotic form and he pictured the Rutilov girls in the most seductive poses. But the longer he had to wait the more annoyed he became. No longer could he hear the music that had barely stirred his dull, unreceptive senses. Night came swiftly and silently, and all around were ominous footsteps and whispers. Two shafts of light from the drawing-room fell across the fence and accentuated the surrounding darkness, and beyond the fence dark log walls were visible. Deep down in the Rutilovs' garden the trees grew black and menacing, and they seemed to be whispering to each other. From the street came the sound of slow, shuffling footsteps – not very far away. What if he were attacked and robbed, murdered even, while he was standing there? He pressed against the wall, hid in the shadows and nervously waited. Suddenly the broad beams of light were broken by long shadows, doors banged, voices could be heard behind the porch door. He cheered up. They're coming at last! he joyfully thought. And amorous visions began to fill his mind again – the vile offspring of his meagre imagination.

The sisters were standing in the hall. Rutilov came out to the gate to see if anyone was coming down the street. There wasn't a soul to be seen. 'It's all clear,' he whispered to them through his cupped hands. He stayed in the street to keep watch and Peredonov joined him. 'They're coming out to speak to you right now,' Rutilov said.

Peredonov stood by the gate and peered through one of the narrow gaps between the gate and the post. He looked mournful again, scared almost, and all the erotic imaginings and day-dreams faded, leaving a vague, aching desire.

Darya was the first to appear. 'And how can I tickle your appetite?' she asked.

Peredonov remained sullenly silent. Darya went on, 'I'll make you the most delicious pancakes, piping hot, but you'll have to watch you don't choke yourself!'

Lyudmila shouted over her shoulder, 'And I'll go and collect all the gossip every morning and come back and tell you all about it. That should be great fun!'

Valeriya's mischievous delicate face popped up between the two cheerful faces and she said in her frail voice, 'I wouldn't tell you for anything in the world how I'd please you – try and guess for yourself!'

The sisters scampered off in fits of laughter and the sound of their voices died away behind the door. Peredonov turned away, not really satisfied. They just babbled something and left, he thought. They should have written it all down on bits of paper. I don't want to stand around here waiting at this late hour.

'Well, did you have a good look? Have you decided?' asked Rutilov.

Peredonov gloomily reflected for a moment. Of course, he finally decided that he'd better choose the youngest. What did he want with the oldest one?

'Let me see Valeriya again,' he said with determination in his voice.

Lyudmila peered furtively through the window, trying to make out what they were saying, but was unsuccessful. Then footsteps rang out on the planked path in the yard. The sisters became quiet and sat there, excited and embarrassed. Rutilov came in again.

'He's chosen Valeriya and he's waiting by the gate,' he announced.

The sisters laughed, but Valeriya turned slightly pale. 'Well, well,' she repeated. 'I need him badly, ever so badly!'

Her hands trembled as her sisters started to dress her for the wedding, all three of them bustling around her. As always she was very fussy and took her time. Her sisters made her hurry up. Rutilov couldn't stop talking for excitement. He was naturally overjoyed – and very pleased with himself for arranging everything so well.

Darya asked him in a worried voice, 'Have you ordered the cabs?'

Rutilov was annoyed at her stupidity and replied, 'How could I do that? Do you think we want the whole town at the wedding? Varvara would drag Peredonov home by his hair!'

'So how shall we get there?'

'We'll walk in pairs to the square and take a cab from there. It's very simple. First you go with the bride, then Larisa with the groom. Lyudmila and I will stop off for Falastov, they can go together, and then I'll pick up Volodin.'

Peredonov, who had been standing by himself, had sweet visions of Valeriya in all the enchantment of their wedding night: naked, bashful but happy. So frail, so delicate . . .

As he day-dreamed like this he took the remaining caramels out of his pocket and sucked them.

Then he recalled that Valeriya was a coquette. She would certainly want a new dress every week, nice furniture. It would be impossible to put some money by every month as he'd have to spend all his savings. She might create scenes and wouldn't deign to show her face in the kitchen. And they might slip poison into his food there – Varvara could very well bribe the cook out of sheer spite. No, thought Peredonov, she's much too delicate for me. I just wouldn't know how to handle her. How could I swear at someone like her, beat her, spit on her? She'd cry her heart out and make my name mud all over town. No, life with her would be sheer hell. Now, Lyudmila's far less complicated – why not take her?

Peredonov went over to the window and tapped the frame with his walking-stick. After a few moments Rutilov stuck his head out and anxiously asked, 'What do you want?'

'I've changed my mind,' Peredonov growled.

'Well?' Rutilov cried out in alarm.

'I want to see Lyudmila,' Peredonov said.

Rutilov went away from the window.

'He's the devil in spectacles,' he grumbled and went to speak to his sisters.

Valeriya was overjoyed. 'You're the lucky one, Lyudmila,' she said gaily.

Lyudmila fell back in her armchair and just couldn't stop laughing.

'Well, what shall I tell him?' Rutilov asked. 'Is it all right with you?'

Lyudmila couldn't speak for laughter and merely waved her hands.

'Of course it is,' Darya answered for her. 'You'd better go outside quickly in case he gets tired of waiting.'

Rutilov went into the drawing-room and whispered through the window, 'She won't be a moment.'

'Tell her to hurry up!' said Peredonov crossly. 'What are they up to in there?'

Her sisters dressed Lyudmila quickly and she was ready in five minutes. Peredonov was still undecided. True, she was plump and cheerful. But she laughed too much. Most likely she'd laugh at him, and that he couldn't stand. Although Darya was rather lively she was at least steadier and quieter. And prettier too. A far better proposition. He knocked on the window once more.

'There he goes again,' said Larisa. 'It must be you this time, Darya.'

'He's a real devil!' roared Rutilov and rushed to the window.

'Who do you want now?' he whispered angrily. 'Changed your mind again?'

'Let me see Darya,' Peredonov answered.

Rutilov was in a blind rage. 'Wait here!' he said.

Peredonov was already revising his opinion of Darya and his short-lived admiration of her gave way to fear. She was far too boisterous and cheeky for him and she'd make his life hell. Why am I standing here like this? he thought. I might catch cold. Perhaps someone's hiding in the ditch along the street, or in the grass under the fence, just waiting to jump out and bump me off! And he felt really depressed. None of them had any money to speak of, and they had no influence at all with the education authorities. Varvara would complain to the princess. And as it was the headmaster had a grudge against him.

He began to feel angry with himself. What on earth was he getting mixed up with Rutilov for? It seemed he'd cast a spell over him. Yes, that was quite possible. He must recite a counter-charm at once. He turned round and round, spat in all directions and muttered, 'Chur-churashki, churki-balvashki, buki-bukashki, vedi-tarakashki. Evil spirits keep away. Away, away.'

His face showed intense concentration, as if he were performing some solemn ritual. Feeling he'd done what was necessary he now considered himself safe from Rutilov's sorcery. He banged on the window with his stick, furiously muttering to himself, They should be reported for trying to trap me. 'No, I don't want to get married today,' he declared to Rutilov, who was poking his head out.

'You can't back out now, Ardalyon. Everything's ready,' said Rutilov, trying to prevail upon him.

'I don't want to get married,' Peredonov replied decisively. 'Come round to my place for a game of cards.'

'He's a real devil, no mistake!' cursed Rutilov. 'He doesn't want to get married – he's got cold feet,' he announced to his sisters. 'But I'll talk that old fool into it yet, don't you worry. Now he wants me to play cards with him!'

The sisters simultaneously hurled abuse at Peredonov.

'And after all this you're going to play cards with that scoundrel?' cried Valeriya.

'Yes! I'll take all his money off him. He's not going to get away with it as easily as that,' Rutilov said, trying to sound sure of himself but in fact feeling very awkward.

The sisters' anger soon turned to laughter. Rutilov set off for Peredonov's and they ran to the window.

'Mr Peredonov!' called Darya. 'Why can't you make your mind up? This is no way to go on.'

'Old sourpuss!' Lyudmila cried, laughing out loud.

Peredonov felt aggrieved that the sisters weren't shedding sad tears at having been rejected by him. They're only pretending! he thought as he walked out of the yard without saying one word. The girls ran to the front windows and he was followed by their taunts all the way down the street until the darkness swallowed him up.

V

Peredonov was utterly miserable that there were no caramels left: it both saddened and infuriated him. Almost the whole way home Rutilov did all the talking, still singing his sisters' praises. Only once did Peredonov enter into conversation, when he angrily asked, 'Does a bull have horns?'

'Yes it does. What of it?' Rutilov replied in amazement.

'Well, I don't want to be a bull,' Peredonov explained.

'You'll never be a bull, Ardalyon, since you're a perfect pig,' Rutilov replied, thoroughly vexed.

'That's a lie!' Peredonov morosely replied.

'No, I'm not lying, I can prove it,' Rutilov gloated.

'Go on,' said Peredonov.

'If you wait a moment, I shall,' Rutilov replied, still gloating.

Both fell silent. Peredonov waited apprehensively and his annoyance with Rutilov had a wearying effect on him.

'Ardalyon, do you have a pyatachok?' [1] Rutilov suddenly asked.

1. Pun, meaning both 'five-copeck piece' and 'pig's snout'.

'Yes, I do, but you're not having it,' Peredonov spitefully replied.

Rutilov burst into loud laughter. 'Well, if you have one of those, how come you're not a pig?' Rutilov gleefully exclaimed.

Peredonov clutched his nose in horror. 'You're lying. I've a human snout, not a pig's snout,' he muttered.

Rutilov guffawed. Peredonov glanced indignantly and anxiously at Rutilov and said, 'You took me past some thorn-apple[1] today on purpose and drugged me with it to make me marry one of your sisters. One witch is bad enough already, without marrying three at once!'

'You silly ass, how come *I* wasn't drugged by it too?'

'You have some secret remedy,' Peredonov said. 'Perhaps you breathed through your mouth and didn't let it go up your nose. Or you may have recited some special words. I don't know what to use against witchcraft. Until I thought of that counter-charm I was thoroughly drugged.'

Rutilov roared with laughter. 'What did you say then?' he asked, but Peredonov ignored him. 'Why are you so stuck on Varvara?' Rutilov went on. 'Do you think you'll be better off if you get the job through her? Then she'll really have you in her clutches.'

Peredonov could understand none of this. She's really doing this in her own interests, he thought. She'll reap the benefit when I become an inspector and earn lots of money. That means *she* should be grateful to *me*, not the other way round. And in any event I feel more at ease with her than with anyone else.

The truth was that Peredonov was used to Varvara and felt an irresistible attraction towards her. Perhaps it was because he enjoyed making fun of and being cruel to her. He'd certainly never find another like her, not even made to order.

It was getting late and the light from Peredonov's room shone brightly on the pavement against the darkness of the street. Grushina (who now came to see Varvara every day), Mrs Prepolovensky and her husband Konstantin, a tall man of about forty with a pale matt skin, black hair, and of remarkable taciturnity, were drinking tea at the table. Varvara, decked out in her best white

1. Durman: the thorn-apple, a poisonous plant of the nightshade family, with narcotic properties.

44

dress, was very worried that Peredonov had been away so long and when Volodin cheerfully bleated that he had gone off somewhere with Rutilov her anxiety grew. When at last the men returned they were greeted with jeers and stupid dirty jokes.

'Varvara, where's the vodka?' Peredonov angrily asked.

Varvara smiled guiltily, rushed from the table and quickly returned with a large coarsely cut decanter.

'Let's drink,' he said morosely.

'Wait a moment,' said Varvara. 'Claudia will bring us some savouries. Get a move on, you great lump!' she shouted into the kitchen.

But Peredonov was already pouring the vodka. 'Why wait?' he muttered. 'Time doesn't wait!'

They drank up and ate pies filled with blackcurrant jam. All that Peredonov ever kept for entertaining his guests were playing-cards and vodka. But as it was impolite to start playing before tea was served all they could do was go on drinking. Meanwhile Claudia brought them some savouries to help them with the vodka. She forgot to shut the door when she went out into the kitchen, which annoyed Peredonov no end. 'You're always leaving the doors wide open,' he growled.

He was scared of draughts – one could catch cold. With the doors shut the whole time the flat was always stuffy and evil-smelling.

Mrs Prepolovensky took a hard-boiled egg. 'What nice eggs!' she said. 'Where did you get them?'

'They're not too bad,' Peredonov replied. 'But my father had a hen that regularly laid two large ones a day all the year round.'

'That's nothing!' Mrs Prepolovensky replied. 'In our village we had a hen that laid two eggs a day and a spoonful of butter.'

'Yes, yes, ours too!' Peredonov said, not realizing his leg was being pulled. 'There was no hen like ours. She was quite remarkable.'

Varvara laughed. 'Let them have their little joke,' she said.

'It really makes me sick, all this drivel,' Grushina said.

Peredonov looked at her fiercely and savagely retorted, 'If your ears are drooping you should have them pulled off.'[1]

This remark disconcerted Grushina who said plaintively, 'Really, Mr Peredonov! You're always saying things like that!'

1. Peredonov has taken Grushina's remark literally, the idiom for 'It makes me sick to hear this talk,' being translatable as 'It's enough to make my ears droop.'

Everyone laughed in sympathy. Volodin blinked, shook his head and explained, 'If your ears start drooping it's best to have them pulled off. No good having them flapping about to and fro, to and fro.' Volodin demonstrated by tugging his ears.

Grushina shouted at him, 'Can't you think of a joke of your own? Always apeing other people!'

Volodin took offence and replied pompously, 'What does it matter, as long as one has a good time, in nice company? I can make jokes too. But if this is not to your liking, then you know what you can do.'

'Well said, Pavel,' Rutilov laughed approvingly.

'Mr Volodin certainly knows how to stand up for himself,' Mrs Prepolovensky said with a wry grin. Varvara cut a slice off the loaf and kept the knife in her hand as she listened spellbound to Volodin's fine speeches. The edge glittered and Peredonov took fright: was she going to cut his throat? He cried out, 'Varvara! Put that knife down!'

Varvara shuddered. 'You frightened me out of my life with your shouting!' she said, putting it down. 'He's like that at times,' she explained to the silent Mr Prepolovensky, who was stroking his beard and seemed about to say something.

'That kind of thing does happen. I knew a fellow once who was afraid of needles,' he said in a sad, cloying voice. 'He thought someone might stick one right into him one day and whenever he saw a needle he was terribly scared, as you can imagine . . .' And he rambled on and on, unable to stop, telling different versions of the same story, until someone interrupted. Then he lapsed into silence again.

Grushina started to tell smutty stories. She told everyone how her late husband had been jealous and how she had been unfaithful. Then she told some story she'd heard from a friend in St Petersburg about the mistress of an important government official, who met him once while driving in the street and shouted, 'Hullo, my dear old Jean!'

'I ask you,' Grushina said, '*in the street*!'

Peredonov retorted, 'I've a good mind to report you to the police. You shouldn't be allowed to say such stupid things about important officials.'

Grushina was taken aback and mumbled, 'That's what I was told. I don't believe in keeping things to myself.'

Peredonov sat angrily, not saying a word, and drank his tea from the saucer, his elbows on the table. In the house of a future inspector it was very bad form talking so disrespectfully about dignitaries. He was furious with Grushina. And there was something highly suspicious about Volodin's eternal references to him as the future inspector. On some previous occasion Peredonov had even told Volodin, 'My dear chap, I can see how jealous you are. Yes, I'm going to be an inspector and you're not!'

To this Volodin had forcefully replied, 'Each to his own, Ardalyon. We're both experts – in our own fields.'

'Did you know that our Natasha got a job with a police officer immediately she left here?' announced Varvara.

Peredonov shivered and a look of horror appeared on his face. 'You're lying, of course?' he said questioningly.

'Why should I lie?' Varvara replied. 'Go and ask him for yourself if you like.'

This unwelcome information was confirmed by Grushina. Peredonov was speechless. She might tell him anything, the police officer would take note and probably report him to the Ministry. It looked very bad.

At this moment some books on the shelf over the chest of drawers caught his attention. The fat ones were bound volumes of *Annals of the Fatherland*[1] and the thinner ones the works of Pisarev. Peredonov turned pale and said, 'We must hide them at once or I'll be reported.'

Peredonov used to keep these books prominently displayed, to show everyone that he was a man of liberal ideas, although in reality he had neither ideas nor any inclination whatsoever for thought. He only kept them for show – he never opened them and it was a long time since he had read anything. He did not take any newspapers and obtained all his news from other people. But then nothing counted as news for him, as nothing in the outside

---

1. Leading journal (1839–84) of the Westernizers and progressive writers, numbering among its contributors Belinsky, Herzen and Turgenev. It was closed for political reasons.

world interested him. He would even laugh at his friends who were stupid enough to spend time and money on newspapers. *His* time was far too precious!

He went up to the shelf and grumbled, 'In this kind of town they'd report you right away. Help me with these, Pavel,' he asked Volodin. Trying to look sympathetic and understanding, Volodin carefully took the books Peredonov handed him. Peredonov let him carry most of them and Volodin followed him into the parlour.

'Where are we going to hide them, Ardalyon?' he asked.

'Wait and see,' Peredonov replied with his habitual surliness.

'What's that you're taking out, Mr Peredonov?' asked Mrs Prepolovensky.

'Banned books,' replied Peredonov as he passed through the room. 'If they know I've got these I'll be reported.'

In the parlour Peredonov squatted in front of the stove and piled the books high on the iron grating. Volodin followed suit. Then he stuffed one book after another into the narrow opening as fast as he could. Volodin, who had adopted the same position behind him, handed him the books and tried to make his sheeplike face look highly serious, his lips puffed out with importance and his sharp forehead bowed from the mental effort. Varvara kept looking at them through the door and said, laughing, 'He's up to his tricks again!'

Grushina cut in, 'Don't talk like that, dear. He can get into serious trouble if they find out, especially as he's a teacher. The governors are terribly scared that the teachers might be putting revolutionary ideas into the boys' heads.'

When they had finished their tea all seven sat down to a game of cards around the card-table in the parlour. Peredonov played with abandon but very badly. Every twenty points he had to pay the other players, particularly Mr Prepolovensky, who took the money for himself and his wife. In fact, the Prepolovenskys were clearly winning more than anyone else. By prearranged signs – such as a slight cough or knocking on the table – they each knew the other's hand. That day Peredonov's luck was out right from the start. He was in a terrible hurry to recoup his losses but Volodin dealt very slowly, meticulously shuffling the cards.

'Hurry up and deal, Pavlushka!' Peredonov cried out impatiently.

Volodin, who felt he was the equal of all the others, assumed an important expression and asked, 'Why do you call me Pavlushka? Out of friendship, or what?'

'Out of friendship, friendship,' Peredonov replied casually. 'Now, deal a bit quicker.'

'Well, if it's out of friendship, then I'm very pleased,' Volodin said with a happy stupid laugh as he dealt. 'You're a good man, Ardalyon, and I'm very fond of you. If it weren't out of friendship it would be quite a different matter, but if it is, I'm glad. I've dealt you an ace for it!' Volodin added and led with a trump.

In fact Peredonov was dealt an ace, but not a trump, and he had to pay a forfeit. 'You dealt me an ace all right,' Peredonov growled, 'but the wrong one. There's something going on here! I needed the trump, but what did you deal me? What do I need that teak-bellied[1] ace for?'

Rutilov picked up the phrase with a laugh and said, 'He's dealt you an ace with a large belly because your own is getting fat!'

'The future inspector's getting his tongue in a twist. Puz, puz, karapuz!'[2] cried Volodin.

Rutilov chattered incessantly, repeated scandal, all kinds of anecdotes, some of which were quite *risqué*. To tease Peredonov he related how scandalously the boys at school were behaving, especially those who lived out. They smoked, drank vodka and chased the girls. Peredonov believed him and Grushina confirmed this account. The stories gave her particular pleasure: after her husband's death she had wanted to take in three or four boarders, but the headmaster was well aware of her reputation in that town and in spite of Peredonov's intervention refused to give her a licence. Now she began to tell malicious lies about landladies who were accorded that privilege.

'They bribe the headmaster,' she announced.

'All landladies are bitches,' Volodin said with conviction. 'Take

1. A spoonerism on Peredonov's part. He has transposed the initial letters of pikovy tuz (ace of spades), giving tikovy puz (teak belly).
2. Volodin subsequently attempts punning the word puz (belly), making karapuz, a chubby child.

mine, for example. When I first took the room she agreed to bring me up three glasses of milk every evening. It was all right for the first month or so.'

'You didn't drink yourself silly, did you?' Rutilov laughed.

'Why should I do that?' Volodin replied indignantly. 'Milk is good for you. And I like to have three glasses before going to sleep. Then I noticed that she was bringing me only two glasses. I asked the maid why and she said, "Madam is very sorry but the cow isn't giving much milk just now." What did that have to do with me? After all, an agreement's an agreement. Why should I go thirsty because of the confounded cow? So I sent the maid back with the message, "Tell your mistress that if there's no milk I'll make do with water. I must have my three glasses, two's not enough."'

'Did you know our Pavlushka's a hero?' said Peredonov. 'Tell them about your argument with the general.'

Volodin was only too willing to repeat the story. But this time he was laughed down and he indignantly stuck out his lower lip.

During supper everyone got drunk, even the ladies. Volodin suggested another attack on the walls, to the delight of all present. Before they had even finished the meal they got down to work and wildly enjoyed themselves. They spat on the wallpaper, poured beer all over it and fired paper darts tipped with butter at the walls and the ceiling, which was spattered with pieces of chewed-up bread. Then they had a competition to see who could tear off the largest strip of wallpaper and the Prepolovenskys won a further one-and-a-half roubles.

Volodin had no success at all and the combined effects of this and his intoxication brought on a sudden depression. He began to complain bitterly about his mother. His face full of reproach and his arm thrust downwards for some reason, he said, 'Why did she bear me? And what were her thoughts at the time? Look at my life now. She was never a mother to me, only the person who bore me. A real mother cares about her children, but when I was a few years old she bundled me off to an orphanage.'

'But it didn't do you any harm by the look of it,' Mrs Prepolovensky said.

Volodin stared at the floor, shook his head and said, 'You're wrong. I lead a dog's life. Why, why did she give birth to me? What were her thoughts?'

Peredonov suddenly remembered the erli of yesterday. There you are, he thought. He's complaining about his mother and why she bore him, so he doesn't want to be Pavlushka Volodin. He must be jealous. Perhaps he wants to be in my shoes and marry Varvara?

He looked sadly at Volodin: he must get him married to someone as soon as possible.

That night, in the bedroom, Varvara told Peredonov, 'Do you think all those young girls who are chasing after you are so beautiful? If you really want to know, they're absolute rubbish. I'm prettier than the lot of them.'

She quickly undressed and with a provocative smile showed Peredonov her beautiful pale pink, shapely, supple body. Though she was still reeling from drink and her flabby lascivious face would have inspired nothing but disgust in most men, her body had a strange allure. It was the lovely body of a gentle nymph with a faded whore's head attached to it by some perverse magic. And this beautiful body was for those two drunken filthy-minded wretches merely the source of the basest pleasures. Indeed, as is so often the case in our day and age, beauty is debased, abused.

Peredonov mournfully laughed as he looked at his naked mistress. All night long he dreamed of women of all kinds, naked and disgusting. Varvara really believed that following Mrs Prepoloven-sky's advice and rubbing herself daily with nettles had helped her put on weight. Whenever she met a friend she would ask. 'Don't you think I've filled out a little?' And she thought that Peredonov would waste no time in marrying her when he saw how much weight she'd put on, and especially when he'd received the letter.

Peredonov, however, was in a far less optimistic frame of mind. The headmaster was his deadly enemy – of that he had long been convinced. In fact the headmaster considered Peredonov lazy and incompetent. Peredonov, on the other hand, thought that the headmaster was purposely encouraging the boys to be rude, which of course was nothing but a stupid invention of his own.

However, it convinced Peredonov that he must defend himself and he tried to get his own back by inventing scandalous stories about the headmaster and telling them to the senior boys, many of whom were only too ready to listen. And now, as he was hoping to become an inspector, this hostility on the headmaster's part was particularly unwelcome. If she so wished, the princess could presumably use her influence to overcome the headmaster's machinations. All the same, they were a possible source of danger.

And there were others in the town, as Peredonov had recently noticed, who were hostile and who wanted to block his promotion. Volodin, for instance, who obviously for some good reason kept on using the words 'future inspector'. There had been cases where people had impersonated others and subsequently prospered. Of course, for Volodin actually to take the place of Peredonov himself would prove rather difficult, but there was no knowing what crazy things an imbecile like that might get up to. And then the Rutilovs, Vershina and Marta – partners in jealousy – would jump at the chance to do him harm. But how could they? They could make him out to be extremely unreliable, blacken his name before the authorities – that was quite obvious.

Therefore Peredonov was faced with two problems: to show how very reliable he was, and to make himself safe from Volodin by ensuring he married some rich woman.

So one day he asked Volodin, 'Would you like to marry Miss Adamenko? Or are you still pining for Marta? Isn't a whole month rather a long time to get over it?'

'Why should I be pining for Marta?' Volodin replied. 'I did her a great honour by proposing, but if she doesn't want me what do you expect me to do? I won't have much trouble finding someone else. There's as good fish in the sea . . .'

'Yes, but Marta made a fool of you,' Peredonov teased.

'I just don't know what kind of husband they're looking for,' Volodin said in a hurt voice. 'I wouldn't care, but she hasn't even any money. I think it's you she's after, Ardalyon.'

'If I were you I'd smear her gates with tar,' Peredonov advised.

'It could be nasty if I were caught.'

'Hire someone, why do it yourself?' Peredonov said.

'She deserves it, by God she deserves it!' Volodin said with animation. 'She doesn't want to enter into lawful wedlock, yet she lets young men in through the window – what sort of behaviour is that! Some people have no shame, no conscience.'

VI

Next day Peredonov and Volodin went to see Nadezhda Adamenko. Volodin had dressed himself up for the occasion, wearing his new tight-fitting jacket, a freshly starched shirt and a bright neckerchief. His hair was heavily greased and he had sprayed himself with scent. He was in very high spirits.

Nadezhda Vasilyevna Adamenko lived with her brother in a small red-brick house. Not far from the town she had a small estate, which she leased out. About two years previously she had left the local high school and now her sole occupation was lying on a divan reading novels of every description. She also gave lessons to her eleven-year-old schoolboy brother, who complained when she was too strict with him by angrily declaring, 'It was better when Mama was alive. She would only stand the umbrella in the corner.' Nadezhda's aunt lived with her – a shrivelled-up anonymous old woman who had no say in the running of the house. Nadezhda was very choosy about her friends. Peredonov rarely visited her, but thought that a slight acquaintance was a good reason for supposing she would marry his friend Volodin.

She was very surprised at this unexpected visit, but welcomed her uninvited guests most graciously. She wondered how she could entertain them and, remembering that Peredonov taught Russian literature, started to discuss educational matters, high-school reforms, literature, Symbolism and journals. She touched on all of these topics but all she received by way of reply were rather puzzling rebuffs, which showed her visitors weren't in the least interested. She realized that the latest scandal would be the only possible topic of conversation, but in a last desperate attempt at serious conversation she asked, 'Have you read Chekhov's "Man in a Case"? It's very well written and observed, isn't it?'

As this question was addressed to Volodin he grinned pleasantly and asked, 'Is it an article or a novel?'

'It's a short story,' Nadezhda explained.

'By a Mr Chekhov, you said?'

'Why, yes,' Nadezhda replied, smiling.

'Where did it appear?' asked the inquisitive Volodin.

'In *Russian Thought*'[1] the young lady graciously replied.

'In which number?' Volodin asked yet again.

'I really don't remember, I think it came out in the summer,' Nadezhda replied, still graciously but somewhat startled at all these questions.

A small schoolboy suddenly poked his head round the corner. 'It came out in May,' he said, leaning against the door with one hand and surveying his sister and guests with his cheerful blue eyes.

'You're too young to be reading fiction,' snapped Peredonov. 'You should be studying what you're given at school instead of reading obscene rubbish.'

Nadezhda glared at her brother. 'That's very nice behaviour, listening behind the door.' She crossed her fingers at a right angle. Two little fingers crossed meant that he had to stand in the corner for ten minutes. The schoolboy frowned and vanished. He went back to his room and stood in the corner looking at the clock. Sadly he thought, It was better when Mama was alive, she only stood the umbrella in the corner.

Back in the drawing-room Volodin made a solemn promise to get hold of the May issue of *Russian Thought* and read Mr Chekhov's story. Peredonov listened with an expression of undisguised boredom. Finally he said, 'I haven't read it either. As I said, I don't read rubbish. In novels and stories they only write stupid nonsense.'

Nadezhda smiled politely and said, 'I think you're being very hard on contemporary literature. You must admit some good things are being written these days?'

'I read all the books worth reading a long time ago,' Peredonov announced. 'And I don't intend reading any of this modern stuff.'

Volodin looked at Peredonov with respect. Nadezhda gently sighed and, as there was nothing else she could do, engaged in idle talk and gossip to the best of her ability. Although she never indulged in trivial small talk she managed to keep the conversation going with all the skill and vivacity of an intelligent, confident young woman.

The guests cheered up. Nadezhda was incredibly bored but her

1. 'Man in a Case' was first published in the July issue of *Russian Thought* in 1898.

guests thought that she was being particularly nice to them. Peredonov ascribed this to Volodin's inescapable infectious charm.

When they were outside in the street Peredonov congratulated Volodin on his success. Volodin, who had clearly forgotten the refusals of the past, jumped up and down for joy.

'Now stop leaping about like a four-year-old ram,' Peredonov told him. 'And don't be too sure of yourself, she might still make a fool of you.' However, he meant this as a joke: he really believed his matchmaking had been successful.

Grushina went to see Varvara almost every day and Varvara visited her even more often, so the two were rarely apart. Varvara was very worried that Grushina was taking so long with the letter. Grushina assured her that it was very difficult to make a fair copy from such awkward handwriting.

Peredonov was still unwilling to arrange a date for the wedding and once again insisted on being appointed inspector before he took any such step. Reminding her how many girls were waiting for him he threatened Varvara more than once (as he had done the previous winter) with the words, 'I'm going off to get married right now. And when I come back in the morning with my wife I expect you to be gone. This is the last night you'll be spending here.' And with these words he would go off to play billiards. Sometimes he would come straight home in the evening, but more often than not he would make merry in some disreputable drinking-den with Rutilov and Volodin. When this happened Varvara would lie awake the whole night and as a result suffered from migraine. It wasn't so trying for her if he came home around midnight, but when he returned in the early morning she could hardly get through the day.

Grushina at last finished the letter and showed it to Varvara. They scrutinized it very carefully, comparing it with the princess's letter of the previous year. Grushina maintained that the princess herself would never tell the difference. Although there was little similarity Varvara believed her. Also, she realized that Peredonov would have only the faintest recollection of such unfamiliar hand-writing and thus would never detect the forgery.

'Well!' she happily exclaimed. 'I was really beginning to lose patience. But what about the envelope? What shall I tell him if he asks?'

'I can't forge the envelope, because of the postmark,' Grushina chuckled, glancing at Varvara with her crafty, different-sized eyes: the right one was a little larger than the left.

'What shall I do then?'

'It's quite easy, dear. Just tell him you threw it into the fire – why should you keep the envelope?'

Varvara's hopes rose. 'If only he'd make up his mind and marry me there wouldn't be any more of this running around. I'd make sure *he* did the running!' she told Grushina.

After dinner on Saturday Peredonov went off to play billiards. He was feeling unusually depressed. It's terrible living with all these jealous, hostile people, he thought. But what can I do? Not everybody can be an inspector! That's what they mean by survival of the fittest!

At the intersection of two streets he had the bad luck to meet a police officer, Lieutenant-Colonel Nikolay Rubovsky, a short stocky man with jolly grey eyes and thick, bushy eyebrows. His limp made his spurs jingle unevenly and loudly. He was very charming and therefore well liked in local society. He knew everything about everyone in the town and loved listening to gossip, but he himself was a model of tact and discretion.

They greeted each other and chatted for a while. Then Peredonov frowned, looked all around and cautiously remarked, 'I hear our Natasha's working for you now. I wouldn't believe a word she says about me, she's a born liar.'

'I don't listen to maids' gossip,' Rubovsky replied with dignity.

'She's the lowest of the low,' continued Peredonov, ignoring Rubovsky's rejoinder. 'She has a Polish lover and perhaps she came to you just to filch some secret document.'

'You needn't worry on that score,' the lieutenant-colonel coldly replied. 'I don't have blueprints for fortresses at my house.'

The mention of fortresses worried Peredonov. It seemed to him that Rubovsky was hinting that he could easily lock him away in one. 'Well, I didn't really mean fortresses,' he muttered. 'That's the last thing on my mind. It's just that, in general, people are talking all sorts of stupid nonsense about me, mainly out of sheer envy. Don't you believe any of it. They want to inform on me to divert suspicion from themselves, but I'm quite capable of informing myself.'

Rubovsky was mystified. 'I do assure you,' he said, shrugging his shoulders and jingling his spurs, 'no one's reported you to me. Obviously someone made the threat as a joke – people can say all sorts of things.'

Peredonov did not believe him. He thought that the police officer was hiding something and suddenly he felt terrified.

Every time Peredonov passed Vershina's garden she would stop him and try and lure him in with her bewitching movements and words. And he would go in, unwillingly submitting to her gentle witchcraft. Perhaps she had a better chance of achieving her ends than the Rutilovs? After all, he was equally remote from everyone, so why shouldn't he marry Marta? But it was now apparent that the morass Peredonov was sinking into was so tenacious that no sorcery could ever succeed in extricating him from it and dropping him into another. And now, after his encounter with Rubovsky, he was once again enticed into the garden by Vershina, who was dressed as usual in black.

'Marta and Vladya are going into the country today,' she said, fondly gazing at him through a haze of cigarette smoke. 'How about joining them? A workman's come for them in a cart.'

'It would be too cramped,' Peredonov said sullenly.

'Nonsense,' Vershina replied, 'there's plenty of room. And even if you are a bit cramped it's not very far – only about four miles.'

Just then Marta came out of the house to ask Vershina something. The excitement of the trip had stirred her a little from her customary lethargy and her face was livelier and more cheerful than usual. The two of them tried to persuade Peredonov to make the trip.

'You'll be very comfortable,' Vershina assured him. 'You can sit with Marta in the back and Vladya will be in front with Ignaty. Look, the cart's over there.'

Peredonov followed Marta and Vershina into the yard where the cart was waiting. Vladya was busy packing some things into it. The cart looked roomy but Peredonov cast a mournful eye over it and said, 'I'm not going in that. Certainly not enough room for four – and that's not allowing for Vladya's things.'

'If you really feel like that,' Vershina said, 'Vladya can walk.'

'I don't mind at all,' Vladya said with a friendly but forced smile. 'I can easily walk it in one-and-a-half hours. I'll start now and I'll get there before you.'

Then Peredonov objected that the cart would shake him up and down too much. They returned to the summer-house. Everything was ready, but Ignaty was still gorging himself in the kitchen in the most leisurely fashion.

'How is Vladya getting on at school?' Marta asked Peredonov.

If anything annoyed Vershina it was Marta's complete inability to talk to Peredonov about any other topic except her brother.

'Shocking. He's lazy and inattentive.'

Vershina liked a good grumble now and again and she began to give Vladya a good telling-off. Vladya flushed and smiled alternately and shrugged his shoulders as if shivering with cold, raising one shoulder higher than the other, as was his habit.

'But the year's only just begun,' he protested. 'There's plenty of time yet.'

'You must work from the beginning,' Marta said, speaking like an elder sister and as a result blushing slightly.

'And he's mischievous into the bargain. He plays around just like a street urchin and on Thursday he said something very rude to me!'

Vladya suddenly flared up and hotly retorted, 'I said nothing of the kind! I only told the truth. He missed everybody else's mistakes in last week's homework and gave me the lowest mark for the best work.'

'That doesn't alter the fact that you were impertinent,' said Peredonov.

'I wasn't. I only said I would tell the inspector,' Vladya said heatedly, 'that you gave me the lowest mark for nothing!'

'Vladya! You're forgetting yourself,' Vershina crossly said. 'What about apologizing instead of keeping on saying the same thing?'

It suddenly dawned on Vladya that Peredonov might marry Marta, so it was bad policy to annoy him. He blushed a deeper red, fumbled with his belt and stuttered, 'I'm sorry, I only wanted you to look at my work again and give me the right marks.'

'Be quiet, please!' Vershina interrupted. 'I won't have this arguing.' Her whole dried-up body trembled almost imperceptibly. And she proceeded to shower him with many reproaches, puffing at her cigarette and wryly smiling as she always did, whatever the conversation. 'I shall have to tell your father to punish you,' she concluded.

'A good thrashing is what he needs,' said Peredonov with an angry look in the direction of the offending Vladya.

'Exactly,' Vershina agreed. 'A real good hiding.'

'Yes, a nice birching,' said Marta and blushed.

'That's why I'm coming with you today,' Peredonov continued. 'I shall tell your father to thrash you – and I'll see he does it properly.'

Vladya said nothing and looked at his tormentors. He shrugged his shoulders and smiled through his tears. His father was very strict and Vladya tried to console himself with the thought that they were only threatening him, nothing more. How could they spoil his holiday for him? After all, a holiday was almost a sacred day, on which nothing connected with school or work could ever happen.

But Peredonov liked seeing young boys in tears, especially when he was the one who saw to it that they wept and confessed. Vladya's confusion, his suppressed tears, his timid, guilty smile – all this delighted him. He decided to go with Marta and Vladya.

'Oh all right, I'll come then,' he told Marta.

Marta was glad but rather apprehensive. Of course, she wanted Peredonov to come along – rather, Vershina had wanted this for her and had instilled this desire in her with her powers of persuasion. But now that he had actually agreed to go with them, she felt ill at ease because of poor Vladya and sorry for him.

It was painful for Vladya as well. Was Peredonov going just because of him? He thought he might placate him and said, 'Mr Peredonov, if you think you're going to be uncomfortable, I'll go on foot.'

Peredonov looked at him suspiciously and said, 'Oh no, not on your life! We don't want you running off on your own. No, we'll take you to your father's and he can give you a good thrashing.'

Vladya flushed and sighed in despair. He felt so uneasy and miserable, so upset by his stern torturer, that he sank into a deep gloom. In an attempt to please Peredonov he tried to make more room for him. 'I'll arrange your seat so that you have a nice comfortable journey,' he said and he hurried off to the cart.

Vershina watched him, still smiling and still smoking. 'They're all scared of their father, he's terribly strict with them,' she told Peredonov quietly.

Marta blushed.

Vladya dearly wanted to take his new English fishing-rod, for which he had saved up all his money. And there was something else too, but all this would have taken up a lot of room so he took everything back into the house.

It was a warm day but the heat was not oppressive. The sun was just setting and the road, still wet from the morning rain, bore very few traces of dust. The cart rolled its way smoothly over the small cobblestones, carrying its four passengers out of town. The well-fed little grey mare trotted as if she had no weight at all to pull. With a barely perceptible movement of the reins, so delicate that only the expert eye would have noticed it, the silent, lethargic Ignaty put her into a fast trot.

Peredonov had taken his place next to Marta. Vladya had made so much room for him that it was extremely uncomfortable for her. But Peredonov was quite blind to her discomfort, and even if he had noticed he wouldn't have done a thing about it – after all, *he* was the guest.

Peredonov was in the best of moods and decided he would have a friendly chat with Marta and amuse her with a few jokes. He began: 'Well now, isn't it time you had a rebellion?'

'A rebellion?' Marta asked.

'Yes, you Poles are always having them but they never succeed.'

'Nothing could be further from my mind,' Marta said. 'None of us wants to rebel.'

'Aha! You only say that. In fact you hate the Russians.'

'Not at all,' Vladya said, turning round from the front where he was sitting with Ignaty.

'We know how you're plotting the whole time. We're not going to give you Poland back. We defeated you and at the same time brought you many benefits. No matter how well you feed a wolf he'll still hanker after the forest.'

Marta didn't attempt to contradict him. Peredonov said nothing for a moment and then he suddenly remarked, 'The Poles are a lot of brainless nitwits.'

Marta went very red in the face. 'Every country has its share of idiots,' she said.

'What I'm telling you is true,' insisted Peredonov. 'The Poles are stupid. All they can do is show off. Now take the Jews – they're a clever lot.'

'Jews are swindlers and not at all clever,' Vladya said.

'On the contrary, the Jews are very clever. A Jew will always fool a Russian, but never the other way round,' Peredonov retorted.

'But one shouldn't swindle,' Vladya said. 'Is that what you call clever, being able to cheat and swindle?'

Peredonov looked angrily at him. 'Cleverness consists in studying hard – which you don't!'

Vladya sighed, turned round and watched the mare's even trot.

Peredonov continued, 'Jews are clever at everything, including studying at school. If Jews were allowed to become professors, then all professors would be Jews. Polish women are all sluts.'

With much pleasure he watched Marta blush furiously and said, out of kindness, 'Don't think I mean you. I know for a fact you'd make a good housewife.'

'All Polish women make good housewives,' Marta replied.

'Hm, yes. They're clean on the surface but their petticoats are filthy. But then you had your Mickiewicz.[1] He's much better than our Pushkin. I have his portrait in my room. Pushkin used to hang there but I took him down and hung him in the lavatory. Pushkin was nothing but a court flunkey.'

'But you're Russian yourself,' Vladya said, 'so how can you prefer our Mickiewicz to Pushkin? They're both very good poets.'

'Mickiewicz is superior,' Peredonov repeated. 'The Russians are stupid. All they've done is invent the samovar.' Peredonov looked at Marta, blinked and said, 'You've got too many freckles. It doesn't look nice.'

'What can I do to get rid of them?' Marta asked, smiling.

'I've got them as well,' said Vladya, turning round and knocking the silent Ignaty with his elbow.

'You're only a boy,' Peredonov said. 'Besides, it doesn't matter with men. But with women' (he turned to Marta) 'it's positively unsightly. No one will marry you like that. You ought to try some cucumber brine.'

1. Adam Mickiewicz (1798–1855), Polish national poet. A friend of Pushkin.

Marta thanked him for the advice. Vladya smiled at Peredonov.

'What are you smiling about?' asked Peredonov. 'You wait, you're going to get such a thrashing once we get you to your father's!'

Vladya didn't know whether to take him seriously and stared him straight in the face. Peredonov couldn't bear being stared at and snapped, 'Why are you gawking at me like that? Do I have pretty patterns on my face? Or are you trying to cast an evil spell over me?'

Vladya turned his eyes away in fright. 'I beg your pardon . . . I didn't mean to stare on purpose.'

'Do you believe in the evil eye?' Marta asked.

'That's nothing but a stupid superstition,' Peredonov said irately. 'But it's terribly rude to stare like that, don't you think?'

An awkward silence followed, broken by Peredonov saying, 'It's true that you haven't much money, isn't it?'

'No, we're not rich,' replied Marta. 'At the same time, we're not so poor. We all have something put away.'

Peredonov looked at her disbelievingly and said, 'I know you're poor. At home you go around without any shoes the whole time.'

'But that's not because we're poor,' replied Vladya brightly.

'Because you're rich then?' Peredonov broke into loud bursts of laughter.

'*Not* because we're poor,' Vladya said, blushing. 'It's healthy and toughens us up – and it's very pleasant in summer.'

'You're lying,' said Peredonov gruffly. 'Rich people don't go around in bare feet. Your father has lots of children and he earns next to nothing. He can't afford to buy shoes for everyone.'[1]

1. See variant 4, p. 272.

VII

Varvara had no idea where Peredonov had gone and as a result spent a night sleepless with worry. When he arrived back in town in the morning Peredonov didn't go straight home but went to the church instead, where he was just in time for Mass. He thought that he was running a great risk by not appearing every now and then in church – he would be reported for that.

At the church gates he met a friendly-looking schoolboy with a healthy red face and angelic blue eyes. Peredonov said, 'Hullo, Mashenka,[1] bought any nice skirts lately?'

Misha Kudryatsev blushed to the roots of his hair. It was not the first time that Peredonov had teased him this way and he couldn't understand why. But he didn't have the courage to complain. Several of his stupid schoolfriends standing in a crowd near by laughed at Peredonov's remark. They too found teasing Misha great fun.

St Elijah's was an ancient building, dating back to the time of Tsar Mikhail. It stood in the square facing the school. On church holidays and for vespers the boys had to assemble and stand in rows to the left, by the side-chapel of St Katherine; behind them stood an assistant master to keep order. Next to them, and nearer the centre of the church, stood the form masters, the headmaster and the inspector, with their families. Most of the Orthodox boys went to the services, apart from a few who had permission to attend their parish churches with their parents. The choir was noted for its singing and the church was patronized by important merchants, civil servants and landowning families. Very few peasants or labourers worshipped there, especially as Mass was celebrated much later than in other churches, at the headmaster's special request.

Peredonov went to his usual place, from which he could see all the choirboys. He screwed up his eyes and thought that they were

1. Peredonov has made Misha into a girl's name.

standing very raggedly: *he* would have pulled them up for that if he were an inspector!

Kramarenko, for example, that small dark-faced frail and fidgety boy was behaving particularly badly. He was turning this way and that, whispering and smiling. It was most strange that no one stopped him, as if they couldn't be bothered.

An absolute disgrace, thought Peredonov. Those choirboys are lazy good-for-nothings. Kramarenko thinks he can smile and talk just because he has a good voice. And he frowned.

Next to Peredonov stood the inspector of national schools, Sergey Bogdanov, who had arrived late. He was an old man with a stupid dark face. He always gave the impression of wanting to explain something that he didn't understand himself. No one was easier to shock or intimidate than Bogdanov. Whenever he heard something new or disturbing his forehead would wrinkle up in intense pain and he would let forth a stream of incoherent, confused exclamations.

Peredonov bowed and whispered, 'I hear one of your schoolmistresses has taken to wearing a red blouse.'[1]

This news frightened Bogdanov and his white goatee bobbed nervously up and down on his chin. 'What's that you say?' he whispered hoarsely. 'Which one?'

'The fat one with the loud mouth. I can't remember her name,' Peredonov whispered back.

'Loud-mouthed, loud-mouthed,' muttered the perplexed Bogdanov as he tried to remember. 'Hm, that sounds like Miss Skobochkina.'

'That's the one,' said Peredonov.

'In a red blouse! I can't believe it. Did you see her yourself?'

'I did. And she's taken to parading it at school. What's even worse, she wears a peasant tunic, just like a country girl.'

'Go on! I must get to the bottom of this. We can't have teachers going around in red blouses. She'll have to be dismissed, that's certain. I might have expected something like that from her.'

1. According to a ruling of the Ministry of Education, male teachers had to wear white linen shirts without stripes. Peredonov has extended this to women. In addition, red calico blouses and shirts, very popular among the peasantry at this time, were also looked upon as a symbol of the adoption of the simple life.

Mass was over and as they were leaving the church Peredonov stepped up to Kramarenko and said, 'You black-faced street Arab! Why were you smiling in church? Wait till I tell your father.'

Kramarenko looked at him in amazement and ran past without saying a word. He was one of the majority of boys at the school who found Peredonov coarse, stupid and unfair. For this they hated and despised him. Peredonov was sure that these were the ones whom the headmaster was inciting against him – if not personally, then through his sons.

Outside the church Volodin came up to Peredonov, happily chuckling. His face had a blissful expression, as if it were his birthday. He wore a bowler hat and swung his cane dashingly.

'What do you think, Ardalyon!' he said gaily. 'I've persuaded Cherepnin to smear Marta's gates with tar.'

Peredonov reflected for a moment and then suddenly produced a morose laugh. Just as suddenly, Volodin stopped grinning, looked sheepish and said, gazing up at the sky and swinging his cane, 'What wonderful weather! But I think it might rain this evening. Well, let it. I shall spend a nice evening at home with the future inspector.'

'I'm too busy right now to stay at home this evening,' said Peredonov. 'I've things to see to in town.'

Volodin pretended to understand, although he had no idea what Peredonov suddenly had to see to. Peredonov was quite sure that it was imperative to make several visits. In fact yesterday's chance encounter with the police officer had convinced him of the need to talk to all the important people in town and make them believe he was trustworthy and above suspicion. If he were successful he would have many defenders in the town who would testify that politically he was beyond reproach, should the need arise.

'Where are you off to, Ardalyon?' asked Volodin when he saw that Peredonov was turning from his normal route home from church. 'Aren't you going home?'

'Yes, but I'm going a different way, I don't like that street anymore.'

'Why not?'

'There's a lot of thorn-apple growing there and it smells very strong. It sends me into a complete daze. My nerves are weak enough as it is. Life is nothing but unpleasantness at the moment.'

Volodin once more tried to look sympathetic and understanding. On the way Peredonov picked some thistles and stuffed them into his pocket.

'What do you want those for?' Volodin asked, grinning.

'They're for the cat,' Peredonov gloomily replied.

'Are you going to stick them in its fur?'

'Yes.'

Volodin gave an idiot-like laugh. 'Mind you don't start without me, won't you?' he said. 'It should be quite amusing.'

Peredonov invited him to come immediately, but Volodin excused himself. He suddenly felt that it wasn't the done thing *not* to have business to see to, and Peredonov's enterprise in calling on everyone had encouraged him to call on Nadezhda Adamenko and tell her that he had some excellent new sketches that he was going to frame. Perhaps she might like to look at them. Besides, she might give him some coffee.

So Volodin did just that. What was more, he had now thought of another ingenious plan: he would offer to give her brother carpentry lessons.

Nadezhda really thought he needed the money and readily agreed, suggesting he came three times a week for two-hour lessons. She would pay him thirty roubles a month. Volodin was in raptures, not only because of the money but also because of the opportunity of seeing her frequently.

As always, Peredonov returned home in a wretched mood. Varvara, pale from a sleepless night, raved at him, 'You might have told me yesterday that you weren't coming home.'

Peredonov, teasing her, told her that he had gone to Marta's. Varvara said nothing. After all, she had the letter. Even though it was a forgery, still . . .

Over breakfast she sniggered, 'While you were gallivanting around with Marta I had a reply from the princess.'

'Did you actually write to her?' Peredonov asked. His face came alive with a gleam of expectation.

'Now stop being so silly!' Varvara laughed. 'Didn't you yourself tell me to?'

'Well, what does she say?' Peredonov anxiously asked.

'Here's the letter, read it yourself.'

After a great deal of fumbling in her pockets, she found the letter and handed it to Peredonov. He dropped his knife and fork and eagerly pounced on it. He read it through and was overjoyed. Here at last was a clear and definite promise. Now he had no doubts at all. He gulped down the rest of his food and rushed to show the letter to his friends.

Filled with grave excitement he entered Vershina's garden. As always she was standing at the gate smoking. She was delighted: formerly she had been obliged to employ all her charms to coax him in, now he came of his own accord.

That trip with Marta is having results! After a few hours in her company he's come running! I wonder if he's made up his mind and wants to marry her? she wondered, both nervously and happily.

Peredonov disillusioned her at once by showing her the letter. 'And you didn't believe it,' he said. 'Well, here's proof for you, it's from the princess herself. Read it and see for yourself.'

Vershina looked at the letter suspiciously and blew tobacco smoke over it several times. Then she smiled wryly and asked in her quiet, rapid voice, 'Where's the envelope?'

Peredonov suddenly took fright. He realized that Varvara could have tricked him and written the letter herself. He must demand the envelope from her at once.

'I don't know,' he said. 'I must ask Varvara for it.'

He bade Vershina a hurried farewell and dashed off home. He had to discover the origin of the letter – and as soon as possible. This sudden doubt was truly excruciating for him.

Vershina stood at the gate and watched him go, smiling and puffing at her cigarette for all she was worth, hurrying as if trying to finish some lesson in time.[1]

His face full of despair and terror, Peredonov ran all the way home. Before he had even reached the dining-room he shouted in a voice hoarse with agitation, 'Varvara, where's the envelope?'

'What envelope?' Varvara asked in a trembling voice.

She looked at Peredonov quite brazenly and would have turned red had she not been smothered with rouge.

'The envelope of the princess's letter that came today,' Peredonov explained, looking apprehensively and malevolently at her.

Varvara forced a laugh. 'I burned it. What use was it to me? Do

1. See variant 5, p. 277.

you think I'm starting an envelope collection? You don't get your money back on them like beer bottles you know.'

Peredonov sulked around the house and growled, 'There's all kinds of princesses, you and I know that. Perhaps this one's living right here.'

Varvara pretended not to have any idea that he suspected something but she was scared out of her wits.

Later that evening Peredonov was stopped by Vershina as he was walking past her garden.

'Have you found the envelope?' she asked.

'Varvara says she's burned it,' he replied.

Vershina laughed and fine white clouds of smoke drifted in front of her in the calm mild air.

'How very strange of your cousin to be so careless! Such an important letter and suddenly it's got no envelope! At least you could have told where and when it was posted from the stamp.'

Peredonov was furious and in vain Vershina tried to lure him into the garden, in vain did she offer to tell his fortune with cards – Peredonov left. All the same, he still showed his friends the letter and boasted about it. They believed it was genuine.

But Peredonov didn't know whether to believe it was genuine or not. At all events, he decided to begin his self-justificatory visits to all the important people in town on Tuesday – Monday was a bad day.

VIII

As soon as Peredonov had gone off to play billiards Varvara went to see Grushina. They had a long talk, at the end of which they decided to put matters right with a second letter. Varvara knew that Grushina had friends in St Petersburg and through them it would not be difficult to have a letter sent back.

As before, Grushina took a long time to be persuaded. 'But Varvara, dear! I've still got the shivers from doing the first one. Whenever I see a policeman near the house I'm scared stiff thinking he's come to lock me up.'

After a whole hour and much cajolery, the promise of gifts and payment in advance, Grushina agreed. Their plan of action was as follows: Varvara would say that she had written to the princess to thank her. A few days later they would receive an answer from her, stating even more definitely that there were some posts vacant and that she would ensure Peredonov was offered one if they married straight away. Like the first one, Grushina would write the letter, seal it in an envelope with a seven-copeck stamp and send it in another envelope to a friend in St Petersburg, who would post it back to her. Then they both set out for a shop right on the other side of town, where they bought a packet of narrow envelopes with a floral-pattern lining and some coloured paper. They bought up the whole stock, a precaution that Grushina had thought of to help conceal the forgery. Narrow envelopes were chosen so that the forged letter could easily be enclosed in another.

When they returned to Grushina's they set about writing the letter from the princess. Two days later it was ready and they sprayed it with potent sandalwood perfume. Then the envelopes and paper that were left over were burned as an extra precaution. Grushina wrote and told her friend exactly when to post the letter They worked it out so that it would arrive on a Sunday – then Peredonov would be at home to receive it from the postman himself, which would be additional proof of its genuineness.

On the Tuesday, Peredonov very much wanted to get home earlier from school. Luck was on his side, for the classroom where he took the last lesson of the day was opposite the clock, near which the school porter, a doughty army reservist, stood with his gong.

Peredonov sent him to the common-room for the register and while he was gone put the clock forward a quarter of an hour. No one noticed. When he arrived home, Peredonov said he didn't want any lunch and asked for his dinner to be kept for him when he came back: he had important business in town.

'They're all trying to trap me and I must escape from their clutches,' he said angrily, thinking of the snares his enemies were setting for him.

He put on a tailcoat which he seldom wore: it was tight and uncomfortable. Over the years he had grown fatter and the coat itself had shrunk. This and the fact that he had no medals exasperated him. All the others had them, even Falastov at the town school. There was no doubt that the headmaster was behind this – not once had he recommended him. He felt that he could be sure of his rank as a minor civil servant – that the headmaster couldn't take that away from him. But what was the use if there were no visible signs of it? Well, it would show on his new uniform. It was nice to know that the epaulettes would correspond to his rank, not the type of position he held. Once he had his new uniform with its epaulettes – like a general's – and its one large star, then everyone would be able to see at once that a State councillor was coming down the street. I must order that uniform as soon as possible, he thought.

He went out into the street and only then did he wonder where to go first. It seemed that the people who could help him most were the district police officer and the district attorney. So he must start with them. Or perhaps the marshal of the nobility? But the thought of going to see them terrified him. Marshal Veriga was a general and in the running for a governorship. The police chief and attorney were two terrible symbols of law and order. I must start rather lower down, he thought. Then I can have a good sniff around, find out what they think of me, what they're saying. So he decided it would be best to visit the mayor first. Although he was a merchant, and had only been to a parish school, he was in great demand and was highly respected in that town. Into the bargain, he had friends in quite high places in other towns, even in St Petersburg.

So Peredonov summoned up his courage and set off for the mayor's house.

The weather was miserable. Leaves fell submissively from the trees, as if too tired to hold on any longer. Peredonov felt rather scared. In the mayor's house the smell of newly polished parquet floors mingled strangely with a faintly discernible, pleasant smell of food. It was very quiet, even depressing. The children, a boy at the high school and a teenage daughter who in the mayor's words was 'under the supervision of a governess', were where they should be, in their room, which was cheerful and bright and looked out on to the garden. The furniture looked comfortable. There were all kinds of toys there and in the garden, and their voices rang out gaily.

On the first floor, which looked on to the street and where guests were received, everything was stiff and severe. The mahogany furniture seemed to have been taken from a doll's house and magnified many times. For everyone but the weighty master of the house, who sat on them quite comfortably, the chairs were as hard as stones. The archimandrite of a nearby monastery, who was a frequent visitor, called them 'soul-saving', to which the mayor would reply, 'Yes, I don't like all that soft effeminate stuff you find in other houses, when you get shaken up and down on springs. You shake – and the furniture shakes with you. What's the good of that? Besides, doctors don't approve of soft furniture.'

Yakov Skuchayev, the mayor, met Peredonov at the door of his living-room. He was a tall stout man with short black hair. He held himself with dignity and was slightly overbearing and condescending to those without much money.

After he had sat bolt upright in one of the hard chairs and returned the preliminary compliments Peredonov said to his host, 'There's something I want to discuss with you.'

'Good. How can I help you?' Skuchayev politely inquired.

A scornful glint showed in his cunning black eyes. He thought that Peredonov had come to ask for money and made up his mind not to lend him more than one hundred and fifty roubles. Many officials in town owed Skuchayev fairly substantial sums. Although he never reminded his debtors when the money was due, he would never again lend to anyone who didn't pay up on time. The first loan was always fairly generous, but depended on the cash he had to hand and on the solvency of the borrower.

'Since you're the mayor and the most important person in this town I must talk to you,' said Peredonov.

Skuchayev assumed an important look and bowed slightly from his chair.

'All kinds of rubbish is being said about me in this town,' Peredonov said sadly. 'It's all invented, of course.'

'You can't stop other people talking, you know,' the host said. 'But there are scandalmongers around here who have nothing better to do than wag their tongues.'

'They say I don't go to church. That's not true for a start. I do go. True, I wasn't there on St Elijah's Day, but that was because I had stomach-ache. Otherwise I'm always there.'

'Yes, I saw you myself. But even I don't go every day. It's long been a family tradition to drive out to the monastery instead.'

'They're saying all sorts of rubbish,' Peredonov continued. 'That I tell the boys dirty jokes. That's nonsense. It's true I sometimes tell them something funny, just for a laugh. You have a son yourself at the school – he hasn't said anything about me, by any chance?'

'Nothing at all, rest assured. Boys are a cunning lot, at times they only say what they really have to. Of course, my boy is young enough to say something stupid. But he's said nothing to me so far.'

'Yes, and in the senior forms they already know everything. I've never said anything indecent to them, either.'

'Well, of course. A school isn't a market-place.'

'But it's considered the normal thing in this town to concoct all sorts of fiction. That's why I came to see you, as you're the mayor.'

Skuchayev was extremely flattered by Peredonov's visit. He wasn't quite sure what it was all about, but was diplomatic enough to pretend that he understood perfectly.

'And they've been saying other nasty things about me. That I'm living in sin with Varvara, that she's not my cousin at all, but my mistress. Well, she *is* my cousin, but a distant one, three times removed. One's allowed to marry that kind. And I do intend marrying her.'

'Quite so. But a little walk to the altar would settle everything.'

'I couldn't marry her earlier, there were important reasons. It was quite impossible – I'd have done it long ago if I could have, believe me.'

Skuchayev assumed a dignified air, frowned and tapped the dark tablecloth with his puffy white fingers. 'I believe you. If what you're saying is true, then it's a different matter. I believe you now, but I must confess, if you will permit me to say so, that I did find it rather dubious, your living with your . . . companion without being married! I say dubious, because youngsters are very sharp. They're liable to distort anything they hear and see the worst side of everything. It's difficult to teach them what's good – and what's bad needs no tuition! That's why it looked so dubious. At any rate, whose concern is it? – that's my considered opinion. I'm flattered that you've come to me. Although I'm an ordinary sort of chap, who didn't go further than the district school, I still enjoy the trust and respect of society . . . I've been mayor for three years, so my word counts for something among the people of this town.'

The more Skuchayev rambled on in this way, the more he became entangled in his own thoughts and it seemed that his maundering would never stop.

He abruptly broke off and sadly thought, Anyway, I'm wasting my time. The trouble with these educated men is that one can never understand what they want. Everything is as clear as daylight to a scholar as long as he has his books. But the moment he takes his nose out of them he's all at sea – and he makes sure others are too.

He became hopelessly confused and stared wearily at Peredonov. His keen eyes had lost their fire, his stout body slumped back in his chair and no longer did he seem the vigorous man of action of before, but a tottering, stupid old man.

Peredonov also sat silently, as if drugged by Skuchayev's speech. Then he screwed up his eyes and said with a vague, morose expression on his face, 'You're the mayor of this town, so you can tell them it's all a load of nonsense.'

'About what?' inquired Skuchayev warily.

'They might report me for not going to church or something. You could speak up for me, should they come and ask questions.'

'That we can do. You can rely on me, have no fear,' the mayor said. 'Why shouldn't I stand up for a respectable man and put in a good word for him? I could even get the town council to send a testimonial if need be. That we can do. Or make you an honorary citizen. All that's possible.'

'So I can depend on you,' Peredonov said gloomily, as if replying to something very unpleasant. 'The headmaster's always persecuting me.'

'Go on!' exclaimed Skuchayev, shaking his head in sympathy. 'That can only be because of all this slander that's going around. Nikolay Khripach has always struck me as a sound man who wouldn't offend anyone for no reason. I can tell that from his son. A fine, serious man. He's strict and only shows leniency where it's due. He's quite impartial, a very sound man. It can only have been because of all this malicious gossip. What have you been quarrelling about?'

'We just don't see eye to eye,' Peredonov explained. 'And some of the teachers are jealous – they all want to be inspectors. But Princess Volchansky promised *me* the position, so they're all mad with envy.'

'Quite, quite,' Skuchayev said, taking care not to contradict him. 'To change the subject, why are we having such a dry conversation? Let's have a drink and something to eat.'

He pressed the button of an electric bell near the table lamp. 'Useful gadget, isn't it?' he told Peredonov. 'All the same, I think it might be a good idea if you took up a post somewhere else. Dashenka, bring us some of the nice savouries and some hot coffee – understand?'

'Yes, sir!' replied Dashenka, a heavily built, pleasant-looking girl. She glided off with a remarkably light step considering her size.

'As I was saying, I think you ought to take up another post. Had you thought of going into the Church? If you wanted to take holy orders I'm sure you would make an excellent high-minded priest. And I could help you – I've quite a few friends who are high up in the Church.'

Skuchayev enumerated several diocesan and suffragan bishops.

'No, I don't want to take holy orders,' Peredonov replied. 'I'm scared of the incense. It makes me feel sick and gives me a headache.'

'In that case, the police would be a good idea. You might become a district commissioner. If I may ask, what rank do you hold in the civil service as a teacher?'

'I'm a State councillor,' Peredonov said pompously.

'Go on!' Skuchayev exclaimed. 'Teachers certainly reach high rank these days. And all for teaching young boys! Well now, education must be really something! However, although it has its critics, it's true you can't go far without it. I myself only went to a district school, but I'm sending my son to university. I have to help him through school almost by force, you know, but once he's at university he won't need any pushing. Not that I ever thrash him. Only when he's lazy or misbehaves, I take him over to the window and say, "Do you see those birches over there?" and he replies, "Oh yes, Papa, I can see them. I'll behave in future." It really does work and the lad turns over a new leaf, just as if he'd been given a good hiding. Oh, children, children!' Skuchayev concluded with a sigh.

Peredonov stayed about two hours at the mayor's. When the business was finished refreshments in abundance were served.

Skuchayev was the most solemn of hosts and, as in everything he did, entertained his guest as if conducting some very serious business. All the same, he liked to introduce a few artful little tricks.

Mulled wine would be served in large glasses, just like coffee. The vodka glasses had been broken off and rounded at the stem so it was impossible to put them down on the table.

Another visitor arrived, Tishkov the merchant. He was small, grey-haired, very lively for his age, and wore a long frock-coat and boots like large bottles. He drank a great deal of vodka, kept rattling off nonsense rhymes and was evidently very satisfied with himself.

Peredonov at last decided that it was time to leave and rose from his chair.

'Don't be in such a hurry,' the host said. 'Stay a while.'

'Please stay here and keep good cheer,' rhymed Tishkov.

'No, it's time I went,' Peredonov replied anxiously.

'Time to leave or his "cousin" will grieve,' Tishkov said, winking at Skuchayev.

'I've things to see to,' Peredonov said.

'A busy chap we can only clap,' Tishkov instantly replied.

Skuchayev accompanied Peredonov to the hall. They embraced as they parted. Peredonov was pleased with the visit. The mayor's on my side, he confidently thought.

Returning to Tishkov, Skuchayev said, 'It's all idle chatter about that man.'

'It's idle chatter and the truth doesn't matter,' Tishkov immediately caught up, pouring himself a glass of English bitters. Clearly, he never paid attention to the meaning of what people said to him but was only interested in words that he could rhyme.

'He's all right, a good fellow and an expert tippler,' Skuchayev continued, filling his glass and ignoring Tishkov's rhyming.

'If he's a good toper he can't be a moper!' Tishkov cried as he emptied his glass.

'And what if he is larking about with a mam'selle!' Skuchayev said.

'From a mam'selle's head you get bugs in your bed!' Tishkov replied.

'He who hasn't sinned against God is not responsible to the Tsar.'

'All of us transgress for one sweet caress.'

'But he wants to conceal his sin under the altar.'

'Hiding sin under a wedding wreath leads to fighting and gnashing of teeth.'

Tishkov always spoke like this if the conversation didn't concern him. He would have bored everyone to death but they were used to him and ignored his rapidly delivered tongue-twisters. Only now and then did they let him loose on a stranger. But Tishkov could not care less whether they listened or not. He just couldn't resist picking up words other people said and rhyming them, and he functioned with the unwavering efficiency of a cunningly devised boredom machine. Looking at his brisk, precise movements for long might make one think that this was no living person, that he had died or had never even lived, was blind to the real world and heard nothing but words with a deathly ring to them.

IX

Next day Peredonov went to see the district attorney, Avinovitsky. Once again the weather was miserable. A blustery wind whirled clouds of dust before it. Evening was drawing in and everything was suffused with a melancholy light that filtered through a thick haze and didn't seem to come from the sun at all. A deathly silence hung over the streets. The wretched, hopelessly tumbledown houses seemed to have been built for no purpose at all beyond that of creating a soulless uniformity and drabness and timidly hinted at the dreary, miserable lives dragging on within their walls.

People walked along the streets slowly, aimlessly, as if weighed down by a lethargy they had no desire to shake off. Only children, those eternal tireless vessels of divine joy on earth, showed any life as they ran and played – but they were already showing signs of being afflicted with inertia. Some faceless and invisible monster seemed to be perched on their shoulders, peering every now and then into their blank faces with eyes full of menace.

Tormented by vague fears, Peredonov walked amidst all this squalor and depression, over an earth that seemed alienated from heaven, impure and impotent. The lofty gave him no comfort, the earthly brought him no joy, and now, as always, he looked on the world with lifeless eyes, like some solitary demon consumed by fear and dejection.

Sluggish in perception, his squalid mind contaminated every sensation, transforming it into something obscene and loathsome. He delighted in seeing imperfection in everything. Whenever he passed an upright, freshly painted column or pillar he felt a savage desire to break it or cover it with filth. He loved to see objects soiled in his presence and would laugh for joy. Well-scrubbed schoolboys were anathema to him and he would persecute them, calling them 'soap addicts' – the slovenly, scruffy ones he understood much better. He loved nothing and no one, and as a result the real world could only have a depressing effect on him. And so it was whenever he met people, especially strangers and people he didn't know and to whom it was impossible to be rude. Happiness consisted in doing absolutely nothing, in cutting himself off from the world and in pampering his stomach.

And now he had to face the utter vexation of actually having to go and talk to someone whether he liked it or not. How tiresome! Even the consolation of being able to daub the walls of the attorney's house would be denied him. The house itself only strengthened and gave definite form to his feeling of oppression and fear. Indeed, it had an evil, angry look. The high roof seemed to frown over the windows, forcing them down on to the ground. The weatherboards and roof had once been painted a bright, cheerful colour, but time and the elements had turned them a dreary grey. The huge, heavy iron gates, higher than the house itself and apparently built to resist attackers, were kept constantly locked and behind them a mastiff rattled its chain and growled at every passer-by.

All around was a wilderness – waste ground, overgrown kitchen gardens and ramshackle huts. Opposite the house was an unpaved square where rank grass grew around a small hollow in the middle. The only lamp there was the one outside the attorney's house. Slowly and reluctantly Peredonov climbed the four steep steps up to the porch with its sloping roof and pulled the blackened copper bell-handle. A sharp continuous tinkling could be heard just inside. Soon there was a sound of muffled footsteps. Someone tiptoed to the door and stood there very quietly, probably looking at him through a hidden chink. Then an iron bolt rattled and the door opened to reveal a scowling, black-haired, pock-marked girl who stared at him with the utmost suspicion.

'Who do you want?' she asked.

Peredonov replied that he had come to see Mr Avinovitsky on important business. As soon as he was in the hall Peredonov recited a magic charm. And only just in time too, he thought. Before he'd had time to remove his coat Avinovitsky's strident, angry voice echoed from the drawing-room. It was absolutely terrifying – but he could never speak any other way – and in this angry, thunderous voice he now bellowed a welcome to Peredonov, showing how pleased he was that at last he'd come to see him.

Aleksandr Avinovitsky, a grim-looking man, seemed to have been born to reprimand and bully others. He enjoyed superb health and went swimming the whole year round. But his thick black beard, tinged with blue, had grown so large that it made the rest of him look thin. If he didn't frighten people with his continual shouting, he certainly intimidated them, constantly fulminating and issuing threats of hard labour in Siberia.[1]

'I've come to see you on business,' Peredonov said, rather confused.

'Have you brought your confession with you? Is it murder, arson or mail-robbery?' Avinovitsky angrily asked as he showed Peredonov into the drawing-room. 'Or perhaps you yourself have been the victim of a crime, which is more than possible in this town. It's an iniquitous place and the police are even worse. It makes me wonder why dead bodies aren't found every morning out there on the square! Please sit yourself down. Now, what can I do for you? Are you the criminal or the victim?'

'No,' Peredonov said, 'I haven't committed a crime. I know that the headmaster would love to have me hauled off to court but I haven't done anything wrong, absolutely nothing.'

'So you haven't come here to confess?' Avinovitsky asked.

'No, nothing of the sort,' Peredonov replied in a trembling voice.

'If that's the case,' the attorney said, fiercely stressing every syllable, 'then we can proceed to other matters.'

He took a handbell from the table and rang it. No one came. Then he took the bell in both hands, shook it furiously, flung it on to the floor, stamped his feet and wildly shouted, 'Malanya! Where the devil are you!'

There was a sound of hurried footsteps and a schoolboy entered.

1. See variant 6, p. 277.

It was Avinovitsky's son, a stocky dark-haired lad of about thirteen with an air of supreme self-confidence. Unruffled, he bowed to Peredonov, put the bell back on the table and said, 'Malanya's in the kitchen garden.'

Avinovitsky calmed down for a moment. He looked at his son with a tenderness that was foreign to such a fierce, rugged face and said, 'Run along and tell Malanya to bring us some food and drink, there's a good boy.'

The obedient son ambled out of the room, watched by his proudly smiling father. He got no further than the door, however, when his father suddenly frowned and shouted in such a terrifying voice that Peredonov almost jumped out of his skin, 'And don't take all day about it!'

The boy ran off and they could hear one door after the other being slammed. Avinovitsky listened, smiled with his thick red lips and then said in the same angry voice, 'My sole heir. Not a bad boy, eh? I wonder how he'll turn out. What do you think? He may turn out a complete idiot, but a scoundrel, coward or milksop – never!'

'Of course –' mumbled Peredonov.

'People nowadays are travesties of the human race, ne thundered on. 'They think that health is something to be sneered at. If I had my way I would have sentenced the German who invented the undervest to hard labour. Just the very thought of my Vladimir wearing one! All last summer in the country he went around without any shoes – and to think of him in a thick woollen vest! Why, when he's had a bath he runs naked in the freezing cold and rolls in the snow. My son in an undervest – I ask you! That damned German should be given a hundred lashes!'

After the unfortunate inventor of the undervest other transgressors came in for abuse.

'The death penalty, my dear sir, is not in the least inhuman. Science now tells us that people are born criminals. Then they should be exterminated! It's the State that has to feed them. With the law as it is, a man who's an inveterate murderer, an arsonist, a sex maniac, is given a nice warm cell in a penal settlement and has nothing to worry about for the rest of his life. The taxpayer has to foot the bill. If you ask me, it's cheaper – and more just – to hang them straight away. Yes, that just about sums it up!'

The round table in the dining-room was covered with a white cloth with a red border, on which were laid plates of fat sausages of every variety, pickles, smoked herring and all sorts of cured fish. Interspersed with the plates were decanters and bottles of various shapes and sizes containing different kinds of vodkas, brandies and liqueurs. All this was very much to Peredonov's taste; even the slight disorderliness in the appointments pleased him. The host continued his diatribe. The presence of food turned his thoughts to shopkeepers and then he changed his attack to ancestry, for no apparent reason.

'The importance of ancestry and breeding shouldn't be over-looked!' he furiously shouted. 'It's stupid, ludicrous and immoral that peasants can enter the landowning class. The soil is getting poorer, the towns are filling with tramps, harvests are bad, illiteracy is rampant, the suicide rate goes up. Is that something to be pleased about? Educate a peasant if you like but don't give him any status. Otherwise the peasantry itself will become impoverished and will always remain riff-raff, cattle. And the landowning gentry itself suffers from this influx of uncouth rabble. A peasant may well stand out amongst his own people in a village, but once he moves into higher circles he brings something coarse, uncouth and ignoble with him. He's really only interested in earning enough to live on and stuffing his belly. No, sir, castes were a wise institution.'

'And that headmaster of ours allows all kinds of scum into the school,' Peredonov said angrily. 'There are even peasant boys – and quite a few shopkeepers' children.'[1]

'A fine state of affairs I must say!' shouted the attorney.

'A Government paper[2] was recently published, stating that such riff-raff shouldn't be admitted, but Khripach goes his own sweet way and almost never refuses anyone,' complained Peredonov. 'He says that life is poor in this town and there are so few high-school students as it is. What does he mean, too few? It would be better if there were even fewer! But it's as much as we can do to mark their

1. See variant 7, p. 277.
2. Reference to the notorious 'sons of cooks' White Paper, issued in 1887 by the Minister of Education, where it was stated, '. . . sons of coachmen, footmen, cooks, laundresses, small shopkeepers and so on . . .' should not be admitted to high schools.

work, let alone do any reading. And they deliberately use dubious words in their essays so that you have to keep checking them in the dictionary.'

'Drink some herb vodka,' Avinovitsky suggested. 'You still haven't told me why you've come.'

'I have enemies,' Peredonov muttered and he mournfully peered into his glass of yellow vodka before drinking it.

'There once was a pig that had no enemies,' Avinovitsky replied, 'but they still slaughtered it. Have a slice, will you? – a very good pig it was too.'

Peredonov took a slice of ham and said, 'Some people are spreading malicious lies about me.'

'Yes, I think I'm right in saying there's no worse town than this when it comes to slander!' Avinovitsky fiercely shouted. 'What a town! The moment you put a foot wrong those pigs start grunting about it.'

'Princess Volchansky promised me an inspector's post and that's set them all talking. It could really harm my prospects. And it's all out of jealousy. And the headmaster's let the whole school go to rack and ruin. The boys who live out smoke, drink and run after the girls. And local boys do the same. Khripach has let things go to the dogs and now he's persecuting me. I bet someone's been trumping up ridiculous stories about me and told him. It could go even further and reach the princess!'

Peredonov proceeded to give a lengthy and confused description of everything he felt he had reason to fear. Avinovitsky listened angrily and from time to time interrupted by shouting furiously, 'The swine! Bastards! Scum!'

'And to say I'm a nihilist!' said Peredonov. 'It's really quite funny. I have an official cap with a badge,[1] although I don't always wear it and sometimes wear a hat. And as for the portrait of Mickiewicz in my room, I hang it there because of his poetry, not because he was a rebel. What's more, I've never even read *The Bell*.'[2]

1. A cap with a badge or cockade was part of the formal dress of civil servants and teachers, and also a distinguishing mark of the nobility. The hat as mentioned (often broad-brimmed) was usually associated with nihilists. Thus Peredonov is paranoid about being seen without a badge on his cap, and wearing a hat.
2. Liberal newspaper published by Alexander Herzen in London and Geneva, 1857–67. It was freely smuggled into Russia and was a major vehicle for liberal intellectual ideas.

'You're getting your journals mixed up,' Avinovitsky said unceremoniously. '*The Bell* was published by Herzen, not Mickiewicz.'

'You must be thinking of another *Bell*. Mickiewicz also published one.'

'That's the first I've heard of it. Why don't you have it published – it would be a major discovery. You'll be famous!'

'I can't possibly publish it,' Peredonov crossly retorted. 'I'm not allowed to read banned books. I never read them – I'm a patriot!'

After these lengthy complaints that Peredonov poured out Avinovitsky came to the conclusion that someone was trying to blackmail Peredonov and was spreading rumours to frighten him, thus preparing the ground for a sudden demand for money. That he himself hadn't heard anything yet he attributed to the skill of the blackmailer, who was obviously operating in Peredonov's immediate circle – after all, it was only Peredonov he had to work on.

'Whom do you suspect?' asked Avinovitsky.

Peredonov reflected for a moment. The name of Grushina happened to spring to mind first and he had a vague recollection of their recent conversation during the course of which he had interrupted her and threatened to inform on her. Or had he? Whether *he* had been doing the informing or whether someone had been informing on *him* wasn't clear. The idea that he'd threatened to inform on Grushina became indissolubly linked in his mind with the concept of informing in general. One thing was clear, however: Grushina was an enemy. And, worst of all, she had seen him hide the Pisarev. He must find another place at once.

'There's that Grushina woman,' he said.

'Yes, I know. A bitch of the first order,' Avinovitsky summed her up.

'She's always coming to our place and nosing around,' Peredonov complained. 'Never satisfied with what she can get. Perhaps she wants to blackmail me with the Pisarev? Or perhaps she wants me to marry her. She won't get any money out of me, and I already have a fiancée. Let her inform – the police will find nothing. Only it could all be very unpleasant for me if there were a scandal – it could damage my promotion prospects.'

'She's a notorious charlatan,' the attorney said. 'She used to tell fortunes from cards and cheated some poor fools, but I told the police that she had to be stopped. On that occasion they had the sense to do what I told them.'

'And she's still at it,' said Peredonov. 'Whenever she told my fortune she always saw a long journey and an official letter.'

'She knows just what to say to everyone. I bet you she'll set some kind of trap and then try and extort money from you. If she does, come and see me right away. She'll get a hundred of the best!' This was one of his favourite expressions and was not meant to be taken literally. All it meant was a severe reprimand.

And so Avinovitsky promised to defend Peredonov. But his visitor left in an even worse frame of mind, tormented by fears that had no discoverable cause but which were strengthened by Avinovitsky's threatening attitude and thunderous tirades.

Every day Peredonov set out on one of his visits, before dinner. He never managed more than one a day because of the time needed to make a full deposition. In the evenings he usually went off to play billiards.

Vershina still succeeded in luring him into her garden, Rutilov still sang his sisters' praises, Varvara was more insistent than ever that they marry as soon as possible – but still he came to no decision. Sometimes he thought that the best thing would be to marry her and have done with it. But what would happen if the princess were to trick him? He'd be the laughing-stock of the whole town. And this consideration kept holding him back.

That the women kept pursuing him, that all his friends were jealous – these were more figments of his imagination than anything else – all this, together with the plots he thought were being hatched against him, made his life dreary and miserable, just like the weather, which for several days on end had been wretched, often culminating in long periods of nasty, cold, slowly falling rain. Life really was turning out to be horrible, he felt. But soon, he thought, he would be an inspector and then everything would take a turn for the better.

X

On Thursday Peredonov went to see General Veriga, marshal of the nobility. The marshal's house was like one of those spacious country villas one sees in Pavlovsk or Tsarskoye Selo, eminently suitable for summer or winter. It wasn't strikingly luxurious but the newness of much of the furnishings seemed unnecessarily pretentious. Veriga was waiting for Peredonov in his study. He pretended he was hurrying to greet his guest and that he'd been too busy to come earlier.

Veriga held himself extremely stiffly, even for a retired cavalry officer. It was rumoured that he wore a corset. His smooth face was of a uniform red, as if it had been powdered. His hair was cut very short indeed to distract attention from his bald patch. His eyes were grey and friendly, though they revealed a certain aloofness. He was very civil to everyone and had fixed and positive views. A good military training was apparent in every movement and at times he bore himself like the governor he hoped to be one day.

Peredonov told him why he had come, from the opposite side of the carved oak table. 'All sorts of rumours are being spread about me and since I belong to the nobility I am appealing to you. People have been saying the most ridiculous things about me, Your Excellency!'

'I haven't heard anything,' Veriga replied with an expectant smile. He stared at Peredonov with his piercing grey eyes. Peredonov stared into one corner of the room. 'I've never been a Socialist. I may have said something I shouldn't have at some time or other – who doesn't get carried away when they're young? But I never think such things now.'

'So you were once a keen Liberal?' Veriga asked with a friendly smile. 'You wanted a constitution, didn't you? Well, we all did when we were young. Would you care for one?' Veriga held out a box of cigars, but Peredonov was too scared to take one and refused. Veriga lit one himself.

'Of course we did, Your Excellency,' Peredonov confessed. 'At university I too wanted one – only a different kind from the others.'

'And *what* kind exactly?' Veriga asked, a note of increasing dissatisfaction creeping into his voice.

'I wanted a constitution without a parliament,' Peredonov explained. 'In parliament all they do is squabble.'

Veriga's grey eyes twinkled: this was very good entertainment!

'A constitution without a parliament!' he said dreamily. 'That sounds most practical!'

'But all that was a long time ago,' Peredonov said hastily, 'I don't think about such things now.'[1]

He looked hopefully at Veriga, who blew a fine smoke-ring, paused for a moment and then said, 'Well, you're a teacher. However, my duties happen to keep me in contact with the schools too. I'd be interested to know which type you prefer, the local Church schools or these so-called district ones?' Veriga knocked the ash from his cigar and stared right into Peredonov's face with an amiable, over-attentive look.

Peredonov frowned and looked away. Then he said, 'The district schools need thoroughly overhauling.'

'Overhauling?' Veriga repeated in a vague voice. 'Quite so.' And he looked down at his smouldering cigar as if preparing himself for a lengthy explanation.

'The teachers there are nihilists and the women teachers don't believe in God. They just stand in church and blow their noses.'

Veriga gave Peredonov a swift glance, smiled and said, 'We all have to do that sometimes, you know!'

'Yes, but the one I'm talking about blows hers like a horn to make the choirboys laugh,' Peredonov said angrily. 'She does it deliberately. Her name is Skobochkina.'

'That's not so good,' Veriga said, 'but that's more from ill-breeding than anything else. I must admit she does have quite appalling manners. None the less, one can't deny she's a very conscientious teacher. But in any event it's not very nice, she ought to be told about it.'

'What's more, she goes around in a red blouse. And sometimes she even walks barefoot, in a peasant tunic. And she plays knuckle-bones with the boys. They're allowed to do just what they like at school. There's no discipline and no one is ever punished. Anyhow,

1. See variant 8, p. 277.

peasant children can't be treated the same as children of the gentry: they should be whipped.'

Veriga calmly looked at Peredonov and appeared to be embarrassed by his tactlessness. He looked down and said in a cold, almost magisterial voice, 'I feel it is incumbent on me to say that I have witnessed much that is good in district-school pupils. There is no doubt that in the great majority of cases they apply themselves to their work conscientiously. Of course there are lapses at times but this applies to children everywhere. It is a recognized fact that misconduct can take more violent forms as a result of bad upbringing and unfavourable environment. This is all the more so since, among the rural population of Russia today, the sense of duty and respect for private property are sadly lacking. The schools must deal strictly with behaviour of this sort. When all attempts at persuasion have failed, and in serious cases, then more extreme measures must be taken to avoid the necessity of expelling the pupil. This applies to all children, even of the nobility. I am, however, in complete agreement with you inasmuch as the system of teaching in district schools is deficient and not wholly satisfactory. Madame Shteven[1] has written a very interesting book on the subject. Have you read it by any chance?'

'No, Your Excellency,' said Peredonov in embarrassment. 'I never have time for reading as I'm so busy at school. But I shall read it.'

'It's not all that important,' Veriga replied with an amused smile, as if giving Peredonov to understand that he was excusing him from the task. 'This Madame Shteven was very indignant when two of her pupils, both lads of seventeen, were sentenced to be birched by the district court. They held their heads high, those young lads, and I think all of us suffered while that shameful sentence was hanging over their heads – as you know, that kind of thing was later abolished. If I were in Madame Shteven's place I would not rest until I had let all Russia know about that outrage. Put on trial for stealing apples – I ask you! They were her best pupils, she writes, and yet they stole apples! That says a lot for

---

1. A. Shteven (1865–1933), educational reformer, author of *Memoirs of a Country Schoolmistress* and founder of a group of primary schools in the Nizhny Novgorod region in the 1890s.

their education! It must be frankly admitted that there's no respect for property these days!'

In his excitement Veriga got up, took two steps forward, but then immediately composed himself and sat down again.

'I would do things differently if I became inspector of district schools,' Peredonov said.

'So you have that appointment in view?' Veriga asked.

'Yes, Princess Volchansky promised me.'

Veriga smiled pleasantly. 'I shall look forward to shaking your hand then. I have no doubt that, under your direction, there will be a distinct and rapid improvement.'

'But what concerns me, Your Excellency, is that certain people in this town are talking all sorts of nonsense about me. Who knows, someone might report me to the authorities and that would severely damage my prospects. There's no truth in any of it.'

'Is there anyone you suspect of spreading these false rumours?' Veriga asked.

This question disconcerted Peredonov and he muttered, 'Whom should I suspect? I have no idea. People talk and it worries me because it might harm my career.'

Veriga decided that it wasn't all that important for him to know: after all, he hadn't been appointed governor yet. Then he slipped back into his marshal's role and delivered a speech that Peredonov listened to in fear and trembling.

'I am deeply appreciative of the confidence you have shown me in asking for my intervention' (Veriga almost said 'patronage' but stopped himself in time) 'in this very nasty affair. According to your statement, damaging rumours are being promulgated. Although they have not yet reached my ears you can rest assured that they are circulating in the dark and obscure places of this town, among the very lowest levels of society, whence they dare not emerge into the light of day. And there they shall remain. It affords me the greatest pleasure that you, who have been appointed to your present position by government authorities, value public opinion so highly, as well as the dignity of the position you occupy as nurturer of youth; you are one of those dedicated souls, in short, to whose enlightened guidance we, as parents, entrust our most priceless possessions, namely, our children, sole heirs of all we have. In your status as servant of the State, you owe allegiance to your highly respected headmaster. But as a member of society, and as a gentleman, you may always count upon the . . . co-operation of the marshal of the nobility in matters appertaining to your honour, your dignity as a human being and as a gentleman.' Still declaiming, Veriga stood up, pressed heavily against the edge of the table with the fingers of his right hand and gave Peredonov the kind of disinterested paternal look of an orator who has just delivered a well-intentioned lecture to a large audience.

Peredonov also stood up, crossed his hands over his stomach and looked mournfully at the carpet under the general's feet. Veriga continued his peroration. 'I am glad that you came to see me since at the present time it is particularly useful for members of the ruling class to remember that, above all else, they are noblemen and must duly value their membership of that class – not only on account of its privileges but also its code of honour. As you know, noblemen in Russia are principally civil servants and, strictly speaking, all government positions, except the very lowest, should of course be theirs for the asking. The presence of commoners in the civil service is one reason for such undesirable incidents as have disturbed your peace of mind. Intrigue and slander are the weapons of the lowest orders, of those not brought up in accordance with fine, gentlemanly traditions. But I hope public opinion will not hesitate to speak out loud and clear in your support – and in this you may count on my wholehearted co-operation.'

'My most humble thanks, Your Excellency,' Peredonov said. 'I know that I can count on you.'

Veriga smiled amiably and remained on his feet to show that the conversation was now over. He felt that, having delivered his speech, he had wasted his words, and that Peredonov was nothing but an impostor, a spineless adventurer who went around pestering people in pursuit of their protection. He said goodbye to Peredonov with the icy contempt he had come to feel for him on account of his disreputable life.

As Peredonov was helped on with his coat in the hall by a footman and heard the distant sounds of a piano, he thought that the proud people in that house really knew how to lord it and had high opinions of themselves. He's after a governorship, he concluded with a twinge of envious awe.

On his way downstairs he met Veriga's two small sons who had just returned from a stroll with their tutor. Peredonov looked at them with sullen curiosity. They're so clean, he thought. Not a speck of dust in their ears. They look so alert, so well disciplined and obedient. I bet they're never flogged. He watched them angrily as they raced up the stairs, gaily chatting. He was astonished that their tutor treated them as equals and didn't grumble or shout at them.

He arrived home to find Varvara standing in the drawing-room with a book in her hands, a rare occurrence. It was an old, tattered cookery book – the only one she ever used. The black binding depressed Peredonov immediately.

'What are you reading, Varvara?' he crossly asked.

'What do you think? It's a cookery book. I don't read rubbish.'

'But why a cookery book?' Peredonov asked in horror.

'What do you mean? I thought I'd try a new dish for you, as you're so fussy with your food,' Varvara explained with a proud, self-satisfied smile.

'I won't eat from a black book,' Peredonov said determinedly, snatched the book and rushed into the bedroom with it.

A black book! And preparing meals from it! he thought in terror. This was the last straw: they were going to get rid of him by black magic and quite openly at that! I must burn it at once, he thought, ignoring Varvara's shrieks of protest.[1]

On Friday he went to see the president of the local landowners' association, Ivan Kirillov.

Everything in that house suggested that its owners liked to live simply, but by no means austerely, and to work for the common good. Many of its contents immediately put one in mind of the simple, rural life: an armchair with a back made of a harness arch and axe-handles for arms; an ink-well shaped like a horseshoe and an ashtray like a peasant's bast shoe. In the living-room, on the window-sills, on the floor, on tables, were scattered corn measures containing various types of grain. Here and there were bits of famine bread[2] and filthy clods of earth resembling peat. In the drawing-room were designs and models for agricultural machinery.

1. See variant 9, p. 277.
2. Baked from husks instead of flour during famines, which were particularly severe in 1891, 1893 and 1899.

The study was cluttered with piles of books on rural economy and educational matters. On the table there were heaps of papers, bills and shoeboxes filled with different-sized cards. There was much dust everywhere and not one picture.

The host, Ivan Kirillov, tried very hard to combine the life of an elegant European with that of a respected landowner. Full of contradictions, he seemed to consist of two completely different and contrasting halves welded together. That he was industrious could be seen from the house and estate. But if one looked at him closely, one soon realized that all this activity was mere dilettantism, that his work was nothing more than a pastime, and that his real concern was with the future, into which he peered with dull eyes. It was as if someone had extracted his soul, put it away for safe keeping and replaced it with an ingenious boredom machine, which worked with monotonous and ruthless efficiency. He was rather short and thin and looked so young and rosy-cheeked that at times he resembled a small boy who had glued on a beard and become very successful in apeing the habits of grown-ups. Every movement was quick and precise. Whenever he greeted someone he would bow deeply and elaborately, shuffle his feet and appear to be gliding on the soles of his smart boots. He wore a grey jacket, a soft fine linen shirt with turned-down collar, a bright blue cord tie, narrow trousers and grey socks. One was tempted to call this ensemble fancy dress. And his almost invariably courteous speech also had two sides to it. One moment he would speak most solemnly and suddenly he would break into childlike smiles and behave like a young boy; the next he would withdraw into his shell again and become serious. His wife was a quiet, demure woman who seemed older than her husband and came into the study on several occasions while Peredonov was there, to ask for some detailed advice on local matters.

Their house was run quite chaotically, always full of business visitors and people drinking tea. Peredonov barely had time to sit down when they brought him a glass of lukewarm tea and a few rolls on a plate. Another guest was already there. Peredonov knew him – and in our town who doesn't know everyone else? Only a few have quarrelled and fallen out.

He was Georgy Trepetov, the local doctor, an insignificant-looking man, even smaller than Kirillov, with a sharp-featured pimply face. He was wearing blue spectacles and always looked down or sideways during a conversation, as if too nervous to look the other person in the face. He was incredibly honest but would never part with one copeck to help a friend in need. He detested anyone in government service. When he met civil servants he would shake hands, but he resolutely avoided having a serious conversation with them. As a result he was considered one of the luminaries of the district, like Kirillov, although he knew little and was a bad doctor. He was always intending to take up the simple life and to that end would often closely watch peasants when they blew their noses, scratched the backs of their necks, wiped their lips with the back of their hands; sometimes, when no one was looking, he liked to imitate them. But he was always postponing his own return to nature until the following summer.

Peredonov repeated all his usual complaints about slanderous gossip in the town, about those envious people who wanted to stop him from becoming an inspector. At first Kirillov was flattered by the visit and exclaimed, 'Yes, that's what it's like in the provinces. I've always said that the only salvation for thinking people is pulling together, combining forces. I'm delighted you've come to the same conclusion.'

Trepetov snorted angrily: something had offended him. Kirillov looked at him anxiously. Trepetov then said contemptuously, 'Thinking people!' whereupon he snorted again. After a moment's silence he said in an offended voice, 'I cannot understand how thinking people can support mouldy old theories like that.'

Kirillov replied, without much assurance, 'But you're ignoring the fact that people sometimes have no choice as to their profession.'

Trepetov snorted scornfully, which seemed finally to put paid to Kirillov. He lapsed into deep silence.

Kirillov then turned to Peredonov. Having heard him speak about his hopes of an inspectorship he became worried: he thought that Peredonov was after a post in his own district. Only recently a proposal had been put forward by the district council to establish the post of inspector of schools, with the approval of the Education Committee. If this plan materialized, Bogdanov, who was in charge of schools in three districts, would be transferred to a neighbouring town and the schools in our district handed over to the new inspector. The council already had someone in view for this position, an instructor from a teachers' training college in Safat.

'I have a patron,' said Peredonov, 'only the headmaster here is trying to queer my pitch – and there're others too. You wouldn't believe what nonsense is being talked about me. In case they should come to you for information about me, I'm telling you that it's a pack of lies. Don't believe a word that these gentlemen say.'

Kirillov was quick to reply. 'Mr Peredonov, I haven't the time to probe into all the slander and gossip that circulates in this town. I'm up to my eyes in work. And if I didn't have my wife to help me, heaven knows how I would cope. I don't have time to go anywhere, I never see a soul, I hear nothing. All the same I am quite convinced that there isn't an atom of truth in any of these rumours – I really do believe it's a lot of nonsense. But you may be aware that the appointment doesn't depend on me alone.'

'They might come and question you,' said Peredonov.

Kirillov looked at him in astonishment and said, 'Of course they will. But the fact is we are intending –'

Just then his wife appeared at the door and she asked him to come outside for a moment. She whispered anxiously, 'You'd better not tell that fellow that Krasil'nikov is being considered for the job. I don't trust him at all, I'm sure he'll try and play some dirty trick on Krasil'nikov.'

'You really think so?' Kirillov whispered. 'Well, perhaps you're right. It's a very nasty business.'

He clutched his head in despair. His wife looked at him with businesslike sympathy and said, 'It's best not to say anything to him at all.'

'Yes, dear, you're right,' he whispered. 'But I must get back now or they'll think I'm rude.'

He went back into the study where he vigorously shuffled his feet and showered Peredonov with compliments.

'So I can rely on you –' Peredonov began.

'Rest assured, my dear fellow. You don't have to worry – I shall bear you in mind,' Kirillov quickly said. 'We haven't reached a final decision on the matter yet.'

Peredonov didn't understand what matter Kirillov was referring to and he became apprehensive and depressed again. Kirillov continued, 'At the moment we are preparing a network of schools.

Some experts came specially from St Petersburg and worked on the project the whole summer. That set us back nine hundred roubles. The network has been carefully worked out and it's an amazingly thorough piece of work. All distances in relation to the schools have been plotted on a map.'

And Kirillov proceeded to describe in detail the master plan. The district would be split up into such small sections that each one would have its own school and the children wouldn't have to travel far. Peredonov understood nothing and his dull brain became enmeshed in the web of verbiage that Kirillov was so deftly spinning. Finally he made his farewell and left in a hopelessly depressed state. In that house, he thought, they neither wanted to understand him nor even listen. What Kirillov said was completely unintelligible to him, Trepetov had done nothing but snort the whole time and Kirillov's wife hadn't been at all friendly, coming and going without saying a word to him. Strange people in that house! he thought. A wasted day.

XI

On Saturday Peredonov decided to see the district police chief. Although he isn't such an important bird as the marshal of the nobility, thought Peredonov, he could do me more harm than anyone else. At the same time, if he wants to, he could put in a good word for me with the authorities. After all, the importance of the police cannot be ignored.

He took his cap with the badge out of a box and decided from now on not to wear anything else. The headmaster could wear whatever hat he liked – he was well in with the authorities. But Peredonov wasn't an inspector yet and couldn't count on his patronage, so it was up to him to show himself in the best possible light. A few days ago, before he had embarked on his visits to the powers that be, he had already given the matter some thought but he always ended up wearing his ordinary hat. Now he arranged things differently: he threw it up over the stove so that there would be no chance of picking it up by mistake.

Varvara wasn't at home and Claudia was scrubbing the floors. Peredonov went into the kitchen to wash his hands. On the table was a roll of blue paper out of which some raisins had fallen. They were for the tea-buns and there was a whole pound of them. Peredonov didn't even bother to wash them, but greedily scoffed them as they were, standing at the table with one eye on the door in case Claudia came in unexpectedly. Then he carefully folded the paper and carried it under his jacket into the hall, where he stuffed it in his overcoat pocket so that he could throw it away in the street and thus destroy the evidence.

He went off to the district police chief. Claudia soon discovered the theft and frantically searched all over the house but could find nothing. When Varvara returned and found out she gave her a ferocious telling-off – she was sure Claudia had eaten them.

Outside it was windy, but the streets were quiet. Only a few scattered rain-clouds drifted across the sky. Puddles were drying up. In the sky was a pale joyful glimmer, but Peredonov's heart was full of anguish.

On the way he called in at the tailor's and told him to hurry up with the new uniform he had ordered two days before.

As he passed the church Peredonov took off his cap and crossed himself three times very ostentatiously so that everyone would notice the pious future inspector. He had never done this before, but now he had to be on the alert. Perhaps a spy was stealthily following him, or hiding behind a tree and watching his every movement?

The police chief lived right on the other side of town. At the gate, which was wide open, Peredonov met a constable. As before, this only increased his depression. Outside in the courtyard were several peasants, not of the usual rough type, but unusually quiet and submissive. The yard was muddy and some carts covered with matting stood near the gate.

Peredonov met another constable in the dark hall, a short skinny man, efficient-looking, but miserable. He stood motionless, with a brown leather-bound book under his arm. A dishevelled, barefooted girl appeared from one of the side-doors, took Peredonov's coat and led him into the drawing-room. 'Please wait here, he won't be long,' she said.

The drawing-room ceiling was oppressively low, thought Peredonov. The furniture was ranged close to the wall. Rope mats lay on the floor. From behind the walls to the right and left could be heard whispers and rustlings. Pale-faced women and pock-marked boys, with hungry gleaming eyes, peered out from doors every now and then. Above the whispers Peredonov could make out some questions and answers.

'I brought . . .'

'Where shall I take it?'

'Where would you like this put?'

'It's from Yermoshkin, Sidor Petrovich.'

The police chief soon appeared. He was buttoning up his tunic and sweetly smiling. 'So sorry to have kept you waiting,' he said as he took Peredonov's hand in his huge grasping hands. 'I've had so many callers today. You know, you can't put anything off until tomorrow in the police service!'

Semyon Minchukov was a tall, thickset man with black hair that was thinning on top. He had a slight stoop and his fingers were like rakes, pointing downwards. His continual smile gave the impression that he had just tasted forbidden fruit and was now licking his lips. His nose was bulbous, his lips thick and bright red and his face eager, sensuous and stupid.

Peredonov was perturbed by all he had seen and heard. He muttered a few incoherent words as he sat down in an armchair and tried to hold his cap so that the badge would be seen. Minchukov sat on the other side of the table and his rake-like hands kept opening and closing on his knees.

'They're saying heaven knows what about me,' Peredonov said. 'Things that never even happened. If it comes to informing I'm quite capable of that myself. I'm nothing that they say I am but I could say plenty of things about *them*. Only I don't want to. They talk all kinds of rubbish behind your back and then laugh in your face. You must agree that it's all rather tricky for someone in my position. As a matter of fact I have influential patrons – but these people are doing their best to spoil everything. They're only wasting their time following me around but they're a real nuisance. Wherever one goes, the whole town knows about it. So I hope that I can count on your support, should I need it.'

'Of course. With the greatest pleasure!' Minchukov said, holding out his broad palms. 'Of course, we the police must be informed if there is anyone you have reason to suspect.'

'To be frank, I really don't give a damn,' Peredonov said irately. 'Let them talk if they want to. But I'm afraid they might spoil my chances. They're a cunning lot. You've no idea what they're all saying – Rutilov, for instance. How do you know he's not planning to blow up the Treasury? One way of shifting blame is to throw suspicion on others.'

At first Minchukov thought that Peredonov was drunk and talking utter nonsense. Having heard more, he concluded that Peredonov was accusing someone of slander and wanted steps to be taken.

'Those young people,' Peredonov continued, with Volodin in mind, 'think a lot of themselves. They like to plot against others when they're up to something shady themselves. Of course, it's all too common for young people to be led astray at times. There are even some employed in the police force who go snooping around.'

For a long time he talked about young people, but for some reason he didn't want to mention Volodin. He wanted Minchukov to understand that he had unfavourable information about certain police officers. Minchukov realized that Peredonov meant two police clerks in the constabulary, young and frivolous and always chasing the girls. Minchukov couldn't help being affected by Peredonov's obvious anxiety and worriedly said, 'I shall see investigations are carried out.' After a brief pause for thought he continued, sweetly smiling, 'There are in fact two young clerks in my department whose mothers' milk isn't yet dry on their lips. Can you imagine, one of them is still made to stand in the corner by his mamma!'

Peredonov burst out laughing.

Meanwhile Varvara had gone to see Grushina, who told her a startling piece of news.

'Varvara, dear,' Grushina said hurriedly, hardly giving her time to enter the hall, 'you'll gasp when you hear what I've got to tell you.'

'Well, what is it?' Varvara asked, grinning.

'You wouldn't believe there's such scum in this world. I never knew people could stoop so low to get what they want.'

'Well, I'm waiting.'

'Sit down and I'll tell you.'

The crafty Grushina first gave Varvara some coffee and then sent her little brats out to play in the street, but the eldest daughter stubbornly refused to go.

'You good-for-nothing little slut!' cried Grushina.

'Slut yourself,' the girl insolently replied and stamped her feet.

Grushina grabbed her by the hair, threw her out and slammed the door.

'The obstinate bitch!' she complained to Varvara. 'It's really terrible with those children. I'm all on my own and I just can't cope. If only their father were alive!'

'You must marry again. Then they'll have a father,' Varvara reasoned.

'Well, you never know who you'll get landed with, dear. The next one might bully them to death.'

At this moment the daughter rushed up to the window and showered them both with a handful of sand. Grushina poked her head out and shouted, 'You rotten cow! I'll show you what's what! You wait till I get my hands on you – you filthy slut!'

'Slut yourself! You wicked old fool!' the girl shouted from the street, hopping on one foot and showing her dirty little fists.

Grushina shouted, 'Just you wait!' and shut the window. Then she sat down quite calmly, as if nothing had happened, and said, 'I wanted to tell you the news but I'm not sure if I ought to. But you needn't worry, dear, they won't get away with it.'

'What's it all about?' asked Varvara, who by now was feeling rather frightened. Her coffee saucer shook.

'Well, you know a new boy's joined the school because his aunt's bought an estate here? He's called Pylnikov and he's gone straight into the fifth form. They say he's from Ruban.'

'Oh yes, I know,' Varvara said. 'I saw him when he came with his aunt. A pretty boy. Always blushing though, and just like a girl.'

'But Varvara, dear, it's not surprising he looks like a girl. He *is* one – in disguise!'

'You don't say!' exclaimed Varvara.

'It's all part of a plan to trap Peredonov,' said Grushina rapidly. She waved her hands wildly and felt very pleased that she was the purveyor of such important news. 'This girl has a first cousin, an orphan who went to school in Ruban. The girl's mother took him away from the school there and used his papers to get the girl into school here. You'll notice that he's in lodgings on his own, without any other boys, so that the whole affair will be kept in the dark.'

'How on earth did you find out?' asked Varvara sceptically.

'News travels fast, dear. Anyway, it was suspicious from the start. He was different from the others, so quiet and gentle and very withdrawn. But to look at he seems just like any rosy-cheeked, healthy, broad-chested boy. He's so shy, when the others speak to him he blushes and they tease him for acting like a girl. They don't know how right they are! The landlady doesn't suspect a thing. You can't imagine what a cunning lot they are!'

'But you still haven't told me how you found out,' Varvara repeated.

'Varvara, dear, is there anything that goes on that I don't know about? I know everyone in the entire district. It's common knowledge that they have a boy at home who's the same age as this one. Now, why didn't they send them to school together? They made excuses that he was ill during the summer, that he was to convalesce for a year and then go back to the high school. But that's all nonsense. The real schoolboy is at home. Apart from that, everyone knows that they had a girl. They said she got married and went off to the Caucasus. It's all lies. She didn't go away at all and she's living here disguised as a boy.'

'But what's at the back of it all?' Varvara asked.

'What's at the back of it? Do you mean to say you can't guess?' Grushina replied excitedly. 'To hook one of the teachers. There's no shortage of bachelors. Or they may have someone else in mind. Dressed as a boy she could get into the men's rooms and there's no limit to what she could achieve.'

'You said she was pretty?' asked Varvara apprehensively.

'I should say so! A real beauty. Only she's a little shy. But just give her time to settle down, let herself go a bit, and then she'll turn everyone's head in this town. They're really very clever, you know. As soon as I found out I tried to speak to his landlady – or should I say *her* landlady? I really don't know what to say!'

'Ugh, a real werewolf, heaven help us!' Varvara said.

'I went to their parish church for evening service on St Panteleimon's Day – she's very religious, you know. I said to her, "Olga, why is there only one boy staying with you? You can't make very much out of that." And she replied, "Why should I want more, it's only extra work." So I told her, "You used to take in two or three." And she replied, "They made it a condition that Sasha was on his own. They said that they weren't poor and would pay me extra. They were scared that other boys might be a bad influence." What do you think of that?'

'The crafty devils!' Varvara said spitefully. 'Did you tell her it was a girl?'

'Yes, I told her, "Did you know they've palmed you off with a girl?"'

'And what did she say to that?'

'She thought I was joking and laughed. Then I said, more seriously, "Olga, you know they're saying it's a girl?" She wouldn't believe me and said that it was all a lot of nonsense, that she wasn't blind and that it couldn't possibly be one.'

Varvara was shaken by this story. She believed every word of it and was sure that another attack on Peredonov was being prepared. The girl must be exposed at once. They argued for a long time about what was to be done but without hitting on any plan of action.

Varvara was put into an even worse frame of mind by the missing raisins. When Peredonov returned home Varvara quickly and excitedly told him that Claudia had hidden them somewhere and wouldn't own up.

'And what's more, she's even suggesting that you've eaten them. She says you went into the kitchen while she was scrubbing the floors and that you were there quite a time.'

'I wasn't there very long,' Peredonov said sullenly. 'Just washing my hands. But I didn't see any raisins.'

'Claudia!' Varvara shouted. 'The master says he didn't see any raisins. You must have hidden them somewhere.'

Claudia's red face, swollen from tears, appeared from the kitchen. 'I didn't take your raisins,' she sobbed. 'If it'll satisfy you, I'll pay for them. But I didn't take them!'

'I'll see you do that all right! Do you think I'm obliged to feed you on raisins?' Varvara angrily shouted.

Peredonov burst out laughing and called out, 'Our little piggy's gobbled up a whole pound!'

'It's not fair!' Claudia said and slammed the door.

Over dinner Varvara couldn't resist telling Peredonov all she'd heard about Pylnikov. She didn't stop to consider whether she would gain by this or not, or how Peredonov would take it. She spoke simply out of spite.

Peredonov tried unsuccessfully to remember who Pylnikov was. Up to now he hadn't paid much attention to this new boy, whom he detested for being pretty and well washed, for being well-behaved, a good student and the youngest boy in the fifth form. Varvara's narrative aroused lewd feelings of curiosity in him. Obscene thoughts slowly stirred in his dark mind . . .

I must go to evening service and see this disguised girl, he thought.

All of a sudden Claudia rushed in and triumphantly threw a crumpled ball of blue paper on to the table. 'So I took your raisins, did I?' she shouted. 'Well, what's that! What would I want with your raisins?'

Peredonov realized that he had forgotten to throw the wrapper away in the street and Claudia had found it in his overcoat pocket.

'To hell with it!' he shouted.

'What's this . . . where did you find it?' Varvara asked.

'In the master's pocket,' Claudia venomously replied. 'He ate them and I'm blamed for it. You know what a sweet tooth he has. Why put the blame on others if –'

'That's enough!' protested Peredonov. 'It's all lies. You put it there yourself. I didn't take anything.'

'Why should I put it in your pocket, for God's sake?' Claudia said distractedly.

'How dare you sneak into other people's pockets!' Varvara shouted. 'Looking for money?'

'I never looked in anyone's pocket! I was taking the coat to be cleaned, it was filthy.'

'But why did you go into the pocket?'

'It just fell out. Why should I go looking in other people's pockets?' Claudia pleaded.

'You're lying, piggy!' Peredonov said.

'I'm not your little piggy. You're always making fun of me . . . To hell with you! I'll pay for the raisins and I hope you choke on them. You're the one who scoffed them and I have to pay up! It seems you've no conscience, no sense of decency, yet you call yourselves decent people!'

Claudia went out into the kitchen, crying and swearing. Peredonov had a fit of laughing and said, 'Very touchy, isn't she?'

'I'll see she pays for them,' Varvara said. 'Give them half a chance and they'll gobble everything up, the ravenous devils.'

For a long time afterwards Claudia was teased for eating the raisins. The money was deducted from her wages and they told all their visitors about it.

The cat, attracted by all the shouting, came in from the kitchen, rubbed along the wall and sat near Peredonov, glaring at him with hungry, evil eyes. Peredonov bent down to pick it up. It hissed furiously, scratched his hand and fled under the cupboard, from where it kept looking out, it's narrow green eyes glinting in the darkness. It's just like a werewolf, thought Peredonov apprehensively.

Meanwhile Varvara, still preoccupied with the identity of Pylnikov, said, 'It might be a good idea if you went to see some of the boys in their lodgings instead of playing billiards every night. They know the teachers rarely call on them and that the inspector comes only once a year, so all sorts of shocking things are going on – drunken orgies and gambling. Why don't you go to see this disguised girl? If you went late, about bedtime, then you might catch her by surprise and embarrass her.'

Peredonov pondered for a moment and then burst out laughing. Varvara's a sly bitch and can teach me a thing or two! he thought.

XII

Peredonov went to evening service in the church used by the school. He stood behind the boys and carefully watched how they behaved. Some appeared to be misbehaving – jostling each other, laughing and whispering. He tried to make a mental note of the offenders, but there were so many of them and he cursed himself for not bringing paper and pencil with him. It saddened him to see them behaving so badly and that no one took any notice, although the headmaster and inspector were there with their wives and children.

In reality, the boys were standing in a very orderly fashion. Some crossed themselves, their thoughts far away from religious matters, while others prayed diligently. Only rarely did a boy whisper to his neighbour – and then only a few quiet words spoken with a turn of the head, a quick sideways glance, a shrug of the shoulders, a smile which received a similar response. But these almost imperceptible movements and sounds that the monitors didn't notice appeared to Peredonov's diseased and troubled mind as nothing less than total disorder. Even when in a relatively calm state Peredonov, like all coarse people, saw everything out of proportion: he either completely misjudged things or exaggerated them to a fantastic degree. And, as now, when he was aroused by expectations and fears, his senses betrayed him and gradually the real world became obscured by a fog of vile, evil phantoms.

And what had the boys ever meant to Peredonov? Weren't they simply machines for pushing a pen over paper and repeating what had been said so many times before and so much better! Throughout his life as a teacher he had never so much as tried to understand them or consider that boys were of the same species as adults. Only those students who were beginning to grow beards and to show an interest in the opposite sex were his equals – as far as he was concerned.

After he had stood at the back for a while, Peredonov moved forward to the middle rows, having absorbed enough of these depressing thoughts. At the end of one of them stood Sasha Pylnikov. He was humbly praying and making frequent genuflections. Peredonov was delighted to see him there, kneeling as if he'd been punished, looking anxiously, imploringly at the altar doors, his black eyes, with their long blue-black lashes, full of entreaty and sadness. Dark-skinned and shapely – this was particularly noticeable as he knelt there, calm and upright as if under someone's strict surveillance, and with that broad, prominent chest – he appeared to Peredonov just like a girl.

And now Peredonov finally made up his mind to visit him in his lodgings after the service.

Soon everyone began to leave the church. People noticed that instead of his usual hat Peredonov was wearing a cap and badge.

Rutilov laughed and asked, 'What's this, Ardalyon, showing off your badge now? I think someone's after an inspectorship!'

'Do soldiers have to salute you now?' said Valeriya, pretending to be naïve.

'Don't try and make a fool of me!' Peredonov retorted.

'Don't be so silly, Valeriya,' Darya said. 'What's it to do with soldiers? He's only wearing it to get more respect from his pupils.'

Lyudmila burst out laughing. Peredonov made a hasty farewell to escape their taunts.

It was too early to go and see Pylnikov and he had no desire to go home. He walked along the dark streets and wondered how to spend the next hour. Lights shone from many windows and now and then voices came from them. He could hear gates clicking and doors opening and closing as churchgoers returned. Everywhere there lived strange, hostile people. Perhaps at that very moment some were plotting against him. Perhaps some person thought it strange that he was alone at this late hour and wondered where he could be going. Peredonov thought someone was following him and stealthily creeping up on him. He was frightened and hurried on aimlessly.

In every house he passed someone had died at some time, he thought. Everyone who had lived in those old houses fifty years ago was now dead. A few of them he could even remember. When there's been a death, the house should be burned down, he wearily thought. It's too frightening otherwise.

Olga Kokovkina, with whom Pylnikov lodged, was a paymaster's widow. She had been left a pension and a small house that was large enough for her to let three or four rooms at a time, but she preferred to take in boys from the school and she was always given the quietest boys who worked hard and finished their studies, not as in other houses where most of the students were the type who drifted from one school to another and thus ended up as ignoramuses.

Olga Kokovkina, a tall, thin, upright old woman with an essentially good-natured face – although she always did her best to look strict – was sitting at the table drinking tea with Sasha Pylnikov, a well-fed boy who had been strictly brought up by his aunt.

Today was Sasha's turn to supply the jam, which he had bought in the country, and for this reason he felt that he was the host. His black eyes sparkled as he solemnly served Olga.

Suddenly the bell rang and a moment later Peredonov appeared. Kokovkina was astonished at this late visit.

'I thought I'd just drop in to see how the new boy is getting on,' he said.

Kokovkina offered Peredonov some tea but he refused. He wanted them to drink their tea as soon as possible, so that he could be alone with the boy. When they eventually finished they all went into Sasha's room, but Kokovkina didn't leave them and prattled incessantly. Peredonov looked mournfully at Sasha, who, out of shyness, didn't say a word. I'm wasting my time here, thought Peredonov, highly annoyed.

Fortunately the maid called Kokovkina out for some reason, so Peredonov had his chance. Sasha watched her go and felt dejected. His eyes grew dim and his exceptionally long lashes seemed to cast a shadow over his whole dark-skinned face, which had suddenly turned pale. He felt uneasy in the presence of this sinister man. Peredonov sat down beside him, put his arm clumsily around his waist and with his perpetual blank expression asked, 'Well, Sasha, have you said your prayers nicely?'

Sasha looked at him in terror, blushed, but said nothing.

'Well? Did you say them properly?'

'Yes I did,' Sasha said at last.

'Such rosy cheeks! Confess now, you're a girl, aren't you? Oh yes, you little devil!'

'No I'm not,' protested Sasha and suddenly, angry with himself for being so shy, asked in a shrill voice, 'What makes you think I'm a girl? Just because I don't like filthy words I get teased by the other boys. I've never used them, so why should I repeat them if I don't want to? Why should I use filthy words?'

'Would Mummy punish you?'

'My mother died a long time ago. My aunt looks after me.'

'Would Auntie punish you then?'

'Of course she would if I repeated filthy words. And she'd be quite right.'

'And how would Auntie find out?'

'Firstly, I don't use such words. And if I did she'd find out one way or the other,' Sasha calmly replied. 'I might give myself away.'

'Which of your friends are responsible for these obscenities?'

Sasha blushed again and was silent.

'Come on now, you've got to tell me,' Peredonov insisted. 'It's no good hiding things from me.'

'No one says anything of the sort,' Sasha replied, now thoroughly confused.

'But you just said they did.'

'I didn't.'

'Why do you deny it?' Peredonov asked angrily.

Sasha realized that he had been hopelessly trapped and said, 'All I meant was that some of the boys tease me for being like a girl. But I wouldn't tell tales on them!'

'You don't say! And why not?' Peredonov spitefully asked.

'It's not very nice,' Sasha replied with an indignant grin.

'I shall go and tell the headmaster. Then you'll be forced to tell the truth,' Peredonov gloated.

Sasha looked furiously at Peredonov. 'Please don't tell him, Mr Peredonov,' he begged.

And one could tell from his breaking voice that he was forcing himself to plead with Peredonov when he would have far preferred to shout insolent, threatening words at him.

'No, I must tell him. Then you'll see if it pays to hide filth. You should have complained from the start. Now you're really in for it.'

Sasha stood up and in his confusion fumbled with his belt. Kokovkina entered.

'You have every right to be proud of your little prig,' Peredonov said maliciously.

Kokovkina was frightened. She stumbled over to Sasha (her legs always seemed to give way when she was excited), sat beside him and asked with sinking heart, 'What do you mean, Mr Peredonov?' she asked. 'What's he done?'

'Ask *him*,' Peredonov replied with a grim smile.

'Well, what have you done wrong?' asked Kokovkina, touching Sasha's elbow.

'I don't know,' Sasha said and burst into tears.

'Then why are you crying?' she asked. She placed her hands on his shoulders and drew him towards her, not noticing that this only embarrassed him. He just stood there, stooping, and holding a handkerchief over his face.

Peredonov explained, 'Someone at school is teaching him dirty words and he won't say who it is. He's only too willing to learn and wants to cover up for the others.'

'Sasha! How could you! It's not possible! Aren't you ashamed of yourself?' Kokovkina said in dismay, letting go of him.

'I've done nothing wrong,' Sasha sobbed. 'They tease me because I *don't* know any rude words.'

'Who is using them?' asked Peredonov.

'No one,' answered Sasha in desperation.

'It's obvious the boy's lying,' said Peredonov. 'He needs a good beating. He *must* tell us who the culprits are or the school will get a bad name and we shall be powerless to do anything about it.'

'You must forgive him, Mr Peredonov!' Kokovkina said. 'How can he tell on his schoolmates? His life wouldn't be worth living if he did.'

'It's his duty to tell,' Peredonov angrily said. 'Only good can come of it. Then we can decide how to punish them.'

'But they'll beat him up, won't they?' said Kokovkina querulously.

'They wouldn't dare. If he's scared he can tell us in secret.'

'Tell him, Sasha, we'll keep it a secret. No one will know it was you.'

Sasha wept silently. Kokovkina drew him to her again, put her arm around his waist and whispered in his ear for some time. He kept shaking his head negatively.

'He doesn't want to,' said Kokovkina.

'A good birching will loosen his tongue,' Peredonov said savagely. 'Bring me some rods, I'll make him talk.'

'But why, Mrs Kokovkina?' Sasha exclaimed. 'What for?'

Kokovkina got up and embraced him once more. 'Now that's enough howling,' she said tenderly but sternly. 'No one's going to lay a finger on you.'

'As you like,' Peredonov said, 'but I shall tell the headmaster all the same. I thought it might be easier for him if we had it out at home, but I think Sasha knows more than he's prepared to tell. We still don't know why he's teased for being a girl. Perhaps it's for something quite different. Perhaps he's not the one who's being taught – perhaps *he's* corrupting the others!'

Peredonov stormed out of the room, followed by Kokovkina, who then gave him a taste of her tongue.

'Mr Peredonov! How dare you come here and attack an innocent little boy for heaven knows what! It's just as well he doesn't really understand what you're talking about.'

'Goodbye,' Peredonov replied furiously. 'I shall tell the head-master as soon as I see him. This matter must be investigated.'

He left abruptly and Kokovkina went to console Sasha, who was sitting sadly by the window, looking at the starry sky. His black eyes were calm now and melancholy. Kokovkina silently stroked his head.

'It's all my fault,' he said. 'I let slip why they're teasing me and after that he wouldn't leave me alone. He's a terribly coarse man. None of the boys likes him.'

Next day Peredonov and Varvara finally moved to their new flat. Yershova stood by the gate and she and Varvara swore violently at each other. Peredonov hid behind one of the removal carts.

As soon as they had moved in a blessing was said. Peredonov thought it was essential to show everybody that he was a true believer. During the ceremony the smell of incense drugged him into something akin to religious fervour. One strange circumstance, however, disturbed him. From somewhere a peculiar, dimly out-lined creature darted out – a small, spritely grey demon. It laughed and quivered and bustled around Peredonov, and whenever he stretched out his hand to catch it, it slipped swiftly away and hid behind the door or under the cupboard, only to reappear a moment later, still quivering and mocking.

When the service was drawing to a close Peredonov guessed what it was and whispered a magic charm. The little demon hissed very softly, shrivelled into a tiny ball and rolled away behind the door. Peredonov heaved a sigh of relief. Yes! I hope it's rolled away for good. Perhaps it lives in this house, somewhere under the floorboards, just waiting to come out and tease me. A chill ran over him; he felt depressed. Why are there all these evil spirits in the world? Peredonov forlornly asked himself.

When the service was over and all the guests had departed, Peredonov pondered a long time about where the demon could have hidden itself. Varvara went to see Grushina, which gave him the chance of searching through her things. I wonder if Varvara took it away with her in her pocket? It can't need much room: it could easily hide there until it feels like coming out again! Then his attention was caught by one of Varvara's dresses. It was all flounces, ribbons and bows, and seemed expressly designed to conceal someone. He examined it for a long time and then, partly with his hands and partly with a knife, he tore off the pocket and threw it into the stove. Then he ripped and cut the rest of the dress into small pieces. Strange, confused thoughts filled his mind. His heart was full of hopeless anguish. Varvara soon returned and found Peredonov still cutting up what was left of the dress. She thought he was drunk and swore wildly. Peredonov let her go on and on and then he said, 'What are you snapping at me for, you stupid woman? Don't you realize there might be a devil in your pocket? Am I the one who always has to look after things here?'

Varvara was stunned. Peredonov was glad that he had shocked her into silence. He hurriedly found his cap and went off to play billiards. While he was putting on his coat in the hall Varvara ran out and screeched, 'If anyone's carrying a devil around it's you! I don't have one. Where do you think I'd get one? By mail order from Holland?'

Cherepnin (the subject of Vershina's story of the rain-tub) had wanted to woo her shortly after she lost her husband. Vershina, who really had no objection to marrying again, found him most insignificant. This made him very bitter. So he jumped at Volodin's idea of smearing her gates with tar.

But no sooner had he agreed than he began to have doubts. Supposing he were caught? After all, he was a civil servant. So he decided to get others to do the job for him and bribed two hooligans with twenty-five copecks, promising them a further fifteen copecks each when they'd done the job – and on one dark night the deed was done.

If anyone in Vershina's house had opened a window after midnight they would have heard the shuffling of bare feet in the street, stifled whispers and some other soft noises – as if someone was gently brushing the fence. Then a faint clatter, the sound of those same feet hurrying away ever faster, distant laughter and the barking of awakened dogs.

No one, however, opened the window. And in the morning the gate and fence between the garden and the backyard were covered with bright orange streaks of tar. Filthy words had been written all over the gate. Everyone who went past just gasped and laughed. The news soon spread and the curious came to look. Vershina paced up and down the garden, smoking as ever, smiling even more wryly than usual and muttering angry words. Marta didn't leave the house and she shed bitter tears. Marya the maid tried to wash off the tar and had furious exchanges with the gaping spectators, who kept laughing riotously and making a dreadful racket.

The same day Cherepnin told Volodin who had done it and Volodin was not long in telling Peredonov. Both knew the boys, who had something of a reputation for wild escapades.

On his way to billiards, Peredonov stopped off at Vershina's. She was sitting in the drawing-room with Marta.

'I see your gates have been smeared with tar,' Peredonov said.

Marta blushed. Vershina hurriedly told him that when they had got up they had seen people laughing at their fence and that Marya was now washing it down.

'I know who did it,' Peredonov said.

Vershina looked at Peredonov in bewilderment. 'How did you find out?' she asked.

'I have ways and means,' said Peredonov.

'Who was it then?' Marta angrily asked.

At that moment she struck Peredonov as really quite ugly, with her spiteful tear-stained eyes and her red swollen eyelids.

'Don't worry, I'm going to tell you – that's why I came,' Peredonov replied. 'Those hooligans must be taught a lesson. But you must solemnly promise not to say who told you.'

'But why, Peredonov?' Vershina asked in astonishment.

After a significant silence Peredonov explained. 'They're such a wild bunch, they'd smash my head in if they ever found out who told on them.'

Vershina promised not to breathe a word.

'And don't *you* say that I told you,' Peredonov said to Marta.

'You can rely on me,' Marta hastily agreed, as she was impatient to hear who the culprits were and felt that they should be made to undergo a severe and humiliating punishment for their crime.

'No, you'd better swear on the Bible,' Peredonov said anxiously.

'I swear to God that I won't tell anyone,' Marta assured him. 'But do hurry up and tell us.'

Vladya was listening through the keyhole. He was glad that he'd not gone into the drawing-room, to be made to promise like the others. Now he could tell anyone he liked. The thought that here at last was a chance to take his revenge on Peredonov filled him with delight. Peredonov began, 'Last night, at about one o'clock, I was going home along this street when suddenly I heard someone moving by your gate. At first I thought it must be burglars. Before I had time to think what to do, two figures ran out towards me. I flattened myself against the wall and they didn't see me. I easily recognized them. One had a brush and the other was carrying a bucket. They're well-known ruffians, Avdeyev the locksmith's sons. As they ran off I could hear one saying to the other, "We can't call this night wasted – we've earned fifty-five copecks!" I very nearly stepped out of my hiding-place to stop one of them but I was afraid I might get my face smeared. And I was wearing my new overcoat.'

No sooner had Peredonov gone than Vershina complained to the police chief Minchukov, who at once sent a constable to arrest Avdeyev and his two sons.

The two boys strutted into the police office, certain that they were being brought in for some previous offence. Avdeyev, a tall miserable old man, was convinced however that his sons had committed some fresh outrage. When the police chief told Avdeyev what the charge was, he replied, 'Do what you like, I can't cope anymore. I've ruined my hands from thrashing them.'

'We had nothing to do with it,' insisted Nil, the elder son, who had thick red hair.

'We're blamed for *everything* in this place,' complained Ilya, whose hair was just as luxuriant as his brother's, but fair. 'Once you've done something wrong you have to answer for everything.'

Minchukov smiled his sugary smile, shook his head and said, 'You'd better make a clean breast of it.'

'There's nothing to confess,' Nil gruffly replied.

'Is that so? Perhaps you could tell me who gave you fifty-five copecks for the job, eh?'

Seeing from their obvious bewilderment and startled silence that they were guilty, he told Vershina, 'Yes, these are obviously the ones.'

There were fresh denials but the protesting boys were taken into a storeroom for a good birching. The pain was too much and after a few strokes they broke down and confessed. But they still wouldn't say who had paid them.

'It was our own idea,' they said.

They were thrashed in turn, slowly, until they confessed that it was Cherepnin who had offered them the money. Then they were turned over to their father. The police chief told Vershina, 'Well, they've been punished – I mean, their father punished them – and you know who did this to you.'

'I won't let Cherepnin get away with it as easily as that,' Vershina said. 'I shall take him to court.'

'I wouldn't advise that,' Minchukov said curtly. 'It's best to let the whole matter drop.'

'What? And let those ruffians get away with it! Never!' exclaimed Vershina.

'The main thing is, there's no real proof,' the police chief said calmly.

'What do you mean, if they themselves confessed?'

'Yes, they confessed all right. But once they're in court they'll deny it. No one's going to flog them there!'

'But how can they? There're witnesses – your own constables,' Vershina said with rather less assurance.

'What witnesses? If you flay the hide off a man he'll own up to anything, even something that never happened. Of course, they're scoundrels and they got what they deserved. But you wouldn't get anything out of them in a court of law.'

Minchukov smiled sweetly and calmly looked at Vershina, who went away feeling highly dissatisfied. She admitted, however, after due consideration, that it would be extremely difficult to accuse Cherepnin and that it would only lead to unnecessary scandal and unwelcome publicity.

XIII

In the evening Peredonov went to see the headmaster on business.

Nikolay Khripach's life was governed by a set of rules which could so easily be applied to every eventuality that keeping them was no bother at all. As headmaster he calmly carried out all the regulations or instructions as laid down by the authorities, so the school board, parents and pupils could find no fault with him. He was a stranger to knotty problems, indecision, hesitation – and what was the point of them, anyway? Wasn't there always the education committee to fall back on when there were difficult decisions to be made? And in his personal relationships he gave the same impression of imperturbability and correctness, which was confirmed by his appearance of solidity and good nature. He was short, well built, with shining eyes and a confident voice. He struck one as a man who had got on well and was determined to do even better. His study was crammed with books and he made copious notes from some of them. When he had accumulated a sufficient number of these notes he would classify them, write them out in his own words and incorporate them in a textbook for publication. Although they didn't sell as well as standard textbooks, they still enjoyed respectable sales. He often compiled from foreign books anthologies of impeccable scholarship which were respected but completely useless, and which he then proceeded to publish in a respected but equally useless journal. He had many children, all of whom, both girls and boys, were already showing decided talents – some for poetry and sketching, while one of them was making great strides in music.

Peredonov entered the study and came straight to the point by growling, 'You're always finding fault with me, Mr Khripach. I know some people in this town have been spreading malicious lies about me, but I never say a word about anyone myself.'

'You must excuse me for being so stupid,' interrupted the headmaster, 'but I really don't understand what malicious lies you're talking about. As head of this school I am guided by my own personal observations. May I make so bold as to state that my experience as headmaster is sufficient to enable me to put a correct interpretation on everything I see or hear. As you know, my work comes before everything else and this is a self-imposed rule that I have never broken.' Khripach said this in a distinct, rapid way, and his clear dry voice sounded like thin bars of zinc being snapped in half. He continued, 'And as far as my personal opinion of you is concerned, I stand firmly by my opinion that your work leaves much to be desired.'

'You're obsessed with the idea that I'm no good at all. But the welfare of the school is my constant concern,' snarled Peredonov.

Khripach raised his eyebrows in amazement at this outburst and looked at him quizzically.

'It's obvious that you haven't noticed there's a possibility of a grave scandal in the school. And I'm the only one who's discovered it.'

'What scandal?' asked Khripach with a dry laugh as he briskly paced his study. 'You really do intrigue me, my dear Peredonov. I'd be very surprised if there were a scandal in *my* school.'

'But you don't know about the new boy you've just admitted.' Peredonov said this with such venom that Khripach stopped in his tracks and stared at him.

'I know all the new boys in the school,' he said coldly. 'Class one has a very good record – none of the boys in it has ever been expelled from another school. And the only new boy to join class five has references that place him quite above suspicion.'

'That may be so, but he should have gone to another type of school, not yours,' Peredonov said morosely and with apparent reluctance.

'Please explain yourself, Mr Peredonov,' Khripach said. 'I hope you're not suggesting we send him to an institution for juvenile delinquents?'

'He should go to an establishment[1] where they don't teach Greek and Latin.' Peredonov's eyes gleamed with malice.

Khripach put his hands in his short jacket and looked at Peredonov in utter astonishment. 'What school do you have in mind? Do you know what type of school has that kind of syllabus!? And if you do, how dare you make such an improper suggestion!' Khripach went very red in the face and his voice sounded sharper and dryer than ever. On any other occasion Peredonov would have been flustered by these signs of anger. Now he felt cool and collected.

'You all think that he's a boy,' he said, derisively screwing up his eyes. 'But let me tell you, he's a girl – and no virgin either!'

Khripach burst into a dry, clear, resonant laugh that sounded almost artificial; that was how he always laughed. 'Ha! Ha!' he went, sitting back in his armchair, throwing his head back, as if collapsing with laughter. 'That's a good one, Peredonov! Ha! Ha! Please be so good as to tell me on what evidence you base this

1. In popular speech an establishment (the Russian word is pansion, meaning 'boarding-school') where they don't teach Greek and Latin is a brothel.

amazing revelation – unless it's something you have to keep to yourself. Ha ha!'

Peredonov related all that he had heard from Varvara and at the same time expatiated on Kokovkina's failings. Khripach listened, occasionally breaking into that peculiar, crisp, clear laugh of his.

'I'm afraid your imagination has been playing tricks on you, my dear Peredonov.' He stood up and tapped Peredonov's sleeve. 'Look here, I'm a married man with children, like many of my esteemed colleagues. We're all men of the world. Do you really think that we could be so stupid as to take a disguised girl for a boy? I ask you!'

'You're entitled to your opinion. But what if I'm right? How will it look for you then?'

'Ha! Ha!' went Khripach. 'And what do you think will be the consequences if it really is a girl?'

'It will be the beginning of the complete corruption of the school.'

Khripach frowned and said, 'Now you're going too far. I must say that your story so far hasn't given me the slightest reason for sharing your suspicions.'

That same evening Peredonov made hurried visits to all of his colleagues, from the inspector right down to the assistant masters. Most of them roared with laughter when they were told that Pylnikov was really a girl in disguise, but many began to have doubts as soon as he had left. Their wives believed him at once, almost without exception.

Next morning many of the teachers came into class thinking that he might be right after all. If they were suspicious they didn't tell anyone, nor did they argue with Peredonov, for fear they would look complete idiots if they were wrong, and they answered questions as ambiguously as they could. Many wanted to hear what the head had to say about it. He disappointed them, however, by staying in his room the whole day and when he did finally turn up very late for his only lesson that day, with the sixth form, he stayed an extra five minutes and then went straight to his study without seeing anyone.

Before the fourth lesson started, the grey-haired divinity teacher, together with two others, went to see the headmaster on the pretext of some school matter and the divinity teacher cunningly led up to the subject of Pylnikov. But the headmaster took it all so lightly and laughed so much that all three were immediately convinced it was a load of nonsense. He quickly turned to other topics, related the latest piece of town gossip and then complained of a splitting headache and said he would probably have to send for the school doctor. And then he most genially announced that the lesson he had taken that day had made his headache even worse, since Peredonov happened to be teaching in the next classroom. The boys there had been laughing the whole time, and exceptionally loudly for some reason. After producing his usual dry laugh Khripach said, 'Fate hasn't been kind to me this year. Three times a week I have to sit next to Peredonov's classroom. The laughter goes on the whole time, almost without interruption. I've never heard anything like it. It's strange, don't you think, that an apparently unfunny person like Peredonov should be able to arouse such constant mirth!'

Without giving them time to object he once more changed the subject. In fact a great deal of laughter had been coming recently from Peredonov's room, but it wasn't something he encouraged. On the contrary, a child's laughter had always irritated him. The fault was his, however, in that he was unable to let a lesson pass without making some indecent remark or saying something quite unnecessary. He would tell some stupid story, or tease one of the more defenceless boys. And there were always those troublemakers who were only too glad of the opportunity of creating chaos and who roared furiously with laughter at each of his sallies.

Towards the end of school Khripach sent for the doctor, picked up his hat and went into the park, which lay between the school and the river. It was large and shady. The boys loved to play there and ran around as much as they liked during break. This was why the assistant masters avoided it like the plague: they were afraid one of the boys might do himself an injury. Khripach, however, insisted that the boys spent their recreation there. This was necessary so that he could make his reports to the authorities more impressive.

As he went down the corridor he stopped by the open gymnasium door, stood there a few moments with head bowed and then entered. From his miserable face and slow walk everyone knew at once that he was having one of his headaches.

The fifth form was getting ready for exercises. They were lined up in single file and their instructor, a territorial lieutenant, was just about to shout an order when he saw the headmaster. He went over to him and they shook hands. The headmaster peered absent-mindedly at the boys and asked, 'Any complaints? Are they working hard? Not tiring too easily?'

The instructor had a profound contempt for the boys, who in his opinion would never learn to bear themselves like soldiers in a hundred years. Had they been real cadets, he would have told them what he thought of them – in no uncertain terms. He had to think of his job, however, and therefore didn't dare tell the sad truth about that load of clodhoppers. And so, pleasantly smiling with his thin lips and giving the headmaster a friendly, cheerful look, he said, 'Very well indeed, sir. A fine lot of boys!'

Khripach walked past the file and then stopped by the door to ask, as if he'd suddenly remembered something, 'Are you pleased with the new boy? Is he trying hard? Does he get tired easily?' He said this lazily and sullenly, puting his hand to his forehead.

The instructor told him, 'He's a bit sluggish and he does get tired quickly.'

But the headmaster was no longer listening and already on his way out. The air didn't refresh him very much evidently, and in half an hour he returned to the gym after standing at the door for a while.

Exercises on the apparatus were in progress. Two or three boys with nothing to do, and who knew the instructor wasn't watching them, were lounging against the wall. They didn't notice Khripach return.

'Pylnikov, why are you leaning against the wall?'

Sasha blushed violently, straightened up and said nothing.

'If you get tired so easily then perhaps gym is harmful for you?' Khripach said sternly.

'I wasn't feeling tired, sir,' Sasha said in alarm.

'There're two alternatives,' Khripach continued. 'Either you don't do gym anymore, or ... anyway, come and see me after school.'

He hurried off, leaving Sasha confused and frightened.

'You'll catch it now!' said the others. 'He'll lecture you till midnight.'

Far more painful than any beating in the eyes of the boys were the headmaster's lengthy reprimands, and it was with a sinking heart that Sasha went to the headmaster's study when lessons were over. Khripach almost rushed at him when he entered, and seemed to be rolling along on his very short legs. He went right up to him, looked him straight in the eye and asked, 'Does gym really exhaust you, Pylnikov? You look healthy enough to me, but appearances can be deceptive, as they say. Have you seen a doctor recently? Perhaps you should stop doing gym.'

'I'm quite all right, sir,' Sasha replied, red with embarrassment.

'The fact is, your instructor has been complaining about your sluggishness, that you get tired so easily. And I thought that you looked tired when I saw you today. Or perhaps I was mistaken?'

Sasha didn't know how to avoid Khripach's penetrating stare and mumbled in his confusion, 'I'm sorry. It was just out of laziness, I'm really quite all right. I promise to try very hard in future, really I do!' And suddenly he burst into tears, much to his own surprise.

'So, you see,' Khripach said, 'it's obvious you're tired out, otherwise you wouldn't cry like that. Anyone would think I'd just given you a severe telling-off. Calm yourself.' He put his hand on Pylnikov's shoulder and said, 'I didn't tell you to come in order to give you a lecture, but to get one thing clear ... Sit down, Pylnikov, I can see you're tired.'

Sasha quickly dried his eyes with his handkerchief and said, 'I'm not a bit tired.'

'Now sit down and relax,' Khripach repeated, pushing a chair over to Pylnikov.

'I tell you, I'm not tired, Mr Khripach.'

Khripach took him by the shoulders and sat him down. Then he sat facing him and said, 'We're going to have a nice quiet chat, Pylnikov. *You* can't know the true state of your health. You're a diligent boy, satisfactory in every respect. Therefore I fully understand why you didn't like to ask to be excused gym. As it happens, I've asked the school doctor to come and see me, as I'm not feeling too well myself. He can have a look at you at the same time. No objections, I hope?' Khripach glanced at his watch and, without waiting for an answer, asked Sasha how he had spent the summer holidays.

The school doctor, Yevgeniy Surovtsev, was not long in arriving. He was a small man, dark and sprightly. His favourite topics of conversation were politics and the latest news. Although he didn't have much idea about medicine, he was very conscientious towards his patients and preferred to leave to the course of nature what medicines couldn't cure. As a result he was very successful.

Sasha was told to undress. Surovtsev gave him a thorough examination and found nothing wrong. Khripach was now convinced that Sasha wasn't a girl. Although he had been sure of this all along, he thought it would be useful if the school doctor could verify the fact should he subsequently have to reply to questions from the district council.

Khripach told Pylnikov he could go and as he left gently told him, 'Now we know there's nothing wrong I shall tell your gym instructor to be quite merciless in future.'

Peredonov didn't doubt for one moment that, besides promotion, he would receive a medal for his astonishing revelation. This thought encouraged him to keep a very close watch on the boys' behaviour. As it happened, the weather over the past few days had been cold and wet and the billiard-rooms were almost deserted. Therefore, all he could do was to go on visiting the boys in their lodgings, even those who were living at home. He selected those parents who could be most easily persuaded. He would complain about the boy, who would then be beaten – and Peredonov would be satisfied. The first victim was Joseph Kramarenko, whose father ran a brewery in the town. Peredonov told him that his son had been misbehaving in church. The father believed him and the son was duly flogged. The same fate befell many others. Peredonov kept away from those he knew would defend their sons and who might complain to the authorities.

Every day he visited at least one of the student lodgings, where he would really lay down the law, issuing severe reprimands, orders and threats. But the boys who lived out felt much more independent and occasionally jeered Peredonov. An exception was Mrs Flavitsky, a tall loud-mouthed energetic woman who obliged at once by giving her young lodger, Vladimir Bultyakov, a really good thrashing.

Next day in class Peredonov recounted his exploits. He did not mention any names, but the obvious embarrassment of certain members of the class was enough to give them away.

XIV

Rumours that Pylnikov was a girl in disguise spread like wildfire through that town. Among the first to hear were the Rutilov sisters. The inquisitive Lyudmila, always wanting to see anything new with her own eyes, was dying with curiosity about Pylnikov. Of course, she simply had to take a look at that masquerading little cheat.

She knew Kokovkina very well and one evening she told her sisters, 'I'm going to have a look at this girl for myself.'

'Nosy!' Darya angrily cried.

'And all dressed up for the occasion!' observed Valeriya with a restrained smile.

They were annoyed that *they* hadn't thought of it first and realized that it would be awkward for all three to go at the same time. Lyudmila dressed herself more smartly than usual – she herself didn't know why. However, she loved to reveal more than her sisters dared: her arms were barer, her skirts shorter, her shoes flimsier and her flesh-coloured stockings thinner and more transparent. At home she normally liked to go about in just a skirt and wear shoes over her bare feet; moreover, her skirts and blouses were always far too dressy.

It was cold and windy. Fallen leaves skimmed across ruffled puddles. Lyudmila walked quickly and hardly felt the cold, despite the fact that she was wearing only a light cape.

Kokovkina and Sasha were having tea. Lyudmila eyed them closely but could see nothing out of the ordinary – there they were, both quietly drinking tea, eating rolls and chatting.

Lyudmila kissed Kokovkina and said, 'There's something important I'd like to talk to you about, Olga, but that can wait a bit. In the meantime I'd like a nice hot cup of tea to warm me up. Oh, what a good-looking boy!'

Sasha blushed and bowed clumsily as Kokovkina introduced him. Lyudmila sat at the table and began to give a lively account of the latest news. She was very welcome in most houses, since she knew everything and recounted it with such charm and simplicity. Kokovkina, who hardly ever went out, was genuinely pleased to see her and cordially entertained her. Lyudmila gaily chatted and laughed and, once or twice, as she leaped from her chair to mimic someone, she brushed against Sasha.

'It must be very dull for you, dear, sitting at home all the time with this sour-faced schoolboy. You could at least come and see us some time.'

'At my age?' Kokovkina replied. 'No, I'm too old to start making social visits.'

'Rubbish! You don't have to be invited,' Lyudmila amiably replied. 'Just come and make yourself at home – this little boy doesn't have to be mollycoddled by you.'

Sasha looked hurt and he blushed.

'He's just a baby!' Lyudmila said perkily as she nudged Sasha. 'Well, haven't you anything to say to your visitor?'

'He's very young,' Kokovkina said, 'and very shy with me.'

Lyudmila smiled and said, 'I'm shy too.'

Sasha laughed and innocently replied, 'Shy? At your age?'

Lyudmila burst out laughing. Her laughter had a deep sensuality mingled with gaiety and whenever she laughed she would blush violently and her eyes would become mischievous and guilty – then she would coyly look away.

Sasha was embarrassed and began to stammer out apologies. 'I didn't mean that. What I wanted to say was that I thought you were lively and not shy – not that you were fast!'

Feeling that what he had said wasn't as clear as it would have been in writing, he became confused and went red in the face.

'What a cheek he's got!' Lyudmila laughed, blushing too. 'I think he's perfectly delightful!'

'Look, you've got my Sasha in a real muddle!' Kokovkina said, smiling at them both.

Lyudmila bent forward and with a catlike movement stroked

Sasha's head. He laughed bashfully, wriggled from under her hands and ran into his room.

'I want you to find me a husband, dear,' Lyudmila said, coming straight to the point.

'Well, you've picked a fine matchmaker, I must say!' Kokovkina replied, smiling. It was clear from her smile, though, that she would be delighted to take on the job.

'Why shouldn't you be my matchmaker? Wouldn't I make a nice bride? You wouldn't be ashamed, would you?' Lyudmila put her hands on her hips and performed a little dance in front of Kokovkina.

'I'll give you what for!' Kokovkina said. 'You little flirt!'

Lyudmila laughed and said, 'Do it, even if it's for want of anything better to do!'

'What kind of husband are you looking for, dear?' Kokovkina asked, still smiling.

'He must have brown hair, very dark – that's essential. Dark brown – dark as a pit. Just like your schoolboy's in fact. Yes, the eyebrows must be black, the eyes languishing, the hair black, with a dark blue sheen. And the lashes beautiful and thick – and blue-black! Your schoolboy's so handsome, so *very* handsome! I want someone like him.'

Soon Lyudmila prepared to leave, as it was now getting dark. Sasha wanted to see her off.

'I'll let you come, but only as far as the cab,' said Lyudmila tenderly, guiltily blushing as she caressed Sasha with fond eyes.

In the street Lyudmila was her lively self again and began cross-examining Sasha.

'Are you working hard at school? Do you read a lot?'

'Yes, I read a lot of books. I love reading.'

'Andersen's fairy tales?'

'No, not fairy tales! All sorts of books. I love history – and poetry.'

'So you like poetry. Who's your favourite poet?' Lyudmila asked sternly.

'Why, Nadson[1] of course,' Sasha replied, firmly convinced that there was just *no one* else.

1. S. Y. Nadson (1862–87), a deeply pessimistic poet who enjoyed great popularity, many of his poems being set to music. His poetry was highly musical, but empty and insipid. He wrote mainly on civic themes.

'That's lovely!' Lyudmila replied encouragingly. 'I like Nadson too, but only in the morning. In the evenings I like to put pretty dresses on, dear. How do you like to spend the time?'

Sasha glanced at her with tender black eyes that suddenly became moist. He softly replied, 'I like cuddling.'

'Ooh, what an affectionate boy you are!' Lyudmila exclaimed, putting her hands on his shoulders. 'So you like cuddling. Do you like puddling[1] too?'

Sasha giggled. Lyudmila persisted, 'In nice warm water?'

'In warm and in cold water,' he shyly replied.

'And what kind of soap do you like?'

'Glycerine.'

'And do you like grapes?'

Sasha laughed. 'You're such a tease! They're two different things and yet you ask as if they're the same! But you won't catch me out.'

'As if I would want to do a thing like that!' she laughed.

'Well, I know how you like to make fun of people.'

'Who told you that?'

'Everyone says so.'

'Why, you little scandalmonger!' Lyudmila said, pretending to be annoyed.

Sasha blushed again.

'Here's a cab. Cabby!' Lyudmila shouted.

'Cabby!' shouted Sasha.

The clumsy old drozhky clattered up to them. Lyudmila gave the driver the address. He thought for a moment and then asked for forty copecks.

'You know, it's not very far,' she said. 'I bet you don't know the way.'

'How much then?' the cabby asked.

'Whichever half you want!'

Sasha burst out laughing.

'A right laugh you are, lady, no mistake!' the cabby said, grinning. 'Make it another five.'

'Thank you for seeing me off, dear,' Lyudmila said as she

---

1. Pun on laskatsya (to cuddle) and poloskatsya (to paddle, puddle).

squeezed Sasha's hand and stepped into the cab. Sasha ran home, cheerfully thinking about that cheerful young lady.

Lyudmila was also in high spirits when she arrived home, smiling and thinking about something very amusing. Her sisters were waiting for her in the dining-room at the round table, which was lit by a hanging lamp. On the white tablecloth was an inviting brown bottle of cherry brandy, with bits of glittering silver foil around its neck. It was surrounded by plates piled high with apples, nuts and halva. Darya's face was flushed with drink and her hair hung over her bare shoulders. She was singing very loudly – Lyudmila had just heard the penultimate verse of the familiar ballad:

> Where is her dress, are her pipes no more?
> Naked he draws her to the sandy shore;
> Fear banishes shame, shame banishes fears,
> The shepherdess laments in bitter tears.
> Oh, forget, forget what you have seen![1]

Larisa was there too, prettily dressed, calm and cheerful. She was slicing an apple with a small knife and softly laughing. 'Well? Did you see him?' she asked.

Darya stopped singing and stared at Lyudmila. Valeriya leaned on her elbow, held her little finger out, tilted her head and tried to imitate Larisa's smile. But she was a thin, delicate creature and could only produce a nervous smile.

Lyudmila filled her glass with the cherry-red liqueur and said, 'It's a lot of rubbish about his being a girl. Of course he's a boy – and a very nice one at that. He's got dark brown hair and sparkling eyes. That little boy's the picture of innocence.' All of a sudden she burst into loud laughter. Her sisters joined in.

'So, it's obviously nonsense invented by that Peredonov,' Darya said, waving her hands contemptuously. Then she became thoughtful, leaned forward on her elbows, looked down and said, 'I might

1. From an early eighteenth-century ballad by an unknown author, very popular at the end of the nineteenth century.

as well go on singing,' and she started to sing in an ear-splitting voice.

There was something grimly inspiring in those shrill sounds. A corpse might sing like this if released from the grave on condition it sang and never stopped. The other sisters were long used to Darya's drunken bawling and occasionally joined in, deliberately shrilling their voices.

'She's really letting rip this time!' Lyudmila said, grinning.

It wasn't that she didn't want to hear her sister sing, but she would have much preferred to tell them all about her visit.

Darya suddenly broke off and told Lyudmila very rudely, 'What's the matter? I'm not stopping you!' And she immediately started again where she had left off.

Larisa said in a soft voice, 'Let her sing if she wants to.'

> It's raining hard on me,
> And there's no roof that I can se-ee.

Darya sang shrilly, distorting the sounds and inserting syllables for greater effect, like simple folk-singers do. As a result her song sounded like this:

> It's rai-ning ha-a-ard on me-e-ee!

The sounds on which the accents didn't fall were particularly jarring as she dragged them out, but had a stunning effect: they would have aroused deathly melancholy in someone listening for the first time.

Oh, deathly melancholy, echoing over fields and villages, over the vast expanses of my homeland! A melancholy embodied in wild commotion, a melancholy that devours the living word with its vile flame, reducing a once-living song to demented wailing! Oh, my beloved Russian song of old, can it be that you are really dying . . .?

Suddenly Darya leaped to her feet, put her hands on her hips and sang a cheerful ditty, dancing and snapping her fingers:

> Young lad, go away from me,
> I'm a robber's wife, can't you see?
> All you'll get from me is my sharp knife,
> I'll never be a peasant's wife.

> So, you're handsome – I don't give a damn!
> A tramp for me – oh, that's the man!

As she sang and danced and whirled around, her motionless eyes in their sockets seemed to follow her movements like dead orbiting moons. Lyudmila laughed aloud and her heart feebly fluttered and palpitated, partly from unbridled joy, partly from the effects of that powerful sweet cherry brandy. Valeriya's soft laugh was just like tinkling glass. She looked enviously at her sisters, wishing that she could enjoy herself like them, but for some reason she didn't feel at all cheerful. She felt unwanted, on the shelf, and that was why she was so weak, so unhappy. When she laughed she seemed about to burst into tears.

Larisa winked at her and Valeriya suddenly livened up and became full of fun. Larisa stood up, twitched her shoulders and soon all four were whirling around the room, locked together in a frenzied dance. They followed Darya in bawling stupid words from ever-new ditties, each more stupid and wilder than the last. The sisters were young and pretty and their voices rang out loud and wild. How the witches on Bald Mountain would have envied that dance!

All night long Lyudmila had such torrid, erotic dreams! First she dreamed that she was lying in a hot, stuffy room. The bedclothes slid down to the floor, revealing her burning body. A scaly-ringed snake glided up to her and twined itself around her as if it were climbing a tree, slithering up the branches of her beautiful naked body. Then she was lying by a lake on a hot summer's evening with threatening storm clouds overhead. She was naked, with a bright golden garland on her brow. There was a smell of warm stagnant water, of scorched grass. Over the dark, menacingly calm lake glided a majestic, powerful swan, violently beating the water with its wings and hissing loudly as it approached the bank to embrace her. Everything became dark and terrifying. Both the snake and the swan had Sasha's face, deathly pale, with dark, strangely melancholy eyes with blue-black lashes that drooped heavily, frighteningly, as if they were jealous of those eyes and were seeking to conceal their enchanting gaze.

Then Lyudmila dreamed of a magnificent palace, built with massive low arches. It was full of beautiful strong naked boys – and the most beautiful was Sasha. She was seated on a throne and was watching the naked boys whip each other. They laid Sasha on the floor, his head towards Lyudmila, and beat him. He laughed and cried and she laughed too, as one laughs only in dreams, when the heart suddenly beats faster – a laugh that is long-drawn-out, irrepressible, the laugh of oblivion and death . . .

Next morning, when she woke up, Lyudmila felt that she had fallen passionately in love with Sasha and was tormented by the desire to see him again. But it vexed her to think that she could only see him dressed! How stupid that schoolboys didn't go around naked! Or at least with bare feet, like the street urchins she loved to watch in summer because they wore no shoes or socks and sometimes bared their legs high. As if it were shameful to have a body! she thought. So shameful, that even street urchins hide it.

XV

Volodin went regularly to the Adamenkos' to give Misha his lessons. His hopes that the young mistress of the house would give him coffee every time he went were sadly disappointed. Whenever he entered the house he was taken straight to the small room that had been set aside as a workshop. Misha would usually be standing by the carpenter's bench in his grey overalls, with everything ready for the lesson. He did all he was told cheerfully, but without much enthusiasm. In order to get away with as little work as possible, he would try to draw Volodin into conversation, but Volodin was far too conscientious to allow himself to be sidetracked in this way. He would say, 'Mishenka, let's work for about two hours and then, if you feel like it, we can have a little chat. But not now. Work comes first!'

Misha would softly sigh and set about his task, but by the time the lesson was over he never felt like talking, saying he'd been given so much work. Sometimes Nadezhda would put in an appearance to see how Misha was getting on. Misha noticed that when this happened Volodin was a little more eager to talk and he took advantage of this. However, as soon as Nadezhda saw that he was idling around she would immediately tell him, 'Misha, don't be so lazy!' And as she left she would tell Volodin, 'Forgive me for interrupting, but that brother of mine will just laze around if you let him.'

Volodin was at first embarrassed by these interruptions. First he concluded that she didn't serve coffee in case it gave rise to malicious gossip. Then he thought that there really was no reason for her to come in while he was taking a lesson. But come she did. Could it be because she found it pleasant seeing him? And hadn't she agreed from the beginning that he was to give the lessons, without even stopping to consider the fees? And he interpreted every fact in his favour – and Peredonov and Varvara encouraged this line of thought.

'It's obvious she's in love with you,' said Peredonov.

'What better husband could she hope to find?' added Varvara.

Volodin tried to look modest and was delighted at his success. On one occasion Peredonov told him, 'A fiancé doesn't go around in a scruffy tie like that!'

'I'm not courting yet, Ardalyon,' Volodin replied soberly, trembling with joy nevertheless. 'Anyway, I can easily buy a new one.'

'Get one with a bright pattern,' advised Peredonov, 'so she can see that you're burning with passion.'

'A red one – and the fancier the better,' Varvara said. 'And with a tie-pin too. You can buy one with a stone for next to nothing – that really would look smart!'

Peredonov thought that Volodin probably didn't have the money. Or that he might try to economize by buying a cheap black tie. That would never do, thought Peredonov. Miss Adamenko is a society lady. He can't possibly go and propose in any old tie. She might be offended and refuse him.

So Peredonov told Volodin, 'Why buy a cheap one, Pavlusha? You've won enough from me for a tie. By the way, how much *do* I owe you? One rouble forty?'

'You're right about the forty copecks,' Volodin sniggered. 'Only it's not one rouble but two, I'm afraid.'

Peredonov knew very well that he owed him two roubles, but it would have been far more agreeable to pay him only one. 'You're lying,' he growled. 'How do you make it two roubles?'

'Varvara is my witness,' Volodin assured him.

Varvara smirked and said, 'You'd better pay up, Ardalyon, if you lost. I remember quite clearly that it *was* two roubles forty.'

Peredonov thought that since Varvara was standing up for Volodin she was going over to his side. He scowled, took the money from his purse and said, 'All right then, if you want your two roubles forty. It won't ruin me, I don't suppose. You're a poor man, Pavlusha, so here you are, take it.'

Volodin took the money, counted it and then, with an injured look, lowered his sharp forehead, puffed out his lower lip and bleated in his high-pitched voice, 'Since you owe me the money it's your duty to pay up, but the fact that I'm poor is neither here nor there. I'm not asking for charity from anyone. At least I have butter on my bread – not like some poor devils I wouldn't care to mention.'

He felt quite comforted, bleated for joy at having replied so brilliantly, twisted his lips and started laughing.

Finally Peredonov and Volodin decided to go and arrange the match. They wore their best suits and looked more solemn and stupid than usual. Peredonov sported a white tie, while Volodin wore a bright red one with green stripes.

Peredonov reasoned thus: 'As I'm the matchmaker, my role is a sober one. Therefore I should wear a white tie. You, the suitor, must show the passion that is burning within!'

With great decorum and dignity they sat themselves down in the drawing-room, Peredonov on the divan and Volodin in the armchair. Nadezhda looked at her guests in amazement. They chatted about the weather and the latest news with the air of two visitors who had come to discuss some very delicate matter but just didn't know how to set about it. Finally Peredonov cleared his throat and said, 'We've come on important business, Miss Adamenko.'

'Yes, important business,' Volodin repeated, assuming a significant look as he stuck out his lips.

'It's to do with him,' said Peredonov as he pointed his thumb at Volodin.

'It's to do with me,' confirmed Volodin, pointing his thumb at his chest.

Nadezhda smiled. 'Do go on,' she said.

'I'm going to speak for him, as he's very shy and can't do it himself. He's a kind, worthy man. Never touches a drop. It's true he doesn't earn very much, but to hell with that! People need different things. Some need money, others a man. Well, why don't you say something?' he said, turning to Volodin.

Volodin leaned forward and said in a trembling voice, just like a sheep bleating, 'Of course, I don't earn a great deal, but I'll always have a crust to eat. So what if I didn't go to university? I get by. There's nothing I regret having done. So you see, I have a lot to be thankful for.' He spread out his arms, lowered his head as if preparing to butt and lapsed into silence.

'As you can see,' Peredonov said, 'he's a young man, and a bachelor's life is no good for him. It's time he was married – a married man's life is so much better.'

'All the better if the lady feels the same,' Volodin declared.

'And as you're a spinster it's time *you* got married,' Peredonov continued.

A faint rustling could be heard from behind the door, accompanied by brief stifled sounds as if someone were sighing or softly laughing. Nadezhda looked sternly in the direction of the door and said coldly, 'You're *too* solicitous about me, I assure you,' irritably stressing the 'too'.

'You don't need a rich husband,' said Peredonov, 'since you're rich yourself. You need someone to love and please you in every respect. And you know who I mean. He is not indifferent towards you and maybe you feel the same about him. I have the buyer, you might say, and you have the goods. I mean to say, you *are* the goods.'

Nadezhda blushed and bit her lip to stop herself laughing. The same curious sounds continued from behind the door. Volodin stared at the carpet in blissful humility: he was sure everything was going perfectly.

'What goods?' Nadezhda asked cautiously. 'Do forgive me, but I don't understand.'

'Why don't you understand?' Peredonov said in disbelief. 'I'll tell you then, quite straight. Pavel Volodin is asking for your hand and heart, and I'm asking on his behalf.'

Something collapsed on to the floor behind the door and rolled around, snorting and panting. Her face flushed with stifled laughter, Nadezhda looked at her guests. Volodin's proposal struck her as a ludicrous impertinence.

'Yes, I'm asking for your hand and heart, Miss Adamenko,' Volodin said. He blushed, stood up, scraped one foot heavily on the carpet, bowed and quickly sat down again. Then he stood up, put his hand to his heart, looked fondly at Nadezhda and said, 'Miss Adamenko, allow me to declare my feelings! Since I love you very much, surely you will reciprocate?' He rushed forward, fell on one knee and kissed her hand. 'Nadezhda! Believe me, I swear eternal love!' He raised his arm and brought it down so violently on his chest that the whole place echoed with a deep rumbling.

'Please get up! What are you thinking of?' Nadezhda said, deeply embarrassed.

Volodin stood up and returned to his seat with a hurt look. Once there he pressed both hands to his heart and exclaimed, 'You must believe me! I shall love you until the day I die!'

'I'm very sorry, but it's quite impossible for me to marry you,' said Nadezhda. 'I have a young brother to bring up. Can't you hear him crying behind the door?'

'A brother to bring up!' Volodin said and stuck out his lips. 'I've never heard such an excuse!'

'All the same, it concerns him as much as myself,' Nadezhda said, hurriedly getting up. 'I must ask him. Will you wait a moment?' She swiftly left the room, her bright yellow dress rustling. Outside she grasped Misha's shoulders, ran with him to the door of his room where she stood for a while, hardly able to speak for laughter and lack of breath. 'I suppose it's quite useless asking if you've been listening!'

Misha threw his arms around her waist and leaned his head against her, convulsed with laughter and the effort of controlling it. Nadezhda pushed him into his room, sat on a chair by the door and burst out laughing. 'You heard what that Volodin said. Now come back into the drawing-room with me and don't you dare laugh. And when I ask your consent – don't you dare give it! Understand?'

'O-o-oooh!' cried Misha and stuffed his handkerchief into his mouth to stifle his laughter, but it didn't help very much.

'Cover your face if you think you're going to laugh,' advised Nadezhda as she took him by the shoulders back into the drawing-room. She made him sit down in an armchair, pulled up a chair for herself and sat beside him. Volodin seemed offended and lowered his head like a young ram.

'Just look how he's been crying,' Nadezhda said, pointing to her brother. 'I'm like a mother to him and he suddenly thinks I'm going to leave him.'

Misha covered his face with his handkerchief. His whole body was shaking and he whined in an effort to stop laughing. 'Ooooh!'

Nadezhda embraced him and, unseen by the others, gave him a sharp pinch and said, 'Don't cry, darling, don't cry.'

Misha was suddenly in such agony that his eyes filled with tears. He dropped the handkerchief and glared at his sister.

He might suddenly lose his temper, thought Peredonov, and start biting. They say human saliva is poisonous. He went over to Volodin so that he could hide behind him if need be.

Nadezhda told her brother, 'Mr Volodin's asking for my hand.'

'Hand and heart,' corrected Peredonov.

'And heart,' Volodin said humbly, but with dignity.

Misha covered his face again and almost choked with suppressed laughter. 'No, you mustn't marry him,' he said. 'What would become of me?'

Volodin then said in a voice shaking with indignation and emotion, 'I'm very surprised, Miss Adamenko, that you find it necessary to ask your brother, a mere boy. Even if he were an adult it seems quite ridiculous to me that you can't decide for yourself and have to ask his permission. To see you doing this not only surprises but shocks me.'

'Yes, it's really quite funny, asking a little boy,' Peredonov said glumly.

'Who should I ask, then? My aunt doesn't care and as I have to educate Misha how can I possibly marry you? Anyway, you might treat him roughly. Isn't that so, Misha? Aren't you scared that he might be cruel to you?'

'No,' said Misha, peeping out from under his handkerchief with one eye. 'I'm not scared he might be cruel. Why should he treat me roughly? No, I'm scared Mr Volodin might spoil me and not allow you to put me in the corner.'

'Believe me, Miss Adamenko,' began Volodin, holding his hand to his heart, 'I would never spoil Misha. Why should I? As long as he's well fed, has good clothes, that's all that matters. Besides, I could easily make him stand in the corner if I wanted to. But spoil him – never! And there's more I could do. As you're a spinster – I mean, young lady – and as it would probably be more convenient for you, I could take care of the thrashing!'

'He'll make us both stand in the corner,' wailed Misha as he covered his face again. 'And birch me as well! No, Nadya, don't you dare marry him.'

'Well, you've heard what he said. It's out of the question.'

'I really cannot understand your attitude, Miss Adamenko,' Volodin said. 'I come here and declare my ardent feelings, most ardent, may I say, and you are swayed by the word of a brother. If you're refusing because of a brother, then another might refuse because of her sister or nephew or some other relative. And then no one would marry and the entire human race would come to an end.'

'I shouldn't worry about that, Mr Volodin,' Nadezhda said. 'The world isn't threatened by that just yet. All the same, I don't intend marrying without Misha's consent and, as you have heard, he is against the marriage. And that I can understand, since you promised from the start that you would thrash him. What's more, you might include me.'

'Really, Miss Adamenko! Surely you don't think that I could be guilty of such base conduct?' Volodin said in desperation.

Nadezhda smiled. 'Well, I myself don't feel like marrying at the moment.'

'Perhaps you wish to go into a nunnery?' Volodin said in a hurt voice.

'Or to join the Tolstoyans and manure the fields?' suggested Peredonov.

'I'm quite happy where I am, thank you,' Nadezhda said icily, rising from her seat. 'There's no reason why I should go anywhere.'

Volodin also stood up, puffed out his lips in an offended manner and said, 'Since Misha feels as he does towards me I must give up teaching him. How can I give him lessons in these circumstances?'

'But why not?' Nadezhda retorted. 'This has nothing to do with the lessons.'

Peredonov thought that there was still a chance of persuading her and said in a tomb-like voice, 'You should really think it over very carefully, Miss Adamenko. He's a good man. What's more, he's a friend of mine.'

'No,' Nadezhda said, 'there's nothing to think over. I'm very grateful for the honour, but I cannot accept.'

Peredonov glared at Volodin and stood up. Volodin was a complete idiot, he thought. Fancy not being able to make that young lady fall in love with him!

Volodin stood by his armchair, his head bowed. 'Well, if that's your final decision, Miss Adamenko, there's no more to be said,' he said disdainfully. 'May God grant you every happiness,' he added, waving his hand. 'Oh, such is my wretched lot! A lad once loved a lass, but she didn't love him. God sees all! I'll go and have a good cry – and that's that.'

'You don't know what a good man you're turning down – you won't find another like him in a hurry!' Peredonov said in a didactic tone.

'Ah!' sighed Volodin again as he made for the door. But suddenly he changed his mind and came back to shake Nadezhda's hand, and even Misha's, to show how magnanimous he could be.

Out in the street Peredonov spluttered with rage. Volodin kept grumbling and arguing in his bleating voice the whole way.

'Why did you give up the lessons?' Peredonov growled. 'You don't need the money – is that it?'

'All I said was that if that's how she felt, then I must give up the lessons. But as she didn't say that I should give them up, and as I didn't reply, this meant that she wanted to carry on with them. So, it's up to me. If I want to, I'll refuse. And if I want to, I'll carry on.'

'Why give up the lessons?' Peredonov said. 'Just carry on as if nothing had happened.' Let him get something out of it, Peredonov thought, then he'll have less reason to envy me.

Peredonov felt upset and worried. Volodin still wasn't settled with a wife so he'd better watch out in case he started something with Varvara. What was more, Miss Adamenko might be furious with him for bringing Volodin to propose to her. She had relatives in St Petersburg – if she wrote she could do him a lot of harm. She only had to pick up a pen . . .

The miserable weather didn't improve matters. The sky was overcast, and evil-looking crows circled and cawed right above his head, mocking him and foretelling more, even worse trouble. Peredonov wrapped his scarf more tightly around his neck, thinking he might easily catch cold in such weather.

'What are these, Pavlusha?' he asked Volodin, pointing to some small yellow flowers growing by someone's garden fence.

'They're wolfsbane, Ardalyon,' Volodin said sadly.

Peredonov remembered that there were a lot of them in his garden. What a terrible name they had! Perhaps they were poisonous? Varvara only had to pick a bunch, brew them up instead of tea-leaves and then she could poison him later, when the appointment was officially confirmed. Volodin would then take his place. Perhaps they'd already agreed on it. It was no coincidence he knew the name of that flower!

'Let God be her judge!' Volodin said. 'Why should she insult me like that? I know she's waiting for a rich nobleman, but she doesn't realize there're all kinds and she might yet rue the day, whereas a simple, honest man could make her happy. Anyway, I'll light a candle for her in church and say a prayer. I shall ask God to send her a drunkard who'll beat her, squander all the money and then utterly ruin her. Then she might remember me and regret her mistake when it's too late. She'll wipe away the tears and say, "What a fool I was to turn Pavel Volodin down. There was no one to make me see reason – he was a good man."' Touched by his own words, Volodin shed a few tears and wiped his sheeplike, protruding eyes on his sleeve.

'You should go and smash her windows one night,' Peredonov suggested.

'There's no point in that. I must forget her,' Volodin said sadly. 'Anyhow, I might get caught. And as for that wretched boy! What did I do to deserve such treatment? Didn't I try and do my best for him? And the whole time he was plotting against me! Tell me, what's he going to be like when he grows up? What kind of boy can he be!'

'No, you couldn't even cope with a little boy. A fine fiancé you are!' Peredonov said angrily.

'What do you mean?' retorted Volodin, 'Of course I'm an eligible bachelor. I'll soon find someone else. As long as she doesn't think I'm going to lose any sleep over her.'

'Ugh, a fine fiancé!' jeered Peredonov. 'You even wore a new tie. How come an oaf like you could think he could get into society! A fine fiancé!'

'Well, I was the fiancé and you were the matchmaker. You

raised my hopes, but you couldn't pull it off! A fine matchmaker you are!'

They went on taunting each other and squabbling for some time, as if discussing some business deal.

When she had seen her guests out Nadezhda went back to the drawing-room. Misha was lying convulsed on the divan, roaring with laughter. Nadezhda dragged him off by the shoulders and said, 'You seem to have forgotten that listening through keyholes is not allowed.' She began to cross her fingers, the sign for him to go to the corner, but suddenly she burst out laughing. They embraced and both went on laughing for some time.

'I still think you should stand in the corner for eavesdropping.'

'Well, there's gratitude for you! I saved you from Volodin and that's how you treat me!'

'Who saved whom? What about the birching he said he would give you? Now into the corner!'

'I prefer to just kneel down here,' Misha said.

He fell on his knees at his sister's feet and put his head in her lap. She stroked and tickled him. Misha laughed and crawled across the floor on his knees. Suddenly Nadezhda pushed him away and sat on the divan, leaving Misha by himself. He stayed on his knees for a few moments and looked at her questioningly. She settled down to read a book, but kept peeping over the top to watch Misha.

'I feel so tired now,' he said plaintively.

'Well, I didn't tell you to kneel, did I?' she said, smiling over her book.

'I've been punished enough, let me go now,' Misha pleaded.

'Did I tell you to kneel?' Nadezhda repeated, pretending not to care. 'Now, leave me in peace!'

'I shan't get up until I'm forgiven.'

Nadezhda laughed, put the book down and drew Misha to her by his shoulders. He squealed and rushed to embrace her, exclaiming, 'Pavlusha's bride!'

XVI

Lyudmila was captivated by the dark-eyed boy and couldn't stop talking about him to her sisters and friends, and often at quite the wrong time. She dreamed about him almost every night, sometimes as just an ordinary shy, inoffensive little boy, but more often in some wild or fantastic setting. Her sisters were now so used to hearing about her dreams that soon they started asking her every morning what she had dreamed the night before. And all her spare time was spent just day-dreaming about him.

On Sunday Lyudmila persuaded her sisters to invite Kokovkina over after Mass and to delay her as long as they could: she wanted to see Sasha on his own. She herself didn't go to church and asked her sisters to make the excuse that she had overslept. They were amused by her little plan, but of course they agreed. The sisters really got on very well and this suited them perfectly: the fact that Lyudmila was so taken up with a young boy would be less competition for themselves. And so they kept their promise and invited Kokovkina after Mass.

Meanwhile Lyudmila put on a bright, pretty dress and sprayed herself with a light jasmine perfume. Into her white beaded handbag went a full bottle of scent and a small sprinkler. She hid behind the curtain by one of the drawing-room windows, so that she could see if Kokovkina was coming. She had thought of taking the scent to spray him with earlier – she didn't want him smelling of Latin books and school. Lyudmila loved perfumes; she had them sent from St Petersburg and used them a lot. She also loved highly fragrant flowers and her room was always full of an almost overpowering smell – of pine, flowers, newly gathered young birch twigs and some exotic perfume.

The sisters duly appeared with Kokovkina along the road. Lyudmila joyfully ran through the kitchen, across the vegetable garden, through the wicket gate and down a side-street in order to avoid the landlady. She smiled gaily as she briskly walked to Kokovkina's house, playfully swinging her white handbag and parasol. The warm autumn day put her in high spirits and she seemed to be radiating her own unique brand of gaiety.

At Kokovkina's the red-cheeked maid told her that her mistress was out. Lyudmila laughed noisily and jokingly remarked, 'Perhaps you're not telling me the truth. Perhaps your mistress is hiding somewhere.'

'Ooh! Why should she?' the maid giggled. 'Come in and see for yourself if you don't believe me.'

Lyudmila looked into the drawing-room and mischievously cried, 'Is everyone dead in here? Aha! A schoolboy!'

Sasha was peering out of his room and was delighted when he saw Lyudmila, whose spirits rose even more at the sight of his cheerful eyes.

'And where's your landlady?' she asked.

'She's not back yet. I think she went on somewhere straight after church. I've been back a long time.'

Lyudmila pretended to be surprised, waved her parasol and said in a mock-serious voice, 'I don't understand. Everyone else is home from church. Yes, everyone's home, but there's no sign of her! You must have driven her out of the house with all your noise!'

Sasha smiled and didn't reply. He loved Lyudmila's voice, her ringing laughter. He was already wondering what was the best way of offering to see her to a cab when she left, just to be with her a few minutes longer. But Lyudmila had no intention of leaving for a long time. She looked at Sasha with a crafty smile and said, 'Well, aren't you going to ask me to sit down, my charming young man? You must understand, I'm tired from walking all that way. I want to rest a little.' She went into the drawing-room, laughing and fondling Sasha with her gentle darting eyes. Sasha was embarrassed, blushed deeply, but was glad none the less that she was going to stay.

'Would you like me to spray you?' asked Lyudmila in a lively voice.

'Really, you're so funny!' Sasha replied. 'You've only just arrived and now you want to strangle[1] me! What have I done to deserve such cruelty?'

Lyudmila laughed with her ringing laugh and leant back in her armchair. 'Strangle you!' she exclaimed. 'You stupid boy, you've

1. Dushit' means both 'to strangle' and 'to perfume'.

completely misunderstood. I don't want to strangle you, I want to spray you with perfume!'

Highly amused, Sasha replied, 'Oh, with perfume! I'd love that!'

Lyudmila took the sprayer from her bag and turned the beautiful dark red bottle with its golden design, rubber bulb and bronze nozzle towards him and said, 'You see, I bought this yesterday and forgot to take it out of my handbag at home.' Then she took out a large bottle of perfume with the name *Guérlain of Paris Rao Rosa* written on the brightly coloured label.

'What a deep handbag!' Sasha said.

Lyudmila gaily replied, 'Now don't think you're getting anything else! I haven't brought you any gingerbread.'

He watched Lyudmila open the bottle with great curiosity and inquired, 'How are you going to pour it without a funnel?'

Lyudmila gently replied, 'You can get me one.'

'I don't have a funnel,' Sasha replied, highly embarrassed.

'Use what you like, but you must get a funnel,' Lyudmila insisted.

'I could borrow one from Malanya, but she's been using it for paraffin.'

Lyudmila laughed. 'How slow you are! Fetch me some paper if you can spare some – and I'll show you how to make one.'

'Oh, of course!' he cheerfully exclaimed. 'You can make one by rolling it up. I'll go and get some right away.' Sasha ran into his room. 'May I tear a page out of an exercise book?' he shouted.

'I don't care,' Lyudmila cheerfully replied. 'Take it from a text-book if you like, from your Latin grammar. It doesn't bother me!'

Sasha laughed and shouted, 'No, I'd better take it out of an exercise book!' He found a new exercise book, tore out the middle pages and was just about to run back into the drawing-room when he saw Lyudmila at the door.

'Have I permission to come in, young sir?' she asked mischievously.

'Of course, I'm delighted!'

Lyudmila sat at his table, made a funnel from the paper and then, with a solemn businesslike expression, poured the perfume into the sprayer. The sides and bottom of the funnel were darkened and moistened by the fragrant stream, which formed a little pool and then slowly dripped downwards. There was a sweet smell of roses mingled with the pungent odour of spirits. Lyudmila poured half the bottle out and said, 'I think that's enough.' She screwed the top of the sprayer and then crumpled the wet funnel and rubbed it between her hands. 'Smell that,' she said, holding her palm to his face.

Sasha bent over, closed his eyes and took a deep sniff. Lyudmila laughed, gave him a gentle slap on the lips and kept her hand to his mouth. Sasha went deep scarlet and kissed her warm scented hands with a gentle touch of his trembling lips. Lyudmila sighed and for a moment a look of tenderness ran over her pretty face. And then she became her usual radiant, ebullient self again.

'Just sit there and don't move!' she said. And she squeezed the rubber bulb. A fine fragrant mist filled the air and settled on Sasha's shirt in myriads of tiny glistening drops. He laughed and turned obediently whenever Lyudmila pushed him.

'Do you like it?' she asked.

'It's lovely,' Sasha cheerfully replied. 'What's it called?'

'Just like a baby you are! Why don't you look at the label?' she said in a teasing voice. Sasha read it and said, 'It smells like attar of roses.'

'Attar of roses!' she said scornfully and gently slapped his back. Sasha squealed with laughter and stuck out his tongue, rolling it into the shape of a tube. Lyudmila got up and began to inspect his school books. 'Mind if I have a look?' she asked.

'Please do.'

'Where are the ones and the noughts?'

'So far I haven't had that pleasure!' Sasha retorted with an injured expression.

'Don't tell fibs,' Lyudmila said emphatically. 'I'm sure you've blotted out all the noughts! I know that's what you get.'

Sasha silently smiled.

'Do you find Greek and Latin boring?' asked Lyudmila.

'No, why should I?' As usual Sasha clearly found the conversation about school work tedious in the extreme. 'It's boring having to swot,' he admitted, 'but I've a good memory. What I like is doing problems.'

'Will you come and see me tomorrow after dinner?' Lyudmila asked.

'Thanks, I'd love to,' Sasha replied, blushing.

He was delighted at the invitation. Lyudmila asked him again, 'You *will* come, won't you? Do you know where I live?'

'Yes, I know where you live. Yes, I'll come.'

'And mind you don't forget!' Lyudmila warned. 'I'll be waiting for you, do you hear?'

'Supposing I have a lot of homework,' Sasha said, more from a feeling of guilt than from any doubt that he might go.

'Rubbish. You must still come. Perhaps they won't give you a one.'

'But why do you want me to come?' Sasha laughed.

'I just want you to. There's something I'd like to tell you – and show you,' Lyudmila said, skipping, lifting her skirt and humming as she stuck her tiny pink fingers out. 'Do come, my delicious, delightful, golden boy!'

Sasha laughed and asked, 'Why can't you tell me today?'

'That's impossible. And if I did tell you, you wouldn't come tomorrow. You'd have no reason!'

'All right, I promise. That's if Kokovkina lets me.'

'Of course she will! She doesn't keep you chained up, does she?'

Lyudmila kissed Sasha goodbye on the forehead and held out her hand towards his lips. He had to kiss it. And Sasha found it extremely agreeable kissing that soft white hand again, but he did feel shy. It was impossible not to blush!

Lyudmila smiled coyly and artfully as she left and looked back several times.

How nice she is! thought Sasha, now he was alone. She didn't stay very long! Suddenly she was gone before I knew what was happening. If only she'd stayed just a little longer. And he felt ashamed that he hadn't offered to see her off. If only I could walk a little with her! If I ran I could catch her up, perhaps? She can't have gone far. No, she'd only laugh and think I was a nuisance.

So he decided against it and as a result felt uneasy and depressed. The soft touch of her kiss still lingered on his lips and the kiss on his forehead was still burning. How tenderly she kisses! he mused. Just like a loving sister. His cheeks were burning. The sensation was sweet – and shameful. Dim visions came crowding into his mind. If only she were my sister! Then I could kiss her whenever I liked, embrace her, whisper some fond words to her. I'd call her my darling Lyudmilochka. Or some other special name – Dragonfly or

Honeysuckle. It would be sheer bliss if she answered to them! But she's not my sister, he sadly thought. She just came and went and she's probably forgotten all about me by now. All that's left is a sweet smell of roses and lilac, the feel of two tender kisses and a strange excitement in my heart, giving birth to sweet dreams, just as the waves gave birth to Aphrodite.

Kokovkina wasn't long in returning. 'Ugh, it really smells in here,' were her first words. Sasha blushed.

'Lyudmilochka called,' he said, 'but you were out. She sprayed me with scent and then she left.'

'Such tenderness!' the landlady said in surprise. 'And you're calling her Lyudmilochka now.'

Sasha gave an embarrassed laugh and ran off to his room. Kokovkina had always thought that the Rutilov sisters were cheerful loving girls, capable of leading old and young men astray with their endearments.

Next morning Sasha awoke in high spirits: he was excited by the invitation. Impatiently, he waited until dinner time and then, red with embarrassment, he asked Kokovkina if he could go to the Rutilovs' until seven o'clock. Kokovkina was surprised but let him go. Sasha cheerfully ran off, having carefully combed his hair – he even put grease on it. He felt very happy but rather apprehensive, as if something important and wonderful was in store for him. He thought of the kisses that would be exchanged: he would kiss her hand and she would kiss him on the forehead when he arrived, and it would be the same when the time came to leave. He had sweet visions of Lyudmila's soft white hand.

He was met in the hall by all three sisters. They loved to sit by the window and look out into the street, so they had seen him coming. In their pretty dresses, they surrounded him in a wild whirlwind of merriment, filling the room with their noisy bird-like chatter. Immediately he felt at ease with them.

'Here's my mysterious hero!' Lyudmila joyfully exclaimed.

Sasha kissed her hand graciously and with much pleasure. Then he kissed Darya's and Valeriya's hands (he couldn't very well leave them out), which he also found highly agreeable. All the more so since all three replied by kissing him on the cheek: Darya's kiss was noisy but impersonal, as though she were kissing a blank wall;

Valeriya kissed him tenderly, lowered her crafty eyes and giggled as she barely touched him with her gentle eager lips: to Sasha it was as if apple blossom had fallen on his cheek, light and fragrant; Lyudmila's kiss was firm, noisy and uninhibited.

'He's *my* guest,' Lyudmila announced determinedly. Then she led him off to her room.

Darya immediately lost her temper. 'If he's yours, then go and kiss him!' she angrily shouted. 'You've a real treasure there! No one's going to steal him from you.'

Valeriya smiled and said nothing. It couldn't be very interesting talking to a young boy like that! What could he possibly understand?

Lyudmila's room was spacious and cheerful and very light because of two large windows overlooking the garden, flimsily curtained in yellow tulle. The chairs and armchairs were covered in golden-yellow chintz with a barely distinguishable white pattern. Everything was neat and bright and a sweet smell of perfume hung in the air. There were different kinds of bottles and phials of perfume, toilet water, little jars, ornamental boxes, fans and a few Russian and French novels.

'I dreamed about you last night,' laughed Lyudmila. 'You were swimming by the town bridge. I was sitting on it and I fished you out.'

'And did you put me in a jar?' Sasha asked playfully.

'Why a jar?'

'Where else then?'

'I didn't put you anywhere. I caught you by the ears and threw you back into the river.' And she laughed long and noisily.

'You *are* strange!' said Sasha. 'I can't wait to hear what you have to tell me.'

Lyudmila laughed long and loud.

'You've brought me here on false pretences. You *promised* to show me something,' Sasha said reproachfully.

'Oh, I shall! Would you like something to eat?'

'I've just had dinner,' Sasha said. 'Oh, you're so deceitful!'

'As if I would want to deceive you! Ugh, is that you reeking of hair oil?' she suddenly asked. Sasha blushed. 'I cannot stand hair oil!' Lyudmila said testily. 'You're just like a girl!' She ran her hand through his shiny hair and slapped his cheek with her greasy palm. 'Don't you dare do that again, do you hear?'

Sasha was quite taken aback. 'All right, I promise,' he said. 'You're so strict with me! But you sprinkle yourself with perfume!'

'Perfume and hair oil are completely different, you stupid boy! You can't compare them,' Lyudmila said persuasively. 'I never use oil on my hair. Why should I stick my hair with glue? Perfume's quite different. Let me spray you again. Would you like that? How about lilac?'

'That would be lovely,' Sasha replied, smiling. It was a pleasant thought, going home smelling sweetly of perfume and surprising Kokovkina again.

'Who wants some?' she asked again, taking the bottle of jasmine perfume in her hand and giving Sasha a questioning, cunning look.

'I want some,' Sasha said.

'Then what are you barking[1] for? Yes, you're barking for it!' Lyudmila gaily teased him.

Sasha and Lyudmila laughed happily.

'Aren't you scared I might strangle you?' Lyudmila asked. 'Do you remember what a coward you were yesterday?'

'I wasn't a coward at all,' Sasha said, flaring up.

Softly laughing and still teasing him, Lyudmila started spraying him with jasmine. Sasha thanked her and kissed her hand again.

'And see you get a haircut!' Lyudmila said sternly. 'You'll frighten the horses with that long hair of yours!'

'All right then, I'll have it cut,' Sasha replied. 'You're terribly strict! My hair's very short, only half an inch long. Even the school-inspector's never passed any comment on it.'

'I love to see young boys with short hair, so don't forget that,' Lyudmila said, solemnly threatening him with her finger. 'I'm not an inspector, but you must still obey me!'

From that day onwards Lyudmila's visits to Kokovkina's became more and more frequent. She tried – particularly at the beginning – to time her visits when Kokovkina would be out and she sometimes resorted to all kinds of cunning to lure the old woman away from the house. Once Darya told her, 'You're such a coward!

1. Pun on kto zhelayet? meaning 'who wants?' and kto zhe layet? meaning 'who's that barking?'

Scared of that old woman! Why don't you go when she's there and then take Sasha out for a walk?'

Lyudmila followed her advice and began to go whenever she felt like it. If Kokovkina happened to be at home she would talk to her for a short while and then she would take Sasha out for a brief walk, never keeping him away for very long.

Although the friendship between Sasha and Lyudmila soon became deep, it was by no means a tranquil relationship. Lyudmila herself didn't notice that she excited strange urges and desires in the boy, feelings he was still too young really to understand. Sasha often kissed her hands and her slender, supple wrists covered with soft, pliant skin – through its yellow-pink tissue he could see her delicate twisting blue veins. And it was easy to kiss her long shapely arms right up to the elbows by rolling up her broad sleeves.

Sometimes Sasha didn't tell Kokovkina that Lyudmila had called. It wasn't that he lied – he just didn't say anything. There was no point in telling lies with a maid around the house. And he found it very difficult not to talk about Lyudmila; all the time her laughter rang in his ears: he wanted to tell everyone about her, but for some reason felt too embarrassed. Sasha soon became very friendly with the other sisters. He kissed their hands as well and before long was calling them Dashenka, Valerochka, Lyudmilochka.

XVII

One day Lyudmila met Sasha in the street. 'The headmaster's wife is giving a birthday party for her elder daughter tomorrow. Is the old girl going?' she asked.

'I don't know,' Sasha replied. And a feeling of joyous hope stirred in his heart – not so much hope as desire. He knew that Lyudmila would come as soon as Kokovkina had gone and would stay with him. That evening he reminded Kokovkina about the party.

'Oh yes, thanks for reminding me,' Kokovkina said. 'Of course I'm going. Such a nice girl, the headmaster's daughter.'

And as soon as Sasha came home from school Kokovkina went to the Khripachs'. Sasha was overjoyed at the thought that he had helped to get her out of the house. Now he was certain that Lyudmila would find time to come.

And come she did. She at once kissed Sasha on the cheek and gave him her hand to kiss. She laughed merrily, but he blushed furiously. Her clothes smelled of a mixture of rose and iris — the sensuous, voluptuous iris dissolved in the sweet dreamy fragrance of roses. She had brought a long narrow box wrapped in thin paper, through which Sasha glimpsed a yellowish label. She sat down, placed the box in her lap and gave Sasha an equivocal look.

'Do you like dates?' she asked.

'I love them,' Sasha replied with an amused grin.

'Well, I've brought you some,' she said solemnly. Then she unwrapped the box and ordered, 'Eat up!' She took out the dates one by one and popped them into Sasha's mouth: after each one he had to kiss her hand.

'Ooh, my lips are all sweet and sticky!' he said.

'What's wrong with that?' she replied gaily. 'You may kiss me as much as you like. I shan't be offended!'

'I'd rather let you have all the kisses at once, right away,' Sasha laughed. He reached out for a date.

'You'll cheat me, I know it!' Lyudmila cried. She shut the box with a bang and slapped him across the fingers.

'I'm an honest boy. I wouldn't cheat you,' Sasha assured her.

'I don't believe you.'

'Would you like payment in advance?' Sasha suggested.

'Now you're talking business!' Lyudmila eagerly exclaimed. 'Kiss me.'

She held out her hand and Sasha took her long, slender, delicate fingers, kissed them once and asked, artfully smiling and still holding her hand, 'You promise not to cheat, Lyudmilochka?'

'Do you really think I'm dishonest?' Lyudmila cheerfully replied. 'You need have no worries, just go ahead and kiss me. I shan't cheat you.'

Sasha bent over her hand and started kissing it all over, making rich smacking sounds with his wide-open lips. He was delighted that there was so much to kiss. Lyudmila carefully counted the kisses and when he reached ten she said, 'It must be very awkward for you, having to lean over all the time.'

'Yes, I'll make myself more comfortable.'

He dropped on to his knees and continued kissing her with great ardour. He loved nice things to eat and was delighted that Lyudmila had brought him something sweet. For this he loved her even more tenderly.

Lyudmila next sprayed Sasha with a lusciously aromatic perfume. Sasha was amazed at its fragrance, sweet but strange, overpowering, radiantly misty like a sinful golden sunrise glimpsed through a milky haze.

'What a strange perfume!' he said.

'Try some on your hand.'

And she gave him an ugly four-cornered jar with rounded edges. Sasha held it up to the light. The liquid was bright yellow and the large gaudy label bore the name *Cyclamen Maison de Piveur*.[1] Sasha pulled out the flat glass stopper and sniffed. Yes, cyclamen! Then he did what Lyudmila loved doing: he put his palm over the mouth, turned the jar upside down and then stood it upright again, rubbed the drops of cyclamen between his hands and smelled carefully.

The spirit had evaporated, leaving the pure aroma. Lyudmila looked at him with nervous excitement.

Sasha said, rather hesitantly, 'It smells a bit like candied bedbugs!'

'Don't talk such nonsense!' Lyudmila said irritably.

She too put some perfume on her hand and sniffed it.

'Yes, like bedbugs,' Sasha repeated.

Lyudmila suddenly flared up so much that little tears glistened in her eyes. She struck Sasha across the cheek and exclaimed, 'Ugh, you wicked boy! Take that for your bugs!'

'That was quite a smack!' Sasha said, laughing and kissing Lyudmila's hand. 'Darling Lyudmilochka! Why are you so angry? Well, what does it smell like to you?' The blow across the cheek

1. Famous nineteenth-century French perfume house.

146

didn't make him angry at all: he was too enchanted with Lyudmila.

'Smell like?' she asked, seizing his ear. 'I'll tell you in a moment. But let me pull this first.'

'Oh! Oh! *Please*, darling Lyudmilochka, I promise not to say silly things again,' Sasha said, wincing from the pain.

Lyudmila let go of the reddened ear, gently drew Sasha towards her and sat him on her knee. 'Let me tell you all about the three scents that live in the cyclamen,' she said. 'The first is ambrosia – that's for the worker bees. You should know that cyclamen's called sowbread¹ in this country.'

'Sowbread,' Sasha repeated, laughing. 'What a funny name!'

'Don't you laugh, you little rascal,' Lyudmila said, seizing his other ear and continuing, 'There's the sweet ambrosia with the bees humming over it – that's the flower's joy. Then there's the scent of mild vanilla, which is not for the bees but for the lover of whom we maidens dream. That is the flower's desire, with the golden sun shining above. The third scent is of a tender, sweet body – this is the poor flower's love, in the sultry noonday heat. Bees, sun, sultry heat – do you understand, my precious?'

Sasha silently nodded. His dark face was burning and his long dark eyelashes trembled. Lyudmila dreamily gazed into the distance, her face flushed. 'The tender sunny cyclamen brings joy, sweet and shameful desires, and stirs the blood. Do you understand, my treasure, what it is to know sweetness, to feel joy and pain, when one wants to weep, all at once? Do you? Let me show you!'

And she clung to Sasha's lips in a long kiss.

Lyudmila stared straight ahead thoughtfully. Suddenly a cunning smile flickered over her lips. Gently she pushed Sasha away and asked, 'Do you like roses?'

Sasha sighed, opened wide his eyes, smiled sweetly and softly whispered, 'Oh yes!'

'Large ones?' Lyudmila asked.

'All kinds, large ones, small ones,' Sasha replied, getting up from her lap with a swift movement, just like a young boy.

1. Dryavka: this would appear to be *cyclamen hederifolium*, the dwarf variety. An odd-sounding word to the Russian ear.

'And do you like rozochki?'[1] Lyudmila tenderly asked, her resonant voice shaking with suppressed laughter.

'Yes I do,' Sasha quickly replied.

Lyudmila laughed and blushed. 'Stupid! You like rozochki, but there's no one to whip you!'

They both laughed and blushed. For Lyudmila the whole charm of the affair lay in its enforced innocence; and though they were stirred by desires, they were yet far from consummating them.

They had a quarrel as to who was the stronger.

'Well, you may be stronger,' said Lyudmila, 'but it's agility that counts.'

'I'm agile too,' Sasha boasted.

'As an elephant!' Lyudmila teased.

They continued quarrelling for some time, until Lyudmila proposed they had a fight to settle the argument.

Sasha laughed and cried, 'You don't stand a chance with me!'

Lyudmila replied by tickling him.

'Oh, that's what you want, is it?' laughed Sasha and grasped her around the waist.

A furious tussle commenced. Lyudmila saw at once that Sasha was the stronger, so she resorted to cunning. At the right moment she tripped him and he fell on to the floor, taking Lyudmila with him. With a swift movement Lyudmila wriggled out of his grasp and pressed him to the floor. Sasha cried out in despair, 'That's not fair!' Lyudmila stuck her knees into his stomach and held him pinned down. Sasha made desperate but futile attempts to escape. Lyudmila started tickling him again. Sasha's sonorous laughter mingled with hers. She laughed so much that she had to let him go.

He leaped to his feet, red in the face and quite angry. 'Rusalka!',[2] he cried.

But the nymph simply lay on the floor and laughed.

Then Lyudmila took him on her knee. Exhausted after the battle, they looked tenderly, joyfully into each other's eyes and smiled.

1. Pun, meaning both 'small roses' and 'birch-rods'.
2. Water-nymph who lured her victims and then drowned them. A kind of mermaid.

'I'm too heavy for you,' Sasha said, 'I'll squash your knees if you don't let me go.'

'Never mind, sit still,' Lyudmila replied affectionately. 'And you told me you liked a cuddle!' She stroked his hair and Sasha clung close to her. 'You know, you're very handsome, Sasha.'

He blushed and burst out laughing. 'Tell me more!' he said. He found it somewhat disconcerting if anyone talked about good looks when he was the subject. As yet he had never been curious enough to find out whether others thought he was handsome or an ugly brute.

Lyudmila pinched his cheek so hard that a red spot appeared: it looked quite pretty. Sasha smiled. Lyudmila did the same to his other cheek. Sasha didn't resist but took her hand, kissed it and said, 'Please stop pinching, it hurts. And you'll spoil your fingers.'

'Of course it hurts,' Lyudmila said, 'but you've become quite the little flatterer!'

'I must be going, I've so much homework. Give me one more cuddle, just for luck, so that I get a five for Greek.'

'So you're throwing me out!' Lyudmila said. She seized his hand and rolled the sleeve up above the elbow.

'Are you going to slap me?' Sasha asked, blushing with guilt and embarrassment. But Lyudmila was content to admire his arm and turned it this way and that.

'What a beautiful arm!' she said in her resonant voice – and suddenly she kissed it near the elbow. Sasha turned red and tried to pull it away. But Lyudmila held on and kissed it several times more before letting go. Sasha didn't say a word and looked down at the floor. His bright half-smiling lips took on a strange look and his burning cheeks began to turn pale beneath the shadow of his luxuriant eyelashes.

They said goodbye and Sasha saw her to the gate – as far as she would let him go with her this time.

'Please come more often, dear, and don't forget to bring some nice sweet gingerbread.'

Impulsively she embraced him once more, kissed him and ran off. Sasha stood there as if stunned.

*

Sasha had promised to go and see her. The appointed time had arrived, but not Sasha. Lyudmila impatiently fidgeted and fretted, her eyes glued to the window. Whenever she heard footsteps in the street she would look out. Her sisters laughed and she angrily and excitedly told them, 'To hell with you! Leave me alone!' And she hurled reproaches at them for laughing at her.

It was obvious by now that Sasha wasn't coming and Lyudmila wept with grief and disappointment.

'Oy, oy, oy! Where's your little boy?' teased Darya.

As she sobbed her heart out, Lyudmila was so grief-stricken that she forgot all about being angry with her sisters and softly told them, 'The old bitch is keeping him in to do his Greek homework.'

In a crude attempt to be sympathetic Darya said, 'He's such a country bumpkin he doesn't know how to get out of it!'

'Fancy getting involved with a little boy!' Valeriya said disdainfully.

Despite their laughter, both sisters felt sorry for Lyudmila. They loved one another tenderly, but not deeply. Tender love is never deep!

'Why on earth are you crying your eyes out over a little milk-sop?' Darya said. 'One could say it's an affair between the boy and the devil.'

'Who's the devil?' Lyudmila cried heatedly and turned deep purple.

'Why *you*, dear,' Darya calmly replied. 'Granted you're young, but still . . .' She didn't finish and broke into a piercing whistle.

'Rubbish!' Lyudmila said in a strangely resonant voice.

A peculiar cruel smile shone through her tears, lighting up her face as a fiery ray at sunset shines through the last weary rainfall.

'Please tell me what you find so interesting about him?' Darya asked irritably.

With that same peculiar smile Lyudmila replied slowly and deliberately, 'He's . . . beautiful! So full of untapped possibilities!'

'That's nothing,' Darya said determinedly. 'All boys are like that.'

'I don't agree,' Lyudmila indignantly replied. 'Other boys are disgusting.'

'And is he so *pure*?' asked Valeriya, contemptuously dragging out 'pure'.

'A fat lot you understand!' Lyudmila cried, but then immediately slipped back into her soft, dreamy voice. 'He's . . . innocent!'

'Go on!' Darya scoffed.

'The best age for boys is between fourteen and fifteen,' Lyudmila said. 'At that age they can't do anything, nor do they understand anything, yet they are just beginning to respond. And they don't have revolting beards.'

'That's a lot to be thankful for, I'm sure,' Valeriya said with a disdainful grin. She was sad: she was conscious of being so small, frail and delicate, and envied her sisters – Darya her cheerful laugh and even Lyudmila her tears.

'You don't understand *at all*,' Lyudmila repeated. 'I don't love him the way you think. Anyway, a boy's better than some monstrosity with whiskers. My love is pure and innocent. I want nothing from him.'

'If that's so, why do you keep tormenting the boy?' Darya rudely retorted.

Lyudmila blushed and a guilty expression appeared on her face. Darya was sorry and went up to embrace Lyudmila.

'Don't be upset, we didn't mean to be spiteful,' she said. Lyudmila again burst into tears and put her head on Darya's shoulder.

'I know that it's hopeless,' she sadly said, 'but if only he would caress me a little – I don't mind how.'

'Oh, what misery!' Darya said peevishly. She walked away from Lyudmila, put her hands on her hips and started to sing:

> Yesterday I left my dear love,
> And went home to spend the night –

Valeriya broke into delicate tinkling laughter; Lyudmila's eyes brightened and took on a lascivious look. She quickly went to her room and sprayed herself with corylopsis.[1] Its sweet, heady, voluptuous smell enveloped her with an insinuating seductiveness. Smartly

1. A shrub of the hazel family, with an exquisite scent.

dressed and excited, she went out into the street, smelling provocatively of that tempting perfume.

Perhaps I'll meet him, she thought.

And meet him she did.

'You're a fine one, I must say!' she cried reproachfully, yet overjoyed at seeing him.

Sasha felt both embarrassed and delighted. 'I really didn't have the time,' he stammered. 'I had so much homework, so much studying. That's the truth.'

'You're lying, my dear. Now come straight home with me.'

Laughingly, he refused at first, but he was obviously delighted that Lyudmila was taking him home with her.

'Here he is!' she announced triumphantly to her sisters as she led Sasha to her room. 'You wait, I'm going to get even with you,' she said threateningly and bolted the door. 'No one's going to help you now.'

Sasha put his hands inside his belt and stood awkwardly in the middle of the room, feeling both happy and frightened. The room had been freshly sprayed with sweet-smelling perfume, but there was something irritating about it, something that set one's nerves on edge, like the touch of small, scaly, nimble, joyous snakes.

XVIII

Peredonov was returning from one of the boys' lodgings when he was caught by a shower of fine, penetrating rain. He wondered where to take shelter as he didn't want his new silk umbrella ruined.

Across the road stood a detached two-storey stone house. Over the gate was a sign N. N. GUDAYEVSKY. PUBLIC NOTARY. Peredonov decided to call on him and at the same time complain about his son, who was in the second form.

He found both parents at home and they greeted him with a great deal of fuss – as always in that house.

Nikolay Gudayevsky was a small, thickset, balding man with a long dark beard. His movements were jerky and erratic. He did not walk so much as hop like a sparrow and it was impossible to predict from his movements or facial expression what he was going to do next. In the middle of a serious conversation he would suddenly throw out one knee, bewildering rather than amusing his audience by its very pointlessness. Whether he was at home or out visiting he would sit calmly for a few minutes, then suddenly leap to his feet and for no apparent reason pace the room, shouting and kicking. In the street he thought nothing of stopping dead, squatting and turning a somersault, or performing some other gymnastic exercise, and then continuing on his way. On the deeds and documents that he witnessed he liked to write funny remarks. Instead of *Ivan Ivanov, residing in Moscow Square, in Mrs Yermilov's apartment house*, he would write, *Ivan Ivanov, living in the market square in that abominable tenement where it is impossible to breathe for the stench* and so on. He even noted the number of hens or geese kept by the person whose signature he was witnessing. His wife Julia was a tall, thin, demonstrative and dreadfully sentimental woman. Strangely, despite the great difference in their figures, she had the same mannerisms as her husband – the same erratic, impulsive movements, quite incongruous with everyone else's. She wore bright dresses that were far too young for her and she had a strange liking for long ribbons of assorted colours, with which she adorned her dresses and her hair in great profusion, and which were always streaming out behind her when she moved quickly.

Their son Antosha, a slightly built alert-looking boy, politely clicked his heels to Peredonov who, the moment he was seated in the drawing-room, started complaining about Antosha's behaviour. Peredonov told the parents that he was lazy and inattentive, that he laughed and talked in class and that he was always misbehaving during break. Antosha was astonished at these fantastic accusations – he had no idea he was as bad as that – and stoutly defended himself. Both parents became very excited.

'Allow me to ask,' shouted the father, 'precisely what he's done wrong?'

'Nikolay! Don't take the boy's side!' the mother shouted. 'He shouldn't misbehave!'

'But what has he done?' insisted the father, prancing around the room on his short legs.

'He's always up to mischief,' said Peredonov mournfully, 'fighting and playing around. He's always misbehaving.'

'I don't fight,' pleaded Antosha. 'Ask anyone you like, I've never fought anyone.'

'And he bullies the others,' Peredonov said.

'Right, I shall go to school myself and find out from the inspector,' Gudayevsky said with determination.

'Nikolay! Do you distrust the word of a teacher? Do you want Antosha to become a lazy good-for-nothing? A good thrashing is what he needs.'

'Rubbish!' shouted the father.

'I'm going to thrash him – that's for certain!' shouted the mother as she grabbed Antosha by the shoulders and dragged him into the kitchen. 'Come on, dear!' she shouted, 'I'm going to give you a nice thrashing!'

'I won't allow it!' shouted Gudayevsky, trying to pull Antosha back. But Julia would not let go and Antosha cried out in despair as his parents struggled.

'Help me, Mr Peredonov!' Julia cried. 'You hold that brute while I deal with Antosha.'

Peredonov went to her aid. Gudayevsky, however, tore his son out of his wife's grasp, shoved her to one side, rushed over to Peredonov and shouted, 'You keep out of it! Don't meddle in other people's affairs! I'll give you what for!'

Dishevelled, his face flushed and covered in sweat, he waved his fist in the air. Peredonov went back on his heels, muttering something inaudible. Julia ran around her husband, trying to catch hold of Antosha, but the father shielded the boy behind his back, pulling him by the arm to the right and left. Julia's eyes blazed as she shouted, 'He'll grow up to be a bandit! He'll end up in prison. He'll be sent to hard labour!'

'Shut your trap, you silly old cow!' Gudayevsky roared.

'You tyrant!' screamed Julia. She rushed over, struck him in the back with her fist and then ran from the room.

Gudayevsky, fists clenched, rushed up to Peredonov. 'You've come just to make trouble. So Antosha's been misbehaving, has he? That's a lie. He never gets up to mischief. If he'd been misbehaving

I would have known without you telling me. But I don't want to speak to the likes of you. You go around this town hoodwinking people stupid enough to believe you, and thrashing the boys. I suppose you're after a diploma – Master of Flagellation! But this time you've found the wrong man. Sir, I must ask you to leave this house at once!'

As he said this he leaped over to Peredonov and forced him into a corner. Peredonov was so terrified he would have fled there and then, but Gudayevsky was so incensed that he didn't notice he was blocking the exit. Antosha seized his father's coat-tails and pulled him towards himself. His father angrily shouted at him to stop and started kicking out. Antosha smartly jumped to one side, but didn't let go of his father's frock-coat.

'I'm warning you!' Gudayevsky shouted. 'Behave yourself!'

'But Papa!' Antosha said, still tugging. 'You're standing in Mr Peredonov's way!'

Gudayevsky quickly jumped back and Antosha barely managed to get out of the way.

'I beg your pardon,' said Gudayevsky, pointing to the door. 'That's the way out, so don't let me detain you any longer.'

Peredonov hurried from the drawing-room. Gudayevsky stuck two fingers up at him and then did a high knee-jerk, as if to help him on his way. Antosha tittered, at which his father turned round and angrily shouted, 'I'm warning you, Antosha! You wait, I'm going to school tomorrow and if it turns out to be true I shall hand you over to your mother for punishment.'

'I didn't misbehave, he's lying,' Antosha said in a pathetic, squeaky voice.

'Antosha! Remember where you are!' his father shouted. 'He's not lying – he's mistaken. Only children lie, adults are *mistaken*.'

Meanwhile Peredonov had escaped into the half-dark hall. After much groping he managed to find his coat and tried to put it on, but he was trembling so much that he couldn't get his arms into the sleeves. No one came to his aid. Suddenly Julia came running from a side-door, her ribbons streaming and rustling behind her. She waved her hands, danced about on the tips of her toes and frantically whispered something to him. Peredonov didn't understand at first.

'I'm so terribly grateful,' he at last made out, 'it's so noble of you, so very noble, to show such concern. People are so indifferent, but you saw things from a poor mother's point of view. You just cannot imagine how hard it is bringing up children. I've only two and they nearly drive me insane. As for my husband, he's a tyrant, a terrible, terrible man. Don't you agree? Well, you saw for yourself.'

Peredonov mumbled, 'Yes . . . your husband . . . shouldn't carry on like that . . . I go to all this trouble and he –'

'Oh, you don't have to tell me,' Julia whispered, 'he's a terrible man. He won't be satisfied until he's driven me into the grave. Then he'll be able to corrupt my children, my little Antosha. But not while I'm alive. Antosha's going to get a thorough thrashing whatever happens.'

'He won't let you,' Peredonov said, jerking his head in the direction of the drawing-room.

'Don't worry. I'll do it when he's gone to the club. He won't take Antosha there! I shan't say a word until he goes, as if I agree with him, and the moment he's left I shall thrash him – and you can help me. You will help me, won't you?'

Peredonov thought for a moment and then said, 'Of course, but how will I know when to come?'

'I'll send you a note,' Julia happily whispered. 'Just wait. The moment he's gone I'll send for you.'

Later that evening Peredonov received the following note from Julia:

Dear Mr Peredonov,
My husband's gone to the club and I'm free from his barbarity until midnight. Please do me a favour and come as soon as you can and help me punish my delinquent son. I realize that it must be thrashed out of him while he's still young, or it'll be too late.
Yours sincerely,

Julia Gudayevsky

PS Please come at once or Antosha will have gone to bed and we'll have to wake him up.

Peredonov quickly put on his overcoat, wrapped his scarf around his neck and was ready to leave.

'Where are you going this time of night?' asked Varvara.

'I've an important matter to see to,' Peredonov replied gruffly and hurriedly left.

Varvara wearily realized that she wouldn't get much sleep that night. If only she could get him to marry her without any more delay. Then she would be able to sleep night and day. What bliss that would be!

Out in the street Peredonov began to have doubts. What if this were a trap? Supposing Gudayevsky was at home all the time, just waiting to get his fists into him? Hadn't he better turn back?

The silent, dark, cool night surrounded him and forced him to walk slowly. He could smell the freshness of nearby fields. In the deep grass that grew along the fences could be heard faint rustlings and shuffling sounds, and everything appeared suspicious and strange. Perhaps someone was creeping up on him from behind? Enveloped in darkness, all objects looked mysterious and it seemed that a new kind of life was stirring in them, nocturnal, hostile and incomprehensible to man. Peredonov quietly walked down the street and muttered, 'You're wasting your time. I'm not doing anything wrong. I'm only going about my work, my friend. Oh yes.'

At last he reached Gudayevsky's house. A lamp was burning in only one of the five windows facing the street, the others were in darkness. Peredonov tiptoed up the steps, stopped for a moment, put his ear to the keyhole and listened. All was quiet. He gently pulled the brass bell-handle and a faint tinkling sound echoed in the distance. But faint though it was, it frightened Peredonov and seemed to be the signal for all the hostile forces that were threatening him to rouse themselves and come to the door. Peredonov quickly ran down the steps and pressed close to the wall, behind a post.

A few moments passed. Peredonov's heart stopped and then pounded away. He heard some light footsteps, the sound of a door being opened. Julia peered out into the darkness, her dark passionate eyes gleaming. 'Who's there?' she whispered.

Peredonov moved a little way from the wall, glanced from down below into the dark narrow doorway and whispered in a trembling voice, 'Has he gone?'

'Yes, he's gone,' Julia happily whispered and nodded.

Peredonov looked timidly around and then followed her into the dark hall.

'Do forgive me, I put the lights out in case anyone sees – you know how people talk.'

She led Peredonov up the stairs into a corridor where a small lamp was burning, casting a dim light on the uppermost steps. Julia laughed softly and this made her ribbons dance up and down.

'Yes, he's gone,' she joyfully whispered as she looked round and turned her passionate, burning eyes on Peredonov. 'I was afraid he would stay at home as he was in such a filthy mood. But he can't do without his game of whist. And I've sent the servant out. There's only Liza's nanny. Otherwise we might be disturbed. You know what people are like these days.'

Julia seemed to be smouldering and her whole body was as dry and hot as a flaming torch. When she caught Peredonov by the sleeve he felt as if small dry sparks were running all over his flesh. Quietly they tiptoed down the corridor, past some closed doors, until they came to the last one. It was the door to the nursery . . .[1]

Peredonov left Julia after midnight, when she was expecting her husband back any minute. He walked gloomily along the dark streets, quite certain someone had been hiding in the shadows by the house and was now following him.

'I was only doing my duty,' he muttered. 'It wasn't my fault. She was the one who wanted it. You won't catch *me* out – you've got the wrong man!'

Varvara was still awake when he returned and a pack of cards lay spread out before her. Peredonov thought that someone might have slipped in unseen when he entered the house. Or perhaps Varvara herself had let the enemy in. He said, 'Once I'm in bed you'll start practising witchcraft with those cards. Let me have them, I don't want you casting a spell over me.'

He snatched the cards and hid them under his pillow. Varvara grinned and said, 'Stop making a fool of yourself. As if I could practise witchcraft – and as if I'd want to!'

Peredonov was both frightened and annoyed to see her grinning:

1. See variant 10, p. 278.

158

that meant she didn't need cards to bewitch him. And there was the cat crouching under the bed, its green eyes glinting in the darkness – she could easily bewitch him by stroking sparks from its fur. And there was the little demon again, darting about under the chest of drawers – perhaps she was summoning it at night with her whistle-like snoring?

That night Peredonov had a terrible, vile dream: Pylnikov came and stood by the door, beckoning and smiling. Peredonov was mysteriously compelled to follow him through the dark muddy streets while the cat, its evil eyes glinting, ran at his feet.[1]

XIX

Each day Khripach became increasingly perturbed by Peredonov's weird behaviour. He consulted the school doctor as to whether Peredonov had gone out of his mind. The doctor laughed and replied that Peredonov had no mind to go out of and that he was acting strangely because he was such a stupid man. Many complaints had been coming in. The first was from Miss Adamenko, who sent him her brother's exercise book: he had been given a very low mark for perfectly good work.

During one of the breaks the headmaster sent for Peredonov. Yes, he really does look like a madman, thought Khripach when he saw the turmoil and terror on Peredonov's dull, miserable face.

'I've a bone to pick with you,' Khripach said in his dry patter. 'Every time I take a class in the room next to yours my head literally splits from all that laughter in your room. May I request you to make your lessons a little less light-hearted? "Joking, always joking – how can you bear it?" '[2]

'It's not my fault if they laugh,' Peredonov said angrily. 'One

---

1. See variant 11, p. 281.
2. A slight misquotation from Griboyedov's *The Misfortune of being Clever*, one of the most famous Russian comedies.

can't always keep on about spelling or analyse the satires of Kantemir.[1] Sometimes you only have to say something and immediately they collapse with laughter. They're very lax and really need taking in hand.'

'It's desirable, in fact even necessary, that classwork should be conducted in a serious manner,' Khripach said. 'And there's another thing.' He showed Peredonov two exercise books. 'They're in your subject. One is Adamenko's, the other is my son's. They're both in the same class. I've carefully compared them and am obliged to say that you are not giving your work the attention it deserves. Adamenko's last piece of written work, which was excellent, is given the very low mark of one, while my own son gets a four for poor work. It's obvious you've given them each other's marks. Although to err is human, I must ask you to avoid such mistakes in future. Such slipshod marking arouses deep discontent among parents and pupils – and rightly so.'

Peredonov muttered some inaudible reply.

In the classroom he embarked on a ruthless campaign of teasing those small boys who had recently been the victims of his complaints: this he did out of sheer spite. Kramarenko was particularly singled out for attack. The boy would say nothing, turn pale under his deep suntan and his eyes would flash.

That day, after lessons, Kramarenko did not hurry home, but stood by the school gates. He waited until Peredonov came out and then started following him, keeping a short distance behind, waiting until the few passers-by had gone. Peredonov walked slowly. He was depressed by the miserable weather. Over the past few days his expression had become even more blank and stupid. His gaze seemed to be fixed on some distant object, or strangely wandering, and in his eyes everything appeared double, blurred and confused.

Who was he trying to see? Obviously, informers. They were hiding everywhere, laughing and whispering to each other. His enemies had dispatched a whole army of them against him. Sometimes he tried to surprise them, but they were always too quick for him and disappeared just as if the earth had swallowed them up . . .

Peredonov heard quick determined footsteps behind him along

1. Eighteenth-century satirical poet who wrote in a heavy archaic style.

160

the pavement and turned round in terror – Kramarenko was gaining on him and looking at him determinedly and malevolently with his burning eyes. He resembled some small, pale, ineffectual warrior about to attack his enemy. The way he looked frightened Peredonov. What if he suddenly bites me, thought Peredonov. He quickened his pace, but Kramarenko kept up. Peredonov stopped and angrily shouted, 'Who the hell do you think you're following around, you filthy guttersnipe? I'll take you straight to your father if you don't clear off!'

Kramarenko stopped too and continued to stare at Peredonov. They were now standing face to face on a loose wooden pavement in a deserted street, near a grey, blank-looking fence.

Quivering all over, Kramarenko hissed, 'You bastard!' He laughed and turned to go, but after three steps he turned round again and shouted even louder, 'What a bastard! Reptile!'

He spat and went off. Peredonov watched him with gloomy eyes and turned towards home, his head swimming with vague, uneasy thoughts.

Vershina called out to him. She was standing, as usual, by her garden gate, wrapped in a large black shawl and smoking. Peredonov didn't at first answer her – she seemed sinister, like a black sorceress blowing magic smoke to bewitch him. He spat, muttering a charm. Vershina laughed and asked, 'What's wrong, Ardalyon?'

Peredonov looked at her blankly and said, 'Oh, it's you! I didn't recognize you.'

'That's a good sign,' said Vershina. 'It means I'll soon be rich.'

This did not please Peredonov at all: he wanted to be rich himself. 'Why do you want to be rich? You should be satisfied with what you've got.'

'But I'm going to win twenty thousand roubles in the lottery,' Vershina said with her wry smile.

'How can you? *I'm* going to win, not you,' he argued.

'I'll win in one draw and you in the other.'

'Rubbish. You never have two wins in the same town. I tell you, I'm going to win.'

Vershina noticed his increasing anger so she decided to end the argument. Opening the gate, she tried to lure him into the garden.

'Why are we standing here?' she said. 'Please come in, Murin's here.'

This name he associated with what was highly agreeable – food and drink – so he went in.

In the drawing-room, which was darkened by the trees outside, were a radiant Marta, with a red sash and a silk scarf around her neck, Murin, looking more dishevelled than ever and particularly pleased for some reason, and a sixth-former, Vitkevich, who was pursuing Vershina and who thought that she was in love with him. He dreamed of leaving school, marrying Vershina and managing her estate.

Murin rose to greet Peredonov with an exaggerated show of pleasure. His eyes glistened and his face took on an even more sickly expression, none of which went with his sturdy figure and his tousled hair, which harboured a few wisps of hay.

'I'm here on business,' Murin said in a loud husky voice. 'I have business everywhere. This time I'm lucky, as these charming ladies are spoiling me with tea.'

'I never knew you had any business!' Peredonov angrily replied. 'You have money, but you don't work for it. I'm the one who's here on business.'

'Well, all business boils down to getting hold of other people's money!' Murin retorted with a loud laugh.

Vershina slyly smiled and seated Peredonov at the table. On a small round table were glasses of rum, cups of tea and blackberry jam, as well as a filigree silver dish covered with a knitted doily and piled high with teacakes and home-made almond cakes.

Murin's glass smelled strongly of rum and Vitkevich had heaped a great deal of jam on his oyster-shaped glass plate. Marta, with undisguised pleasure, was consuming dainty slices of teacake. Vershina offered Peredonov something – he refused the tea. It might be poisoned, he thought. Poisoning's the easiest thing in the world. You can drink and not notice a thing, because poison can taste sweet. I'd just go home and turn up my toes.

He was annoyed that they had brought Murin some of their best conserves and that they hadn't offered him any of the better jam. After all, they had other kinds besides bramble jelly.[1]

And Vershina was paying Murin a lot of attention. Realizing

---

1. Jams made from wild berries, such as blackberries and cloudberries, were regarded as inferior, which explains Peredonov's annoyance.

that there was very little hope with Peredonov, she was looking somewhere else for a husband for Marta. Now she was trying to lure Murin. This landowner, who had grown completely out of touch with society as a result of his pursuit of hard-earned profit, rose eagerly to the bait. He liked Marta very much. Marta was glad, for she constantly dreamed of settling down with a nice husband and having a good home – then her cup would be full. She looked at Murin with love in her eyes and that huge man, past forty and coarse-featured, with his gruff voice and simple face, seemed to her in every way the very paragon of vigorous manhood, of youth, beauty and goodness.

The loving glances exchanged between the two did not escape Peredonov – he was expecting Marta to admire him instead. In an angry voice he told Murin, 'Just like a fiancé you are, sitting there with that blissful look on your face.'

'It's because I'm so pleased,' Murin replied in an excited, cheerful voice. 'I've managed everything very nicely.'

He winked at the ladies. They both smiled in turn. Peredonov scornfully screwed up his eyes and asked crossly, 'So you've found yourself a wife, have you? I suppose there's a large dowry?'

Murin continued as if he hadn't heard. 'Dear Natalya Vershina, God bless her, has agreed to take care of my Vanyusha. He'll be living in clover here. And I shan't have to worry about him being spoiled.'

'He and Vladya will start fooling around together,' Peredonov said dolefully. 'They'll both burn the house down.'

'Vanyusha wouldn't dare!' Murin cried with conviction. 'You need have no worries on that score, my dear Natalya. He'll be at your beck and call.'

Vershina thought it was time to put an end to this conversation and said, 'I fancy something sourish.'

'Would you like some bilberries and apples? I'll fetch some,' Marta said, quickly getting up.

Marta hurried out of the room. Vershina didn't even give her so much as a look: she took her services for granted, as if it were her due. She settled herself comfortably on the sofa, puffed blue clouds of smoke and compared the two men who were talking: Peredonov, dull and angry, Murin cheerful and lively.

Of the two she far preferred Murin. He had a kind, good-natured face, whereas Peredonov was incapable of smiling. Murin pleased her in every way. He was big, fat, attractive, gently spoken and was very polite to her. At times Vershina even thought she might try and arrange things so that he became engaged to herself, not Marta. But she always ended by magnanimously surrendering him to Marta. Anyone would marry me for my money, she thought, so I can take my pick. That schoolboy for instance. And she found it pleasant looking at his impudent yet handsome face. Vitkevich, who said little and ate a lot, kept cheekily smiling at her.

Marta brought the bilberries and apples in an earthenware dish and started telling them about last night's dream. She was a bridesmaid at a wedding and was eating pineapple and pancakes with honey. In one of the pancakes she found a hundred-rouble note, which someone snatched from her, making her burst into tears, and when she woke up she was crying.

'You should have quietly hidden it so no one noticed,' Peredonov said indignantly. 'If you can't look after your money in your dreams what good would you be as a housewife!'

'Well, you shouldn't be upset about the money,' Vershina said. 'You see all sorts of things in dreams.'

'But I *am* upset about losing it, terribly upset,' Marta said ingenuously. 'A hundred roubles!' Tears welled up in her eyes and she forced herself to laugh in order not to cry.

Murin fussed about in his pocket and produced a wallet. 'Now don't you upset yourself, Marta dear! We'll soon put things right.'

He took out a hundred-rouble note, put it on the table in front of Marta, slapped his fist on it and said, 'Please take it. No one's going to take it away from you now!'

Marta was about to rejoice when she blushed deeply and replied in an embarrassed voice, 'Oh, Mr Murin! How could I accept it! What *are* you thinking of? Really!'

'Well, if you don't, I'll be most offended,' Murin said. He laughed softly and left the money where it was. 'Just to show you that dreams can come true!'

'No, I really can't. Not for anything. I feel quite ashamed,' she replied, looking hungrily at the bright green note.

'Why are you so stubborn,' said Vitkevich, 'if someone's giving you it? Some people are just born lucky,' he added with an envious sigh.

Murin stood in front of Marta and said persuasively, 'My dear Marta, believe me! I mean it with all my heart. Please take it. And if you don't want it for nothing, we can say it's for looking after my Vanyusha. That's what we agreed upon, Natalya Vershina and I . . . for looking after him.'

'But it's far too much,' Marta said hesitantly.

'It's for the first six months,' Murin said, bowing low to Marta. 'I shall be offended if you refuse it. Now take it and be like a second sister to my Vanyushka.'

'Well, what are you waiting for?' Vershina said. 'Take it and thank Mr Murin.'

Coyly and joyfully blushing, Marta took the money. Murin began thanking her profusely.

'You'd better get married now, it will be cheaper in the long run,' Peredonov said venomously. 'Just listen to him gushing!'

Vitkevich laughed but the others pretended not to hear. Vershina started telling them about her dream, but Peredonov didn't want to hear and got up to leave. Murin invited him round for dinner.

'No, I must go to evening service,' Peredonov said.

'Since when have you been such an ardent churchgoer?' Vershina asked mockingly.

'I've always gone to church!' he replied. 'I believe in God, not like some others I know. I think I'm the only one in the school who does. That's why I'm persecuted. The headmaster's an atheist.'

'Well, just tell me when you're free,' said Murin.

Peredonov angrily crumpled his hat and replied, 'I've no time for social visits.' But then he suddenly remembered that Murin was the most liberal of hosts. 'Well, I could come on Monday,' he said.

Murin was delighted and wanted Vershina and Marta to come too. Peredonov, however, didn't give them time to answer and said, 'We don't need any ladies. If we get tipsy one of us might blurt out something that should have been censored!'

When Peredonov left, Vershina grinned and said, 'Mr Peredonov's been behaving most peculiarly. There's nothing he wants more than to be made an inspector, but Varvara's probably stringing him along. That would explain his odd behaviour.'

Vladya, who had been hiding while Peredonov was there, came into the room and said with a spiteful snigger, 'Someone's told the locksmith's sons that it was Peredonov who gave them away.'

'They'll break his windows!' Vitkevich exclaimed with a happy laugh.

Everything outside struck Peredonov as hostile and malevolent. A ram standing at the crossroads blankly looked at him. It resembled Volodin so much that Peredonov was frightened. He thought that Volodin had perhaps turned into one so he could follow him around without arousing suspicion. How do we know? he wondered. It might well be possible. Science hasn't managed it up to now, but perhaps there's someone who does know. Take the French. They're a learned lot and there're a lot of sorcerers and magicians in Paris at the moment. And he began to feel terrified. That ram could give me a nasty kick, he thought.

The ram bleated and it sounded just like Volodin's laugh – sharp, piercing, unpleasant.

Then he met Rubovsky the police officer again. He went up to im and whispered, 'Miss Adamenko needs watching. She's corresponding with Socialists and I do believe she's one herself.'

Rubovsky looked at him in mute astonishment. Peredonov walked on and the perplexing thought crossed his mind, Why do I keep bumping into him? He must be investigating me and he's stationed constables everywhere to keep an eye on me.

The muddy streets, the overcast sky, the wretched little houses, the sluggish, ragged children, all combined to produce an impression of dreariness, squalor and hopeless melancholy. This is a wicked town, he thought. Everyone in it is evil and rotten. I'd better get out of it as soon as possible. At least in other towns all the teachers would bow low and the boys would tremble and whisper, 'The inspector's coming!' Yes, officials have a better time of it altogether in this world! 'Inspector of the second district of Ruban,' Peredonov muttered to himself. 'His Excellency, Peredonov. That will be my title. Do you know who you're talking to? His Excellency, Ardalyon Peredonov, head of the national schools of Ruban Province, councillor of State! Hats off there! You'd better resign! Clear off! I'll make it hot for you!'

His face took on an arrogant look; his meagre imagination had for once conjured up an illusory sense of power.

When Peredonov arrived home he was greeted by high-pitched

noises from the direction of the dining-room as he was still taking off his coat.

It was Volodin laughing. His heart sank. He's managed to get here before me, he thought. Perhaps he and Varvara are conspiring to make a fool of me. That's why he's laughing – he's glad Varvara's on his side.

Spiteful and depressed, he went into the dining-room where the table was already laid for dinner. Varvara met Peredonov with a worried look. 'Ardalyon!' she exclaimed. 'What do you think has happened? The cat's run away!'

'Well, why did you let it out?' Peredonov cried in horror.

'You didn't expect me to sew it by the tail to my apron, did you?' Varvara said indignantly. Volodin sniggered. Peredonov was sure that the cat had gone straight to the police station to purr out to the police everything it knew about him, where and why he went out at night. It would reveal all it knew about him – and might even tell them things that never even happened! This was really something to worry about! Peredonov sat at the table, his head bowed, crumpling up the end of the tablecloth and immersed in depressing thoughts.

'Cats always return to their old home,' said Volodin. 'They get used to a house, but not to their master. You should always make a cat dizzy before you take it to a new house. But you mustn't let it see the way, otherwise it's bound to run away.'

Peredonov was somewhat consoled by this. 'So you think he's gone back to the old flat, Pavlusha?' he asked.

'There's no doubt about it, Ardalyon.'

Peredonov stood up and shouted, 'What do you say to a drink, Pavlusha?'

Volodin chuckled. 'That's something I never say no to!'

'But we must get the cat back,' Peredonov decided.

'Such a little treasure!' Varvara said with a smirk. 'I'll send Claudia to look for it after dinner.'

They sat down to eat. Volodin was in a good mood and talked and laughed a great deal. To Peredonov his laughter sounded just like that bleating ram in the street. What's he cooking up now, I wonder? What does he want from me? he thought.

He felt that he might be able to win him over to his side, so he said, 'Listen, Pavlusha. If you don't do me any harm I'll buy you a pound of the best-quality fruit drops every week. You can suck them to your heart's content.'

Volodin laughed, but then he looked quite offended and said, 'I would *never* do you any harm, Ardalyon. But I don't want any fruit drops because I don't like them.'

Peredonov looked glum. Varvara grinned and said, 'Stop being so stupid, Ardalyon. Why should he want to hurt you?'

'Any fool can play all sorts of dirty tricks,' he replied mournfully.

Volodin took great offence at this, puffed out his lips, shook his head and said, 'If that's your considered opinion, Ardalyon, then all I can say is thank you very much! What am I supposed to do now? How am I supposed to take it, in what sense?'

'Have some vodka, Pavlusha, and pour me some,' Peredonov said.

'Don't take any notice of him, Pavel,' Varvara said consolingly. 'He doesn't know what he's saying half the time.'

Volodin didn't reply and, still looking offended, began pouring out the vodka from the decanter. Varvara grinned and asked Peredonov, 'How come you're not scared of accepting a drink from him? It's possible he's cast a spell over it – just look how he's twitching his lips.'

A look of horror appeared on Peredonov's face. He seized the glass and threw its contents on to the floor. Then he recited: 'Keep away, keep away! A curse on the plotter, may the evil tongue wither, may the evil eye burst! Sudden death to him. Keep away, keep away!' Then he turned to Volodin with a bitter look, stuck out a finger and said, 'That's for you! You'll get nothing out of me. You may be clever, but I'm even cleverer.'

Varvara laughed and Volodin said in a high-pitched, hurt voice, just as if he were bleating, 'You're the one, Ardalyon, who knows all the magic words and how to recite them. As for me, I've never dabbled in black magic. But I never cast a spell on your vodka – nor would I on anything else. Perhaps *you've* been spiriting prospective brides away from me!'

'That's going too far!' Peredonov said furiously. 'I don't want your women, I can get far better ones any time.'

'You cast a spell on my eye to make it burst,' Volodin said, 'but mind your spectacles don't shatter first!'

Peredonov grabbed his spectacles in fright. 'What are you

blabbering about now? I think your tongue's run away with you,' he said.

Varvara looked anxiously at Volodin and retorted angrily, 'Don't be so nasty, Pavel. Eat your soup or it will get cold. Oh, you're so spiteful!' She thought that Peredonov had perhaps recited the charm just in time.

Volodin started eating his soup. All were silent until Volodin said in an injured voice, 'It was no coincidence that I dreamed last night I was being smeared with honey. You were the one who was doing the smearing, Ardalyon.'

'And I'd be surprised if you didn't need smearing,' Varvara said angrily.

'What for? Please tell me. I don't think I've done anything to deserve that,' said Volodin.

'Because you've a foul tongue,' explained Varvara. 'One shouldn't go around blabbering the first thing that comes into one's head – there's a time and place for everything.'[1]

XX

In the evening Peredonov went to the club, where he had been invited to a game of cards. Peredonov was terrified when he saw Gudayevsky was there. But the notary didn't make any trouble and Peredonov was able to relax.

Peredonov and company played for a long time and drank a lot. Towards midnight, while they were at the buffet, Gudayevsky suddenly went over to Peredonov and without any explanation struck him several times on the face, breaking his spectacles, and then disappeared. Peredonov offered no resistance and, pretending he was drunk, fell on to the floor and started snoring. The others gave him a rough shaking and took him home.

Next day the whole town was talking about the incident. That

1. See variant 12, p. 284.

same evening Varvara succeeded in stealing the first of the forged letters from Peredonov. It was essential for her to have it, as Grushina had insisted, in case Peredonov found it and later compared it with the other one. Peredonov always carried the letter with him, but on this occasion happened to leave it at home. When he changed into his frock-coat he had taken it out of his pocket, put it under a textbook in the chest of drawers and immediately forgotten all about it. Varvara soon found it and burned it over a candle at Grushina's.

When Peredonov returned late that night and Varvara saw his broken spectacles, he told her that they had broken of their own accord. She believed him and decided that Volodin's evil tongue was to blame. Peredonov believed this too. However, on the following day, Grushina told her about the incident at the club, down to the last detail.

It was in the morning, when he was getting dressed, that Peredonov first missed the letter. He couldn't find it anywhere and he was terrified.

'Varvara! Where's the letter?' he wildly shouted.

Varvara didn't know what to say. 'What letter?' she asked, looking at Peredonov with frightened, evil eyes.

'The one from the princess!' he shouted.

Varvara somehow pulled herself together and said with a brazen smile, 'How do I know where it is? You must have thrown it in the waste-paper bin, or Claudia might have burned it. Have another look in your room, it might still be there.'

Peredonov went to school in a gloomy frame of mind. He remembered yesterday's unpleasant events. How dare that guttersnipe Kramarenko call him a bastard! Obviously Kramarenko wasn't afraid of him. Did he know something? Perhaps he did and was going to report him to the police!

In class Kramarenko stared fixedly at him and smiled, which frightened Peredonov even more.

During the third break the headmaster asked to see Peredonov. He went to his study, vaguely anticipating something highly unpleasant.

Khripach had been hearing stories of Peredonov's behaviour from all over town and that same morning had been informed of yesterday's incident at the club. The previous day, after school,

Volodya Bultyakov, recently punished by his landlady at Peredonov's instigation, had come to see him. The boy feared a second visit, so he complained to the headmaster.

In his dry, sharp voice, Khripach repeated what he had heard, adding that all the reports were from reliable sources. According to them, Peredonov had been going round to the boys' lodgings, giving false information about their conduct and their progress to their parents or tutors, demanding that they be severely beaten. Naturally, this had given rise to much unpleasantness with the parents, as last night's incident at the club all too clearly showed.

Peredonov listened indignantly but apprehensively. When Khripach had finished he said angrily, 'A fine state of affairs, I must say! *He* started fighting – surely you can't condone that sort of behaviour. He had no right to sock me on the jaw. He doesn't go to church and he believes in the apes. What's more, he's teaching his son the same heathen religion. And he should be reported to the police for being a Socialist.'

Khripach looked at Peredonov closely and said in a tone of reprimand, 'That doesn't concern me, and I really don't know what you mean by that most original expression "believes in apes". It's my considered opinion there's no need to enrich the history of religion with any newly invented ones. As for the insult you suffered, you should have taken Gudayevsky to court. However, I consider the best course of action for you is to leave this school altogether. It would be the best solution both for yourself and for the school.'

'But I'm going to be appointed inspector,' Peredonov angrily protested.

Khripach continued, 'Until that time I must ask you to refrain from making these odd perambulations. You must agree that such conduct is unbecoming to a teacher and diminishes his dignity in the eyes of his pupils. Is it right for a teacher to go round to the boys' lodgings and not be satisfied until they are flogged . . .?' Khripach didn't finish and shrugged his shoulders.

'But it was for their own good –' protested Peredonov.

'Please don't let's start an argument,' Khripach brusquely interrupted. 'I must have your solemn assurance that this sort of thing is not repeated.'

Peredonov simply glared at the headmaster.

*

In the evening Varvara and Peredonov decided to give a house-warming party, to which they invited all their friends. Before the party began, Peredonov went through all the rooms to ensure everything was in order and that nothing incriminating had been left lying about. Everything seems all right, he thought. No banned books, the icon lamps are lit, the tsars' portraits are in the place of honour on the wall.

Suddenly, Mickiewicz winked at Peredonov from the wall.

He could put me in a spot, he thought apprehensively. So he quickly removed the portrait and hung it in the toilet, putting Pushkin in its place. After all, Pushkin was a courtier, he reflected as he hung him in the dining-room.

Then he remembered that in the evening they would be playing cards. So he decided to inspect them first. He took an unsealed pack, which had only been used once, and started to examine each card as if he expected to find something. He didn't like the court cards' faces at all – they had such big eyes! Recently, when they'd been playing, the cards seemed to be grinning just like Varvara. Even the humble six of spades had taken on an insolent look and was wiggling about indecently.

Peredonov collected all the cards and with a sharp pair of scissors poked out the eyes of the kings, queens and jacks so that they couldn't spy on him anymore. At first he did this to all the used cards, then he opened new packs and mutilated them too. All the time he was doing this he kept looking round, fearing someone might come in and catch him. Luckily Varvara was busy in the kitchen: he knew that she would never leave Claudia alone with all that food; the moment she was gone Claudia would help herself. So whenever Varvara needed something she sent Claudia for it, and every time she came in Peredonov trembled, hurriedly stuffed the scissors into his pocket and pretended to be playing patience.

While Peredonov was thus depriving the kings and queens of the ability to annoy him with their spying, something unexpectedly unpleasant was creeping up on him from another direction. The hat that he had thrown on to the top of the stove in the other flat had been found by Yershova. She was convinced that it hadn't simply been forgotten, but had been left there on purpose by her former tenants (who had good reason to wish her harm), and it was highly likely that it bore a curse which would stop anyone else taking the flat. Terrified and infuriated, she took the hat to a friend who practised black magic and who, after inspecting it, whispered something very mysterious over it and spat on the corners. 'They've played a dirty trick on you and now we can give them a taste of their own medicine. That sorcerer was a powerful one, but I can make an even stronger spell that will have him in convulsions.'

She continued muttering incantations over the offending hat and, when Yershova had paid her very generously, told her to give the hat to the first redheaded boy she came across and ask him to take it to Peredonov's, where he was to give it to the first person he saw there and then run off without looking back.

It so happened that the first redheaded boy she met was one of the locksmith's sons, who had good reason for wanting to get even with Peredonov for giving him away to the police. He was only too willing to oblige for five copecks, and on the way to the house he heartily spat on the hat of his own accord. Meeting Varvara herself in the dim hall, he shoved it into her hands and disappeared so smartly she had no time to see who it was. Peredonov had just managed to blind the last jack when Varvara rushed into the room in a terrible state. Her voice shook as she told him, 'Look at this, Ardalyon!'

Peredonov looked and almost dropped from fright. The hat he thought he had got rid of once and for all was now in Varvara's hands, crumpled, dusty and with scarcely a trace of its former grandeur. 'Where did you find it?' he asked, breathless with horror.

In a trembling voice Varvara proceeded to tell him how she had received the hat from a fleet-footed boy, who seemed to have sprung out of the earth right in front of her, only to be swallowed up again. 'It looks like Yershova's work,' she said. 'If I know her, she's put a curse on it, that's for certain.'

Peredonov muttered something unintelligible and his teeth chattered from fear. Once again dark misgivings and forebodings took possession of him. He walked up and down, frowning, while the little grey demon ran about under the chairs and tittered.

The guests arrived early. They brought a large quantity of pies, apples and pears. Varvara eagerly took the presents and for politeness' sake said, 'Oh, you didn't have to! You really shouldn't have bothered!' But she became very angry if anyone brought some cheap rubbish; nor did she like it if two guests brought the same present.

Without wasting any time they sat down to play whist, at two tables.

'Dear me!' exclaimed Grushina. 'My king's blind!'

'And my queen hasn't any eyes either!' Mrs Prepolovensky said as she peered at her cards. 'Nor has the jack.'

Everyone laughed and looked to see if their cards had suffered the same treatment. Mr Prepolovensky said, 'Yes, when I felt my cards I thought they were rough – and this is the reason. I kept running my hand over them and thought how rough the backs were. Yes, they kept catching on each other because of the holes. It's these little holes that are to blame.'

Everyone was amused at this, except Peredonov, who was his usual gloomy self. Varvara smiled and said, 'You know how my Ardalyon likes playing tricks. He's always thinking up something new.'

'Why on earth did you do it?' Rutilov asked with a mighty guffaw.

'What do they need eyes for? They don't need to see, do they?' Peredonov said mournfully.

Everyone roared, with the exception again of Peredonov, who remained morose and silent. He thought that the blinded cards were making faces at him, grinning and winking with the gaping holes where once there had been eyes. Perhaps they've discovered a way of seeing with their noses? Peredonov wondered.

He lost, as usual, and he thought the expressions on the faces of the court cards were particularly mocking and malevolent. The queen of spades gnashed her teeth, evidently furious at losing her eyesight.

Finally, after having to pay a very large forfeit, Peredonov seized the pack and savagely tore it to shreds. Everyone roared with laughter.

Varvara grinned and said, 'He always acts strangely when he's had a drop.'

'You mean when he's *drunk*,' Mrs Prepolovensky said viciously. 'Have you heard, Mr Peredonov, what your "cousin" really thinks of you?'

Varvara flushed and retorted, 'Why do you distort everything I say?'

Mrs Prepolovensky smiled and didn't reply.

The torn pack was replaced with a new one and the game went on.

Suddenly there was a terrific crash and a large stone came sailing through the window and landed near the table where Peredonov was sitting. Someone was heard to whisper and laugh under the window – then followed the sound of fast-receding footsteps. Everyone jumped up in panic. As usual the women screamed. Someone picked the stone up and examined it with trepidation. No one dared to go up to the window. First they sent Claudia out into the street and only when she had seen that the street was empty did the guests begin to inspect the damage. Volodin concluded that the stone had been thrown by boys from the school. This seemed a likely guess and everyone looked at Peredonov as if expecting an explanation. Peredonov frowned and muttered something unintelligible. The guests started complaining that schoolboys were impudent and corrupt. Of course, it wasn't boys from the school, but the locksmith's sons.

'The headmaster's put them up to it,' Peredonov suddenly announced. 'He's always picking on me. He doesn't know what to torment me with next, so he's thought of this.'

'And a nice little trick too!' Rutilov said, roaring with laughter.

Everyone laughed, except Grushina, who said, 'What do you expect from that nasty Khripach. He's capable of anything. He doesn't do anything himself, but lets his sons do his dirty work for him.'

'It doesn't seem to mean a thing that they're aristocrats,' Volodin bleated. 'You can expect *anything* from that lot!'

Many of the guests thought that perhaps he was right and stopped laughing.

'You seem to be having bad luck with your glass, Ardalyon,' said Rutilov. 'First your spectacles were smashed and now your window.'

This produced another outburst of laughter.

'Broken windows mean long life,' Mrs Prepolovensky said with a suppressed smile.

When Peredonov and Varvara went to bed, Peredonov thought that Varvara had something nasty in mind, so he took all the knives and forks and hid them under the bed.

'I know you too well,' he muttered in a faltering voice. 'Once we're married you'll report me to the police, just to get rid of me. You'll get a pension and I'll be working the treadmill in the Petropavlovsk prison.'

That night Peredonov was delirious. Obscure, terrifying shapes silently walked up and down; kings and jacks waved their sceptres. They whispered to each other, tried to hide from Peredonov and crawled towards him under the pillow. But soon they grew more daring and began running and bustling around everywhere – along the floor, up and down the bed, over the pillows. They kept whispering and teasing Peredonov, poking their tongues out, pulling horrible faces and twisting their mouths into ugly grimaces. Peredonov could see that they were small and playful, that they were not going to kill him, but were only mocking him and warning him of some imminent disaster. All the same, he was terrified and first muttered incantations, parts of spells he had heard in his childhood, and then he cursed them and tried to drive them away by waving his arms and shouting hoarsely.

Varvara woke up and angrily asked, 'What are you yelling about, Ardalyon? You won't let anyone sleep in this house.'

'The queen of spades keeps sneaking up on me underneath the mattress cover.'

Varvara got up, grumbling and cursing as she tried to calm him down with some kind of drops.

In the local paper there appeared a brief article about how, apparently in our town, a certain Mrs K. had taken to whipping schoolboy lodgers, sons of the best local families. Gudayevsky the notary was highly indignant and spread the news all over town.

And various other absurd rumours about the local high school were doing the rounds. There was talk of a girl disguised as a schoolboy, and then Pylnikov's name gradually came to be associated with Lyudmila's. Sasha's schoolfriends began to tease him for being in love with Lyudmila. At first he didn't take their little jokes seriously, but then he would occasionally flare up and defend Lyudmila, assuring his friends that nothing of the kind had happened in the past, nor was it the case now.

And as a result he began to feel ashamed of visiting Lyudmila, yet the urge to go became even stronger. Confused, agonizing feelings of shame and attraction disturbed him and fed his imagination with vaguely erotic visions.

XXI

On Sunday, when Peredonov and Varvara were having lunch, someone entered the hall. In her usual stealthy way Varvara crept up to the door and just as quietly returned.

'It's the postman. We ought to give him some vodka – he's brought another letter.'

Peredonov nodded – he wasn't mean enough to grudge anyone a small drop of vodka.

'Postman, come in!' Varvara shouted.

The postman came into the dining-room, ferreted about in his bag and pretended to be looking for a letter. Varvara poured him a large glass of vodka and cut him a thick slice of pie. The postman watched her with lustful eyes. Meanwhile Peredonov was wondering who he reminded him of. Finally he remembered – surely he was that redheaded pimply jack of hearts who'd tricked him into paying such a large forfeit just recently? And he'll do it again if I'm not careful, Peredonov wearily thought and secretly cocked a snook at him.

The redheaded 'jack' handed the letter to Varvara. 'It's for you, madam,' he said politely, thanked her for the vodka, gulped it down, grunted, grabbed a chunk of pie and left.

Varvara turned the letter over in her hands. But she didn't open it. She gave it to Peredonov. 'See what it says. I think it's from the princess,' she said, grinning. 'Another long letter saying absolutely nothing, I suppose. She ought to give you the job, instead of just writing.'

Peredonov's hands trembled as he tore open the envelope and quickly read the letter. Then he jumped up from his chair, waved the letter in the air and whooped with delight. 'Hurrah! I've been offered three posts as inspector. I can choose any one I like. Hurrah, Varvara, our luck's really changed!' He started to dance and career around the room. With his motionless red face and dull eyes he looked just like a large clockwork doll. Varvara grinned and gleefully watched him.

'It's settled once and for all, Varvara!' he shouted. 'Let's get married!'

He grasped Varvara by the shoulders and whirled her around the table, stamping his feet. 'The trepak, Varvara!' he shouted.

Varvara put her hands on her hips and sailed off, while Peredonov danced Cossack style before her.

At this moment Volodin came in and happily bleated, 'So the future inspector's taken up the trepak!'

'Dance, Pavlusha!' cried Peredonov.

Claudia looked out from behind a door. Laughing and grimacing, Volodin shouted to her, 'Come and join us! All together, in honour of the new inspector!'

Claudia shrieked and joined in the wild dance, wriggling her shoulders. Volodin cut all sorts of capers, flinging his legs out, whirling around, jumping and clapping his hands. He looked particularly dashing when he raised one knee and clapped his hands beneath it. The floor simply shook under their heels. Claudia was delighted at having such a skilful, dashing partner.

When they were tired they all sat down at the table and Claudia ran back into the kitchen, shrieking with laughter. They drank vodka and beer, smashed the bottles and glasses on the floor, guffawed, gesticulated wildly and embraced each other. Then Peredonov and Volodin went off to the club – Peredonov couldn't wait to tell everyone about his success.

In the billiard-room they found the usual players. Peredonov showed his friends the letter. It produced a great impression and no one doubted its authenticity. Rutilov turned pale and mumbled something, sending out a spray of saliva.

'With my own eyes I saw the postman bring it! Peredonov exclaimed. 'And I opened it myself. That *proves* it's genuine.'

His friends looked at him in awe. A letter from a princess!

From the club Peredonov made haste to Vershina's. He walked quickly and smoothly, rhythmically swinging his arms and muttering to himself. His face was quite without expression, as motionless as that of a clockwork doll. But a strange, hungry fire burned in his eyes with a deathly glimmer.

It was a fine, warm day. Marta was sitting in the summer-house, knitting a sock. Her thoughts were vague and pious. First she reflected on sin. Then she turned her thoughts to more pleasant subjects, such as virtue. This only made her feel drowsy, and the sleepier she became, the more her reflections lost their philosophic content and became hazy dreams. The Virtues arrayed themselves before her, like huge beautiful dolls in white dresses, sweetly smelling and radiant. They promised her rewards, keys tinkled in their hands and white wedding veils fluttered from their heads.

One of them was rather strange and unlike the rest. She promised nothing and looked disdainful, her lips moving in silent menace. It seemed that if she were to say something it would be terrible. Marta guessed that she was Conscience. That awesome visitor was dressed in black, and her eyes and hair were black. She said something rapidly, distinctly – and she seemed just like Vershina. Marta shuddered and answered her questions almost mechanically, until once again she was overcome by drowsiness.

Whether it was Conscience or Vershina seated opposite – that calm, determined visitor who was telling her something rapidly and lucidly, but nevertheless incomprehensibly, who was smoking exotic cigarettes and demanding that everything should be carried out according to her dictates – Marta could not tell. She wanted to look this importunate visitor straight in the eye, but for some reason she couldn't. The visitor smiled so strangely, kept grumbling, and her eyes were constantly wandering and then coming to rest on remote, mysterious objects that Marta was afraid to look at . . .

The sound of loud voices woke her from her day-dreams. Peredonov was in the summer-house, greeting Vershina in a loud voice. Marta looked around in fear. Her heart was pounding, her eyelids still heavy with sleep and her thoughts still confused. Where was Conscience? Or had she imagined it all?

'You were sitting there dozing,' Peredonov told her, 'and snoring your head off. Now you're a pine tree!'[1]

Marta didn't understand the pun, but she smiled, guessing from the smile on Vershina's lips that Peredonov had said something that was supposed to be funny.

Peredonov sat on the bench beside Marta and said, 'I have some extremely important news for you.'

'Well, don't keep it from us,' said Vershina.

'Guess,' said Peredonov in a triumphant but gloomy voice.

1. Pun on so sna, meaning 'from sleep' (i.e., awake), and sosna, meaning 'pine tree'.

'How do you expect us to guess? Why don't you just tell us, then we'll know.'

Peredonov wasn't at all pleased that they didn't want to guess his news. He sat silently, awkwardly hunched up, and looked vacantly in front of him. Vershina smoked and smiled wryly, revealing her dark yellow teeth.

'All right,' she said after a brief pause, 'I'll see what the cards say. Marta, get me a pack from the drawing-room.'

Marta got up, but Peredonov angrily stopped her.

'Sit down, I don't want them. Guess how you like, but leave me in peace. You won't guess my news the way you want, anyway. I'm going to show you a trick now which will make you gasp.'

Peredonov swiftly produced a wallet from his pocket, took out a letter in an envelope and showed it to Vershina without letting go of it. 'You can see the envelope. And here's the letter.'

He took the letter out and read it slowly with a dull expression of triumphant malice in his eyes. Vershina was stunned. To the very last she had not believed in the princess, but now she realized that it was all over as far as Marta was concerned. With a wry vexed smile she said, 'It seems your luck's in!'

Marta's face was all astonishment and she smiled in dismay.

'That'll teach you to think I'm stupid!' gloated Peredonov. 'You thought you were clever, but I'll show you! And you mentioned the envelope – well, here it is. No, it's all plain sailing for me now.' He banged the table with his fist, but not very hard and without making much noise. And his movements and the sound of his words were strangely apathetic, as if he were in another world.

Vershina and Marta exchanged bewildered glances.

'What are you staring at each other for?' Peredonov said rudely. 'There's no point in that, it's all settled. I'm going to marry Varvara. And to think of the narrow escapes I've had.'

Vershina sent Marta for some cigarettes and she joyfully ran from the summer-house. As she walked down the sandy path strewn with colourful, faded leaves, she felt she could breathe freely. And when she met barefooted Vladya near the house she become even more cheerful.

'He's going to marry Varvara, it's all settled,' she said gaily, lowering her voice as she led her brother into the house.

Meanwhile Peredonov, without bothering to wait until Marta came back, suddenly got up to leave. 'I can't stay here wasting time like this. Getting married is not like tying your shoelaces, you know!'

Vershina didn't detain him and bade him an icy farewell.[1] She was bitterly disappointed – and highly indignant. Up to then she had felt that there was a faint chance of arranging a marriage between Peredonov and Marta, with Murin reserved for herself. And now the last hope had vanished.

Marta really did catch it from Vershina that day and many tears were shed.

After he left Vershina, Peredonov thought that he would like a smoke. Suddenly he saw a policeman standing on the corner of the street, shelling sunflower seeds – and his heart sank. He's a spy, he thought. They're trying to catch me out one way or the other.

He didn't dare smoke his cigarette, but went up to the policeman and timidly asked, 'Officer, is smoking allowed here?'

The policeman touched his cap and politely inquired, 'Smoking what, sir?'

'Just a small cigarette,' Peredonov replied. 'Can I smoke one here?'

'There's no law against it as far as I know, sir,' the policeman replied.

'No law against it?' asked Peredonov sadly.

'None at all. We've no orders to stop gentlemen smoking. If any law *has* been passed, that's the first I've heard of it.'

'In that case I'd better not start,' Peredonov replied deferentially. 'I'm a law-abiding citizen. To prove it I'll throw the cigarette away. After all, I'm a senior civil servant, a councillor of State.'

Peredonov crumpled up the cigarette and threw it on to the ground. He was already beginning to fear that he'd said one word too many, so he hurried home. The policeman watched him go, uncomprehendingly. He finally concluded that the gentlemen was still under the influence from last night and thought no more about it.

'The road's standing on end,' muttered Peredonov.

1. See variant 13, p. 286.

The road took a sharp turn upwards along the slope of a hill and then descended abruptly the other side. At the top, two hovels stood outlined against the dark blue melancholy evening sky. Life in this squalid part of the town seemed to be withdrawn from the outside world and weighed down by continual misery and sadness. The trees hung their branches over the fences so that they obstructed the paths. There was a strange mockery in their menacing whispers. A sheep stood at the crossroads and eyed Peredonov blankly. Suddenly he heard a bleating laugh. It was Volodin, who appeared from nowhere and came up to greet him. Peredonov looked at him gloomily and thought about the sheep that had been there just a moment ago and had suddenly disappeared. It's obvious Volodin can turn himself into a sheep whenever he likes. He doesn't look like one for nothing! Sometimes I can't tell whether he's laughing or bleating.

He was so occupied with these thoughts that he didn't hear Volodin greet him at all.

'Why do you have to kick me, Pavlusha?' he asked morosely.

Volodin smiled and bleated, 'I'm not kicking you, Ardalyon, I'm merely shaking hands. Where you come from they might kick with their hands, but in my part of the world they do it with their feet. And even then, if I may say so, it's the horses that kick, not the people.'

'I know you're just waiting to butt me,' Peredonov growled.

Volodin took offence and replied in a trembling voice, 'My horns haven't grown yet. Ardalyon. But maybe yours will grow quicker.'

'You've a long tongue and you talk a lot of rubbish with it,' said Peredonov.

'If that's how you feel, Ardalyon, I'd better keep my mouth shut.'

His face became the picture of misery and his lips stuck out even further. However, he walked along with Peredonov – he hadn't had dinner yet and was counting on eating at Peredonov's, where he'd been invited that morning to celebrate with him.

Some important news was awaiting Peredonov when he arrived home. Before he had gone far into the hall he could tell something momentous had happened from the commotion and shrieks of anguish. At first he thought dinner wasn't ready, that they hadn't been expecting him home so early and now they were panicking. He was delighted to see that they were all so afraid of him! But the cause of the general commotion was something quite different. Varvara ran out into the hall and shouted, 'They've found the cat!'

In her excitement she didn't notice that Volodin was with Peredonov. As usual she was looking very scruffy in her grey grease-spotted blouse, filthy skirt and worn-out slippers. Her hair was uncombed and hung over her eyes.

'We have Irishka Yershova to blame for this!' she excitedly told Peredonov. 'She's played a new trick on us, out of spite. A boy came back with the cat and just threw it down. Someone's tied rattles to its tail and they're making a terrible racket . . . It's under the couch and won't come out.'

Peredonov was terrified. 'What are we going to do now?' he asked.

'Pavel,' Varvara said, 'you're younger than he is, try and see if you can chase it out.'

'Yes, let's chase it out,' Volodin chuckled as he went into the living-room.

Somehow they managed to drag the cat out and they removed the rattles from its tail. Peredonov found some thistles and began to rub them against the cat, which hissed fiercely and escaped into the kitchen.

Tired from all this excitement, Peredonov sat in his usual position – elbows on the arms of the chair, fingers clenched, legs crossed and his face motionless and sullen.

He guarded the princess's second letter even more closely than the first. He always kept it in his wallet and would show it with a mysterious air. He watched it with an eagle eye, in case someone should want to steal it, and he never let anyone hold it – each time he showed it he would put it straight back into his wallet, which he stuffed into a side pocket of his jacket, buttoned it up very carefully and then surveyed his audience with a solemn, grave expression.

Sometimes Rutilov would ask as a joke, 'Why do you always carry it around with you?'

And back would come the grim reply, 'Just a precaution: why, *you* might try and filch it!'

'You'd get sent to Siberia for that, no doubt,' laughed Rutilov as he slapped Peredonov's back.

But he did not ruffle Peredonov's rock-like solemnity. Recently everyone had noticed that he was behaving more pompously than usual. 'I'm going to be an inspector,' he would often boast. 'While you're stagnating here I'll have two districts – or even three – under my control. Ha! Ha!'

He was quite convinced that within a very short time he would be appointed inspector and more than once told his fellow teacher Falastov, 'I'll see you get out of this dead-and-alive hole, my friend.'

And from that time onwards Falastov treated Peredonov with the greatest respect.

XXII

Peredonov's visits to church became more and more frequent. He stood where everyone could see him, crossed himself far more often than was necessary and then stiffened up and looked vaguely towards the altar. Behind every pillar, so it seemed, lurked spies who kept peeping out, trying to make him laugh out loud. But he wouldn't give in.

He could hear the soft laughter and whispers of the Rutilov sisters in his ears. At times the noise swelled and became almost overwhelming: it was just as if those cunning girls were giggling right in his ears to make him laugh and get him thrown out of church. But he wouldn't give in.

And sometimes, between the thick clouds of incense, he could see a bluish demon, like a wisp of smoke. Its eyes seemed to be giving off sparks. At times it flitted through the air with a tinkling sound, but not for long: most often it would dart about among the feet of the congregation, mocking him and persistently tormenting him. Obviously it wanted to frighten him out of church before Mass had been celebrated. But he saw through its evil designs – and would not give in.

The church service, which for its mystique rather than for its liturgy and ritual has so much attraction for churchgoers, was quite incomprehensible to Peredonov and therefore it frightened him. The censing horrified him, like a mysterious magic spell.

What's he waving that thing about for? he wondered. The robes of the celebrants, in his eyes, were annoyingly gaudy bits of coarse rags. Whenever he looked at the priest's vestments he felt like ripping them to pieces and smashing the holy vessels. To him the church rituals and mysteries were a form of evil witchcraft, a means of enslaving and stupefying the masses. Now he's crumbled the wafer into the wine, he thought angrily about the priest. It's cheap wine and they cheat the congregation into giving them more money for their ceremonies. The mystery of the eternal transubstantiation of inert matter into a force capable of surviving putrefaction he was never to know. He was no more than a walking corpse. And how absurd that he felt he could reconcile his belief in Christ and a living God with his belief in witchcraft!

The congregation began to leave the church. The village schoolmaster Machigin, a simple-minded young man, came up to the girls, smiled and chatted away with them. Peredonov thought that this overfamiliar behaviour was quite improper in the presence of a future inspector. Machigin was wearing a straw hat, but Peredonov remembered that he'd seen him wear a cap with a badge during the summer, just outside the town. He decided to complain about it.

Inspector Bogdanov happened to be near by and Peredonov took the opportunity of going up to him and saying, 'Did you know that Machigin's been wearing a cap with a badge? He's obviously trying to look like a *gentleman*!'

Bogdanov jumped in terror and his little grey goatee trembled. 'He has no right, none whatsoever, to wear a badge,' he said anxiously, blinking with his small red eyes.

'Of course he hasn't. And yet he persists in wearing one,' Peredonov complained. 'He needs a severe reprimand, as I told you long ago. We'll soon have any oafish peasant wearing a badge at this rate!'

Bogdanov, who had been frightened enough at first by Peredonov now felt even more terrified. 'The impudence!' he said dolefully. 'I'll summon him at once – yes, at once – and give him a severe talking-to.' He then said farewell to Peredonov and hastily trotted off home.

Volodin walked beside Peredonov and scornfully bleated, 'I ask you! Wearing a badge! Anyone would think he held an official's rank. How could he?'

'And you're not allowed to wear one either.'

'I know I'm not, and I don't need to. True, I do wear one sometimes, but *I* know the right time and place for it. When I'm right out in the country I sometimes put one on. It gives me so much pleasure and there's no one to stop me. You get much more respect from the peasants.'

'A badge doesn't suit your ugly mug, Pavlusha,' Peredonov said. 'And keep away from me, you're covering me with dust with your ram's hoofs.'

Volodin was deeply hurt and fell silent, but still walked on beside him.

'Those Rutilov girls will have to be reported too,' Peredonov said anxiously. 'All they go to church for is to giggle and chatter. They tart themselves up and off they go. And they steal incense to make scent – that's why they're always reeking of perfume.'

'Well I never!' exclaimed Volodin, shaking his head and goggling his vacant bulging eyes.

The shadow of a storm cloud glided swiftly over the ground and filled Peredonov with terror. Amidst the clouds of dust along the road he occasionally caught a glimpse of the little grey demon. Whenever the grass stirred in the breeze Peredonov thought he could see it running around in it, biting off blades and gorging itself. It's a disgrace there's all this grass in the town! It should be rooted out.

On a nearby tree a twig quivered, shrivelled up, turned black and flew off with a loud cawing. Peredonov shuddered, gave a wild cry and rushed home. Volodin followed him anxiously, his protruding eyes full of utter incomprehension. As he ran he clutched his bowler hat and swung his stick.

That same day Bogdanov summoned Machigin to his house. Before he entered Machigin stood with his back to the sun, took off his hat and combed his hair with his fingers.

'Well, young man, what's it all about? What have you been up to?' Bogdanov said, going straight into the attack. 'What have you been up to, eh?'

'What's *what* all about?' Machigin replied nonchalantly, toying with his straw hat and swinging his left foot. Bogdanov didn't allow him to sit – it was far better reprimanding him if he were standing up.

'How is it that you, young man, have been wearing a badge, eh? What made you break the rule, eh?' He assumed an air of the utmost gravity and shook his little grey goatee.

Machigin flushed but answered boldly, 'What about it? Haven't I the right to wear one?'

'Do you think you're a civil servant, eh? Or a government official?' Bogdanov said excitedly. 'What sort of official are you, eh? A copy clerk, eh?'

'A badge is a sign of my professional status as a teacher,' said Machigin daringly, and the thought of its importance brought a sweet smile to his face.

'A *stick*. Yes, a stick – that's the sign of *your* status,' Bogdanov advised him with a shake of the head.

'But please reconsider, Mr Bogdanov,' replied Machigin in a hurt voice. 'An ordinary stick! Anyone can have one of those, but a badge carries *prestige*.'

'What do *you* want with prestige, eh? *What* prestige?' Bogdanov replied, going into the attack again. 'What prestige do *you* need, eh? Do you think you're a government official?'

Machigin tried to reason with him and said, 'Please, Mr Bogdanov, a badge immediately wins the respect of the illiterate peasantry – they've been bowing much lower since I've been wearing one.' He smugly stroked his red moustache.

'It's quite impossible young man, quite impossible,' Bogdanov said, mournfully shaking his head.

'Please, Mr Bogdanov! A teacher without a badge is exactly the same as the British lion without its tail – a caricature!'

'Tail? What have tails got to do with it, eh? What tails do you mean, eh?' Bogdanov said excitedly. 'And why do you have to bring politics into it, eh? What business is it of yours to discuss politics, eh? No, young man, you must do as I say and remove that badge. You can't go around doing just as you please. Anyone could find out, God forbid!'

Machigin shrugged his shoulders and wanted to say something else, but Bogdanov interrupted him: what seemed to him a brilliant idea had flashed through his mind. 'Well, you came here today without a badge, didn't you? So that shows you yourself feel it's wrong.'

Machigin didn't know what to say at first, but soon came up with an apt retort. 'Since we're country schoolmasters, we need only country privileges. But in town we're looked upon as third-rate intellectuals.'

'No, young man! I must tell you once again,' Bogdanov said angrily, 'that it's *not allowed*, and if I hear of it again we shall be forced to dismiss you.'

From time to time Grushina gave small parties for the young bachelors in the town, from among whom she hoped, sooner or later, to hook another husband. So as not to make her intentions too obvious, she invited married friends too.

At one of these parties the guests arrived early. On the walls of Grushina's living-room were some paintings covered over with thick muslin – not that there was anything indecent about them. When Grushina raised the muslin with a provocative smile, all the guests had to admire were very badly painted naked women.

'Why is this one so crooked?' Peredonov asked glumly.

'She's not at all crooked,' Grushina said, quickly stepping to the picture's defence. 'She's just bending over.'

'She's crooked,' insisted Peredonov, 'and her eyes are different sizes, like yours.'

'A fat lot you understand about art!' Grushina said, deeply offended. 'These pictures are very good and they cost a lot of money. Artists always paint like that.'

Peredonov suddenly laughed out loud, remembering the advice he had given Vladya a few days before.

'What are you guffawing about?' asked Grushina.

'Nartanovich, one of the boys in my class, is going to set fire to his sister Marta's dress. I told him to do it.'

'He wouldn't be so damned stupid!' retorted Grushina.

'Of course he'll do it,' Peredonov replied with conviction. 'Brothers and sisters are always quarrelling. When I was small I was always playing nasty tricks on my sisters. I beat the little ones and ruined the older ones' dresses.'

'Not all brothers and sisters quarrel,' said Rutilov. '*I* don't quarrel with mine.'

'What do you do then? Hug and kiss them?' Peredonov asked.

'You, Ardalyon, are a swine and a scoundrel. For two pins I'd give you a punch on the nose,' Rutilov said, very calmly.

'I don't like that kind of joke,' replied Peredonov, edging away from Rutilov. He looked as if he really meant it, he thought. In actual fact there's something really sinister about his face. 'She has only one dress, and that's black,' he went on, referring to Marta.

'Vershina is going to make her a new one,' Varvara said with the utmost envy and spite. 'She'll make her whole trousseau for her. Marta's such a beauty even the horses take fright!' she said softly, looking menacingly at Murin.

'It's time you were married too,' Mrs Prepolovensky said. 'What are you waiting for, Mr Peredonov?'

The Prepolovenskys already realized that after Peredonov had received the second letter he had finally made up his mind to marry Varvara. And they too thought it was genuine. They maintained that they had been on Varvara's side from the start. But there was no sense in quarrelling with Peredonov – it was highly profitable playing cards with him. As for Genya, they'd have to wait until someone else came along. Mr Prepolovensky began, 'Of course you should get married. You'd be doing a good deed as well as pleasing the princess. Yes, the princess will be pleased that you're getting married, so you'll be obliging her and doing a good deed. That's all very good, because you'll be doing the right thing, and pleasing the princess . . .'

'I entirely agree,' said Mrs Prepolovensky.

But Mr Prepolovensky couldn't stop and when he saw that everyone was moving away from him he trapped a young civil servant and started repeating everything he had just said.

'I've decided to get married,' announced Peredonov, 'only Varvara and I don't know how to go about it. Something has to be done, but I don't know what.'

'Well, it's really quite simple,' Mrs Prepolovensky said. 'If you like, my husband and I will make all the arrangements. You won't have to worry about a thing.'

'Good,' said Peredonov, 'I accept. But you must see that everything is done properly and in style. Money is of no importance.'

'Everything will be perfect, you won't have to worry about a thing,' Mrs Prepolovensky assured him.

Peredonov continued to list his requirements. 'Some people are so stingy they have thin silver-gilt rings. I don't want anything like that. I want solid gold. Actually, I would prefer bracelets to rings – they're more expensive and look much more impressive.'

Everyone laughed.

'You can't wear bracelets for a wedding,' Mrs Prepolovensky said, faintly smiling. 'You must have a ring.'

'Why not bracelets?' Peredonov asked peevishly.

'It's just not done.'

'Well, perhaps it is,' Peredonov said sceptically. 'I'll go and see the priest. He knows best.'

Rutilov tittered. 'You'd better order some wedding belts while you're about it, Ardalyon,' he advised.

'I can't afford that,' Peredonov replied, missing the joke. 'I'm not a merchant banker. Only recently I dreamed that I was being married. I was in a velvet tailcoat and Varvara and I were both wearing golden bracelets. Behind us were two headmasters holding garlands over our heads and singing "Hallelujah".'

'I had a most interesting dream too last night,' said Volodin, 'but I'm foxed as to what it can mean. I was sitting on a throne with a golden crown and in front of me was a broad stretch of grass with nothing but flocks of sheep grazing on it and baaing! They walked – like this – and shook their heads – like this – and went baa-baa-baa!' Volodin proceeded to walk up and down the room. He shook his head, stuck his lips out and bleated. All the guests laughed. Then he found himself a seat and blissfully surveyed the scene, screwing up his eyes with pleasure and laughing his sheeplike laugh.

'Well, what happened next?' Grushina asked, winking at the others.

'That was all. Just sheep, lots and lots of them. Then I woke up.'

'A sheep has sheepish dreams,' Peredonov growled. 'It's no great shakes being tsar of the sheep!'

'I had a dream too,' Varvara told Grushina with an impish smile, 'but it's strictly for the ladies. I'll tell you when the men have gone.'

'That's very strange, Varvara, I had one like that too,' Grushina said. She giggled and winked at everyone.

'Come on, tell us. We're modest gentlemen, just like the ladies,' said Rutilov.

The other men tried to prevail upon Varvara and Grushina to tell them their dreams, but the two women only exchanged meaningful glances and laughed obscenely.

Everyone sat down to play cards. Rutilov assured the company that Peredonov was a brilliant player and Peredonov believed him. But as usual he lost and Rutilov won. As a result, Rutilov was overjoyed and his conversation became much livelier than usual.

The little demon started playing tricks on Peredonov. It would hide somewhere close by and then reappear every now and then, sticking its head out from behind a table or someone's back and then hiding again. It seemed to be waiting for something. Peredonov was terrified. The mere sight of the cards frightened him – he saw the queens double. Then he turned the queen of spades over to see if a third was hiding on the back. Rutilov said, 'Mr Peredonov's looking under his queen's petticoat!'[1]

Everyone roared with laughter.

Meanwhile the two young police clerks sat down to play Fools on their own – and a very lively game was soon under way. The winner laughed for joy and thumbed his nose at the other; the loser became very angry.

There was a smell of food. Grushina invited the guests into the dining-room. They all got up, jostling one another and behaving with exaggerated politeness. Somehow or other they took their places at the table.

'Eat up, ladies and gentlemen!' said Grushina. 'Eat until your bellies burst!'

'Eat your cake for your hostess's sake!' Murin joyfully cried. The sight of vodka and the thought that he had won put him in a very good mood.

Volodin and the two young police clerks tucked in more heartily than anyone else. They took the best pieces of pie and didn't spare the caviare.

Grushina forced a laugh and said, 'Our Pavel Volodin may be drunk, but he can still tell the difference between cake and bread.'

As if she'd bought all that caviare just for him to hog! Pretending they were for the ladies, she put all the best dishes out of his reach. Volodin didn't seem to mind and contented himself with whatever

1. Pun on rubashka, meaning 'back of a playing-card' and 'petticoat'.

was left. He'd managed to scoff much of the best food at the start and now he couldn't care less.

Peredonov looked at them munching away and it struck him that they were all laughing at him – he wondered why. He stuffed the food blindly and ravenously into his mouth, greedily and messily devouring everything he could lay his hands on.

After dinner they sat down to another game of cards. Peredonov soon got tired of losing. Throwing down the cards in disgust he said, 'To hell with you! I never have any luck. I'm fed up – Varvara, we're going home.'

Many of the others followed them.

In the hall Volodin noticed that Peredonov had a new walking-stick. Grinning, he turned it round and asked, 'Ardalyon, why are there curled fingers carved on it? What does that mean?'

Peredonov angrily snatched the stick from him, put its knob with the curled fingers carved in ebony to his nose and said, 'It means a fig[1] for you – with butter!'

'Excuse me, Ardalyon,' he said, 'I enjoy bread and butter, but not figs and butter.'

Without listening to him Peredonov carefully swathed his scarf around his neck and buttoned up his coat. Rutilov laughed and said, 'Why are you wrapping yourself up, Ardalyon? It's quite mild outside.'

'Health is more precious than anything else,' Peredonov replied.

In the street it was quiet and dark. In fact the street itself seemed to have settled down to sleep and was softly snoring. It was damp and miserable. Heavy clouds scudded across the sky. It's got so dark. Now why is that? he wondered. But he wasn't afraid, for Varvara was with him.

A fine penetrating rain was falling. All was quiet, except for the sound of the rain, which seemed to be murmuring some dreary, melancholy, incomprehensible message to Peredonov.

He felt that in nature was a true reflection of his own depression, a projection of his own fears. He was oblivious of that inner,

1. Peredonov has had a V-sign carved on the knob of his walking-stick. The word here, shish, means 'fig', in such expressions as, 'A fig for you!' 'A fig with butter!' signifies a snub, i.e. 'Damn-all for you!' But Volodin has taken the word to mean a fig, literally.

indefinable life that is in the whole of nature, that life which alone creates deep and genuine relations between man and nature. Therefore all of nature was permeated with petty human emotions in his eyes. Blinded by the illusions of personality and his alienated existence, he had no understanding of those elemental Dionysian ecstasies triumphantly echoing throughout nature. He was pathetic and blind to them – like many of us.

XXIII

The Prepolovenskys undertook all the arrangements for the wedding. It was to be held quietly, in the country, about four miles from town. Varvara didn't want to get married in town – after all, they had been living together for so many years, pretending that they were related to each other. The date was kept a secret: the Prepolovenskys spread the rumour that it would be on Friday, but in fact it was to take place on Wednesday afternoon. The idea was to stop the curious coming from town. Varvara had repeatedly told Peredonov, 'Mind you don't give the date away, Ardalyon. There're plenty who'd like to put a stop to it.'

Peredonov reluctantly gave Varvara money for the expenses, mocking her as he did so. Sometimes he would bring his walking-stick with the carved fingers on the knob and say, 'Only if you kiss the fingers will I give you some money.'

And Varvara would kiss them. 'Well, my lips won't split,' she would say.

And so the wedding date was concealed until the day itself, even from the best men, in case they let the cat out of the bag. At first Rutilov and Volodin were invited to be best men and both willingly agreed. Rutilov expected something very funny to happen, while Volodin was flattered to be asked to play such an important part in the life of such a distinguished man. Then Peredonov decided that one best man for him wasn't enough.

'One's all right for you, Varvara, but I need two. I'm very tall, so it'll be difficult for one person to keep holding the wedding wreath over my head.'

And so Peredonov invited Falastov to be his second best man.

'What the hell do we need him for?' Varvara grumbled. 'We've two already, why do we need more?'

'He wears gold-rimmed spectacles. It will look more impressive.'

On the morning of the wedding Peredonov washed, as always, in hot water, to avoid catching cold. Then he powdered himself with rouge. 'I must give myself a touch of colour every day now,' he explained. 'Otherwise they might think I am going senile and they won't make me inspector.' Varvara didn't like Peredonov using any of her make-up, but was forced to give in – and Peredonov put rouge on his cheeks. 'General Veriga paints himself to look younger,' he muttered to himself. 'How can I get married with white cheeks?'

Then, in case Volodin should attempt to change places with him, he locked himself in the bedroom and marked himself in ink with a black P on his chest, stomach, arms – and on various other places. Volodin should really be marked too. But how? He'd rub it off straight away.

Then he thought it wouldn't be a bad idea if he wore corsets, just in case he was taken for an old man if he happened to bend over in church. He asked Varvara for a pair, but they were too tight and wouldn't fasten across the middle.

'We should have bought some earlier,' he growled. 'You never think of anything.'

'And what man wears corsets?' Varvara retorted. 'Tell me that.'

'Veriga does.'

'But he's an old man, and you're in your prime, thank God.'

Peredonov looked into the mirror with a self-satisfied smile and said, 'I dare say I'll live another hundred and fifty years.'

At that moment the cat sneezed under the bed. Varvara grinned and said, 'That means it's going to come true.'

But Peredonov frowned. The cat aroused nothing but fear in him, and its sneeze was part of some evil, cunning trick. It might sneeze something it shouldn't! he thought and got under the bed to try and chase it out. The terrified animal mewed wildly, pressed back against the wall and suddenly, with a loud, piercing mew, darted between his hands and escaped from the room.

'A Chinese devil!' Peredonov swore angrily.

'Yes, it's a devil, all right,' Varvara agreed. 'It's really gone wild and never lets you stroke it. I'm *sure* it's got a devil inside.'

Early that morning the Prepolovenskys sent for the bridesmen. By ten o'clock everyone had assembled at Peredonov's. Grushina came with Sofya and her husband. The guests were served vodka and savouries. Peredonov ate very little and worried about how best to distinguish himself from Volodin. He's got curly hair, just like a sheep, he thought malevolently and suddenly realized that he too could have a special hairstyle. He rose from the table and said, 'Please carry on eating and drinking. I don't mind how much. I'm off to the barber's for a Spanish hairdo.'

'What's that?' asked Rutilov.

'Wait and see.'

When Peredonov had gone, Varvara said, 'He's been acting very strangely lately. Says he keeps on seeing devils. That's what comes of drinking all that cheap brandy, the old soak!'

'Once you're married and Mr Peredonov's an inspector he'll calm down,' Mrs Prepolovensky said with a cunning smile.

Grushina giggled. The secrecy of the marriage amused her and she felt a keen desire to throw a small spanner into the works without being implicated herself. On the evening before the wedding she had furtively told some of her friends the time and place of the wedding. Early next morning she bribed the locksmith's younger son with five copecks to wait outside the town, just where the newly-weds would pass, and tip some refuse over their heads. The boy was only too pleased to oblige and gave his solemn promise not to tell a soul. 'Don't forget how you betrayed Cherepnin the moment they started whipping you,' Grushina reminded him.

'We were fools then,' the locksmith's son replied. 'They'd have to put us on the gallows now to get anything out of us.' And to confirm his oath he ate a handful of earth, for which noble act Grushina gave him another three copecks.

At the barber's Peredonov insisted on having his hair cut by none other than the proprietor himself. A young man, who had just finished his training and who now and then borrowed books from the district library, he was just putting the finishing touches to a local squire whom Peredonov didn't know. The barber soon finished and went over to Peredonov.

'Wait until he's gone,' Peredonov said angrily.

When the squire had paid and left Peredonov sat down in front of the mirror. 'I want an extra-special haircut, in the Spanish style,' he said. 'I've got something very important on today.'

The barber's young assistant, who was standing at the door, snorted with laughter and the barber looked daggers at him. He had never been asked to do a Spanish haircut. He had no idea what it could be and doubted whether there was such a style. But the customer knew best and had to have what he asked for. As he didn't wish to display his ignorance the barber politely said, 'I'm afraid that's impossible with your hair, sir.'

'Why is that?' asked Peredonov, taking offence.

'Your hair is in a very poor condition, sir,' explained the barber. 'Very poorly nourished.'

'Do you expect me to pour beer over it?' growled Peredonov.

'No, sir!' laughed the barber, smiling amiably, 'not beer! But you must understand that your hair's too thin for a Spanish haircut.'

Peredonov felt quite shattered at the impossibility of a Spanish haircut. 'Well, cut it as you like,' he said dejectedly. I bet this barber has been bribed not to give me a special haircut. I shouldn't have said anything at home. Obviously, while he was on his way to the barber's, walking solemnly and sedately down the street, Volodin had sneaked round by the back, like a little sheep, and conspired with the barber.

'Some spray, sir?' the barber asked when he'd finished.

'Yes, mignonette, and don't be mean with it. Since you've cropped me any old how you could at least smarten it up with mignonette.'

'I'm very sorry, sir, but we don't have any mignonette,' the barber said in an embarrassed voice. 'Would you like opoponax?'

'You can't do anything right!' Peredonov said dolefully. 'Yes, hurry up and spray me with whatever you've got.'

Peredonov returned in a terrible temper. It was a windy day. Gates banged everywhere and seemed to be laughing and yawning. Peredonov looked at them dejectedly. How could he face the journey? Everything, however, had been arranged.

The three carriages were waiting. They had to leave at once, in order not to attract attention – if that happened crowds of people curious to see the wedding would flock to the church. They settled in their seats and the carriages drove off – Peredonov with Varvara, the Prepolovenskys with Rutilov, and Grushina with the men on the bride's side.

In the square a huge cloud of dust was rising and the noise of axes could be heard. At least, so it seemed to Peredonov. Through the dust he could just glimpse a great wooden wall: they were building a fortress. Everywhere were savage-looking peasants, dressed in red shirts and going about their work grimly and silently.

The carriages sped across the square and the terrible vision was lost: Peredonov looked back in horror, but now there was no trace of peasants or fortress. He decided not to tell a soul about what he had seen.

All the way to the church he felt utterly depressed. Everything looked at him with hostile eyes, everything held a hidden menace. The sky was overcast and the wind blew right in his face and seemed to be sighing about something. The trees gave no shade – they seemed to have kept it all for themselves.

The dust rose like a long grey semi-transparent serpent. For some reason the sun had gone in behind the clouds – was it spying on him? The road was very bumpy. Bushes, copses, clearings came unexpectedly into view from behind small hills; streams ran beneath echoing arched wooden bridges.

'The eyebird's just flown by,' Peredonov gloomily remarked, peering into the misty white expanse of the heavens. 'It consists of just one eye, two wings – nothing else.'

Varvara grinned. She thought that Peredonov was still drunk, but she didn't pick a quarrel with him: he might lose his temper and call off the wedding.

Rutilov's four sisters were already at the church. They had hidden themselves in a dark corner, behind a pillar. Peredonov did not see them at first, but later, during the actual ceremony when they came out of their hiding-place he was terrified that they might insist he throw Varvara out of the church and take one of them instead. But they made no such demand. All they did was laugh the whole time, softly at first, but as their laughter steadily grew louder, more spiteful, Peredonov thought a hundred furies were laughing in his ears. Except for one or two old women there were only the wedding guests in the church. And it was just as well, for

Peredonov behaved most peculiarly and ridiculously. He yawned, muttered under his breath, nudged Varvara and constantly complained that the whole church stank of incense, wax and peasants.

'Those sisters of yours are always laughing,' he growled at Rutilov. 'They'll do themselves an injury one of these days.'

In addition, the little demon was being very troublesome. This time it had covered itself with dirt and dust and kept hiding under the priest's robes.

Varvara and Grushina were highly amused by the pomp and ceremony of the service and giggled the whole time. The passage about a woman cleaving to her husband was a particular source of merriment. Rutilov giggled too – he considered it his duty to amuse the ladies at all times and places. Volodin on the other hand behaved irreproachably, kept crossing himself and maintained an expression of the utmost seriousness. For him the ceremony was nothing but a long-established ritual, the sole purpose of which was to create a feeling of well-being and to ease the conscience. Every Sunday he would go to church and be absolved of his sins; and then, after sinning again, would repent the following week and return to be absolved once more. All this was delightfully convenient – all the more so, since outside the church he didn't have to bother about religious matters at all and could live according to a completely different set of moral principles.

The ceremony had just finished and the congregation were still in the church when something totally unexpected happened. Into the church burst a crowd of drunks – it was Murin and company.

Murin, drab and dishevelled as ever, heartily embraced Peredonov and shouted, 'You can't hide anything from us, old man! You thought you'd keep it from us, you old rogue! And we're supposed to be bosom pals!'

And other recriminations followed: 'Rotter for not inviting us!', 'But we're here all the same!', 'We still found out!' and so on.

The new arrivals all embraced and congratulated Peredonov.

'We would have given you the pleasure of our company earlier if we hadn't got drunk and lost the way,' Murin said.

Peredonov scowled and ignored their congratulations. He was absolutely fuming. Everyone's persecuting me, he thought dejectedly. 'You might at least have crossed yourselves!' he snarled, 'Or perhaps you've something nasty in mind?'

The guests crossed themselves, guffawed and blasphemed. The young clerks particularly distinguished themselves in this until the deacon rebuked them and told them to stop.

Among the visitors was a young man with a red moustache whom Peredonov had never set eyes on before. He was remarkably like a cat. Perhaps it was their own cat transformed? That would explain why he was always sniffing about – he hadn't got rid of his feline habits.

'Who told you about the wedding?' Varvara angrily asked the intruders.

'Oh, some nice young woman,' Murin replied, 'but I can't remember her name for the life of me.'

Grushina turned and winked at them. Murin and company chuckled to themselves, but didn't give her away. Murin said, 'Whether you like it or not, Ardalyon, we're coming to your place to drink to your health and we want champagne. Don't be such a skinflint! You can't treat bosom pals like this! Fancy trying to get married on the sly!'

The sun was setting when the newly married couple drove from the church, but the sky was still ablaze with a golden light. This didn't please Peredonov at all. 'Someone's been sticking pieces of gold to the sky and they're already falling off. What a terrible waste!'

Outside town the locksmith's sons, together with a crowd of street urchins, greeted them with hoots and jeers. Peredonov trembled with fear. Varvara swore violently, spat at them and stuck two fingers up. The other guests and bridesmen thought it a huge joke.

At last they reached the house. Everyone poured in, whistling and making a dreadful racket. First champagne and then vodka were consumed, after which they all sat down to cards. The drunken orgy lasted the whole night. The exultant Varvara danced and got terribly drunk. Peredonov was exultant too – no one had tried to take his place. As always, the guests treated Varvara like the whore she was, but she was well aware that this was in the order of things.

There was little change in the Peredonovs' way of life after the wedding. The only marked difference was Varvara's increased confidence and independence. Although, through long habit, she was still afraid of Peredonov, she didn't run around so much for him now. He still shouted at her – also through long habit – and sometimes he beat her. But even he sensed that she had acquired much more confidence with her new status, and this depressed him utterly. He thought that the reason she didn't fear him so much as before was that she was even more determined to carry out her diabolical plan to get rid of him and replace him with Volodin. I must be on my guard the whole time, he concluded.

Varvara's triumph was complete. Together with Peredonov she called on all the ladies of the town – even those she didn't know very well – and on each occasion she behaved with ridiculous affectation and gaucheness. She was received everywhere, although with much astonishment in many houses. For these visits she had ordered, in good time, a new hat from the best milliner in town, and she was enraptured with the large bright flowers that profusely adorned it.

They began with the headmaster's wife, then they went to see the wife of the marshal of the nobility.

On the same day that the Peredonovs went to the Khripachs' (the Rutilovs, needless to say, had known about this beforehand) the Rutilov sisters, curious to see how Varvara would behave, decided to call on Mrs Khripach, and soon afterwards the Peredonovs arrived. Varvara curtseyed to the headmaster's wife and in a more than usually jarring voice said, 'So, here we are. I hope you'll be nice to us!'

'Charmed, I'm sure,' replied the headmaster's wife stiffly as she showed Varvara to the sofa.

Delighted at this reception, Varvara spread her rustling green dress out wide as she sat down and tried to hide her embarrassment by pretending to be at ease.

'Once I was a mamzell, but now I'm a madam! Did you know we're namesakes? But we've never visited one another. Before I was married I used to stay at home most of the time. That was no life! But now Ardalyon and I intend being a lot more sociable. You're always welcome at our place, and we'll come and see you, moosyure to moosyure, madam to madam!'

'But from what I hear you won't be living here much longer,' the headmaster's wife said. 'I believe your husband's going to be transferred.'

'Yes, we're just waiting for the papers. But until then we have to show ourselves a little more.'

Varvara hoped against hope that Peredonov might get the job after all. She had written to the princess immediately after the wedding, but up to now had received no answer. So she decided to write again, towards the New Year.

'And you led us all to believe you'd marry Pylnikov's sister,' Lyudmila said.

'You should know by now I couldn't marry just anyone,' Peredonov angrily replied. 'I need someone with influence.'

'All the same why didn't it work out with Mademoiselle Pylnikov?' Lyudmila teased. 'Weren't you courting her? And didn't she refuse you?'

'She did, but I'll show her up for what she is,' Peredonov growled.

'Mr Peredonov has what you might call an *idée fixe*,' the headmaster said with a dry little laugh.

XXIV

The Peredonovs' cat had been acting like a creature demented. It kept hissing, it didn't come when called and was completely out of control. Sometimes Peredonov pronounced exorcisms over it. Does that do any good? he wondered. It's the strong electric charge in the fur that's at the root of the trouble.

One day he took it into his head to have the cat shorn. No sooner thought of than done. Varvara was out – she had gone to Grushina's with a bottle of cherry brandy in her pocket – so no one could interfere. Peredonov tied the cat to a strong cord, having made a collar out of a handkerchief, and took it off to the barber's. The poor animal mewed savagely, struggled and kept refusing to budge. Sometimes it threw itself in despair at Peredonov, who pushed it away with a stick. A crowd of jeering and hooting boys followed close behind. Passers-by stopped and stared and people looked out of their windows to see what the noise was. Peredonov remorselessly dragged the cat along, quite unperturbed. Somehow he got it there and he told the barber, 'I'd like its fur cut – and the shorter the better!'

The boys crowded the entrance to the shop, roaring with laughter and making funny faces. The barber was furious and went red in the face. In a wavering voice he said, 'I'm very sorry, sir, but we don't do such things here. And whoever heard of shaving a cat? If it's the latest fashion it certainly hasn't reached us yet.'

Peredonov listened in blank astonishment. 'Why don't you admit you can't do it – charlatan!' he cried. And he walked out of the shop, dragging the screeching cat. On the way back he pondered dejectedly the fact that no one wanted to help him and that everywhere people were laughing at him. His heart was heavy with sadness.

Peredonov went to the club with Volodin and Rutilov for a game of billiards, but an embarrassed marker explained as soon as they arrived, 'I'm very sorry, but you can't play today, gentlemen.'

'Why not?' snarled Peredonov. 'It's *us*, and you're telling us we can't play?'

'I'm most terribly sorry, sir, but there aren't any balls.'

'Someone lifted them while he wasn't looking, the dozy devil,' said the barman in a menacing voice as he leaned across the counter.

The marker trembled and suddenly his red ears twitched like a hare's. 'They've been stolen, sir,' he whispered.

Peredonov cried out in alarm, 'Well, tell us who took them!'

'We can't say, sir. There didn't seem to be anyone around at the time and then, all of a sudden, I noticed that all the balls had gone!'

Rutilov sniggered and exclaimed, 'A fine story!'

Volodin looked hurt and told the marker, 'If people start stealing your billiard-balls and you happen to be in another place at the time, then you ought to have provided others right away, so that we have something to play with. We came here to play billiards – how can we play without any balls?'

'Stop whining, Pavlusha,' Peredonov said. 'It's sickening enough as it is.' Then he turned to the marker and said, 'Now you go and look for them, as we want to play. Without fail. In the meantime you can bring us three beers.'

They drank their beer but soon grew bored. The balls couldn't be found anywhere. They swore at one another and cursed the marker, who felt it was all his fault and didn't say a word.

For Peredonov the theft was a dirty new trick on the part of his enemies. Why did they do it? he thought wearily, uncomprehendingly.

He went into the gardens and sat down on a bench near the pond. It was the first time he'd sat there. He stared blankly into the still green water. Volodin sat beside him, sharing his grief and looking abjectly into the pond with his sheeplike eyes.

'Why is this mirror so dirty, Pavlushka?' Peredonov asked, pointing his walking-stick at the water.

Volodin grinned and replied, 'It's not a mirror, Ardalyon, it's a pond. As there's no wind to ruffle the surface, you can see the trees in it. That's why it looks like a mirror.'

Peredonov looked up. Beyond the pond was a high fence, which separated the gardens from the street. 'Why's that cat sitting there?' he asked.

Volodin looked in the same direction and laughed out loud. 'There was one, but it's gone now.'

In fact there had been no cat. That terrible tireless enemy, with its green eyes full of evil cunning, was nothing but a figment of his imagination.

Peredonov's thoughts turned to the lost billiard-balls. Who could have wanted them? Had the little demon swallowed them? No, I haven't seen it today, he thought. I bet it's gorged itself on them and gone somewhere to sleep it off.

He trudged wearily homewards.

The sun was sinking. A small rain-cloud was wandering across the sky, gliding stealthily and silently (clouds have soft shoes!) – it was spying on him. On its dark edges was a faint, enigmatic silver light. Above the stream that flowed between the gardens and the town, shadows of houses and bushes quivered and whispered to each other, as if they were searching for someone. And on the earth, in that dark and perpetually hostile town, lived only evil, mocking people. Everything conspired in hostility towards Peredonov. Dogs laughed at him, people barked.

The ladies of the town began to visit Varvara. Some, filled with curiosity, had come two or three days after the wedding to see the house. Others didn't come until a week later. And some, like Vershina, didn't come at all.

Every day the Peredonovs anxiously awaited return visits and noted on a piece of paper those who hadn't yet been. They were particularly impatient about the headmaster and his wife and were on tenterhooks the whole time in case they should suddenly turn up.

A week went by and still the Khripachs didn't come. Varvara became terribly bad-tempered and kept cursing. All this waiting plunged Peredonov into a really deep depression. His eyes lost their fire and at times became like those of a corpse, vacant and blank. He was tormented by the most absurd fears. For no apparent reason even the simplest object became a source of terror. For several days now he had been obsessed with and tormented by the thought that someone might cut his throat. Anything sharp terrified him and he hid all the knives and forks in the house. Perhaps they've been bewitched. I could easily cut my own throat on them! he thought. And as a result they didn't have any meat for a whole week but made do with cabbage soup and gruel instead.

'What do we need knives for?' he asked Varvara. 'Chinamen eat with chopsticks, you know.'

Varvara wanted to avenge the torments Peredonov had made her suffer before the wedding and whenever possible she confirmed his suspicions, telling him he wasn't imagining things for nothing. More than once she told him that he had many enemies: indeed, why shouldn't people be jealous of him? And more than once she had teased him by saying that there was no doubt at all that people had informed against him, both to the authorities and the princess herself. She took much delight in seeing how frightened he was.

Soon it became apparent to Peredonov that the princess was dissatisfied with him. Surely she could have sent him an icon, or some cake as a wedding present? He racked his brains as to how he could please her. But how? By telling her lies? By slandering someone, spreading malicious gossip, reporting someone to the police? All women loved scandal, so it might not be a bad idea to invent some salacious story about Varvara – he could even make it amusing – and write to her about it. She would be tickled pink and he would get the job. But he couldn't bring himself to write anything of the sort – what a terrible thought, writing to the princess in person! And so the plan was forgotten.

When Peredonov was entertaining, guests of no particular importance had to make do with vodka and the cheapest port. But for the headmaster he bought a three-rouble bottle of madeira. He was convinced that this was a lot of money for madeira, so he kept it in the bedroom and would show it to less fortunate guests with the words, 'It's reserved for the headmaster.'

Once, when Rutilov and Volodin were present, Peredonov showed them the madeira.

'We can't tell what it's like by just looking at it,' Rutilov laughed. 'Come on, give us some of your expensive madeira!'

'The idea!' Peredonov angrily replied. 'And what shall I give the headmaster?'

'He can make do with a glass of vodka,' Rutilov said.

'Headmasters don't drink vodka! Headmasters drink *madeira*!' Peredonov reasoned.

'But supposing he wants vodka?' Rutilov persisted.

'You don't really think that an important person like him would drink vodka, do you?' Peredonov replied confidently.

'Give us some of that madeira, all the same,' Rutilov said.

But Peredonov hastily took the bottle away and they could hear him locking the little cupboard where he kept his wine. When he returned he started talking about the princess – just to change the subject.

'As for the princess,' he said gloomily, 'she used to sell rotten apples in the market. God knows how she managed to hook a prince!'

Rutilov guffawed. 'So princes go shopping in markets, do they?'

'She knew how to catch him all right, don't you worry,' Peredonov said.

'You can't expect us to believe that cock-and-bull story,' said Rutilov. 'The princess is a real lady.'

Peredonov glared at him and thought, He's standing up for her. That can only mean he's in league with her. She must have bewitched him – even though she lives as far away as St Petersburg.

The little demon darted around, silently laughing and convulsed with mirth. Its presence set a whole train of alarming thoughts in motion. Peredonov nervously looked around and whispered, 'In every town there's an officer from the secret police. During the day he doesn't wear uniform and he works in the civil service, or does business deals or something. But at night, when everyone's asleep, he puts on a blue uniform and in two seconds he's a police officer.'

'Why does he put on a uniform?' Volodin inquired in a business-like voice.

'No one dares appear before the authorities without one. He'd get flogged for it,' Peredonov explained.

Volodin sniggered. Peredonov went close up to him and whispered, 'And sometimes he even becomes a werewolf. And you're mistaken if you think it's simply a cat we have in the house. It's really a police officer in disguise. No one can hide from a cat – it can hear everything you say.'

After about two weeks the headmaster's wife finally decided to pay them a visit. She came with her husband one day in the week, at four o'clock in the afternoon. She had put on one of her best dresses and smelled sweetly of violets. The Peredonovs were very much taken by surprise, as they had been expecting the Khripachs on a Sunday, and somewhat earlier in the day. They got into a dreadful panic. Varvara was in the kitchen at the time, half dressed and filthy. She dashed off to get changed, while Peredonov received the guests looking as if he had just got out of bed.

'She won't be long,' he mumbled. 'She's just changing. She's been cooking. We've a new maid, you know, and that stupid cow doesn't know how to do things our way yet.'

Varvara soon appeared in some old dress she'd hurriedly put on. She was very red in the face and seemed frightened. She held out a dirty, sweaty hand to the visitors. In a trembling voice she said, 'I'm so sorry to have kept you waiting, we didn't expect you on a weekday.'

'I seldom go out on a Sunday,' Mrs Khripach said. 'There are too many drunks on the streets. I usually let the servants have the day off then.'

After awkward beginnings the conversation got under way. Varavara was somewhat encouraged by the headmaster's wife's rather condescending, but none the less friendly, attitude. In fact

Mrs Khripach spoke to her as if she were addressing a repentant sinner who had to be treated kindly, but on whom one could nevertheless soil one's hands. She gave Varvara a few little words of advice, as if in passing, about clothes and furniture.

Varvara did her best to please Mrs Khripach, but her red hands and chapped lips kept trembling with fear. This had a somewhat inhibiting effect on Mrs Khripach, so she tried to be even more friendly. However, an involuntary feeling of revulsion took possession of her. By her whole attitude she tried to give Varvara to understand that there could never be any intimate friendship between the two of them. But she did this with such grace and charm that Varvara completely misunderstood and concluded that she and the headmaster's wife would be the greatest of friends.

Khripach felt like a fish out of water, although he skilfully and bravely concealed the fact. He refused the madeira: he wasn't in the habit of drinking wine so early in the day, he said. They discussed the latest town gossip, forthcoming staff changes in the district court. It was only too apparent, however, that he and Peredonov moved in completely different circles.

They didn't stay long and Varvara was delighted when they left: it had been short and sweet. As she changed she gaily remarked, 'Well, thank God they've gone. I just didn't know what to say to them. That's how it is with people you don't know very well – you never know what line to take with them.'

Suddenly she remembered that when the Khripachs had said goodbye they hadn't invited them back. At first this disturbed her, but then she pointed out, 'They'll send us an invitation, giving the time and date. People like them do everything in their own sweet time. It might be a good idea if I took up French, I just haven't a clue how to speak it.'

When she arrived home the headmaster's wife told her husband, 'What a pathetic, dreadfully vulgar woman! It's quite impossible to treat her as an equal. There's nothing about her that corresponds with her position.'

'She corresponds with her husband in every way! I can't wait until they remove him.'

After the wedding Varvara had begun to drink for the sheer joy of it, and her constant companion was Grushina. Once, when she'd had a drop too much and Mrs Prepolovensky was there, she let slip about the letter. She didn't tell all, but gave quite enough away. It was enough for the cunning Sofya Prepolovensky: suddenly the truth dawned on her and she blamed herself for not having guessed right away. She told Vershina – in strict confidence of course – about the forged letters and as a result the whole town soon knew all about it.

Whenever Mrs Prepolovensky met Peredonov she couldn't help laughing at his credulity and would say, 'How gullible you are, Mr Peredonov.'

'Not at all,' he would reply. 'I was at university, you know.'

'You may have been. But that doesn't alter the fact that it's easy for anyone to take you in.'

'*I* can fool anyone if I want to,' Peredonov would reply.

Mrs Prepolovensky would smile and leave. Peredonov would watch her go in blank bewilderment. What can she mean? he'd wonder. It must be out of spite – that's it! Of course, *everyone* was his enemy. And he would stick out two fingers after her. 'You'll get nothing out of me,' he said to console himself. But he was tormented with fear.

There was little substance to these hints of Mrs Prepolovensky's. Obviously she didn't want to tell him the whole truth, in so many words. Why should she pick a quarrel with Varvara? From time to time she sent him anonymous letters in which the hints grew stronger. But still Peredonov didn't catch on.

In one letter she wrote. *Why don't you have a look round? Perhaps the princess who wrote those letters is living quite near you.*

Peredonov took this to mean that the princess had in fact come all the way from St Petersburg to keep an eye on him. Obviously she's fallen for me and wants to take me away from Varvara, he thought. And these letters both frightened and angered Peredonov. So he kept asking Varvara, 'Where's the princess? I hear she's in town.'

Avenging herself for her previous sufferings, Varvara tormented him with vague hints, taunts and nasty cowardly *double entendres*. With an impudent smile, and in the uncertain voice of someone who lies without much hope of being believed, she would tell him, 'How on earth should I know where she lives!'

'You're lying! You do know!' Peredonov said in horror.

He didn't know what to believe – the message conveyed by her words, or the lying tone of voice in which they were spoken. And this, like everything he didn't understand, terrified him.

'Well, whatever next!' Varvara retorted. 'Perhaps she's visiting from St Petersburg. She doesn't have to ask my permission.'

'So perhaps she's really here?' Peredonov asked timidly.

'Yes, perhaps she's really here,' Varvara replied, mimicking him. 'She's fallen for you and she's come to feast her eyes on you.'

'You're lying! Do you think she'd fall in love with *me*?'

Varvara gave a spiteful laugh.

From that time onwards Peredonov kept a close lookout for the princess. Sometimes he thought that she was looking through the window, listening at the keyhole, or whispering to Varvara.

The days went by and still the eagerly awaited papers didn't come, nor did he hear anything privately. He did not dare ask the princess herself – Varvara kept frightening him off by telling him that she was very important. Besides, he himself felt that if he wrote to her in person there could be very nasty consequences. He couldn't say exactly *what* they would do to him if the princess should complain, but the thought itself was enough to frighten the wits out of him.

'Surely you know what aristocrats are like?' Varvara said. 'Just be patient. They'll do what's necessary. And you'd only get her back up by reminding her. Aristocrats think a lot of themselves. Very proud they are – and they like to be trusted. No, you'd only make matters worse.'

And for the moment Peredonov believed her. But he was still furious with the princess. At times he even thought that she might report him, just to free herself of her obligations. Or perhaps she might do it because she was angry with him for marrying Varvara, when she herself was in love with him. That explained why she had planted spies all around him – so many that they gave him no breathing-space at all. They were constantly following him. Not for nothing was she so distinguished – she could do anything she liked with him. Out of sheer spite he began to invent the most absurd lies about her. He told Rutilov and Volodin that he had been her lover and that he had been generously rewarded for his services. 'Only I've spent it all on drink,' he said. 'What the hell do I need the money for? What's more, she promised me a life pension, but she didn't keep her word.'

'And would you have accepted it, anyway?' Rutilov tittered.

Peredonov was silent: he didn't understand the question. Volodin answered for him, most sensibly, 'Why shouldn't you take the money if she's rich? She had her pleasure, so she ought to pay for it.'

'I wouldn't care if she were anything to look at,' Peredonov said wearily. 'She's covered in spots and she's snub-nosed. If she hadn't paid me so well at the time I wouldn't have even deigned to spit in the old she-devil's face. But she must get me that job.'

'You're lying, Ardalyon,' Rutilov said.

'So I'm lying, am I? Do you really think she paid me for nothing? She's jealous of Varvara. That's why she's taking so long about the job.'

Peredonov had no qualms at all about pretending that the princess had paid him for his services. Volodin was a ready audience and the absurdities and contradictions in Peredonov's stories completely escaped him. Rutilov, though, in spite of his objections, still thought that there's no smoke without fire and that there really was something between the two.

'She's as old as the hills,' Peredonov said with conviction, as if it were an established fact. 'But please don't tell a soul – I'd be in deep trouble if she got to hear of it. She smothers herself with mascara and tries to make herself look as young as a piglet by injecting herself with something. You'd never tell how old she is. She must be a hundred.'

Volodin nodded and smacked his lips. He believed every word.

It turned out that on the day after this conversation Peredonov happened to read Krylov's fable 'The Liar'[1] in class. For several days afterwards he was too frightened to cross the town bridge and went by boat instead – you never know, bridges can collapse.

'I was telling you the truth about the princess, only the bridge might suddenly not believe me and just collapse to hell,' he explained to Volodin.

---

1. This fable features a bridge that allows no liars to cross it, tossing them into the water.

XXV

Rumours about the forged letters spread like wildfire through the town and were a constant source of gossip and amusement. Almost everyone praised Varvara and was glad to see Peredonov made to look a complete fool. And all those who actually saw the letters unanimously affirmed that they had guessed the truth from the start.

The Vershina household in particular had good reason to gloat. Although Marta was going to marry Murin, she had still been turned down by Peredonov; Vershina would have liked Murin for herself, but had to surrender him to Marta; and Vladya had his own delicate reasons for hating Peredonov and rejoicing in his failure. Although he was annoyed that Peredonov was still teaching at the school, this was more than compensated for by the news that Peredonov had been duped. Moreover, it was constantly rumoured among the boys that the headmaster had informed the director of district schools that Peredonov had lost his reason. Soon they would be sending someone down to officially certify him and then he'd be put away somewhere.

Whenever Varvara happened to meet any of her friends, they made it perfectly clear by the way they winked and by the obscene jokes they made that they knew all about the forgery. She would smile at them brazenly and would neither confirm nor deny it, not wishing to get into an argument with them.

Others, however, gave Grushina to understand that they knew about her part in the forgery. She was very alarmed at this and told Varvara off for having let the cat out of the bag. Varvara only grinned and reassured her. 'Don't be so silly! As if I would tell anyone!'

'Well, how does the whole world know about it?' Grushina said excitedly. 'I wouldn't be so silly as to tell anyone.'

'And *I* didn't tell anyone,' Varvara protested.

'You'd better give me the letter,' Grushina insisted. 'He might examine it more carefully this time and then he'd see it's a forgery from the writing.'

'Let him find out!' Varvara snapped. 'I'd like to see the expression on that idiot's face!'

At this point Grushina's different-sized eyes flashed and she shouted, 'It's all right for you to talk, you've got what you wanted, while I'll end up in prison because of you! No, do whatever else you like, but give me that letter. Peredonov could get a divorce with it, you know.'

'That's nonsense!' Varvara exclaimed, standing before her quite brazenly with hands on hips. 'Even if you shout it in the market, nothing can break up our marriage.'

'It isn't nonsense!' cried Grushina. 'There's no law that says you can marry by false pretences. If he takes it to the authorities, it would go to the Senate, and they'd grant him a divorce.'

Varvara was frightened at this and said, 'Don't lose your temper, I'll give you the letter. Don't be scared – I won't give you away. Do you think I'd be such a bitch? I have a soul too!'

'What's it got to do with souls?' Grushina rudely replied. 'There's no such thing, anyway. Whether you're a dog or man, you only have breath, but no soul. You live your life and that's that!'

Varvara decided that she would have to steal the letter, although this would be difficult. But Grushina kept pressing her. There was only one hope: to catch Peredonov the next time he was drunk and steal it then. He'd been drinking a lot recently and often turned up inebriated at school, where he said such shameless things that even the worst boys were disgusted.

One day Peredonov returned from the billiard-rooms more drunk than usual: they had been toasting the new balls. But not once did he let the letter out of his sight, and after somehow managing to undress he stuffed it under his pillow.

He slept fitfully but deeply, and in his delirium talked aloud about something terrible and monstrous that scared the wits out of Varvara. She comforted herself with the thought that she was safe as long as he didn't wake up. She then tried to see if nudging would wake him but he only muttered something unintelligible, cursed violently but didn't wake up. She lit a candle and carefully placed it where the light would not fall on his eyes. Numb with terror, she got out of bed and slowly inched her hand under Peredonov's pillow. The wallet wasn't very far away, but for a long time it kept slipping out of her fingers. The candle burned dimly and flickered, casting frightening shadows over the walls and the bed – they darted about like murderous little devils. The air was heavy with the smell of stale vodka and the whole room was filled with snoring and the sound of drunken delirium. That place was the very incarnation of a nightmare.

With trembling hands she pulled the letter out and replaced the wallet. When Peredonov woke up in the morning he automatically felt for the letter and when he discovered that it was gone he cried out in horror, 'Varvara, where's the letter?'

Varvara was terribly frightened but concealed her terror and told him, 'How do you expect me to know, Ardalyon? You keep showing it to everyone, so you must have dropped it somewhere. Or perhaps one of those friends you go carousing with at night has stolen it?' Peredonov was certain one of his enemies was the thief, most likely Volodin. Now he had the letter all the official papers would fall into his clutches, he would be appointed inspector in his place – and Peredonov would be left a penniless dupe.

So he decided to defend himself. Every day he drew up a report about his enemies: Vershina, the Rutilovs, Volodin and his fellow teachers, all of whom were after the same job it seemed. In the evenings he took these reports to Rubovsky.

The police officer lived quite close to the school in an open place by the square. Many people could see Peredonov going up to the house from their windows, but he was sure he wouldn't be noticed if he crept up by the back door with his notebook under his coat. Anyone could see at once that he was hiding something. If he had to shake hands with someone he kept hold of the papers under his coat with his left hand. He was sure no one would guess he was hiding anything and if anyone asked where he was going he told some clumsy lie which satisfied only himself.

'They're all traitors,' he explained to Rubovsky. 'They pretend to be friends so they'll have a better chance of betraying me. But what they don't know is that I have sufficient information to have them all sent to Siberia.'

Rubovsky listened without saying a word. He sent the first denunciation, which was obviously quite absurd, to the headmaster. He did the same with some later ones, but others he kept back just in case he should need them later. The headmaster then wrote to the director of national schools that Peredonov was showing unmistakable signs of severe mental disturbance.

At home Peredonov constantly heard rustlings – unbroken, tiresome, mocking. Mournfully he complained to Varvara, 'Someone's walking around on tiptoe, this house is swarming with spies. You're not taking proper care of me, Varvara!'

Varvara didn't understand one word of Peredonov's ravings. She sometimes taunted him and sometimes felt terribly scared. 'God knows what you can see when you're drunk,' she said spitefully and apprehensively.

The door into the hall seemed particularly suspicious: it did not shut tightly and the little gap seemed to hint that something was lurking there, hiding. Could it be the jack of clubs spying on him? An eye gleamed there, evil and piercing.

The cat followed him everywhere with its staring green eyes. Now and then it winked and then mewed terrifyingly. Obviously it was just waiting for the chance to catch Peredonov off guard, but so far it hadn't succeeded and was venting its anger. He tried to ward it off by spitting, but still it followed him.

The little demon ran squeaking under the chairs and into every corner. It was filthy, repulsive, evil-smelling and terrifying. There was no doubt that it was Peredonov's mortal enemy and had appeared on the scene just for him: it had never even existed before. It had been created and then a spell had been cast over it. And there it was, a fantastic creature which could take many shapes and which was born to terrify and destroy him.

It followed him everywhere, deceiving and mocking him. It would roll over the floor or turn into a rag, a ribbon, a twig, a flag, a small cloud, a dog, a cloud of dust in the street. Everywhere it crawled or ran after him to weary and exhaust him with its quaking dance. If only someone could rid him of it with a magic charm or deal it a swingeing blow to the head. But he had no friends here, no one would come to his rescue. He must find a way before that evil creature destroyed him.

And at last he thought of a way: he smeared the whole floor with glue so that the demon would get stuck. Unfortunately all that did stick were the soles of Varvara's shoes and the hems of her dresses, and the demon gaily rolled on, shrilly laughing. Varvara cursed him to high heaven.

Peredonov was gradually being worn down by his constant dread of persecution and he became more and more submerged in a wildly illusory world. One could see it in his face, which had become as immobile as a mask, with horror written all over it.

He no longer went to play billiards in the evenings. After dinner he would shut himself in the bedroom and barricade the door with chairs and tables, and he would try and ward off evil by repeating exorcisms and crossing himself. Then he would sit down and write reports about anyone he could think of. He wrote denunciations not only of people, but of the four queens in the pack of cards. As soon as he had finished he would take his reports straight to the district police officer. All his evenings were spent in this way.

Everywhere he looked he could see kings, queens and jacks strutting about like real people. Even the humbler cards took to parading themselves. They were people with bright buttons – schoolboys and policemen. Then there was the fat ace of spades, so fat it seemed all belly. Sometimes the cards turned into people he knew, and sometimes living people mingled with these weird spectres.

Peredonov was convinced that the jack of clubs was hiding behind the door and that it had the power and authority of a policeman and could whisk him away somewhere, perhaps to some grim gaol. And beneath the table sat the little demon. Peredonov was too scared to look there – or behind the door . . .

The elusive boyish eights in the pack mocked him – they were really schoolboys who had turned into playing-cards. They raised their legs with strange lifeless movements, like the arms of a pair of dividers, only their legs were covered with hair and for feet they had hoofs. In place of tails they had birch twigs and each time they swished them they whistled and shrieked out loud. The demon grunted from under the table, highly amused at their antics.

It infuriated Peredonov to think that the demon wouldn't have dared enter the house of a more important official. It wouldn't be allowed past the front door, he thought enviously. The footmen would have driven it off with mops.

At last Peredonov could stand the demon's evil, shrill, mocking laugh no longer. He fetched a chopper from the kitchen and with one mighty blow split the table in half. The demon squealed pitifully and malevolently, rushed out and rolled away. A shiver ran down Peredonov's spine. It might bite me, he thought. He shrieked with terror and sat down. The little demon had peacefully disappeared – but not for long . . .

Sometimes Peredonov would take the cards and savagely poke out the heads of the court cards with a penknife – the queens in particular. Whilst decapitating the kings he would keep looking round, in case someone saw him and charged him with treason. But even these purges didn't help for long. Guests brought new packs, which once more became a hiding-place for evil spies.

Peredonov had already convinced himself that he was a deadly enemy of the State. Indeed, he imagined that he had been under police surveillance from his student days. This was why they were still following him and this both horrified him and made him feel important.

The wind suddenly rustled the wallpaper. It flapped with a quiet, sinister sound and dim half-shadows crept over its bright patterns. There's a spy hiding there, behind the paper, he thought dejectedly. What wicked people! That explains why they hung the paper so loosely, so that some wafer-thin, cunning, patient spy would have room to hide. It's an old trick. He had dim recollections about someone who had got what he deserved for hiding behind wallpaper – he had been stabbed with a dagger – or was it an awl?

He immediately went out to buy an awl. When he returned, the wallpaper was still stirring and flapping in the wind – perhaps that spy was trying to creep further into the wall as he sensed the danger. A shadow jumped up to the ceiling and danced about menacingly.

Boiling with rage, Peredonov made a swift thrust at the paper with the awl. A shudder ran all along the wall. He gave a howl of triumph and started dancing about the room, waving the awl.

Then Varvara came in. 'What's this, dancing on your own, Ardalyon?' she asked with her usual stupid brazen grin.

'I've killed a beetle,' Peredonov gloomily explained.

His eyes shone in wild triumph. Only one thing troubled him: the terrible smell. It was the executed spy stinking behind the wallpaper as he rotted away. He trembled with fear and exultation: he had killed his enemy! With this murder his heart was hardened beyond redemption. It wasn't a murder but to Peredonov it seemed so. Mad terror had forged in him a readiness to commit crime.

And now the deep, unconscious notion of some future crime that lurked in the lower strata of his spiritual life, a tormenting urge to commit murder, oppressed his depraved will. This urge, still alive many generations after Cain of old, found satisfaction in smashing and ruining things, in chopping with an axe, in cutting with a knife, in felling trees in the garden to prevent spies from peering out from behind them. And that ancient demon, the spirit of primeval chaos and confusion, rejoiced in the destruction of things, while a lunatic's wild eyes reflected the horror of some monstrous death agonies.

Again and again the same illusions returned to torment him. Varvara, enjoying her fun at Peredonov's expense, would sometimes creep up to the room where Peredonov was sitting and whisper through the keyhole in some disguised voice. Peredonov would be scared stiff and tiptoe to the door to catch the enemy, only to find Varvara.

'Who were you whispering to?' he would ask miserably.

'Why, you're imagining things, Ardalyon,' she would reply with a grin.

'Not everything is imaginary,' he would wearily mutter. 'There is some truth in this world.'

Yes, even Peredonov was striving towards the truth, according to the universal law of all conscious life, and the effort exhausted him. He himself didn't realize that he was seeking the truth, like everyone else, therefore he was plagued with fear and anxiety. He couldn't find the truth for himself and so he was becoming caught in the toils – and perishing.

Even Peredonov's friends now began to laugh at him for being taken in as he had been.

People often spoke about the deception to his face, with that cruelty towards the weak so typical of this town. Mrs Prepolovensky, for example, asked with a crafty smile, 'How is it you haven't taken up your new appointment yet, Mr Peredonov?'

Varvara, suppressing her anger, would answer for him, 'The moment we receive the confirmation you won't see us for dust.'

Questions like these only depressed Peredonov. Life just won't be worth living if I don't get that job, he thought.

*

And he kept devising new ways of defending himself from his enemies. He stole the chopper from the kitchen and hid it under his bed. Then he bought a very sharp clasp-knife, which he always kept in his pocket. Constantly he locked himself up in his room. At night he surrounded the house with traps and even put some in the rooms. In the morning he examined each one. Needless to say, these traps were so clumsily constructed that no one could possibly get caught in them. They gripped but they did not hold, and it was the easiest thing to shake them off. Peredonov was hopeless with his hands and he had no brains either. Every morning, when he saw that no one had been caught, he concluded that his enemies had wrecked his traps. This terrified him even more.

Peredonov was now keeping a particularly close watch on Volodin. More than once he went to his house when he knew he wouldn't be in and rummaged among his papers to see if he had stolen any important documents from him.

Peredonov began to suspect that the princess wanted him to become her lover again. But he thought she was old and repulsive. She's a hundred and fifty years old, he thought spitefully. But despite her age, she's very influential. And his repulsion mingled with feelings of desire. She's barely warm and smells like a corpse, Peredonov imagined, and a feeling of wild lust made him feel quite faint. Perhaps I could bring myself to sleep with her and then she might relent. What if I wrote to her?

And this time, without more ado, he sat down and wrote a letter to the princess as follows: *I love you because you are cold and remote. Varvara sweats too much and it's like an oven in bed with her. I want a cold, distant mistress. Come then, and let us share our love.*

As soon as he had posted the letter he was sorry. What's going to happen now? he thought. Perhaps it was quite the wrong thing to do. I should have waited for her to come of her own accord.

He had been the victim, as in most of what he did, of a sudden impulse. He was like a corpse brought to life at times by strange powers which, it seemed, couldn't be bothered with him for long: one of them would play with him for a while and then abandon him to another.

The little demon soon reappeared and for hours it would roll around Peredonov as if it were on a lasso, constantly teasing him.

Now it made no noise and could laugh only by trembling all over. Then it would flare up with a shower of faint golden sparks and threaten him, evil and shameless, glowing in its triumph, and this he found insufferable. And the cat threatened him too, with its evil glinting eyes, mewing insolently, terrifyingly. What are they all so pleased about? he sadly wondered and suddenly realized that the end was approaching, that the princess was already with him, close, quite close. Perhaps in that pack of cards.

Yes, there was no doubt about it, the princess was either the queen of spades or hearts. Perhaps she was hiding in another pack, or behind some other cards? But he had no idea what she was really like. The trouble was he had never set eyes on her. It was no good asking Varvara, she would only tell him some lie.

Finally he decided to consign the whole pack to the flames. Let them all burn. If any of his enemies had crept into the packs to spite him it would be their own fault.

Peredonov waited for the right moment – when Varvara was out and the living-room stove was blazing away – and threw the whole pack into it. The cards crackled and went black at the edges as they burned. Mysterious, strangely beautiful pale red flowers unfurled. Peredonov looked at these fiery blossoms in horror.

The cards writhed and twisted and turned, as if trying to escape from the stove. Peredonov seized a poker and started beating them. Tiny bright sparks showered out in all directions – and suddenly, in a swirling, evil-looking welter of sparks, the princess rose up, small, grey as ash and covered with dying sparks. She cried piercingly, hissed and spat on the fire. Peredonov fell backwards and howled in terror. The darkness swallowed him up, tickled him, and its laughter was like a thousand cooing voices.

XXVI

Sasha was enchanted with Lyudmila but he was too shy, it seemed, to discuss her with Kokovkina. Now he feared her visits and when he saw her pinkish-yellow hat flash beneath the window his heart sank and he couldn't help frowning. All the same, he would wait patiently, anxiously, and felt very miserable when she didn't come for some time. Vague, conflicting feelings of guilt and desire stirred within him – wanton for one so young, and for that reason so very sweet!

Lyudmila hadn't been either yesterday or today and Sasha, weary of waiting, had given up. Suddenly she came. His face lit up and he rushed to kiss her hands. 'Where did you get to?' he grumbled. 'It's a whole two days since I saw you.'

She laughed and was happy, and the smell of sweet, languorous, heady Japanese funkia wafted from her, seemingly flowing from her light brown hair.

They went for a stroll together outside the town. They had invited Kokovkina to join them, but she wouldn't go. 'What do you want an old woman like me with you for?' she said. 'I'd only be a nuisance. Go on your own.'

'But we might get up to mischief!' Lyudmila laughed.

The warm motionless air caressed them and evoked what was past recall. Against the tired pale sky the crimson sun shone weakly, as if it were ailing. Dry leaves lay on the dark earth, submissive, dead.

Lyudmila and Sasha climbed down into a hollow. There it was cool and fresh, damp almost. The gentle weariness of autumn reigned on its shady slopes.

Lyudmila led the way. She raised her skirt to show her small shoes and flesh-coloured stockings. Sasha, who was looking down so as not to trip over the roots, saw them. He had thought that she wasn't wearing any and, overcome by a feeling of shame and desire, he blushed. His head went round. How wonderful it would be if I fell in love with her, as if by chance. Then I could pull off her shoes and kiss her tender foot.

Lyudmila seemed to feel instinctively that Sasha was staring at her passionately and sensed his impatient desire. She laughed and turned to him.

'Are you looking at my stockings?' she inquired.

'No, I was only . . .' Sasha mumbled in embarrassment.

'But they're terrible stockings!' Lyudmila said, laughing and ignoring what he said. 'They're simply shocking. I know you're thinking I forgot to put any on. But they're just the same colour as my legs. Don't you think they're silly?' She turned her face towards Sasha and lifted the hem of her dress. 'Aren't they funny?'

'I don't think so,' replied Sasha, his face red with embarrassment. 'They're lovely.'

With a look of feigned surprise Lyudmila raised her eyebrows and exclaimed, 'And when did you become such an expert!'

She laughed and walked on. Burning with embarrassment, Sasha followed, stumbling in her tracks.

They crossed a small gully and sat down on the trunk of a birch tree blown down by the wind. Lyudmila said, 'I've so much sand in my shoes I just can't walk a step further.'

She took her shoes off and shook out the sand, cunningly looking at Sasha the whole time. 'Don't you think it's a pretty foot?' she asked.

Sasha turned even redder and didn't know what to say. Lyudmila took her stockings off. 'Aren't my feet lovely and white?' she asked again, with a peculiar, crafty smile. 'On your knees! Kiss them!' she said sternly with an expression of imperious cruelty.

Sasha nimbly went down on his knees and kissed her feet.

'It's so much nicer without stockings,' Lyudmila said as she stuffed them in her pockets and put her shoes on again. Her face became calm and cheerful once more, just as if Sasha hadn't been kneeling and kissing her bare feet a few moments ago.

'Won't you catch cold like that, dear?' he asked. His soft voice was trembling.

Lyudmila laughed. 'Don't worry, I'm used to it,' she said. 'I'm not as delicate as that!'

One day, just before dark, Lyudmila called at Kokovkina's and asked Sasha to come and help her put up a new shelf. Sasha loved to hammer in nails and had given his promise before to help Lyudmila arrange her furniture. And now he gladly agreed: this was a good excuse to go with her to her room. He felt soothed by the innocent but rather pungent smell of lily of the valley that wafted from her light green dress.

Before they started work Lyudmila changed behind a screen and emerged wearing a short pretty dress with short sleeves; she smelled strongly of seductive, cloying Japanese funkia.

'Oh, you're all dressed up!' exclaimed Sasha.

'What if I am?' Lyudmila laughed. 'But look – my feet are bare!' She spoke these last words slowly, provocatively, but with a certain innocence.

Sasha shrugged his shoulders and said, 'You're always dressing up! Come on, let's start. Do you have any nails?' he asked anxiously.

'Don't be in such a hurry. Sit down here for a little while first. You make me feel as if you find it boring talking to me and that you've just come here to work!'

Sasha blushed and said tenderly, 'Dear Lyudmila, I'd sit here as long as you like – until you tell me to leave, that is – but I've got homework to do.'

Lyudmila sighed softly and said very slowly, 'You're getting prettier every day, Sasha.'

Sasha blushed, laughed and stuck his tongue out, curling the tip. 'Anyone would think I was a girl! Why should I get prettier!?'

'Your face is pretty – but what about your body? Show me it – at least down to the waist.' She snuggled up to Sasha and put her arm around his shoulder.

'Whatever will you think of next!' he exclaimed indignantly and bashfully.

'What's wrong with that?' Lyudmila asked in an unconcerned voice. 'What do you have to hide?'

'Someone might come in,' said Sasha.

'Who, for example?' Lyudmila replied in the same carefree voice. 'We'll lock the door, then no one can come in.'

She briskly went over to the door and bolted it. Sasha realized that she wasn't joking. He blushed so violently that tiny beads of sweat stood out on his forehead. 'There's no need for that, Lyudmilochka,' he said.

'You silly boy! Why not?' she said persuasively.

She pulled Sasha over to her and began to unbutton his blouse. Sasha resisted and tried to catch hold of her hands. He looked terrified – and ashamed. The excitement made him feel weak. Lyudmila frowned and set about undressing him with a determined expression. She took off his belt and somehow managed to pull his blouse off his shoulders. Sasha struggled even more desperately. They both careered around the room, bumping into tables and chairs. Lyudmila's heady perfume intoxicated and weakened him.

With a quick push on the chest Lyudmila knocked him back on to the divan. A button flew off the shirt she was pulling at. She rapidly bared his shoulder and began pulling his arm out of his sleeve. In his wild efforts to break free, Sasha accidentally slapped her on the cheek. He had not meant to do this, of course, but she caught the full force of the blow, which rang out loud and clear. Lyudmila staggered, went very red in the face, but didn't let him go.

'You wicked little boy, fighting like that!' she gasped.

Sasha was terribly embarrassed, dropped his arms and looked guiltily at the white imprints of his fingers on her left cheek. Lyudmila quickly took advantage of his confusion and in a flash had the blouse off both shoulders, down to the elbows. Sasha recovered himself, tried to break free, but it was too late. Lyudmila deftly pulled the sleeves down and the blouse fell to his waist. He felt cold and experienced a strange feeling of shame, which made his head go round. Now he was bare to the waist. Lyudmila held his arm firmly and with her other trembling hand stroked his naked back, staring into his downcast eyes mysteriously gleaming beneath those long blue-black lashes.

And suddenly those lashes quivered, his face became distorted by the pathetic grimace of a child – and he burst into loud sobs. 'You wicked girl!' he cried. 'Let me go!'

'Stop snivelling, you cry-baby!' Lyudmila said, angrily pushing him away.

Sasha turned away to wipe his eyes. He was ashamed of crying and tried to hold back the tears. Lyudmila hungrily eyed his naked back. There's so much pleasure in the world! she thought. Why do people have to hide so much beauty from themselves – why?

Hunching his bare shoulders for shame, Sasha tried to put his shirt on, but it became tangled up with his trembling arms and he just couldn't get them into the sleeves. He made a grab for his blouse – let the shirt stay as it was for the time being!

'I shan't steal your things if that's all you're afraid of!' she said spitefully, her voice full of tears. Then she threw him his belt and turned to the window. She didn't want him like that, the little prig, wrapped up in that nasty grey blouse!

Sasha quickly put it on, somehow smoothed his shirt out and gave Lyudmila a shy, bashful look. He could see that she was brushing the tears from her cheeks so he went timidly up to her and looked straight into her face – and the tears streaming down her cheeks filled him with tender pity and he no longer felt either ashamed or angry.

'Why are you crying, dearest Lyudmila?' he asked in a soft, gentle voice. And suddenly he blushed, remembering how he had struck her. 'Forgive me, I didn't do it on purpose, really,' he said timidly.

'Are you afraid you'll melt, you silly boy, if you sit with bare shoulders?' said Lyudmila. 'Or are you afraid of getting sunburned, or losing your beauty and innocence?'

'But why do you want all this, Lyudmilochka?' Sasha asked with a bashful grin.

'Why?' Lyudmila repeated passionately. 'Because I love beauty. I'm a pagan, a sinner. I should have been born in ancient Athens. I love flowers, perfume, bright clothes, the naked body. There's supposed to be a soul, but I've never seen it. And what should I do with a soul, anyway? Let me die so that nothing is left of me, like a water-nymph, let me melt away, like a rain-cloud in the hot sun. It's the body that I love – strong, agile, naked – the body can *enjoy*.'

'But it can suffer too,' Sasha said.

'But suffering is also good,' Lyudmila whispered passionately. 'In pain there is sweetness. If only to feel the body, to see it in all its nakedness and fleshly beauty!'

'But doesn't it make you feel ashamed, without any clothes?' Sasha timidly asked.

In a sudden impulse Lyudmila threw herself on her knees before him. 'My darling boy, my idol, my little god, just let me admire your beautiful shoulders – only for one moment.'

Sasha sighed, looked down, blushed and awkwardly removed his blouse. Lyudmila embraced him with burning hands and smothered his shoulders, which were trembling with shame, with her kisses.

'There! That's how obedient I can be,' Sasha said, attempting to conceal his embarrassment with a joke.

Lyudmila rapidly kissed Sasha's arms from the shoulder down to the fingers. Sasha did not take them away: he was so excited, filled with passionate, painful longings. Lyudmila's kisses were adoring and she seemed not to be kissing a young boy but a young god as she paid homage to the flowering of the flesh, tremulously worshipping it with her burning lips.

Darya and Valeriya, who had been standing at the door all this time, looking in turn through the keyhole, were swooning with passionate, burning desire.

'It's time to get dressed,' Sasha said after a while.

Lyudmila sighed and with the same expression of adoration in her eyes helped him on with his shirt and blouse as if she were his humble servant.

'So you call yourself a pagan?' Sasha asked.

Lyudmila gaily laughed and answered, 'And what are you?'

'What a fine question!' Sasha replied confidently. 'I know the whole catechism by heart.'

Lyudmila roared with laughter. Sasha smiled at her and asked, 'If you're a pagan, why do you go to church?'

Lyudmila stopped laughing and thought for a moment. 'Well, one has to pray, shed a few tears, light a candle for the dead. I love that kind of thing – the candles, the lamps, the incense, the vestments, the choir – if it's a good one – the icons with all their trimmings. Yes, all that is *so* beautiful. And I love Him . . . who was crucified . . .' Lyudmila spoke these last words very softly, almost in a whisper, blushed guiltily and lowered her eyes. 'Sometimes I dream of Him on the cross, with tiny drops of blood on His body . . .' she said.

From that day onwards Lyudmila would often start unbuttoning Sasha's jacket as she led him to her room. At first he was ashamed to the point of tears, but he soon became used to it and would watch calmly and cheerfully as Lyudmila pulled his shirt down, bared his shoulders, caressed him and stroked his back. In the end he took his clothes off without any assistance. Lyudmila loved holding him half naked on her knees, kissing and fondling him.

One day, Sasha was alone in the house. He thought of Lyudmila looking passionately at his bare shoulders. What does she want of me? he wondered. And suddenly he blushed crimson and his heart pounded violently. He was overcome with wild, uncontrollable excitement. He turned several somersaults, fell on to the floor, jumped on the furniture, propelling himself in a thousand insane movements from one corner of the room to the other. His bright, clear laughter echoed all over the house.

Just then Kokovkina returned and when she heard the unusual commotion went straight to Sasha's room and stood in the doorway, shaking her head in disbelief. 'What the devil's got into you, Sasha? I wouldn't mind so much if you behaved like this with your friends – but on your own! You ought to be ashamed of yourself at your age!'

Sasha stood there and in his embarrassment didn't know where to put his heavy, clumsy hands. He was shaking all over with excitement.

Once Kokovkina came home to find Lyudmila feeding Sasha some sweets.

'You're spoiling the boy,' Kokovkina said. 'He can't resist anything sweet.'

'Yes – and he calls me a wicked girl!' Lyudmila complained.

'Sasha! How could you?' Kokovkina said in a tone of mild reproach. 'Explain yourself!'

'She keeps tormenting me,' he stammered. He glared at Lyudmila and then blushed deep purple. Lyudmila laughed. 'Tell-tale!' Sasha whispered to her.

'How can you be so rude, Sasha,' Kokovkina said. 'I won't have it!'

Sasha smiled at Lyudmila and muttered, 'All right, I won't do it again.'

Every time Sasha came to see her Lyudmila would take him straight to her room, lock the door, take his clothes off and dress him in various costumes. Sometimes she would make him wear a corset under them. In a low-cut dress his plump, naked, delicately rounded arms and shapely shoulders struck her as particularly beautiful. His skin was rather yellow, but of a rarely encountered, even gentle, hue. Everything of hers seemed to suit him – skirts, shoes, stockings – and when he sat there, obediently fluttering his fan, completely dressed as a woman, he really did resemble a young girl – and he tried to behave like one. Only one thing wasn't right – his hair was too short. Lyudmila didn't want to make him wear a wig or fasten a plait of hair to his head – that would look revolting.

She taught him to curtsey. At first he did this awkwardly and self-consciously. But he had a certain grace, although this was combined with the typical clumsiness of a schoolboy. Blushing and laughing, he studied the art of curtseying – and he flirted furiously.

Sometimes Lyudmila would take his bare shapely hands and kiss them. Sasha would offer no resistance and would laugh as he watched her. And sometimes he himself would put his hands to her lips and say, 'Kiss them!'

Most of all he liked some of the dresses that Lyudmila made herself: a fisherman's costume or a young Athenian's tunic, both bare-legged. After dressing him she would stand there admiring him, but with a pale, sad look.

Once he was sitting on Lyudmila's bed, his bare legs dangling, examining the folds of his Greek tunic. Lyudmila stood in front of him and looked at him with a happy but puzzled expression.

'How stupid you are!' Sasha said.

'I may be, but I'm so happy in my stupidity,' she replied, crying as she kissed his hands.

'Why are you crying?' Sasha asked with a carefree smile.

'My heart is smitten with joy! My breast is pierced by the seven swords of happiness. So why shouldn't I cry?'

'You're such a silly girl! So silly!' Sasha laughed.

'And you're so clever!' Lyudmila retorted with sudden anger in her voice. She wiped away some tears and sighed. 'Please understand, you stupid boy,' she continued in a soft, persuasive voice, 'only in madness is there happiness and wisdom.'

'Of course!' Sasha replied disbelievingly.

'You must forget – and forget yourself – then all will become crystal clear,' Lyudmila whispered. 'In your opinion, do wise men think?'

'But what else should they do?'

'They just *know*. It's given to them at once to understand. A wise man only has to look – and all is revealed to him . . .'

The autumn evening gently lingered. At times they could just hear the rustling of the trees in the garden as the wind stirred the branches. They were alone. Lyudmila had dressed Sasha in the fisherman's costume of thin blue linen and made him lie on a low couch, while she sat on the floor at his bare feet, without any stockings, wearing only a shift. She sprinkled Sasha all over with a rich perfume that had a heady grassy smell, like the still air of a mysteriously flowering valley locked between mountains.

Large bright beads shone on her neck and ornate golden bracelets jingled on her arms. Her whole body smelled of orris, which overpowers the senses with its heavy, sensual, exciting perfume; made from the distillations of slow-moving waters it brought on a delightful drowsiness and lethargy. Lyudmila suffered and sighed as she looked at his dark-skinned face, at his blue-black eyebrows, his midnight eyes. She lay her head on his bare knees and her bright hair caressed his dark skin. She kissed his body and its strange, potent smell, mingling with that of his young skin, made her head go round.

Sasha lay quietly with a gentle flickering smile on his face. He was excited by a vague feeling of desire that stirred within him and brought sweet torment. And when Lyudmila tenderly kissed his knees and feet, her soft kisses aroused languorous, almost dreamlike, fantasies. He wanted to do something to her, be it pleasant or painful, tender or shameful – but what? Should he kiss her feet or beat her long and hard with supple birch twigs? Should he make her laugh with joy or cry out with pain? Perhaps she desired both: but that would not be enough. What *did* she want of him? There they both were, half naked, tormented at the same time by desire and shame at their naked flesh. Just what was this mystery of the flesh? And how could he sacrifice his blood and his body, sweetly surrendering to her desires, at the price of his shame?

Meanwhile Lyudmila was longing for him, squirming at his feet, one moment turning pale and cold from desires that could never be fulfilled and burning with passion the next.

'Am I not beautiful?' she passionately whispered. 'Have I not burning eyes, beautiful hair? Embrace me! Take me! Tear off my bracelets! Undo my necklace!'

Sasha was terrified, tormented by what for him were impossible desires.

XXVII

When Peredonov woke up in the morning someone was looking at him, so it seemed, with enormous dim rectangular eyes. Could it be Pylnikov? He went to the window and drenched the menacing spectre with water.

Everything around him seemed to have been bewitched. The little demon squealed wildly, people and even cattle looked at him craftily, malevolently. Everything was hostile towards him and he felt that he was one against many.

During lessons Peredonov made spiteful remarks about his fellow teachers, the headmaster, parents and pupils. The boys listened to him in astonishment. Some of them, boors by nature, expressed their sympathy by humouring him. Others remained grimly silent, but whenever Peredonov attacked their parents they stoutly defended them. Peredonov would look at these boys mournfully and walk away muttering something. Sometimes he amused the class by making ridiculous comments on the texts they happened to be studying.

One day they were reading some poetry by Pushkin:

> In freezing mist dawn awakes to show
> The fields which give no harvest load,
> With his hungry mate in tow,
> The wolf walks out on the road.[1]

Let's stop here,' said Peredonov. 'We must try and understand the poet's meaning. What we have is an allegory. Wolves hunt in pairs, that is to say, the wolf with his hungry mate. *He* is well fed, but she is hungry. Now the wife should always take her turn after her husband. The wife must obey her husband in everything. That's the meaning.'

Pylnikov, who was in high spirits, smiled at Peredonov with his deceptively innocent fathomless black eyes: his face both tormented

1. From *Eugene Onegin*, chapter 4.

and fascinated Peredonov. That damned boy was casting a spell over him with his insidious smile!

But was he a boy? Perhaps there were two of them, brother and sister. He couldn't tell one from the other. Perhaps Pylnikov could even change into a girl when he wanted. That was why he was always so much cleaner than the others – when he wanted to change he sprinkled himself with different kinds of magic water – that was the only way. He always smelled of perfume.

'What have you been spraying yourself with, Pylnikov?' Peredonov asked. 'Patchouli?'[1]

The boys laughed. Sasha turned red at this insult and remained silent. Any genuine desire to please, to look pleasant and tidy, was beyond Peredonov's comprehension. Any such display, even by a boy, he regarded as part of a plot against himself. Any boy who dressed himself smartly was obviously intending to lead him astray. What other reason could there be? A smart appearance and cleanliness were anathema to Peredonov and for him perfume had an evil smell. He preferred the smell of freshly manured fields to any perfume – in his opinion it was very healthy. To dress smartly, to keep oneself clean, to wash – all that needed time and effort. And any thought of hard work depressed and frightened Peredonov. How wonderful if he could do nothing but eat, drink and sleep!

Sasha's friends teased him about the patchouli and about Lyudmila, saying she was in love with him. He flared up and furiously denied any such relationship with Lyudmila, maintaining that she wasn't in love with him and that it was all an invention of Peredonov's, who had been in love with her himself. But she had turned him down, so he was getting his own back by spreading malicious rumours about her. Although his classmates believed him – it was obviously Peredonov's work – they still teased him, just for the fun of it.

Peredonov persisted in letting everyone know about Pylnikov's depravity. 'He's having an affair with Lyudmila,' he claimed. 'They kiss so passionately that she's already given birth to one prep-school student and she's expecting another.'

Lyudmila's love for the schoolboy was grossly exaggerated by the townsfolk, who added many stupid obscene details of their

1. A strongly scented East Indian plant from which perfume is obtained.

own. But few actually believed this story, realizing Peredonov had gone much too far. However, those who loved to tease (and there are quite a number of them in our town) would ask Lyudmila, 'How could you fall for a young boy? It's an insult to the cavaliers of this town!'

Lyudmila would laugh and reply, 'Stuff and nonsense!'

Sasha became a general object of morbid curiosity. A rich general's widow inquired about his age and when she discovered that he was rather too young for her purposes she decided to take him under her wing in two years' time. In the meantime she would keep a close watch on his development.

Sasha was already beginning to reproach Lyudmila at times, since everyone was teasing him because of her. He even gently struck her now and then, which only made her laugh out loud.

To put an end to the ridiculous gossip, and to save Lyudmila from what might easily turn into a very nasty scandal, the Rutilovs, together with their numerous friends and close and distant relatives, waged a fierce campaign against Peredonov to prove that all these stories were the invention of a raving lunatic. Peredonov's wild behaviour convinced many of the truth of what they said.

At the same time denunciations of Peredonov poured into the office of the director of district schools, and from the district offices an inquiry was sent to the headmaster. Khripach referred to his previous reports and made it plain that the continued presence of Peredonov in the school was a positive danger, since his mental state was noticeably deteriorating.

Peredonov was now a hopeless victim of his wild imaginings, and his hallucinations formed a barrier between himself and the world. His vacant demented eyes were never at rest, it seemed as if he were always peering beyond objects, in the hope of finding some illumination, some ray of hope beyond the real world. He talked to himself and shouted wild threats at people, such as, 'I'll kill you! I'll cut your throat! I'll have you locked up!'

Varvara would only laugh and grin. Rave as much as you like! she spitefully thought. She felt that the explanation for his behaviour was nothing other than spite: he had guessed that he had been cheated and now he was furious. But he wouldn't go out of his mind – an imbecile has no mind to go out of! And even if he did, he would at least be happy in his lunacy.

One day Khripach told him, 'Did you know, Peredonov, that you look most unwell?'

'I've got a splitting headache,' Peredonov gruffly replied.

'To be frank, my dear sir,' the headmaster continued in a cautious voice, 'I would advise you not to come to school for a while. You should seek medical treatment, rest your nerves, which are clearly in a pretty bad state.'

Not go to school! thought Peredonov. What could be better! Why didn't I think of that before? I can pretend to be really ill and then I can stay at home and wait and see what happens. So he cheerfully replied, 'No, no, I shan't come. I'm ill!'

Meanwhile the headmaster sent another letter to the director of district schools and was expecting to hear any day that doctors would be coming to examine Peredonov. But, being civil servants, they took their time.

So Peredonov stayed away from school – he too was expecting something. For the past few days he had been sticking to Volodin like a leech. In fact he didn't dare let him out of his sight for fear Volodin might do him some harm. From the time he woke up Peredonov wearily thought of Volodin: where was he at that precise moment? what was he doing? Sometimes he thought that he could see him everywhere: in the clouds that drifted across the sky like a flock of sheep, there was Volodin in his bowler hat, bleating with laughter; or in the smoke pouring from a chimney, pulling the most grotesque faces and leaping about in the air.

Volodin was sure that Peredonov had taken a great liking to him and proudly related the news to everyone. He was certain Peredonov just couldn't live without him. Varvara's done the dirty on him, he thought, and in me he sees a loyal friend. That's why he never leaves my side.

One day Peredonov left the house to call on Volodin and saw him coming towards him, complete with bowler hat and walking-stick, gaily skipping and bleating for joy. On another occasion Peredonov asked him, 'Why are you always wearing that thing?'

'And why shouldn't I wear a bowler?' Volodin replied cheerfully. 'It's not too showy and it suits me very well. I'm not allowed to wear a cap with a badge, and top hats are strictly reserved for aristocrats – they're not for the likes of us.'

'You'll boil[1] to death in that,' Peredonov said sullenly.

Volodin burst out laughing.

They went off to Peredonov's.

'I get so tired of walking,' Peredonov said.

'But it's good for you,' Volodin assured him. 'If you work, walk and eat your food, you'll stay healthy.'

'That's all very well,' objected Peredonov. 'Do you think that people will still have to work two or three hundred years from now?'

'But what should they do? If you don't work, you have no bread. Bread costs money and money has to be earned.'

'But I don't want any bread.'

'You wouldn't have any rolls or pies either,' Volodin chuckled, 'and you wouldn't be able to buy any vodka or have anything to make liqueurs from.'

'But people themselves wouldn't have to work. Machines would do everything. You would only have to turn a handle, like a barrel-organ, and there you are ... But it would be boring to turn it for long.'

Volodin reflected for a moment, lowered his head and stuck out his lips. 'Yes, that would be fine,' he said pensively, 'only we shan't be here.'

Peredonov glared at him and growled, 'You mean *you* won't be here, but I shall.'

'God grant you live two hundred years and crawl around on all fours for three hundred,' Volodin gaily replied.

No longer did Peredonov recite magic charms – let the worst come! He would get the better of everyone. All he had to do was to be vigilant and stand firm.

As he sat in the dining-room at home, drinking with Volodin, Peredonov would tell him about the princess. In Peredonov's mind she was getting uglier and more repulsive by the day. She was an evil old woman, with yellow wrinkled skin, a hunched back and large tusks – that was how he constantly imagined her.

'She must be two hundred years old,' Peredonov said, staring strangely at the opposite wall. 'And she wants me to be her lover – otherwise she won't get me the job.'

1. The word for pot and bowler hat is the same in Russian.

'She's asking a lot, I must say!' Volodin cried, shaking his head. 'The old hag!'

Peredonov talked some delirious nonsense about a murder. With a fierce frown he told Volodin, 'There's a body hidden behind the wallpaper. And I'm going to kill someone else and nail him under the floorboards.'

Volodin took this as a joke and sniggered.

'Can't you smell that stench from behind the wallpaper?' Peredonov asked.

· 'I can't smell anything,' Volodin replied, tittering and pulling funny faces.

'Then you want to clean your nose,' Peredonov said. 'That's why it's so red. The body's there, rotting away behind the wallpaper.'

'It's only a bug!' Varvara cried and burst out laughing. But Peredonov looked deadly serious.

Sinking deeper and deeper into insanity, Peredonov had already begun to write denunciations of the playing-cards, the little demon and the ram, which was obviously an impostor passing itself off as Volodin and after an important position, although it was simply a ram. He wrote denunciations of woodcutters – they had felled all the birches so that there was no fuel for steam baths and nothing to beat the children with, leaving all the aspens intact – and what good was aspen?

Whenever he met some of the boys in the street, his foul and sometimes absurd remarks terrified the younger ones but amused the older boys, who would follow him in a group and rapidly disperse when they saw another master coming. The younger boys ran away of their own accord.

Every object seemed bewitched and harboured some evil spirit. Terrifying hallucinations drew mad howls and shrieks from him. The little demon would appear covered in blood, or on fire. It roared loud enough to split his head with unbearable pain. The cat grew to a fantastic size, stamped on the floor with its boots and pretended to be an ogre with large red whiskers.

XXVIII

Sasha had gone out after lunch and still hadn't returned by seven o'clock, when he was due back. Kokovkina was very worried and thought, Heaven help him if he's caught by a master in the street when he's not supposed to be out. He'd be punished and it would make things very awkward for her. She had the reputation of taking in only well-behaved boys who weren't given to wandering about the streets at night. So she went to look for him – and where else but at the Rutilovs'?

As ill luck would have it, that day Lyudmila had forgotten to lock her bedroom door. In came Kokovkina. And what did she see? Sasha was standing in front of the mirror in a woman's dress, fanning himself. Lyudmila was laughing and arranging the ribbons on his brightly coloured belt.

'Good heavens! What's going on here?' she shrieked with horror. 'I've been worried out of my life looking for him everywhere, and here he is dressed as a woman! What a disgrace, wearing a skirt! And *you* should be ashamed of yourself, Lyudmila!'

Lyudmila, taken by surprise, didn't know what to say at first, but she soon regained her composure, however. With a cheerful laugh she threw her arms around Kokovkina, made her sit down and then proceeded to tell her some cock-and-bull story she'd made up on the spot.

'We're just rehearsing for a little play at home. I'm taking the part of the boy and he's the girl and it will be terribly amusing.'

Sasha stood there red-faced and frightened and with tears in his eyes.

'Don't give me that nonsense!' Kokovkina said angrily. 'He should be doing his homework and not wasting his time with stupid plays. Whatever will you think of next! Get changed at once, Sasha, I'm taking you straight home.'

Lyudmila laughed loud and gaily and kissed Kokovkina. The old woman thought that this cheerful young lady was as irresponsible as a child and that Sasha had been stupid enough to want to do all she asked. Her cheerful laughter, however, showed that this was simply a childish prank which deserved no more than a good telling-off. After a few grumbles and angry looks she calmed down.

Sasha quickly changed behind the screen where Lyudmila's bed stood. Kokovkina took him home and scolded him all the way. Sasha was too ashamed and frightened to attempt any excuses. What will she do when we get home? he thought anxiously.

For the very first time, Kokovkina was strict with him and made him get down on his knees. But after a few minutes she relented, touched by the sight of his guilty face and those silent tears.

'A proper little nancy boy! Heavens! You can smell the perfume a mile off!' she grumbled.

Sasha bowed smartly, kissed her hand, and she was even more touched by the punished boy's politeness.

Meanwhile a storm was gathering over Sasha's head. Varvara and Grushina had sent an anonymous letter to Khripach, in which they stated that Pylnikov was infatuated with Lyudmila Rutilov, that he spent entire evenings with her and that he had given himself up to debauchery. This letter reminded Khripach of a recent conversation he had heard at the house of the marshal of the nobility. Someone, he recalled, had made a pointed remark which no one had picked up, about a young lady who had fallen in love with a boy. The conversation immediately turned to other topics: in Khripach's presence, according to the unwritten law of people who moved in polite society, this was considered an extremely awkward subject for discussion, so they pretended that such conversation was improper in the presence of ladies and that the subject itself was trivial and most implausible. Khripach, of course, was quick to notice this, but was not naïve enough to question anyone about it. He had been absolutely certain all along that he would hear everything sooner or later. And here was this letter with the news he had been waiting for.

Not for one moment did Khripach believe that Pylnikov had become depraved and that there was anything improper about his behaviour with Lyudmila. It's all an absurd invention of Peredonov's, he reflected, encouraged by Grushina's spiteful jealousy. However, this letter does show that undesirable rumours are circulating, which might sully the reputation of the school that has been entrusted to my care. Therefore I must take the necessary steps.

First of all he invited Kokovkina to come and discuss the circumstances that might have encouraged those undesirable rumours. Kokovkina already knew all about it: she had been told in even plainer terms than the headmaster. Grushina had waited in the street for her, had started a conversation and informed her that Lyudmila had already completely corrupted Sasha. Kokovkina was stunned. At home she showered Sasha with reproaches. What annoyed her more than anything else was the fact that all this had happened practically under her nose and she had known very well that Sasha was visiting the Rutilovs.

Sasha pretended to understand nothing. 'What have I done wrong?' he asked.

At first Kokovkina didn't know what to reply. 'What have you done wrong? You mean to say you don't know? Was it so long ago that I caught you wearing a skirt? Have you forgotten already, you shameless boy?'

'So you caught me. What was so particularly bad about it? And you've already punished me for it, anyway! It wasn't as if I'd stolen it.'

Kokovkina was dismayed and said, 'Just listen to the boy argue! It seems I didn't punish you enough.'

'I'm not stopping you,' Sasha replied petulantly with a look of outraged innocence. 'You yourself forgave me, but it seems it's not enough. I didn't ask to be forgiven – I would have stayed on my knees the whole evening. I'm tired of being told off the whole time!'

'Did you know the whole town is talking about you and your Lyudmila?'

'What are they saying?' Sasha asked with naïve curiosity.

Kokovkina again didn't know what to reply. 'You know very well what! You yourself know what people are liable to say. And it's not very flattering. That you're carrying on with Lyudmila – that's what they're saying.'

'Well, I won't misbehave anymore,' Sasha promised, as calmly as if they were discussing a game of five-stones.

He assumed an angelic expression, but his heart was heavy. He kept asking Kokovkina what they had been saying and was scared that he might hear something very nasty. What could people be saying about them? Lyudmila's room overlooked the garden, so no one could have seen them from the street. Besides, she always kept the curtains drawn. And even if someone had been watching them what could they possibly say? Something annoying, insulting, perhaps? Or merely that they'd often seen him going to the house?

Next day Kokovkina received the invitation from Khripach, and this really alarmed the old woman. She said nothing to Sasha, quietly got dressed and left at the appointed time. Khripach told her as gently as he could about the anonymous letter. She burst into tears.

'Calm yourself, we're not accusing you,' Khripach said. 'We know you too well. However, I must ask you to keep a closer watch on the boy in future. For the moment I want you to tell me what actually happened.'

When she returned from the headmaster's Kokovkina once again showered Sasha with reproaches. 'I shall write to your aunt,' she said, crying.

'But I haven't done anything wrong! Let her come. I'm not scared,' Sasha said, also crying.

The following day Khripach asked Sasha to come and see him. As soon as he entered the study he asked in his dry, severe voice, 'I wish to know with whom you've been associating lately in this town.'

Sasha looked at him with deceptively innocent calm eyes. 'Associating with?' he replied. 'Olga Kokovkina knows that I only go to see my friends from school – and the Rutilovs.'

'Exactly,' Khripach continued his cross-examination. 'And what do you do at the Rutilovs'?'

'Nothing in particular, sir,' Sasha replied just as innocently. 'We usually spend most of the time reading. The Rutilov sisters are great poetry lovers. And I'm always home by seven.'

'But perhaps not always?' asked Khripach with an attempt at a piercing look.

'Well, once I was late,' Sasha replied with the unruffled candour of the innocent. 'I really caught it from Kokovkina for that, so I wasn't late again.'

Khripach fell silent. He was disconcerted by Sasha's calm replies. At all events he knew Sasha had to be lectured, reprimanded, but how, and for what? He was afraid that he might have put wicked thoughts into the boy's head that had never been there in the first place (so he believed); or that he might hurt the boy. He wanted to avoid the possibility of any unpleasantness that might occur in the future as a result of such a relationship.

Khripach thought that a teacher's job was difficult and carried a lot of responsibility, especially if one had the honour of being a headmaster. Yes, his was a difficult, responsible task! This trite definition of his duty gave wings to a whole train of thoughts that might have remained dormant. He started talking quickly, distinctly – and trivially. Sasha understood very little of what he said.

'A student's first duty is to learn ... he mustn't be distracted by friends, however pleasant and irreproachable their company may be. At all events, I must say that the company of boys your own age is much more beneficial for you ... you must value your own reputation and that of the school ... to conclude, I must come straight to the point and tell you that I have grounds for supposing that your relations with a certain young lady do not conform with the generally accepted laws of propriety, and that they are characterized by a degree of freedom totally impermissible in someone of your age and not at all in accordance with the generally accepted rules of good conduct.'

Sasha burst into tears. He was mortified to hear that anyone could talk of his darling Lyudmila as someone who allowed liberties to be taken with her. 'On my word of honour, we didn't do anything wrong,' he assured Khripach. 'All we did was read, go for walks, play games – that's to say we had races – nothing worse than that.'

Khripach slapped him paternally on the shoulder and tried to speak in a voice that was sympathetic, but which still sounded cold and dry. 'Now, listen, Pylnikov ...' (Why couldn't he have called him Sasha? Was it because there were instructions from the Ministry, according to which this was not the correct form of address?) 'I believe what you say, that nothing wrong did happen. All the same, I think it would be better if you stopped making such frequent visits. Believe me, it's for your own good. I'm speaking not only as mentor and tutor, but as your friend.'

Sasha thanked the headmaster and bowed his way out, having promised to do what he said – he had no option. And from then onwards he visited Lyudmila only for five or ten minutes at a time, but he still tried to see her every day. He was most annoyed at having to cut short his visits and he projected his annoyance on to

Lyudmila. He would often call her a silly little fool, a she-ass, and would beat her. But all Lyudmila did was laugh.

News spread that the actors from the local theatre were going to present a fancy-dress ball at the club house, with prizes for the best costumes, male and female. There was much far-fetched talk about these prizes. Some said that the women's prize was a cow and the men's a bicycle. These rumours excited the townsfolk. Everyone wanted to win – the prizes were so substantial. Costumes were hurriedly made. No expense was spared and all ideas were jealously guarded, even from close friends, lest some brilliant invention be copied.

When the actual posters announcing the ball appeared – huge placards were pasted on to fences and the printed announcements personally delivered to all the prominent citizens – it turned out that they were not going to award either a cow or a bicycle and that all the women could expect was a fan, and the men an album. This news infuriated and deeply upset those who had been preparing for the ball and there was much grumbling: 'What a waste of money!', 'It's an insult offering prizes like that!', 'They should have told us in the first place!', 'It could only happen in this town,' and so on.

All the same, they continued with their preparations: it wasn't the prize that was so important, they thought, as much as the honour of winning it.

Darya and Lyudmila weren't concerned at all with the prize, neither at the start or later. A fat lot of use a cow would be! And a fan was nothing special. And who would be judging the costumes? What taste did those judges have? But both sisters were enraptured with Lyudmila's idea of sending Sasha dressed as a woman – this way they could fool the whole town and ensure that they won the prize.

Even Valeriya seemed to be in agreement. As jealous and delicate as a child, she was furious that Lyudmila's little friend never came to see *her*, but she didn't want to quarrel with her two elder sisters. However, she couldn't resist remarking with a contemptuous grin, 'He wouldn't dare to go like that!'

'We'll dress him so that no one could possibly recognize him,' Darya said with determination.

When the sisters told Sasha of their plan and Lyudmila informed him, 'You're going as a Japanese lady,' Sasha jumped and howled for joy. Whatever happened at the ball (and especially if no one recognized him), why shouldn't he agree? It would be such great fun fooling everyone!

They immediately decided that he should go as a geisha girl. They kept the whole thing strictly secret and didn't even tell their married sister Larisa, or their brother. Lyudmila made the costume herself by copying the design on the label on a bottle of corylopsis[1] perfume. She used yellow silk on red velvet and the costume was wide and long. She sewed a bright pattern of large, fantastically shaped flowers on to it. The others made a fan from rice-paper and thin bamboo sticks, and a parasol from some fine pink silk, with a bamboo handle. For the legs they bought pink stockings and wooden sandals. Lyudmila, who was very clever with her hands, painted a geisha mask: the face was rather too yellow, but pleasant all the same, with a faint, immobile smile, slanting eyes and a tiny narrow mouth. All they had to do after that was order a black shiny wig from St Petersburg.

The costume took a long time to fit, because Sasha could only stay for a few minutes at a time, and not every day, as he had been hoping. But they found another way: Sasha came in through the window at night, when Kokovkina was asleep. This plan worked very well.

Varvara had also decided to enter for the fancy-dress ball. She bought a grotesque mask and the costume itself was no trouble as she decided to go as a cook. She really looked the part, just like a cook straight from the stove, with a ladle hanging from her waist, a white cap on her head and her arms bare to the elbows and smothered with rouge. If she won the prize, so much the better. If she didn't – well, she didn't need a fan, anyway.

Grushina decided to go as Diana the huntress. This had Varvara in fits of laughter. 'Are you going to wear a collar?' she asked.

'Why should I need one of those?' Grushina asked in amazement.

'Well, you're going as Dianka the dog, aren't you?'

'Whatever gave you that idea!' Grushina laughed. 'No, not Dianka the dog, but Diana, the goddess.'

Varvara and Grushina both changed for the ball at Grushina's

1. A shrub of the hazel family, with exquisitely scented flowers.

place. Grushina's costume was flimsy, to say the least, with bare arms and shoulders, bare back, bare chest, legs bare to the knee, light slippers, no stockings. The very thin dress was of white linen with a red border. Although rather short, it was quite full, with a large number of pleats; she wore nothing underneath.

'It's a bit daring, isn't it?' Varvara sniggered.

'Then I'll have all the men chasing me,' Grushina replied with a saucy wink.

'But why so many pleats?' Varvara asked.

'So that I can stuff them with sweets for my little brats,' Grushina explained.

Grushina's daringly exposed body was really quite attractive, but what contradictions! Her skin was covered with flea-bites, she had coarse manners and used intolerably vulgar language: another example of profaned bodily beauty.

Peredonov thought that the fancy-dress ball was specifically designed to trap him. All the same, he decided to go – not in fancy dress, but in an ordinary frock-coat. He wanted to see for himself what evil plots were being hatched against him.

For some days Sasha had been terribly excited at the prospect of going to the ball. After a time, however, he began to have doubts. How could he escape from the house? And particularly now, after all that unpleasantness? There'd be real trouble if they got to know at school – he'd be expelled immediately.

Recently one of the assistant masters, who was so liberal a young man that he would say 'Mr Thomas Cat' instead of 'Tom', had told Sasha in a portentous voice, when he was giving out the marks, 'You'd better pay more attention to your work, Pylnikov.'

'But I haven't had any low marks,' Sasha had casually replied. His heart sank – what would the teacher say next? But he said nothing and merely gave him a stern look.

When the day of the ball arrived, Sasha's courage completely deserted him. He was terrified. There was one thing, though: the costume was now ready at the Rutilovs' – how could he possibly let them down? Would all their dreams and hard work be in vain? Lyudmila would certainly cry. No, he decided, he had to go.

His habit of being secretive, acquired only over the past few weeks, helped him conceal his excitement from Kokovkina. Fortunately the old woman went to bed early. And so did Sasha. So as not to arouse suspicion, he put his shoes outside the door and his clothes on a chair just by it. Now came the hardest part – getting out of the house. The route had already been worked out – through the window he had used when he went for the fittings. He put on a light summer shirt that was hanging in his wardrobe, a pair of soft slippers, and carefully climbed through the window, choosing the moment when he could hear neither voices nor footsteps near by. It was drizzling and it was cold, dark and muddy. He kept thinking that someone would recognize him and he took off his cap and shoes and threw them back into his room. Then he turned up his trousers and hopped along the slippery, rickety, planked pavement in his bare feet. It would have been hard to distinguish a face in that darkness, especially if the person was running: anyone he happened to meet would surely take him for a boy sent out on some errand.

Valeriya and Lyudmila made themselves complicated but artistic costumes. Lyudmila dressed as a gypsy and Valeriya decided to go as a Spanish lady. Lyudmila's dress consisted of strips of bright red silk and velvet, and the frail, delicate Valeriya's of black silk and lace; in her hand was a black lace fan. Darya decided that last year's Turkish costume was good enough and as she put it on she said with determination, 'It's hardly worth thinking up a new one!'

When Sasha arrived they all rushed to dress him. He was more worried by the black wig than anything else. 'Supposing it comes off?' he asked anxiously.

Finally the sisters solved the problem by fixing it tightly with ribbons tied under his chin.

XXIX

The fancy-dress ball was to take place at the club house, a two-storeyed brick, barrack-like building painted bright red and situated in the market square. The organizer was Gromov-Chistopolsky, the actor and manager of the local theatre.

The entrance was covered by a calico canopy and lit by two lamps. A large crowd shouted their criticism at the people arriving in carriages and on foot and their remarks were mainly disapproving: since they were out in the street, people's costumes were almost entirely hidden under their coats and so the crowd had to rely on guesswork. The policemen in the street did their best to keep order — the chief of police and the district police officer remained in the main hall, as guests.

Each guest was given two cards on arrival: a pink one for the best woman's costume and a green one for the best of the men's. These cards were to be handed to those they considered most deserving.

Many inquired when they arrived, 'Can we take some for ourselves?'

At first the attendant expressed mild surprise and asked, 'Why for yourselves?'

'In case I think my costume's the best!'

When he had been asked the same question several times the young attendant (who had a good sense of humour) would reply with a sardonic smile, 'Help yourselves! Keep the lot!'

The hall was very dirty and from the start most of the guests seemed to be in a high state of intoxication. In those cramped rooms, whose walls and ceilings were black with soot, burned crooked chandeliers. They were huge and heavy and seemed to be greedily drinking up the air. The curtains at the doors looked so moth-eaten that it gave one the shivers just to brush against them. Here and there crowds would gather, and laughter and loud exclamations were heard when someone's costume became the centre of attraction.

Gudayevsky the notary had come as a Red Indian. His hair was decked with cock's feathers and he wore a copper-coloured mask with ridiculous green designs all over it, a leather jacket, a check plaid over one shoulder and jackboots with green tassels. He waved his arms in all directions, leaped about and walked like an athlete, doing violent jerks with his bare knees. His wife was dressed as Ceres. Her costume was made of bright green-and-yellow rags. Ears of corn stuck out on all sides, catching and pricking everyone who went by, in return for which she was bumped and pinched.

'I'll scratch you!' she shouted viciously.

Everyone guffawed and someone inquired, 'Where did she glean all that corn?'

To which someone else replied, 'She's been saving it up since the summer. She stole some from the fields every day.'

A group of smooth-faced, young civil servants, all of them in love with Gudayevsky's wife and all of whom had been told in advance what she would be wearing, followed her around, collecting cards for her where they could, almost resorting to force at times and making rude remarks. Others, who were not particularly courageous, simply had their cards taken off them.

Other ladies in fancy dress made their partners collect cards for them. Some looked hungrily at cards that hadn't yet been handed over, asked if they could have them and received rude replies.

A dejected-looking lady dressed as Night, in a dark blue costume, with a crystal star and paper moon on her forehead, timidly asked Murin, 'May I have your card, please?'

'What do you mean? Give you my card! No – I don't care for your ugly mug!' he rudely replied.

Night mumbled something angrily and glided away. If only she could have just two or three cards to show at home, and could tell them they'd been given her. But modest dreams never come true.

The schoolmistress Skobochkina was dressed as a bear – that is to say, she had simply draped herself in a bearskin, with a bear's head as a kind of helmet over the usual half-mask. It looked dreadful; all the same, it suited her robust figure and stentorian voice. She tramped along and roared so loudly that the lights in the chandeliers quivered. Her costume was a great success and she was handed quite a number of cards. But she was unable to hold on to them as she hadn't found herself a quick-witted partner like the others, and more than half her cards were stolen from her after she had been plied with drink by local tradesmen, who really appreciated her decided talent for mimicking a she-bear.

'Just look at that bear swilling vodka!' people in the crowd shouted. Skobochkina had decided not to refuse vodka: she was convinced that a she-bear would drink it if she were offered it.

Someone dressed as an ancient Teuton stood out on account of his height and sturdy figure. He was admired by many for his robustness and because his powerful arms with their superbly developed muscles were visible.

It was mainly the women who followed him and gathered around him, whispering to each other in terms of adoration. He was soon recognized as Bengalsky the actor. He was a great favourite with everyone in our town, so he was showered with cards. Many reasoned as follows, 'If I don't win the prize then let it go to an actor or actress. If any of our lot wins it, we'll never hear the end of it.'

Grushina's costume was a success; more accurately, a *succès de scandale*. Men swarmed after her, laughing and making obscene remarks. The ladies were shocked and turned away. In the end the district police officer came up to Grushina, sweetly smacking his lips, and said, 'I must ask you to cover yourself, madam.'

'What's that? You can't see anything you shouldn't!' Grushina answered perkily.

'Madam, the other ladies are complaining,' Minchukov said.

'The other ladies can go to hell!' Grushina shouted.

'But I must insist on you covering your bosom and your back, at least with a handkerchief.'

'And supposing my handkerchief's covered in snot?' Grushina retorted with a brazen laugh.

Minchukov was undeterred, however, and continued, 'As you wish, madam. But if you don't cover yourself you'll have to leave.'

Cursing and spitting, Grushina stormed off to the ladies' room, where the attendant helped her rearrange the folds of her costume so that they covered her front and back. She returned more decently attired, but she still eagerly sought admirers, flirting indiscriminately with anyone she came across. When everyone's attention was diverted, she went to the buffet to steal some sweets and fruit. She soon returned to the main hall, showed Volodin two peaches, smiled impudently and told him, 'I helped myself!' And she immediately tucked the peaches up in the folds of her dress.

Volodin beamed. 'Well, I'm off to get some!' he said gleefully.

Soon Grushina was completely drunk and she made a real exhibition of herself, shouting, waving her arms about and spitting on the floor.

'Our huntress is warming up,' they said.

This, briefly, was the fancy-dress ball to which the light-headed sisters had brought the frivolous Sasha. Because of the delay in getting Sasha ready, they all arrived fairly late, in two cabs.

As a result they made a conspicuous entry. The geisha, in particular, met with wide acclaim. It was rumoured that she was Kashtanova, a local actress who enjoyed great popularity with the men. Therefore Sasha was given a lot of cards. In actual fact Kashtanova wasn't there at all – her little son had fallen dangerously ill the previous night.

Sasha was quite intoxicated by the novelty of the situation and flirted madly. The more cards that were thrust into his small hands, the more seductively his eyes gleamed through the narrow slits of his mask. He curtseyed, raised his tiny fingers, laughed softly, fluttered his fan, striking one or two men on the shoulder with it. Every now and then he opened out his pink parasol and shyly hid behind the fan. Although these movements couldn't be described as graceful, they were enough to captivate all of Kashtanova's admirers.

'I hereby present the most charming lady here this evening with my card,' Tishkov said as he handed the geisha his ticket with a dashing bow. He was very drunk and red in the face – he looked just like a doll with that smile on his motionless face, and his awkward figure. And he never stopped making his stupid rhymes.

Valeriya was extremely envious of Sasha's success. She wanted to be the centre of attraction, to have her costume and slender, shapely figure admired by everyone and consequently to win the prize. Now she saw how impossible this was, much to her chagrin, as her sisters had agreed to try and get cards only for the geisha and, should they receive any themselves, to give them to her all the same.

Dancing had started in the hall. Volodin, who had rapidly become inebriated, started dancing a wild Cossack dance, squatting and kicking up his legs, until the police intervened. In a jolly, deferential voice he told them, 'I'll stop if you really object!'

Two shopkeepers, however, who had followed suit and were dancing the trepak, refused to stop. 'You've no right to do that,' they said to the police. 'We paid our fifty copecks!'

They were escorted out of the hall. Volodin went with them, smiling and performing a little dance of his own.

The Rutilov sisters decided that it would be a good idea to find Peredonov, so that they could have a good laugh. He was sitting alone by the window, looking at the festivities with restless eyes. To him, every person, every object was meaningless, but was hostile nevertheless. Lyudmila went up to him in her gypsy costume and said in a deep, guttural voice, 'Can I tell your fortune, my fine sir?'

'Go to hell!' Peredonov shouted, startled by the gypsy's sudden appearance.

'Let me read your palm, my precious sir. I already see from your face that you're going to be rich – and an important official!' Undeterred, Lyudmila took his hand and continued.

'All right, but make sure my fortune's a good one,' Peredonov growled.

'Oh, my sweet sir, you have many enemies. They're going to report you to the police. You'll weep many tears and go and die by a fence.'

'You rotten bitch!' Peredonov shouted as he snatched his hand away.

Lyudmila smartly ran off into the crowd. Then Valeriya came up, sat down beside him and whispered tenderly:

> I am a young Spanish maid,
> You are the height of my desire,
> But by your wife you are betrayed,
> My charming, simple squire.

'You're a lying imbecile,' Peredonov growled.
Valeriya carried on whispering:

> Hotter than noon, sweeter than night,
> Is my Sevillian embrace.
> You must take your wife
> And spit in her stupid face.
> Varvara's not worthy of handsome Ardalyon,
> Why – you're as wise as old Solomon!

'That's true,' Peredonov said. 'But how can I spit in her face? She'd only complain to the princess and then I wouldn't get the job.'

'Why do you want the job? You've a high enough position as it is.'

'No, I just couldn't live if they don't give me it,' he said dolefully.

Darya pushed a letter into Volodin's hand. It had a pink seal.

Volodin opened it with a joyful bleat, read it through quickly and reflected for a few moments. He looked very pleased with himself, but seemed puzzled. The letter was very clear and concise:

My darling!
Meet me tomorrow night by the military bathhouse at eleven.
Yours anonymously,
Zh

Volodin believed it was genuine, but the question was: should he go? Who was Zh for instance? Some girl called Zhenya? Or was it the first letter of a surname? He showed the letter to Rutilov.

'Of course you should go!' urged Rutilov. 'You must go and see what it's all about. It might be some rich girl who's fallen in love with you and whose parents are against the marriage. That's why she wants to declare her feelings this way.'

After much thought Volodin finally decided it wasn't worth going. 'I just can't shake them off!' he said pompously. 'But I draw the line at sluts like her.'

He was afraid he might be beaten up if he went: the baths were in a dark, remote place, right on the outskirts of town.

In the midst of all the uproar and drunken laughter in the various crowded rooms, loud shouts of approval suddenly came from the room near the entrance and everyone immediately flocked there. People said that they had seen the most *awfully* original mask yet. A tall thin man wearing a soiled, patched dressing-gown, with a birch brush under one arm and with a bucket in one hand, was forcing his way through the surging mass. He had a cardboard mask, representing a stupid face, with a tiny beard, side-whiskers, and on his head he wore a cap with an official's badge.

'I was told that there was a fancy-dress ball here, but I can't see anyone washing[1] himself,' he said in a surprised voice, dejectedly swinging his bucket.

The crowd followed him, gasping and displaying unfeigned delight at his brilliant invention.

'I bet he wins the prize,' Volodin said enviously.

1. Maskarad, normally meaning 'fancy-dress ball', is also a jocular term for a bathhouse.

He envied him like many of the others did – spontaneously, without thinking. But Volodin really had no reason to be envious as he hadn't entered the competition. As for Machigin, he was in raptures over the costume, particularly the badge. He laughed joyfully, slapped his knees and told all and sundry, whether he knew them or not, 'A superb caricature. Those lousy bureaucrats are too fond of acting high and mighty, and like nothing more than showing off their badges and uniforms. That's really one in the eye for them. Very neat!'

When he began to feel hot the official in the dressing-gown started fanning himself with the birch brush. 'Phew, it's like a sauna in here!' he exclaimed.

People near by burst into fits of laughter and poured their cards into his bucket.

Peredonov looked at the brush waving about in the crowd: to him it looked just like the little demon. It's turned green, the filthy beast! he thought in horror.

XXX

At last they started counting the cards. The judges were all club stewards and a large crowd gathered outside their room and waited in tense expectation. For a short while it was quiet and boring in the hall. The music stopped and everyone became silent. It made Peredonov feel quite scared. But soon everyone started talking again and there were impatient murmurs. Someone was convinced that both prizes would go to the actors.

'You'll soon see,' someone replied in an irritated hissing voice.

Many believed him. The crowd became restless. Those who had received few cards seethed inwardly; those who had received a large number were agitated, thinking that an injustice was about to be done.

Suddenly a bell tinkled with a faint, nervous, vibrating sound. Out came the judges: Veriga, Avinovitsky, Kirillov and some other stewards. A wave of excitement ran through the hall and then there was a sudden hush. Avinovitsky announced in his stentorian voice, which could be heard all over the hall, 'The prize of an album for the best male costume has been awarded to the gentleman in the Teutonic costume.'

Avinovitsky held the album high above his head and angrily surveyed the surging mass. The tall Teuton started to make his way through the crowd. He met with hostile looks and they didn't even make way for him.

'Stop pushing, please!' the dejected-looking woman dressed as Night tearfully implored.

'Just because he's won the prize he thinks all the ladies have to prostrate themselves in front of him,' someone malevolently hissed from the crowd.

'What do you expect if you won't let me through?' replied the Teuton, trying to control himself.

Somehow he managed to reach the judges and took the album from Veriga. The band played a flourish, but the sound of the music was lost in the ensuing uproar. People shouted abuse. The Teuton was hemmed in and jostled. Some shouted, 'Off with your mask!'

The Teuton didn't reply. He could easily have forced a way through the mob, but was evidently afraid of using all his strength. Gudayevsky grabbed the album and at the same time someone tore the mask off.

'It's the actor!' everyone shouted.

And sure enough it was none other than Bengalsky.

'And what if I am an actor?' he angrily shouted. 'You yourselves gave me the cards, I didn't ask for them!'

Back came the venomous replies, 'You could have slipped some of your own in!', 'You had them printed!', 'More cards have been handed in than there are people here!', 'He brought fifty with him when he came,' and so on.

Bengalsky turned pale and said, 'It's disgraceful, accusing me like that! You can verify it if you like by checking the cards with the number of competitors.'

Here General Veriga came up and told those nearest him, 'Calm yourselves, gentlemen, please. There's been no cheating, you can rest assured. The number of cards corresponds exactly with the number of competitors.'

The stewards, aided by some of the more reasonable guests, somehow managed to pacify the crowd. Then everyone began to wonder who would win the fan.

Veriga announced, 'Ladies and gentlemen, the largest number of cards for the ladies' costume has been received by the lady dressed as a geisha. She therefore wins the fan. Will you please step this way, Miss Geisha, and collect your prize. Ladies and gentlemen! Kindly let her pass!'

The band played a second flourish. The terrified geisha felt like escaping there and then, but the crowd nudged her, made way and led her to the front. With a warm, congratulatory smile Veriga handed her the fan. Sasha had a blurred impression of a sea of brightly coloured costumes as he stood there trembling, his eyes clouded with fear and confusion. He knew that he had to thank the judges, and the customary politeness of a well-brought-up boy showed. The geisha curtseyed, muttered something inaudible, giggled, lifted her tiny fingers. And once again there was uproar, with whistling and catcalls from every corner of the hall. There was a great surge towards the geisha. 'Curtsey again, you hussy!' savagely shouted the dishevelled Ceres.

The geisha made a dash for the exit, but didn't get far. There were angry cries from the milling crowd. 'Make her take her mask off! Don't let her get away! Tear her costume off! Take her fan!'

'Do you realize whom you've given the fan to?' shouted Ceres. 'To Kashtanova the actress! She stole someone's husband, yet she wins the prize! Honest women don't get prizes, only sluts like her!'

And she rushed at the geisha, shrieking and clenching her small bony fists. Others followed – mainly her escort of admirers. The geisha defended herself desperately. A wild scuffle broke out. The fan was seized, broken into small pieces and stamped on. With the geisha in the middle, the crowd moved across the hall in a wild frenzy, sweeping away all in its path. The Rutilovs and the stewards had no hope of reaching the geisha. She was quick and strong, produced ear-splitting shrieks, scratched and bit; at the same time she firmly held on to the mask with whichever hand was free.

'They should all be whipped!' screeched some furious woman.

Grushina, who was quite drunk, hid behind the others and egged on Volodin and some of his friends. 'Pinch her! Pinch the hussy!' she cried.

Machigin, clutching his nose, which was streaming with blood, leaped out and said, 'Look! She scored a direct hit with her fist!'

Some ferocious young man sank his teeth into the geisha's sleeve and tore it in half. The geisha yelled for help. 'Save me!' she cried.

The others began to tear off her dress. Bare flesh appeared. Darya and Lyudmila made desperate attempts to elbow their way to the geisha, but to no avail. Volodin pulled her so hard, squealing and flailing about so much that he got in the way of others who were less intoxicated but more incensed than he was. He didn't do it from spite, but for the sheer fun of it, in an excess of high spirits. He tore one sleeve clean off and tied it around his head. 'That'll come in handy!' he guffawed. Having escaped from the mob, which rather cramped his style, he could now give full rein to his clowning, and he danced on the broken fan with wild shrieks. No one stopped him.

Peredonov looked at him in horror and thought, He's dancing because he's pleased about something. That's how he'll dance on my grave.

Finally the geisha managed to break free – the men who had been clustering around her were no match for those fast-moving fists and sharp teeth. She rushed from the hall. In the corridor Ceres again went into the attack and grabbed hold of her dress. The geisha tried to escape, but was surrounded again. Another scuffle broke out. 'They're pulling her ears!' someone shouted.

A certain lady had seized an ear and was tugging it, at the same time yelling in triumph. The geisha screamed and somehow tore herself away, giving that nasty woman a hard blow with her fist.

Finally Bengalsky, who had meanwhile succeeded in changing out of his costume, fought his way through the crowd to the trembling geisha, whom he took up into his arms, shielded her as much as he could with his huge body and rapidly bore her away, skilfully brushing the mob aside with his elbows, to the accompaniment of shouts of 'Rotter!' and 'Swine!' from the crowd.

Bengalsky was pulled this way and that and punched in the back. 'I won't allow a mask to be torn from a lady. Do whatever else you like, but that I won't allow!' he protested.

He took the geisha along the corridor until they came to a narrow door leading into the dining-room. Here General Veriga managed to hold back the crowd for a time. With truly martial determination he stood before the door, guarding it with his body. 'Gentlemen! You will come no further!' he said.

Mrs Gudayevsky, rustling what was left of her crop of corn, threw herself at Veriga, brandishing her fists and screeching at the top of her voice, 'Get out of the way! We want to come through!' But the general's cold, rock-like face with its determined grey eyes deterred her from any further action. Helpless with rage, she shouted to her husband, 'You could have moved yourself and given her a slap in the face instead of standing there like a ninny!'

'I couldn't get to her,' pleaded the Red Indian with wild gesticulations. 'Pavel Volodin was flailing about like a windmill.'

'You should have bashed him in the teeth and given her one on the ear. Why stand on ceremony?' Mrs Gudayevsky shouted.

The mob pressed against Veriga. Foul abuse rang out. Veriga calmly stood at the door and tried to persuade those nearest him to stop the rioting. Suddenly the kitchen boy opened the door behind him and whispered, 'They've gone, Your Excellency.'

Veriga walked away. The crowd broke into the dining-room, then into the kitchen in search of the geisha, but she wasn't there.

Bengalsky, still carrying her, had run out into the kitchen. She lay motionless and silent in his arms. Bengalsky thought that he could hear her heart beating strongly. On her bare arms, which tightly clutched him, there were several scratches and a bluish-yellow bruise near the elbow. In an agitated voice he told the servants crowding into the kitchen, 'Hurry! An overcoat, a dressing-gown, blankets, anything you have . . . I must save this lady.'

An overcoat was thrown over Sasha's shoulders and somehow Bengalsky wrapped the geisha up. Then he groped his way down the narrow staircase, dimly lit by smoky kerosene lamps, and went through a gate into a side-street.

'Take your mask off, there's less chance of them recognizing you without one . . . it's dark now,' he said rather disjointedly. 'I won't tell anyone.' He was curious to know who it was: one thing was certain – it wasn't Kashtanova. So who was it then? The geisha took her mask off and Bengalsky was confronted by an unfamiliar dark-skinned face, in which all traces of fear had given way to joy at having escaped. A pair of bright, cheerful eyes were looking at him.

'How can I possibly thank you?' said the geisha in a sonorous voice. 'I shudder to think what would have happened if you hadn't saved me!'

She's no coward, this woman. Most interesting! the actor thought. But who is she? Obviously a visitor to this town. Bengalsky knew all the local women and he quietly told Sasha, 'I must take you home immediately. Tell me where you live and I'll call a cab.'

The geisha's face clouded over again. 'No! You mustn't. You really mustn't!' she babbled. 'I can get home on my own. Please let me go.'

'I can't let you walk through all this mud, especially in sandals. You must go by cab,' he confidently assured her.

'No, I'll manage. For goodness' sake, let me go!' the geisha pleaded.

'I give you my word of honour I shan't tell a soul,' Bengalsky reassured her. 'I can't leave you like this, you'll catch your death of cold. I'm responsible for you now and I can't just leave you. Now tell me where you live. Quickly! They're after your blood. You saw for yourself that they're just like savages. That lot's capable of anything.'

The geisha shuddered and tears swiftly rolled down her cheeks. 'They're terribly, terribly evil people!' she sobbed. 'Take me to the Rutilovs' then, I'll spend the night there.'

Bengalsky hailed a passing cab and they drove off. He peered closely into the geisha's dark face. Very strange, he thought. The geisha turned away. Something vaguely dawned on him. Now what was that story about a schoolboy and Lyudmila Rutilov . . .?

'I've got it! You're a boy!' he whispered so that the driver wouldn't hear.

'Please don't tell anyone!' pleaded Sasha, his face as white as a sheet. He stretched his arms out from under his coat towards Bengalsky in an imploring gesture.

Bengalsky laughed softly and repeated, just as softly, 'I shan't breathe a word, so don't worry! All I'm concerned about is getting you home safely. I know nothing else. But you're a desperate character. What if Kokovkina finds out?'

'No one will know — if you don't give the game away,' Sasha said in a gently pleading voice.

'You can rely on me, I'll be as silent as the grave. I was a boy myself once. I used to get up to all sorts of tricks.'

*

The uproar at the club was just beginning to die down when a fresh catastrophe rounded off the evening. While the geisha was being hunted along the corridor, a brightly burning demon darted among the chandeliers, laughing and whispering to Peredonov that he must free it, that he must strike a match and let it loose on those dark, dirty walls; and then, when it had gorged itself on the destruction of that building where such terrifying and incomprehensible events such as this evening's riot were taking place, it would leave Peredonov in peace. He was powerless to resist its insistent prompting. He went into a small sitting-room next to the ballroom. No one was there. He looked around, struck a match and held it to the bottom of the curtains until they caught fire. The fiery demon climbed like a nimble snake, quietly hissing with delight. Peredonov walked out of the room and shut the door behind him. No one had seen him.

The fire wasn't detected until the whole of the front of the building was blazing. The flames spread quickly. Everyone escaped, but the whole building was burned down.

Next day the sole topics of conversation were the geisha-girl scandal and the fire. Bengalsky kept his word and told no one that the geisha was really a boy in disguise.

That night, after he had changed at the Rutilovs' and was an ordinary barefooted boy again, Sasha had run home, climbed through the window and fallen fast asleep. In a town that was alive with gossip, in a town where everybody knew what everybody else was doing, Sasha's nocturnal exploit thus remained a complete secret: for a long time that is, but, of course, not for ever.

XXXI

Yekaterina Pylnikov, Sasha's aunt and guardian, received two letters about her nephew simultaneously: one from the headmaster and one from Kokovkina. She was greatly disturbed by them, dropped everything and hastened from her village over the muddy autumn roads to see Sasha, who was overjoyed when she arrived. He was very fond of his aunt, who had come with the full intention of giving him a thorough telling-off. But he threw himself so joyfully around her neck and kissed her so affectionately that at first she was unable to take a strict tone with him.

'Dear Auntie, how kind of you to come!' Sasha exclaimed as he looked at her plump rosy face with its dimpled cheeks and serious grey eyes.

'Save your welcome for later. I'm going to take you in hand now,' she said, rather indecisively.

'I don't mind,' said Sasha in an unconcerned voice. 'Take me in hand – as long as you have good reason. But I'm still so terribly pleased to see you!'

'You may well say *terribly*,' Auntie repeated in a voice of displeasure. 'Let me tell you the terrible things I've been hearing about you.'

Sasha raised his eyebrows and looked at his aunt with innocent, uncomprehending eyes. 'It's all the fault of one of the teachers,' he complained. 'Mr Peredonov. He invented the whole story that I'm a girl and he never leaves me in peace. Then the headmaster gave me a real telling-off for being friendly with the Rutilov sisters. As if I went to their house to steal! And what's it got to do with them?'

Is he the same little boy as before? Auntie wondered. Or has he sunk so low as to tell me such barefaced lies?

She sat behind locked doors with Kokovkina, had a long talk with her and came out looking very sad. Then she went to see the headmaster and returned dreadfully upset. Sasha felt the full weight of her tongue. He cried bitterly, but stoutly maintained that it was all lies and that he had never allowed himself any liberties with the young ladies. His aunt didn't believe him. She scolded him for some time and threatened him with a severe thrashing that same day, as soon as she'd seen the Rutilovs. Sasha sobbed and assured her that he had done nothing to be ashamed of, that everything had been terribly exaggerated and invented.

His aunt, angry and tearful, went off to the Rutilovs'. She was almost too furious to sit and wait in their drawing-room at all – she wanted to attack the sisters at once with the most savage reproaches and she had already prepared the nasty things she had to say. However, the prettily furnished peaceful drawing-room had a calming effect on her nerves – much against her wishes – and tempered her anger. The unfinished embroidery that was lying on the table, the souvenirs, the engravings on the walls, the carefully tended plants growing in window-boxes and the absolute spotlessness of everything were not what one would expect in a disreputable house. Surely her innocent Sasha couldn't have been seduced by those thoughtful young ladies in such homely, orderly surroundings? All that she had heard or read about Sasha now seemed patently absurd. On the other hand, Sasha's accounts of how he passed the time at the Rutilovs' struck her as perfectly plausible – they had read, talked, joked, laughed, they had wanted to put on a play, which Olga Kokovkina wouldn't allow.

The sisters, however, were extremely worried. They didn't know whether the fact that they'd dressed Sasha up was still a secret or not. But there were three of them and each was ready to help the others. This gave them courage and they assembled in Lyudmila's room to deliberate on a plan of action and whispered to each other.

'We must go to her now,' Valeriya said. 'It's not polite to keep her waiting.'

'Let her cool down a bit first,' Darya replied casually, 'otherwise she'll really let fly.'

All the sisters scented themselves with fragrant clematis and entered the drawing-room calm and cheerful, prettily dressed as ever, and they filled the room with their pleasant chatter, charm and gaiety. Yekaterina Pylnikov was at once enchanted by them – they looked so respectable, so sweet. So *they* are the corrupters! she thought indignantly, with those pedagogues in mind. But then she wondered if all that modesty were not mere pretence. She decided not to submit to their charms.

'You must forgive me for troubling you, young ladies, but there's something I must talk to you about.' She tried to make her voice sound stern and businesslike.

The sisters asked her to sit down and resumed their light-hearted chatter.

'Which one of you . . .?' Yekaterina began hesitantly.

Lyudmila, acting the part of a gracious hostess who was fully aware of a guest's embarrassment, cheerfully said, 'I played the most with your nephew. We have a lot in common.'

'Such a nice boy, your nephew,' Darya said, quite sure that this flattery would make her happy.

'Yes, so nice, and so amusing,' Lyudmila said.

Yekaterina Pylnikov felt increasingly embarrassed. Suddenly she realized that she had no real grounds for complaint and this made her angry. Lyudmila's last words provided her with the chance to speak her mind.

'You may find him amusing, but –' she said angrily.

Darya interrupted her, however, and said sympathetically, 'I can see you've been hearing all those ridiculous stories of Peredonov's. You must know he's quite mad. The headmaster won't even allow him into the school. They're just waiting for a psychiatrist to come and certify him. Then he'll be dismissed –'

'Before you go any further,' interruped Yekaterina in turn, becoming increasingly annoyed, 'I must tell you that I'm not interested in that teacher, only in my nephew. I've heard – if you'll pardon the expression – that you've been corrupting the boy.'

The moment she had used this critical word, in the heat of the moment, she realized that she had gone too far. The sisters looked at one another with such well-simulated incomprehension and confusion that they would have deceived many others besides Yekaterina Pylnikov. They blushed and all of them exclaimed at once, 'That's not very nice!', 'How shocking!', 'That's news to us!'.

Darya said coldly, 'My dear lady, you are not too fussy in your choice of words. Before saying such rude things you should consider whether they are entirely appropriate.'

'Oh, but it's very understandable!' exclaimed Lyudmila with the air of a well-mannered girl forgiving an insult. 'After all, he's not a stranger to you. Of course, all this stupid gossip is bound to upset you. We felt sorry for Sasha, that's why we took him under our wing. The least thing in this town immediately becomes a crime. If you only knew what terrible, terrible people live here!'

'Terrible!' Valeriya softly repeated in her fragile, brittle voice. And she shivered all over, as if she had touched something unclean.

'Ask him yourself, that's the best way,' Darya said. 'You just have to look at him to see he's still a child. Perhaps you've grown used to his naïvety, but we can see more objectively, being outsiders, that he's completely unspoiled.'

The sisters lied so calmly and confidently that it was impossible

259

not to believe them. Indeed, a lie is often more plausible than the truth. *Almost* always. The truth, of course, is never very plausible.

'It's true he comes here rather too often,' Darya said. 'But we shan't let him past the front doorstep in future, if that's what you'd like.'

'I'm going to see Khripach myself today,' said Lyudmila. 'I just can't imagine who put the idea into his head. Surely he can't believe such nonsense?'

'No, I don't think he himself believes a word of it,' admitted Yekaterina. 'But he did tell me that certain nasty rumours are going around.'

'There you are!' exclaimed Lyudmila joyfully. 'Of course he doesn't believe any of it. So why all the fuss?'

Lyudmila's cheerful voice captivated Yekaterina and she asked herself, Could any of this have really happened? Even the headmaster says he doesn't believe a word of it.

For a long time the sisters carried on chattering like a flock of birds, each trying to be the one to persuade Yekaterina of the complete innocence of their friendship with Sasha. To make their case more convincing, they wanted to provide her with a detailed account of exactly what they had been doing with Sasha, and when, but as soon as they started they became terribly confused: they were all such innocent, simple things that it was just impossible for them to remember it all. And finally Yekaterina was fully convinced that her nephew and the delightful Rutilov girls were the innocent victims of stupid slander.

Yekaterina warmly kissed the sisters goodbye and told them, 'You're such nice uncomplicated girls. At first I thought you were – if you'll forgive the expression – tarts.'

The sisters burst out laughing. 'No, we're just ordinary happy-go-lucky girls with rather sharp tongues. That's why we're not too popular with the local geese!' Lyudmila said.

When she returned from the Rutilovs' Sasha's aunt didn't say a word to her nephew. He was thoroughly scared and confused when she came in and he anxiously scrutinized her face. But she went straight into Kokovkina's room and had a long heart to heart with her, at the end of which she decided to go and see the headmaster again.

*

That same day Lyudmila went to see Khripach. She sat for some time in the drawing-room with his wife and then announced that she wanted to see the headmaster himself.

The ensuing conversation in Khripach's study was a lively one, not because the two had very much to say to each other, but because they both liked to talk, and they simply showered one another – Khripach with his quick, high-flown patter, Lyudmila with her melodious babbling. With the irresistible plausibility of what is false, she smoothly poured out her story of her relationship with Sasha. Her chief motive, however, was her very real sympathy for the boy who had been subjected to the whips and scorns of evil tongues, as well as her desire to replace his absent family. All in all, he was such a wonderful, cheerful, open-hearted boy. Lyudmila was so touched by her own story that tiny tears, so beautiful to see, swiftly rolled down her pink cheeks to her lips, which were smiling with embarrassment.

'Yes, I've come to love him like a brother,' she said. 'He's such a wonderful, kind boy who appreciates affection so much. He used to kiss my hands.'

'That's all very laudable,' Khripach replied, somewhat embarrassed, 'and it does credit to your kind feelings. But I think that you've taken too much to heart the simple fact that, as headmaster, I considered it my duty to inform the boy's relatives about the rumours that have reached my ears –'

Without listening Lyudmila went on chattering and her tone became mildly reproachful. 'And tell me, what was so wrong with our taking an interest in a poor boy who's been victimized by that lunatic, Peredonov? When are you getting rid of him, anyway? Can't you see for yourself that Pylnikov is a mere child? Yes, a mere child!'

She clasped her tiny pretty hands, jingled her gold bracelet and laughed softly, as though she were crying; then she took out her handkerchief to wipe away the tears and a delicate fragrance drifted towards Khripach. Now he suddenly felt impelled to tell her that she was as 'enchanting as an angel'[1] and that the whole

1. From Lermontov's poem, 'Tamara'.

regrettable incident 'was not worth one moment of her sweet sorrow'.[1] But he managed to control himself.

Like a stream, Lyudmila's gentle, rapid chatter flowed on and on, scattering like smoke the fantastic edifice of Peredonov's lie. One only had to compare the demented, coarse, filthy Peredonov with that happy, radiant, sweet-smelling, prettily dressed Lyudmila. Khripach didn't care whether she was telling the whole truth or making it up: he felt that *not* to believe her, to quarrel with her, to take some steps or even punish Pylnikov would be tantamount to putting his foot in it and would only bring disgrace on himself throughout the whole district. All the more so since it involved Peredonov, who was generally considered insane.

So he smiled amiably and told Lyudmila, 'I'm very sorry that this has been so distressing for you. Not for one moment did I have any doubts as to the purity of your relationship with Pylnikov. I think you have been inspired in this matter by the noblest of motives, which I value very highly, and not for one moment have I looked upon the rumours circulating in this town as anything other than stupid insane slander, and this has disturbed me deeply. It was my duty to inform Pylnikov's aunt, all the more so since she might have heard even more distorted stories. But I had no intention of troubling you in any way and I had no idea that Mrs Pylnikov would deem fit to reproach you.

'Well, we've patched things up with Mrs Pylnikov,' Lyudmila said gaily. 'But we don't want you to be hard on Sasha because of us. If you think that our house is really so dangerous for schoolboys, then we shan't let him come anymore, if you so wish.'

'You've been very kind to him,' Khripach said rather vaguely. 'We can have nothing against his visiting his friends in his free time, as long as he has his aunt's permission. We don't want to turn the boys' lodgings into places of confinement. However, until the whole affair concerning Peredonov is cleared up I think it would be best if Pylnikov stayed at home.'

The Rutilovs' and Sasha's story was soon confirmed by a terrible event that took place at the Peredonovs' and left no doubt in anyone's mind that all the rumours about Sasha and the Pylnikov sisters were the ravings of a lunatic.

1. From Lermontov's 'The Demon', slightly altered.

XXXII

It was a cold overcast day. Peredonov was returning from Volodin's, feeling sad and weary. Unable to resist Vershina's seductively inviting voice, he was lured into her garden once more. They walked together towards the summer-house, along wet paths strewn with dark rotting leaves. Inside there was an unpleasant damp smell. Through the bare trees the shuttered house could be seen.

'I want you to know the truth,' Vershina muttered, giving Peredonov a quick look and then turning her black eyes away. She was wrapped in a black jacket. Round her head was a black kerchief. Her lips, blue with cold, firmly grasped a black cigarette holder. Thick clouds of black smoke rose into the air.

'You can go to hell with your truth,' Peredonov replied. 'All the way!'

Vershina smiled wryly and replied, 'I don't like to hear you talk like that. I'm so very sorry to hear how you've been cheated.' She spoke this sentence with malicious glee and the spiteful words just rolled off her tongue. 'You relied on someone's patronage, but you were far too trusting. You were fooled because you were so ready to believe. Anyone can forge a letter. You should have known with whom you were dealing. And as for your wife, she has no scruples at all.'

Peredonov had great difficulty in following her muttering and he could find barely any meaning behind all those circumlocutions. Vershina was afraid of speaking too loudly or bluntly: if she spoke too loudly someone might hear and tell Varvara. And things might turn out very nasty, as Varvara wouldn't hesitate to make a scandal. And if she spoke clearly and to the point, Peredonov might lose his temper and even beat her. So it was best to drop hints and let him guess for himself. But he was incapable of guessing. He had been told before, to his face, that he had been fooled. But still he was too stupid to realize that the letters had been faked. And still he thought that the princess herself was deceiving him and leading him up the garden path.

Finally Vershina decided to tell him quite bluntly. 'Do you

really think that the princess wrote those letters? The whole town knows that Grushina forged them because your wife asked her to. The princess knows nothing about the whole affair. Ask anyone you like. Everyone knows that the two of them gave the game away themselves. Then Varvara stole the letters from you and burned them to destroy the evidence.'

Peredonov's brain was filled with dark, oppressive thoughts. He now understood one thing: that he had been duped. But he still couldn't believe that the princess knew nothing of what was going on. No, she knew very well. She hadn't emerged unharmed from the fire for nothing.

'You're lying about the princess,' he said. 'I tried to burn her, but didn't finish her off. She escaped by spitting.'

Suddenly he was seized by a fit of mad rage. Fooled! He struck the table savagely with his fist, leaped up from his seat and dashed home without saying goodbye to Vershina. Joyfully she watched him go, and the black clouds of smoke whirled from her mouth, to be broken up and carried away by the wind.

Peredonov was burning with anger. But as soon as he saw Varvara he was struck dumb by a feeling of agonizing fear.

Next day, as soon as he was up, Peredonov got hold of a small knife which was kept in a leather sheath and he carefully concealed it in his pocket. Throughout the morning, right up to dinner time, he stayed with Volodin, watching him work and listening to his stupid remarks. Volodin was always pleased to have Peredonov for company and found his ridiculous actions quite amusing.

The little demon danced around Peredonov the whole day. It prevented him from having his usual nap after dinner and drove him to distraction. And when at last, towards evening, he was dropping off, an old wild-looking woman suddenly appeared from nowhere. Pug-nosed, very ugly, she came up to his bed and muttered, 'The kvass[1] must be brewed, the tarts must be taken out of the oven, the meat must be roasted.' Her cheeks were dark, but her teeth sparkled.

'Go to hell!' cried Peredonov.

The pug-nosed woman vanished as though she had never existed.

*

1. A kind of beer, usually made from bread with malt.

Evening set in and a melancholy wind moaned in the chimney. The rain beat against the windows, gently, slowly, persistently. Outside it was quite dark. Volodin was at the Peredonovs' – he had been invited that morning for a cup of tea.

'Don't let anyone in, do you hear, Claudia?' said Peredonov.

Varvara sniggered.

'There're some strange women prowling around the house,' Peredonov muttered. 'We must be careful. One of them just sneaked into my bedroom, she wanted a job as a cook. Now what do I need a pug-nosed cook for?'

Volodin laughed – rather, bleated, 'There are women who roam the streets, but they have nothing to do with us. So we shan't let them sit at *our* table!'

The three sat down at the table. They had vodka and savouries and they drank far more than they ate. Peredonov was in a deep gloom. In his eyes everything was like a nightmare, so meaningless, incoherent, chaotic. He had a splitting headache too. One thought tormented him again and again: that Volodin was his deadly enemy and must be got rid of before it was too late. Then all the hostile cunning of his enemies would be exposed. Volodin was soon very drunk and amused Varvara with his gibberish.

Peredonov felt uneasy. 'Someone's coming,' he muttered. 'Don't let anyone in. Tell them I've gone to pray at Cockroach Monastery.'

He was afraid that any visitors might get in his way. Volodin and Varvara were amused, thinking he was only drunk. They winked at each other and went out, one by one, knocked at the door and asked in disguised voices, 'Is General Peredonov at home?' 'One diamond-studded medal for General Peredonov.'

But Peredonov wasn't tempted by any medal that day. 'Don't let them in! Chase them away! Let them bring it in the morning, now isn't the time.' No, he thought, I must be strong today. Today all will be revealed, but meanwhile my enemies are ready to sling anything at me so that they can do away with me once and for all.

'Well, we've got rid of them,' Volodin said. 'They're coming back in the morning.' He sat down at the table again.

Peredonov looked at Volodin with his dull eyes and asked, 'Are you my friend or my enemy?'

'Why, your friend, your friend, Ardalyon!' Volodin replied.

'A true friend's like a cockroach behind the stove,' said Varvara.

'Not a cockroach, but a sheep,' corrected Peredonov. 'Let's drink together, Pavlusha, just the two of us. Varvara! Why don't you join us? That will make two of us.'

Volodin sniggered and said, 'What do you mean? That makes *three* if Varvara joins us, not two!'

'Two,' repeated Peredonov gloomily.

'He means husband and wife are the devil in one,' Varvara laughed.

Up to the very last Volodin didn't suspect that Peredonov wanted to cut his throat. He bleated, played the fool, said stupid things to amuse Varvara. But Peredonov had his mind on the knife the whole evening. Whenever Volodin or Varvara came up to him on the side where he kept it he would shout fiercely and tell them to go away. Now and then he pointed to his pocket and said, 'I've got something here, Pavlusha, that will make you quack.'

Volodin and Varvara laughed.

'I'm very good at quacking, Ardalyon,' said Volodin. 'Quack, quack! It's really quite simple.'

Red-faced and stupefied with vodka, Volodin kept quacking and puffing out his lips. He became more and more insolent towards Peredonov. 'Really fooled you, didn't they, Ardalyon?' he said in a sympathetic and at the same time contemptuous voice.

'I'll fool you in a minute!' Peredonov roared.

In his eyes Volodin now appeared menacing and terrifying. He must defend himself. He pulled out the knife, threw himself on Volodin and with one stroke slit his throat. Blood spurted out in a stream. Peredonov took fright and the knife dropped from his hands. Volodin continued to bleat and tried to grasp his throat. Obviously he was mortally frightened, growing feebler, and could not reach his throat. Suddenly he went numb and fell on to Peredonov, letting out a terrible broken groan as if he were choking. Then he was silent. Peredonov shrieked with horror. He pushed Volodin away and he slumped on to the floor. He made a wheezing noise, kicked his feet out – and was soon dead. His wide-open eyes became glassy and stared straight at the ceiling. The cat came in from the next room, sniffed the blood and mewed evilly. Varvara stood there as if petrified. Claudia came running in to see what the noise was.

'God, they've cut his throat!' she wailed.

Varvara came to her senses and ran screaming out of the dining-room with Claudia.

The news soon spread. Neighbours gathered in the street, in the front garden. The bolder ones came into the house, but didn't dare enter the room for some time. They kept peering round the door and whispering. Peredonov was looking at the corpse with the eyes of a madman, listening to the whispering behind the door. A dull anguish weighed heavily on him ... His mind was a complete blank.

At length the people summoned up courage and came in. Peredonov was sitting there, his head bowed, muttering something incoherent and meaningless.

19 June 1902

VARIANTS

1. Natasha did want to steal a tart and consume it on the sly, but this was impossible. In the first place, Varvara was always hanging around her and there was no way she could get rid of her. Secondly, even if Varvara did leave her on her own and she managed to take a tart from the pan, later on Varvara would count how many there should have been from the marks on the pan and then she would notice the shortage. So it was impossible to steal even one and this made Natasha furious. As usual, Varvara was cursing her maid, taking her to task for being so slipshod in many things and for what was, in her opinion, sheer inefficiency. Her wrinkled yellow face, which still bore a few traces of its former charms, had a peevish, predatory look.

'You lazy cow!' Varvara shouted in her jarring voice. 'Have you gone soft in the head or something? You've only just started in this house and already you don't want to do a thing, you filthy slut!'

'Just tell me if there's *anyone* who'll put up with you!' Natasha rudely replied.

And she was right. Servants never stayed for very long at Varvara's. She fed her maids badly, was constantly swearing at them and was always trying to put off paying them their wages. If she happened to find one who wasn't very bright, she would push her, pinch her and slap her cheeks.

'Shut up, you bitch!' Varvara shouted.

'Why should I? Everyone knows that nobody can stick it here for long, madam. You think no one's good enough! Well, you're not so wonderful yourself. I've never known anyone so fussy as you!'

'How dare you – you filthy cow!'

'Well, I don't even have to dare! How could anyone live with an old hag like you? Who'd want to?'

Varvara completely lost her temper, shrieked and stamped her feet. But Natasha stood her ground. A furious slanging-match followed.

'You starve me to death and yet you want me to work!' shouted Natasha.

'All the refuse in a rubbish dump wouldn't be enough to satisfy you,' Varvara replied.

'And you know who's a rubbish dump, where all the rubbish goes . . .!'

'I may be rubbish, but I'm from the gentry. And you're just a servant. You filthy slut! You wait, I'll give you one in the mug in a minute!' cried Varvara.

'And I can give as good as I get!' rudely replied Natasha, looking down contemptuously on little Varvara from her great height. 'Right in the mug. I know the master keeps bashing you there. But I'm not his mistress, no one's going to pull *me* around by the ears.'

Just then the loud drunken voice of a woman came through the window from outside. 'Hey you, madam! Or should I say young lady? What am I supposed to call you? Tell me, where's your sweetheart?'

'And what's that got to do with you, you pain in the neck?' cried Varvara as she ran to the window.

Down below stood the landlady, Irinya Stepanovna, a cobbler's wife. She was bareheaded and wore a filthy cotton dress. She and her husband lived in a little outbuilding in the yard and rented out the house. Recently Varvara had had lots of violent arguments with her – the woman was constantly turning up half drunk and was always bullying her, as she suspected they intended moving out.

And once again they confronted each other in a heated slanging-match. The landlady was the calmer, while Varvara was beside herself with rage. In the end the landlady turned her back to Varvara and lifted her skirt. Varvara immediately did the same.

Such scenes, all that never-ending shouting, gave Varvara migraines afterwards. But by now she had grown used to that rough disorderly life and could never resist obscene horseplay. She had long lost all respect for herself and for others.

2. Next day, after dinner, while Peredonov was asleep, Varvara set off for the Prepolovenskys'. Earlier she had sent her new maid with a whole sackful of nettles. She was terribly scared, but went all the same.

Seated in a circle around the oval coffee table in the Prepolovenskys' drawing-room were Varvara, the hostess and her cousin Zhenya, a tall plump red-cheeked girl with languid movements and deceptively innocent eyes.

'You can see for yourself,' Sofya Prepolovensky was saying, 'what a red-cheeked fatty we have here – and all because her mother used to whip her with nettles. I whip her too.'

Zhenya blushed crimson and burst out laughing. 'Yes,' she said in a lazy low-pitched voice, 'the moment I start to get thin they immediately treat me to a good stinging and I put on weight again.'

'But isn't it painful?' Varvara asked with cautious surprise.

'Well, so what? It's very healthy,' Zhenya replied. 'We've always done it. Even my younger sister was whipped when she was a little girl.'

'Aren't you scared?' asked Varvara.

'What can I do? No one asks my permission,' Zhenya calmly replied. 'They whip me and that's all there is to it. It's not that I want it of my own free will.'

'What's there to be afraid of?' Sofya said reassuringly and unhurriedly. 'It's not *that* painful, I can vouch for that myself.'

'And does it work?' Varvara asked once more.

'Well, really!' Sofya retorted. 'Can't you see – there's a living example right in front of you! First you lose some weight, but the very next day you start putting it on again.'

Finally the two cousins' assurances and persuasiveness overcame any lingering doubts Varvara might have had. 'All right,' she said, grinning. 'Go ahead! Let's see what happens. But I only hope no one sees us.'

'There's no one here, all the servants have the day off,' Sofya said.

They led Varvara to the bedroom. In the doorway she began to have second thoughts, but Zhenya pushed her from behind – she was a strong girl – and locked the door.

The curtains were drawn and it was half dark in the room. Not a sound could be heard from there. On two chairs lay a few bundles of nettles, their stalks wrapped in handkerchiefs so one could hold them without getting stung.

Varvara was terrified. 'I'd rather not,' she said hesitantly. 'I've a slight headache. Tomorrow would be better . . .'

But Sofya cried, 'Come on! Hurry up and get undressed, there's nothing to be squeamish about.'

Varvara still hesitated and started backing towards the door. The cousins threw themselves on her and forcibly undressed her. Before she knew what was happening, she was lying on the bed with only her petticoat on. Zhenya grabbed both her hands with one powerful hand, whilst with the other she took a bundle of nettles from Sofya and started whipping Varvara. Sofya held Varvara's feet in a firm grip and kept repeating, 'Now stop fidgeting . . . really, you're a terrible fidget!'

Varvara couldn't hold out for long and soon she was screaming with pain. Zhenya whipped her hard and long, changing the bundles several times. She pressed Varvara's head into the pillow with her elbow so that her screams couldn't be heard far away.

Finally they let her go. She got up, sobbing with pain, and the cousins started comforting her.

'What are you howling for?' asked Sofya. 'It's nothing, really! It will smart for just a little while and then the pain will go. But that's not nearly enough. We shall have to repeat the treatment in a few days.'

'Oh my dear, you can't mean it!' Varvara cried plaintively. 'I've suffered enough already.'

'Come now, we didn't make you suffer very much,' Sofya said to comfort her. 'Of course, this treatment must be repeated from time to time. Both of us have been whipped since childhood – and very often too. There's no point in it otherwise.'

'Puff pastry nettles!' Zhenya chuckled.

When he'd had his after-dinner nap, Peredonov went off to the club to play billiards in the restaurant there. In the street he met Mrs Prepolovensky: after seeing Varvara home she had gone to tell her friend Vershina about what had happened, in secret. They were going the same way and walked together. Peredonov took the opportunity of inviting her and her husband to come and play cards that evening, for small stakes. Sofya led the conversation round to why he wasn't getting married. Peredonov remained gloomily silent. Sofya dropped a few hints about her cousin – wasn't Peredonov very fond of nice plump girls like her? She thought that he agreed – he looked just as mournful as ever and didn't argue.

'I do know your tastes with women,' Sofya said. 'You don't fancy skinny ones, so you must choose someone suitable, a girl with some flesh on her.'

Peredonov was afraid to speak – they might be trying to hook him – and he kept angrily glancing at Sofya.

3. On the way Peredonov told Volodin that Zhenya, Sofya's cousin, was Mr Prepolovensky's mistress. Volodin immediately believed him: he was furious with Zhenya, who had turned him down not so long before.

'She ought to be reported to the ecclesiastical court,' Peredonov said. 'After all, she's from a Church family, a bishop's daughter. Yes, they should report her, then she'd be packed off to a convent to do penance – and there they would whip her!'

Volodin wasn't sure whether he should report her. But he decided to be magnanimous and he left her alone. Otherwise he might get involved, be summoned to the court and told to prove the allegation.

4. Still conversing about such matters, they arrived at the village. The house where the lessee – Marta and Vladya's father – lived was low and wide, with a high grey roof and carved shutters. It wasn't new, but it was solidly built. Hiding behind a row of birches it looked comfortable and charming – at least, that was how it appeared to Vladya and Marta. But Peredonov didn't care for the young birches in front of the house – he would have had them cut down or broken off.

Three barefoot children aged from about eight to ten ran out to greet the visitors with joyful shouts. There were one girl and two boys, all with blue eyes and freckles.

The host, a broad-shouldered, powerful-looking Polish gentleman, with a long grey moustache and an angular face, greeted the visitors at the front door. His face put one in mind of those composite photographs where several similar faces are printed at the same time on the same plate. In such photographs all the distinguishing features of a person are lost, leaving only a general impression of what is typical of all, or most, faces. And so it seemed with Nartanovich's face, which had no particular distinguishing features unique to him alone, but only what was typical of all Polish faces. For this reason one of the town wags nicknamed Nartanovich the 'four and forty' Pole. Nartanovich behaved accordingly: he was polite, perhaps over-polite, but he never lost the sense of pride of a Polish gentleman, saying only what was absolutely necessary, as if he were afraid that, should he say too much, he would reveal what concerned him alone, no one else.

He was clearly pleased at having a guest and, like a true country-dweller, gave him a grossly exaggerated welcome. When he spoke his voice would thunder forth, as if competing with the wind, drowning all other sounds and then abruptly breaking off and falling away. After his, all other voices seemed weak and pathetic.

In one of the rooms, which were rather dark and low, where the master could easily have touched the ceiling, a table was quickly laid. A lively peasant girl brought vodka and savouries.

'Please help yourself,' said Nartanovich, accenting his words incorrectly from lack of conversational practice. 'But you'll have to take pot luck.'

Peredonov quickly downed some vodka, ate a few little snacks and then proceeded to complain about Vladya. Nartanovich gave his son a fierce look and kept plying Peredonov with food and drink, without saying very much. However, Peredonov was determined not to eat any more.

'No,' he said. 'I'm here on business, so you listen to me first.'

'Oh, you're here on business,' cried the host. 'So there's a reason for this visit?'

Peredonov maligned Vladya in every way. The father became even more furious. 'Oh, the lazy devil!' he slowly exclaimed, impressively accenting every syllable. 'A good tanning is what you need! I'm going to give you such a thrashing now – a hundred stingers!'

Vladya burst into tears.

'I promised him that I would come with the express purpose of seeing you punish him in my presence,' Peredonov said.

'And for that I'm truly grateful,' Nartanovich said. 'I shall give that idler such a thrashing with the rod that he won't forget it in a hurry.'

Staring fiercely at Vladya, Nartanovich got up and Vladya had the impression he was so enormous he'd forced all the air out of the room. He grabbed the boy's shoulders and hauled him off to the kitchen. The other children huddled around Marta and looked in terror at the sobbing Vladya. Peredonov followed Nartanovich.

'What are you standing there for?' he asked Marta. 'You should come too. Watch how we do it and give us a hand. You'll have your own children one day.'

Marta flushed, gathered all three children into her arms and smartly sped with them out of the house, as far away as she could, so that they wouldn't hear what was going on in the kitchen.

When Peredonov entered the kitchen, Vladya was undressing. His father was standing before him, slowly uttering dreadful words.

'Lie down on the bench,' he said when Vladya was completely undressed.

Vladya obeyed. Tears were streaming from his eyes, but he was trying to control himself. His father didn't like cries of entreaty – that would only make matters worse. Peredonov glanced at Vladya and his father, surveyed the kitchen and grew anxious when he couldn't see the whipping rods anywhere. Was Nartanovich really doing this just for show? He would give his son a good fright and then let him go, unpunished. It was no coincidence that Vladya was acting peculiarly, not at all as Peredonov had expected: he didn't struggle or sob, or go down on his knees (all Poles are grovellers), or beg forgiveness, or run to Peredonov to plead with him. Had Peredonov travelled all that way just to witness preparations for punishment and no more than this?

Meanwhile Nartanovich, without hurrying, tied his son to the bench, fastened his hands over his head with a strap, tied each foot separately to the bench with a rope, one foot to each side of it. For good measure he tied a rope around his waist. Now Vladya couldn't move at all and he lay there trembling with fear, convinced that his father would thrash him to within an inch of his life, since on previous occasions he had punished him for minor transgressions without tying him up. When he had finished, Nartanovich said, 'Now I must break off some rods and whip you, you wretched idler – that is, if the gentleman doesn't find it too repellent seeing you getting your hide tanned.'

Nartanovich gave a sidelong glance at the gloomy Peredonov, grinned as he smoothed his long moustache and went over to the window, beneath which grew a birch tree. 'We don't even have to go out of the house,' Nartanovich said, breaking off some twigs.

Vladya closed his eyes. He felt that he was going to faint right away.

'Now listen to me, you lazy devil!' his father shouted in a terrifying voice over his head. 'For the first offence this year I shall give you twenty strokes, but next time the dose will be increased.'

Vladya felt relieved – this was the lowest number recognized by his father, and the punishment was nothing new to him.

His father started whipping him with long firm rods. Vladya clenched his teeth and didn't cry out. The blood came through in delicate dewy drops.

'That's good!' his father said when he'd finished. 'A sturdy lad!' And he started untying him. Peredonov thought that it hadn't really hurt Vladya.

'It was hardly worth tying him up just for that,' he said angrily. 'It was just water off a duck's back for him.'

Nartanovich looked at Peredonov with his calm blue eyes and said, 'Next time, if you like, he'll get more. But that'll do for today.'

Vladya put on his shirt and wept as he kissed his father's hand.

'Kiss the rod, you black-faced urchin!' his father shouted. 'And get dressed.'

Vladya dressed and ran barefoot into the garden to have a good cry in peace.

Nartanovich took Peredonov around the house and outbuildings and showed him how he ran the farm. But Peredonov didn't find it at all interesting. Although he had often thought of saving up to buy an estate, now, as he looked at everything Nartanovich was showing him, he could see only crude, dirty implements. He had no idea why they should exist at all, and couldn't understand what they were used for or what they had to do with running the farm.

Half an hour later they sat down to supper. Vladya was called to the table too. Peredonov tried to joke at Vladya's expense, but the intended witticisms turned out crude and stupid. Vladya blushed and was close to tears, but the others didn't laugh, which distressed Peredonov. Moreover, he was annoyed that Vladya hadn't cried out during the punishment. It must have been painful – not for nothing had the blood spurted out. But that little devil had kept quiet. An out-and-out little Polish stinker! thought Peredonov. By now he was beginning to think that his journey had been a complete waste of time.

Next morning Peredonov got up early and said he was leaving right away. They tried in vain to persuade him to stay another day – he flatly refused. 'I only came on business,' he said glumly.

Nartanovich produced a faint grin, stroked his long greying moustache and said in his thunderous voice, 'What a shame! A real shame!'

Several times Peredonov teased Vladya, who was absolutely delighted that Peredonov was leaving. Now, after yesterday's punishment, he knew that he could do what he liked at home and that his father wouldn't scold him. He would have been only too pleased to reply to Peredonov's pestering with some impertinence, but during the past few days Vershina had told him more than once that if he really had Marta's welfare at heart he should do nothing that would make Peredonov angry. And so he took great pains to ensure that Peredonov was seated even more comfortably than yesterday evening.

As he stood on the porch, Peredonov watched him running about.

'Well, did he really let fly?'

'Oh yes,' Vladya replied with a bashful smile.

'You won't forget it until the next thrashing?'

'No I won't.'

'So it was a really good one?'

'Very good.'

And the conversation continued in this vein while the cart was being hitched up. Vladya was beginning to think that there were limits as to how polite one could be, but Peredonov drove off and he breathed freely. That day his father treated him as if nothing had happened the previous evening and Vladya's day was a happy one.

Over dinner Nartanovich told Marta, 'That teacher of theirs is so stupid. He doesn't have any children of his own and he goes around making sure other people's are thrashed. What a monster!'

'You could have let Vladya off this time,' Marta said.

Nartanovich looked at her sternly and said peremptorily, 'Even for someone of your age there's nothing to be said against a good thrashing – please remember that. Anyway, he deserved it.'

Marta blushed ... Vladya said with a restrained smile, 'It'll heal in time for my wedding!'

5. Peredonov walked very quickly, almost ran. He was frightened and annoyed by the policemen he happened to meet. What do they want? he wondered. They're just like spies.

6. He knew an astonishing amount about the townsfolk and in actual fact, if every shady deal were to be exposed, with sufficient evidence for submission to the law courts, then the people in that town would have had the opportunity of seeing in the dock citizens who normally enjoyed universal respect. Several of the cases would have proved quite fascinating!

7. There were now one hundred and seventy-seven students in the school, including twenty-eight from lower-middle-class families, eight peasants and only a hundred and five from the gentry and civil service families.

8. 'So that means you're not a Liberal now, but a Conservative.' 'Yes, a Conservative, Your Excellency.'

9. When Peredonov returned home he found Varvara in the sitting-room with a book in her hands – a very rare sight. She was reading a cookery book, the only one she ever opened.

There was a great deal she didn't understand and everything she read in it and wanted to put into practice ended in failure: in no way could she get the different amounts of ingredients she needed right, since the recipes were for six or twelve people, whereas she had to cook for two or three, rarely more. All the same, she sometimes prepared dishes exactly as the book stated. The cookery book was old and tattered and it had a black binding. This binding immediately caught Peredonov's attention and put him in an utterly miserable mood.

'What are you reading, Varvara?' he angrily asked.

'Can't you see? A cookery book,' replied Varvara. 'I have no time for reading silly books.'

'But why a cookery book?' Peredonov asked in horror.

'What do you mean, *why*? I want to prepare a dish especially for you. You're so fussy with your food,' Varvara explained, grinning with an arrogant, self-satisfied expression.

'I refuse to eat anything out of a black book!' Peredonov announced with determination. He seized the book and carried it off to the bedroom.

A black book! What's more, using recipes from it! he thought in terror. That would be the last straw if they tried to get rid of him with black magic, and quite openly at that! I must destroy it, he concluded, ignoring Varvara's strident grumbles.

But how could he destroy it? Burn it? But that might start a fire. Drown it? Of course, it would only come to the surface and fall into the clutches of someone else. Throw it away? No, someone was bound to find it. No, the best thing would be to tear one page out at a time, quietly steal off with them when paper was needed and, then, when they had all been ripped out, to burn the black cover. This made him feel more relaxed. But what should he do about Varvara? She might get hold of a new book of black magic. No, she had to be well and truly punished.

Peredonov went into the garden, broke off some birch twigs and, after looking gloomily up at the windows, brought them into the bedroom. Then he shouted into the kitchen, through the partly opened door, 'Claudia! Tell madam to come into the bedroom – and you can come as well.'

Varvara and Claudia soon came in. Claudia was the first to see the birch twigs and she started giggling.

'Lie down, Varvara!' Peredonov ordered.

Varvara screamed and made for the door.

'Hold her, Claudia!' shouted Peredonov.

Together they lay Varvara on the bed. Claudia held her while Peredonov thrashed her. Varvara sobbed desperately and begged forgiveness.

10. The gentle sound of children's voices came from behind the door and they could hear Liza's silvery laughter.

'You wait here, behind the door,' Mrs Gudayevsky whispered, 'so he won't know you're in the house.'

Peredonov hid in a dark corner of the corridor and pressed close to the wall. Mrs Gudayevsky impetuously flung open the door and entered the nursery. Through a narrow crack in the door-frame

Peredonov could make out Antosha sitting at a table with his back to the door, next to a little girl in a white frock. Her curls touched his cheek and appeared dark, since only the side that was in the shadows was visible to Peredonov. Her hand was lying on Antosha's shoulder. He was cutting something out of paper for her, which made Liza laugh with joy. Peredonov was annoyed that the two of them were laughing: what that boy deserved was a good thrashing, but here he was, amusing his sister instead of weeping tears of remorse. Then a feeling of malice gripped him. You'll be howling in just a few moments, Peredonov reflected, and the thought comforted him.

Antosha and Liza turned round when they heard the door open. From his hiding-place Peredonov could distinguish Liza's rosy cheek and short little nose under her long straight locks of hair, as well as the look of innocent surprise on Antosha's face.

Antosha's mother went impetuously over to him, tenderly put her arms around his little shoulders and said in a bright, determined voice, 'Let's go, Antosha darling.' Then turning to the nanny whom Peredonov couldn't see she added, 'And you stay here with Liza, Maryushka.'

Antosha reluctantly got up and Liza started whining, as he hadn't finished cutting out the paper for her.

'Later, dear, he'll do it later,' her mother told her as she led her son from the room, holding on to his shoulders.

Antosha still didn't know what was going on, but his mother's determined look had already struck fear into him and made him suspect something awful.

When they came out into the corridor and Mrs Gudayevsky had shut the door, Antosha spotted Peredonov, took fright and tried to run back. But his mother gripped him firmly by the hand and quickly hauled him down the corridor.

'Let's go, let's go, darling,' she kept saying. 'I'm going to treat you to some lovely little birch-rods. Your father – that tyrant! – is out, so I'm going to punish you with them. It will be *so* good for you, my darling.'

Antosha burst into tears and cried out, 'But I haven't been naughty, so why should you punish me?'

'Be quiet, my darling,' his mother said, slapped him on the back of his neck and pushed him into the bedroom.

Peredonov followed them, angrily muttering something to himself.

The rods were lying ready in the bedroom. Peredonov wasn't at all pleased – they were so stubby and short. Rods for the ladies, he angrily thought. Antosha's mother quickly sat down on a chair, stood him in front of her and started unbuttoning him. His flushed face was bathed in tears. Antosha shouted, struggled between her hands and lashed out with his feet.

'Mummy, mummy! Please forgive me. I won't ever do it again!'

'It's all right, darling,' his mother replied. 'Come on now, let's get you undressed. It'll be very good for you. Now, there's nothing to worry about, it'll heal in no time,' she said, consoling him as she nimbly undressed him. The half-undressed Antosha kept putting up a fight, kicking out and shouting.

'Help me, Mr Peredonov,' Julia Gudayevsky said in a loud whisper. 'He's such a little ruffian. I knew all along that I wouldn't be able to manage on my own.'

Peredonov took hold of Antosha by the feet while Mrs Gudayevsky started thrashing him.

'Don't be lazy, don't be lazy!' she repeated again and again.

'Don't kick! Don't kick!' Peredonov repeated in turn.

'Oooh! I won't do it again. Oooh, I won't!' cried Antosha.

Mrs Gudayevsky worked so zealously that she soon grew tired. 'That's enough for now, darling,' she said, letting Antosha go. 'That's enough, I can't manage any more. I'm absolutely exhausted.'

'If you're so tired I could take over,' Peredonov suggested.

'Antosha! Thank the gentleman,' Mrs Gudayevsky said. 'Thank him and click your heels. Mr Peredonov's going to whip you just a little bit more with the rods. Lie over my knees, darling.'

She handed Peredonov a bundle of rods, pulled Antosha to her again and pushed his head between her knees. Peredonov suddenly became frightened: he felt that Antosha might break free and bite him. 'That's enough for now,' he said.

'Antosha! Did you hear?' Mrs Gudayevsky asked, lifting him by his ears. 'Mr Peredonov is forgiving you. Now thank him and click your heels. Click them and get dressed.'

Sobbing, Antosha clicked his heels and got dressed. His mother led him by the hand out into the corridor.

'Just a minute,' she whispered to Peredonov, 'there's something else I have to say.'

She took Antosha into the nursery where the nanny was putting Liza to bed and told him to go to bed. Then she returned to the bedroom. Peredonov was gloomily sitting on a chair in the middle of the room.

'I'm so grateful,' Mrs Gudayevsky began. 'I can't tell you how grateful. You acted so nobly, so very nobly. My husband should have taken care of this, but you took his place. He deserves to be cuckolded – if he lets others assume his responsibilities then others should enjoy his privileges too.'

Impulsively she threw herself around Peredonov's neck and whispered, 'Fondle me, darling!'

Then she spoke a few words that cannot be printed here. Peredonov was filled with blank astonishment, but he flung his arms around her waist and kissed her on the lips. She pressed hers firmly to his, in a long greedy kiss. Then she broke away from his embrace, dashed to the door, locked it and quickly began to undress.

11. Antosha was already asleep when his father returned from the club. In the mornings, when Antosha left for school, his father would still be sleeping and he saw him only in the afternoons. He sneaked quietly away from his mother into the study and complained about the thrashing. Mr Gudayevsky flew into a rage and ran around the study. He threw a pile of books on to the floor from his desk and shouted in a terrifying voice, 'That's vile, disgusting, despicable, disgraceful! Damn and blast! Call the police!'

Then he rushed over to Antosha, pulled his trousers down, inspected his slim little body that was marked all over with narrow pink stripes and shouted in a piercing voice, 'Map of Europe, seventeenth edition!' He caught Antosha up in his arms and ran to his wife. Antosha felt both awkward and ashamed and whined pitifully.

Julia Gudayevsky was deep in a novel. When she heard her husband shouting in the distance she guessed what had happened, leaped up, threw the book on to the floor and ran around the room, her dry fists clenched and her brightly coloured ribbons streaming behind her.

Mr Gudayevsky charged into the room, kicking the door open with his foot. 'What's this?' he roared, setting Antosha down and showing her his naked body. 'How did this landscape get there?'

Julia Gudayevsky trembled with rage and stamped her feet. 'I thrashed him!' she shouted. '*I* did it!'

'Vile! Most vile! Hellishly vile!' Mr Gudayevsky shouted. 'How dare you do this without my consent!'

'And I'd do it again. I'll thrash him just to spite you!' Mrs Gudayevsky screamed. 'I'll thrash him every day.'

Antosha struggled free and fled, buttoning himself as he ran and leaving his parents to hurl abuse at each other.

Mr Gudayevsky dashed over to his wife and gave her a hard slap on the face.

She screamed, burst into tears and shouted, 'Monster! Scum of the earth! You want to drive me into the grave!' She smartly rushed at her husband and slapped his cheek.

'Mutiny! Treason! Call the police!' Gudayevsky shouted.

For a long time they fought, flying at each other again and again. Finally they grew tired. Mrs Gudayevsky sat on the floor, crying. 'You scoundrel! You've ruined my youth!' she wailed in a plaintive, dragging voice.

Gudayevsky stood before her and was just about to give her another slap when he changed his mind, sat on the floor opposite his wife and shouted, 'You Fury! Harridan! Tailless witch! You've made my life sheer hell!'

'I'm going to Mother's,' Mrs Gudayevsky whined.

'Go then,' Gudayevsky angrily replied. 'Nothing would give me more pleasure. I'd even take you myself. I'll make music on a frying-pan, play a Persian march on my lips!' He trumpeted a wild harsh tune through his fist.

'And I'll take the children!' shouted Mrs Gudayevsky.

'I won't let you!' shouted Mr Gudayevsky.

Simultaneously they leaped to their feet and carried on shouting, wildly gesticulating.

'I won't let you have Antosha!' shouted the wife.

'And I won't let you have him!' shouted the husband.

'I'm taking him!'

'I won't let you!'

'You'll corrupt the boy, mollycoddle him, ruin him!'

'And you'll tyrannize him!'

They clenched their fists, threatened one another and ran off in opposite directions – she to the bedroom, he to his study. The sound of the two doors being slammed echoed throughout the house.

Antosha was sitting in his father's study, as this seemed the most convenient, safest place. Gudayevsky ran around repeating, 'I won't let your mother have you, Antosha, I won't!'

'Let her have Liza,' advised Antosha.

Gudayevsky stopped in his tracks, slapped his forehead and cried, 'That's a good idea!'

He ran out of the study. Antosha gingerly glanced into the corridor and saw him running into the nursery. From there he could hear Liza crying and the frightened voice of the nanny. Gudayevsky pulled the violently sobbing, terrified Liza out of the nursery by the hand, took her into the bedroom, threw her at her mother and shouted, 'Here's your little girl! Take her, but my son stays with me, on the basis of the seven articles of the seven sections of the Code of Codes!' And with that he ran back into his study, exclaiming, 'What a joke! Now try and be satisfied with just a little, and only give her gentle thrashings! Ho, ho!'

Mrs Gudayevsky grabbed her daughter, sat her on her lap and started comforting her. Then she suddenly leaped up, took Liza's hand and swiftly led her to her father. Once again Liza burst into tears.

From the study father and son could hear Liza howling down the corridor and they looked at each other in amazement.

'What is she up to?' whispered the father. 'She doesn't want her – she's coming for *you*!'

Antosha crawled under the writing-table. But just then Mrs Gudayevsky ran into the study, threw Liza to her father, dragged her son from under the table and struck him on the cheek. Then she grabbed his hand and hauled him along the corridor after her, crying. 'Let's go, darling. That father of yours is such a tyrant!'

And now the father suddenly pulled himself together, grabbed the boy by his other hand, struck him on the other cheek and cried, 'Don't be scared, my boy, I shan't let anyone have you.'

Father and mother tugged Antosha in opposite directions whilst they ran around him. Antosha spun like a top between them and cried out in terror, 'Let go of me, let go! You'll tear my arms off!'

Somehow he managed to free his arms, so that mother and father were left holding only his jacket sleeves. But they were oblivious of this and continued circling Antosha in a wild frenzy. Antosha cried out desperately, 'You're tearing me apart! My shoulders are cracking. Oh, oh, you're tearing me in half. You've torn me in half!'

And in fact mother and father suddenly fell on to the floor on either side of him, each holding a sleeve of Antosha's jacket. Antosha ran off with a desperate cry, 'You've torn me in half, that's what you've done!'

Both father and mother imagined that they had ripped off Antosha's arms. They lay on the floor howling in terror. 'We've torn our little Antosha in half!' they cried.

Then they jumped up and waved the empty sleeves at one another, each trying to shout louder than the other: 'Send for a doctor! He's run away! Where are his arms? Look for his arms!!'

They both crawled around the floor, but they found no arms. Then they sat facing one another. Howling with fear and with pity for Antosha, they set about lashing each other with the empty sleeves, after which they rolled around the floor, locked in combat. The maid and nanny came running in and separated the master and mistress.

12. After dinner Peredonov went straight to bed, which he always did when he wasn't playing billiards. He dreamed of nothing but sheep and cats, which walked around him, bleating and mewing quite distinctly words that were really obscene. Everything they did was shameless.

After his nap he went to see the merchant Tvorozhkov, father of two boys at the school, to complain about them. The success of two previous visits had tickled his palate and he felt that here too he would be successful. Tvorozhkov was a simple, straightforward person, educated on a pittance and now very prosperous. He had a forbidding appearance, said very little and conducted himself sternly and solemnly. His sons, Vasya and Volodya, feared him like the plague. Of course, he was the kind of man who would give them a thrashing that would turn the very devil's stomach.

When he saw how solemnly and silently Tvorozhkov was listening to his complaints, Peredonov felt all the more confident that his assumptions were correct. The boys, fourteen-year-old Vasya and twelve-year-old Volodya, stood stiffly to attention before their father, like little soldiers, but Peredonov was surprised and annoyed to see how calm their faces were, without a trace of fear. When Peredonov had finished and was quiet, Tvorozhkov looked carefully at his sons. They stiffened up even more and looked straight back at him. 'You can go now,' Tvorozhkov said. The boys bowed to Peredonov and left. Tvorozhkov turned to Peredonov.

'It's a great honour for me, my dear sir,' he said, 'that you are so concerned about my sons. It has just come to my notice, however, that you are in the habit of making similar visits, insisting that parents thrash their sons. Is it really possible that boys have suddenly got so out of hand that there's no other way of controlling them? Everything used to run nice and smoothly, but all of a sudden there's just one thrashing after the other.'

'But if they *misbehave*,' Peredonov muttered, rather taken aback.

'They do misbehave,' said Tvorozhkov. 'Everyone knows that. When they misbehave they're punished. But what surprises me very much – please forgive me, dear sir, if I'm saying the wrong thing – what really surprises me is the fact that you alone, of all the teachers, have seen fit to burden yourself with such – if I may use the expression – unbecoming activities. Of course, if a father thrashes his son, well, that's only right and proper – if that's what the son deserves. But spying on other people's sons would appear to be overstepping the mark in your case.'

'But it's for their own good,' Peredonov angrily replied.

'We are quite familiar with the correct procedure in such cases,' Tvorozhkov immediately retorted, not allowing Peredonov to continue. 'If a pupil misbehaves, then he's punished at school, according to the rules and regulations. If he persists, the parents are notified, or are asked to come to school and then the form master or an inspector will tell them what the offence was. And as for dealing with boys in their homes, it goes without saying that the parents will know what to do, depending on the kind of boy and the seriousness of the offence. But there is absolutely no precedent where a teacher takes the law into his own hands and goes round to boys' homes demanding that they are thrashed. One day you might go to a certain house, then someone else might go there the next, then a third the day after that. Am I supposed to thrash my sons after each of these three visits? No, thank you very much, sir, it's quite unacceptable and you should be ashamed of concerning yourself with such absurdities. Ashamed, sir!' Tvorozhkov stood up and added, 'I don't think there's anything more to discuss.'

'Is that all you have to say on the subject?' Peredonov said gloomily, getting up from his chair in great confusion.

'Yes, I think so,' Tvorozhkov replied. 'Now will you please excuse me?'

'So you want to breed nihilists,' Peredonov said maliciously as he clumsily backed towards the door. 'I should report you to the police for that.'

'If it comes to it, I can do my share of reporting,' Tvorozhkov calmly replied.

This reply shocked Peredonov to the core: what was Tvorozhkov going to report him for? It's possible, he thought, that I said something I shouldn't have, gave something away during the conversation, and he's made a mental note of it. Perhaps he has a special machine hidden under the couch that records dangerous words. Peredonov took a terrified look under the couch – and there something seemed to move – it was small, greyish, pulsating, shaking all over with mocking laughter. Peredonov shuddered. I mustn't give myself away, whatever happens, flashed through his mind.

'You won't catch me out – not if I know it!' he shouted to Tvorozhkov and hastily left the room.

13. Of course, Peredonov hadn't noticed this. He was too absorbed in his own happiness.

Marta returned to the summer-house when Peredonov had already left. She entered it rather apprehensively: Vershina might have something to say to her.

In fact Vershina was extremely annoyed. Up to now she still hadn't lost all hope of pairing Marta off with Peredonov and marrying Murin herself. And now everything was in ruins. Quickly and softly she showered her with reproaches as she briskly puffed clouds of cigarette smoke and glared at her.

Vershina loved to have a good grumble. Her vague whims, her fading, languid desires lent support to this feeling of dull discontent and this was expressed most conveniently by grumbling. If she had said it out loud, this would have resulted in sheer nonsense. But if she grumbled, any absurdities would simply slip off her tongue so that neither she herself nor others would notice the incoherence, the contradictions or pointlessness of all those words.

Perhaps it was only now that Marta realized how repulsive she found Peredonov, after all that had happened with him and because of him. Marta never gave much thought to love. She was always dreaming of marrying and keeping a good household. Of course, to do this she needed someone to fall in love with her. Although this was a pleasant thought, at the same time it wasn't the most important thing.

Whenever Marta dreamed about her household, she imagined that she would have exactly the same kind of house, orchard and kitchen garden as Vershina. Sometimes she had sweet dreams that Vershina would make her a present of all this and that Vershina would stay on there to live with her, to smoke her cigarettes and rebuke her for her laziness.

'You just didn't know how to get him interested,' Vershina said quickly and angrily. 'You were always sitting there like a lump on a log. What more could you have wanted? A fine young man, the very picture of health. All I do is worry myself over you and try my very best for you. You could at least have appreciated, understood that. After all, it was for *you*. So you, for your part, might have tried to attract him in some way.'

'But how could I have forced myself upon him?' Marta said softly, 'I'm not like those Rutilov sisters.'

'They're so conceited, these poverty-stricken Polish gentry!' Vershina grumbled.

'I'm afraid of him. I'd better marry Murin,' said Marta.

'Murin! You don't say! You've a pretty high opinion of yourself! Murin! As if he'd have you. He may have whispered some sweet nothings, but it's obvious they weren't intended for you at all. You don't deserve a husband like him, such a sound, steady, respectable man. You like stuffing yourself, but thinking just gives you a headache!'

Marta blushed bright crimson. She really did like her food and would eat frequently – and a great deal. As she had been brought up on country air, and was used to simple rough work, Marta considered plentiful nourishing food one of the principal conditions for a person's well-being.

Vershina suddenly dashed over to Marta, struck her cheek with her small dry hand and shouted, 'On your knees, you lazy bitch!'

Quietly sobbing, Marta went down on her knees and said, 'Forgive me, N[atalya] A[fanasyevna].'

'I'll make you stay there all day!' Vershina cried. 'And mind you don't fray your dress, it cost money. Now stay on your bare knees, lift your dress and take your shoes off. Think you're a fine lady, do you?! You wait, I'm still going to give you a thrashing with birch-rods.'

Marta obediently sat on the edge of the bench, hurriedly took her shoes off, bared her knees and knelt on the bare boards. It was as if she wanted to subjugate herself and to know that her involve-ment in this distressing affair was coming to an end. She would be punished, kept on her knees, even thrashed perhaps – and it was all going to happen very soon, that same day. Vershina kept walking back and forth past the meekly kneeling Marta: she felt sorry for her, yet offended that she wanted to marry Murin. It would have been much more agreeable if she could have married Marta off to Peredonov, or someone else, taking Murin for herself. Murin had such a strong appeal for her – he was big, fat, kind and very attractive. Vershina thought that she would have suited Murin far more than Marta. The fact that Murin had become so taken with Marta and was so tempted by her would soon be a thing of the past. But now Vershina understood that Murin would insist on Marta marrying him and she had no wish to interfere. It was as though she were possessed by some kind of maternal compassion and tenderness towards the girl and that she was contemplating sacrificing herself and surrendering Murin to Marta. This compas-sion for Marta made her feel noble and very proud, while at the same time the heartache brought about by the loss of all hope of marrying Murin inflamed her heart with the desire to make Marta feel the full force of her anger, to make her fully appreciate how kind she'd been to her – and to make her acknowledge that she was the guilty one.

What Vershina found particularly appealing about Marta and Vladya was that she could order them around, have a good grouse at them and occasionally punish them. Vershina loved power and she was very flattered when Marta, after doing something wrong, would unquestioningly go down on her knees when she was ordered to.

'I do everything for you,' she said. 'I'm not an old woman yet. I too could still enjoy life, marry some kind respectable man, instead of running myself off my feet trying to find you a husband. But I care for you more than I do for myself. As you've let one chance slip, I shall have to lure another one for you, just as if you were a little child. But again you'll only turn your nose up and frighten him off.'

'Someone will marry me,' Marta said bashfully. 'I'm no freak and I don't need other people's fiancés.'

'Be quiet!' Vershina cried. 'No freak? Does that make me one then? She's been punished, yet still she answers back! Clearly the punishment wasn't enough! Of course, my dear, what you need is a really good talking-to so that you'll be obedient, do everything you're told and not try to be clever. How can I expect sense from someone who tries to be clever out of sheer stupidity? You, my dear, must first learn to lead your own life. But as things are, you're still going around in other people's clothes, so you must learn to be a little more meek and mild, to do what you're told, otherwise Vladya won't be the only one to get a thrashing.'

Marta trembled as she raised her tear-stained, flushed face and looked with timid, silent entreaty into Vershina's eyes. In her heart there was a feeling of submissiveness and readiness to do all that was required of her, to endure everything they might want to do with her: if only she could discover, or guess what it was they wanted.

Vershina was quite aware of her power over the girl and this went to her head. At the same time, a feeling that was both tender and cruel told her that she should treat Marta with the severity of a parent, for her own good. She's used to thrashings, she thought. It's the only lesson girls of her type understand. It's no use just talking. They only respect those who are hard on them.

'Let's go home, my beauty,' she told Marta, smiling. 'I'm going to treat you to some excellent birch-rods.'

Marta burst into tears, but she was glad that the end of the affair was in sight. She bowed down at Vershina's feet and said, 'You're like a mother to me. I owe you so much.'

'Come on now,' said Vershina, pushing her in the shoulder.

Marta obediently stood up and followed Vershina on her bare feet. Vershina stopped under a birch tree and grinned at her.

'Do you want me to break them off?' Marta asked.

'Yes,' Vershina said, 'and make sure they're good ones.'

Marta started breaking off some twigs, choosing the longer and tougher ones and stripping the leaves off as Vershina watched and grinned.

'That'll do,' she said at length and walked towards the house.

Marta followed her with a huge bundle of twigs. Vladya came out to greet them and gave Vershina a frightened look.

'I'm going to give your sister a good thrashing right now,' Vershina told him, 'and you can hold her for me while I punish her.'

But once inside the house Vershina changed her mind and sat on a chair in the kitchen. Then she made Marta kneel in front of her and bend over her knees. She lifted her dress from behind, gripped her hands and ordered Vladya to whip her. Although Vladya was very familiar with birch-rods, having seen his father thrash Marta more than once, he felt sorry for his sister, but he thought that if punishment had to be carried out it should be done conscientiously. So he whipped Marta as hard as he could, keeping a careful count of the strokes. The pain was excruciating and she cried out in a voice partly muffled by her own dress and partly by Vershina's. Marta tried to keep still, but despite herself her bare legs started flailing about more and more on the floor, until she finally began to kick them out in despair. Her body was already covered with weals and splashes of blood. Vershina had great difficulty holding her.

'Wait a moment,' she told Vladya. 'Tie her legs tighter.'

Vladya brought a length of rope from somewhere. Marta was tightly bound, put on the bench and secured to it with the rope. Vershina and Vladya each took a rod and for a long while they thrashed Marta from both sides. As before, Vladya kept an accurate tally of the strokes, counting them under his breath and calling the tens out loud. At first Marta's screams were loud and shrill, and then she gasped for breath and they became hoarse and intermittent. Finally, when Vladya had counted to a hundred, Vershina said, 'Well, that's enough. She won't forget that in a hurry.'

They untied Marta and helped her to her bed. All the time she kept whimpering and moaning. For two days she couldn't get up. On the third she managed it, bowed down with difficulty at Vershina's feet and moaned and wept when she stood up again.

'It was for your own good,' Vershina said.

'Oh, I do understand,' Marta replied, bowing at her feet again. 'But from now on please don't leave me. Be like a mother to me. Now you must forgive me and not be angry anymore.'

'It's all right, I forgive you,' Vershina said, offering Marta her hand. Marta kissed it.

Discover more about our forthcoming books through Penguin's FREE newspaper...

Penguin Quarterly

It's packed with:

- exciting features
- author interviews
- previews & reviews
- books from your favourite films & TV series
- exclusive competitions & much, much more...

READ MORE IN PENGUIN

In every corner of the world, on every subject under the sun, Penguin represents quality and variety – the very best in publishing today.

For complete information about books available from Penguin – including Puffins, Penguin Classics and Arkana – and how to order them, write to us at the appropriate address below. Please note that for copyright reasons the selection of books varies from country to country.

In the United Kingdom: Please write to *Dept. JC, Penguin Books Ltd, FREEPOST, West Drayton, Middlesex UB7 OBR*

If you have any difficulty in obtaining a title, please send your order with the correct money, plus ten per cent for postage and packaging, to *PO Box No. 11, West Drayton, Middlesex UB7 OBR*

In the United States: Please write to *Penguin USA Inc., 375 Hudson Street, New York, NY 10014*

In Canada: Please write to *Penguin Books Canada Ltd, 10 Alcorn Avenue, Suite 300, Toronto, Ontario M4V 3B2*

In Australia: Please write to *Penguin Books Australia Ltd, 487 Maroondah Highway, Ringwood, Victoria 3134*

In New Zealand: Please write to *Penguin Books (NZ) Ltd,182–190 Wairau Road, Private Bag, Takapuna, Auckland 9*

In India: Please write to *Penguin Books India Pvt Ltd, 706 Eros Apartments, 56 Nehru Place, New Delhi 110 019*

In the Netherlands: Please write to *Penguin Books Netherlands B.V., Keizersgracht 231 NL–1016 DV Amsterdam*

In Germany: Please write to *Penguin Books Deutschland GmbH, Friedrichstrasse 10–12, W–6000 Frankfurt/Main 1*

In Spain: Please write to *Penguin Books S. A., C. San Bernardo 117–6° E–28015 Madrid*

In Italy: Please write to *Penguin Italia s.r.l., Via Felice Casati 20, I–20124 Milano*

In France: Please write to *Penguin France S. A., 17 rue Lejeune, F–31000 Toulouse*

In Japan: Please write to *Penguin Books Japan, Ishikiribashi Building, 2–5–4, Suido, Bunkyo-ku, Tokyo 112*

In Greece: Please write to *Penguin Hellas Ltd, Dimocritou 3, GR–106 71 Athens*

In South Africa: Please write to *Longman Penguin Southern Africa (Pty) Ltd, Private Bag X08, Bertsham 2013*

READ MORE IN PENGUIN

Penguin Twentieth-Century Classics offer a selection of the finest works of literature published this century. Spanning the globe from Argentina to America, from France to India, the masters of prose and poetry are represented by the Penguin.

If you would like a catalogue of the Twentieth-Century Classics library, please write to:

Penguin Marketing, 27 Wrights Lane, London W8 5TZ

(Available while stocks last)

PENGUIN AUDIOBOOKS

Penguin Books has always led the field in quality publishing. Now you can listen at leisure to your favourite books, read to you by familiar voices from radio, stage and screen. Penguin Audiobooks are ideal as gifts, for when you are travelling or simply to enjoy at home. They are edited, abridged and produced to an excellent standard, and are always faithful to the original texts. From thrillers to classic literature, biography to humour, with a wealth of titles in between, Penguin Audiobooks offer you quality, entertainment and the chance to re-discover the pleasure of listening.

Published or forthcoming:

Emma by Jane Austen, read by Fiona Shaw

Persuasion by Jane Austen, read by Joanna David

Pride and Prejudice by Jane Austen, read by Geraldine McEwan

The Tenant of Wildfell Hall by Anne Brontë, read by Juliet Stevenson

Jane Eyre by Charlotte Brontë, read by Juliet Stevenson

Villette by Charlotte Brontë, read by Juliet Stevenson

Wuthering Heights by Emily Brontë, read by Juliet Stevenson

The Woman in White by Wilkie Collins, read by Nigel Anthony and Susan Jameson

Heart of Darkness by Joseph Conrad, read by David Threlfall

Tales from the One Thousand and One Nights, read by Souad Faress and Raad Rawi

Moll Flanders by Daniel Defoe, read by Frances Barber

Great Expectations by Charles Dickens, read by Hugh Laurie

Hard Times by Charles Dickens, read by Michael Pennington

Martin Chuzzlewit by Charles Dickens, read by John Wells

The Old Curiosity Shop by Charles Dickens, read by Alec McCowen

Crime and Punishment by Fyodor Dostoyevsky, read by Alex Jennings

Middlemarch by George Eliot, read by Harriet Walter

PENGUIN AUDIOBOOKS

Silas Marner by George Eliot, read by Tim Pigott-Smith

The Great Gatsby by F. Scott Fitzgerald, read by Marcus D'Amico

Madame Bovary by Gustave Flaubert, read by Claire Bloom

Jude the Obscure by Thomas Hardy, read by Samuel West

The Return of the Native by Thomas Hardy, read by Steven Pacey

Tess of the D'Urbervilles by Thomas Hardy, read by Eleanor Bron

The Iliad by Homer, read by Derek Jacobi

Dubliners by James Joyce, read by Gerard McSorley

The Dead and Other Stories by James Joyce, read by Gerard McSorley

On the Road by Jack Kerouac, read by David Carradine

Sons and Lovers by D. H. Lawrence, read by Paul Copley

The Fall of the House of Usher by Edgar Allan Poe, read by Andrew Sachs

Wide Sargasso Sea by Jean Rhys, read by Jane Lapotaire and Michael Kitchen

The Little Prince by Antoine de Saint-Exupéry, read by Michael Maloney

Frankenstein by Mary Shelley, read by Richard Pasco

Of Mice and Men by John Steinbeck, read by Gary Sinise

Travels with Charley by John Steinbeck, read by Gary Sinise

The Pearl by John Steinbeck, read by Hector Elizondo

Dr Jekyll and Mr Hyde by Robert Louis Stevenson, read by Jonathan Hyde

Kidnapped by Robert Louis Stevenson, read by Robbie Coltrane

The Age of Innocence by Edith Wharton, read by Kerry Shale

The Buccaneers by Edith Wharton, read by Dana Ivey

Mrs Dalloway by Virginia Woolf, read by Eileen Atkins

READ MORE IN PENGUIN

A CHOICE OF TWENTIETH - CENTURY CLASSICS

Ulysses James Joyce

Ulysses is unquestionably one of the supreme masterpieces, in any artistic form, of the twentieth century. A modernist classic, its ceaseless verbal inventiveness and astonishingly wide-ranging allusions confirm its standing as an imperishable monument to the human condition. 'It is the book to which we are all indebted and from which none of us can escape' – T. S. Eliot

The End of the Affair Graham Greene

'One of the most personal and most interesting of Greene's stories, containing not only his mature thoughts on the literary life and the dubious fame it brings, but also on the nature of an adulterous love affair, the joy and guilt it generates in roughly equal proportions' – Anthony Curtis in the *Financial Times*

Tigers are Better-Looking Jean Rhys

Jean Rhys wrote about women – society's victims – with all the passion and despair of a loser. Set in Paris, London and the Caribbean, her bitter-sweet, tantalizingly evocative stories conjure up the loneliness of a rented room, the regrets of a failed love affair and the temporary oblivion of alcohol with astonishing power and poignancy.

Babbitt Sinclair Lewis

In chronicling the follies, ambitions and fantasies of Babbitt, Sinclair Lewis captures with superb realism and biting satire the small-town mentality of America in the twenties. 'One of the greatest novels I have read for a long time' – H. G. Wells

The End of the Chapter John Galsworthy

Here Galsworthy writes about the lives and loves of the Cherrells, cousins of the Forsytes. Galsworthy's grasp of political and social change and its effect on a family, as well as his incisive sense of character, make this a fine trilogy with which to end The Forsyte Saga.

READ MORE IN PENGUIN

A CHOICE OF TWENTIETH - CENTURY CLASSICS

Between the Acts Virginia Woolf

'Her posthumous novel ... suggests several new directions ... Its weave of past and present, quotidian reality and imminent catastrophe, the thin line between civilization and barbarism, its erotic overtones and continual humour make a powerful and prophetic statement' – *The Times*

Gentlemen Prefer Blondes Anita Loos

Gentlemen Prefer Blondes had its first acclaimed appearance in *Harpers Bazaar* and was later made famous on stage and screen. In this brilliant satire of the Jazz Age Anita Loos has created the funniest Bad Blonde in American literature.

The Living and the Dead Patrick White

To hesitate on the edge of life or to plunge in and risk change – this is the dilemma explored in *The Living and the Dead*. 'Scene after scene is worked out with an exactness and subtlety which no second-string novelist can scent, far less nail to paper' – *Time*. 'He is, in the finest sense, a world novelist' – *Guardian*

Go Tell It on the Mountain James Baldwin

'*Mountain* is the book I had to write if I was ever going to write anything else. I had to deal with what hurt me most. I had to deal with my father' – James Baldwin. 'Passionately eloquent' – *The Times*

Memories of a Catholic Girlhood Mary McCarthy

Blending memories and family myths, Mary McCarthy takes us back to the twenties, when she was orphaned in a world of relations as colourful, potent and mysterious as the Catholic religion. 'Superb ... so heartbreaking that in comparison Jane Eyre seems to have got off lightly' – Anita Brookner

READ MORE IN PENGUIN

A CHOICE OF TWENTIETH - CENTURY CLASSICS

The Sea of Fertility   Yukio Mishima

'Mishima's thrilling storytelling is unique; there is nothing like it. His flashing style is perfect for his dark motives and there are times when his words are so splendid, and his concepts so tragic, that reading him becomes a profound experience' – Ronald Blythe in the *Sunday Times*

Nineteen Eighty-Four   George Orwell

'It is a volley against the authoritarian in every personality, a polemic against every orthodoxy, an anarchistic blast against every unquestioning conformist ... *Nineteen Eighty-Four* is a great novel and a great tract because of the clarity of its call, and it will endure because its message is a permanent one: erroneous thought is the stuff of freedom' – Ben Pimlott

The Outsider   Albert Camus

Meursault leads an apparently unremarkable bachelor life in Algiers, until his involvement in a violent incident calls into question the fundamental values of society. 'Few French writers of this century have been more versatile or more influential than Camus ... No one in his lifetime wrote better prose than he, no one better blended conviction and grace of style' – *The Times*

Mittee   Daphne Rooke

Daphne Rooke is one of South Africa's finest post-war novelists and *Mittee*, set in nineteenth-century Transvaal, remains her masterpiece. Juxtaposing violence and sexuality, the novel is a searing indictment of the alienation created by the excesses of Afrikaaner nationalism.

The Home and the World   Rabindranath Tagore

Rabindranath Tagore's powerful novel, set on a Bengali noble's estate in 1908, is both a love story and a novel of political awakening. 'It has the complexity and tragic dimensions of Tagore's own time, and ours' – Anita Desai

READ MORE IN PENGUIN

A CHOICE OF TWENTIETH -CENTURY CLASSICS

The Grand Babylon Hotel   Arnold Bennett

Focusing on Theodore Racksole's discovery of the world inside the luxury hotel he purchased on a whim, Arnold Bennett's witty and grandiose serial records the mysterious comings and goings of the eccentric aristocrats, stealthy conspirators and great nobles who grace the corridors of the Grand Babylon.

Mrs Dalloway   Virginia Woolf

Into *Mrs Dalloway* Virginia Woolf poured all her passionate sense of how other people live, remember and love as well as hate, and in prose of astonishing beauty she struggled to catch, impression by impression and minute by minute, the feel of life itself.

The Counterfeiters   André Gide

'It's only after our death that we shall really be able to hear'. From puberty through adolescence to death, *The Counterfeiters* is a rare encyclopedia of human disorder, weakness and despair.

The Great Wall of China and Other Short Works   Franz Kafka

This volume contains the major short works left by Kafka, including *Blumfeld, An Elderly Bachelor, The Great Wall of China* and *Investigations of a Dog*, together with *The Collected Aphorisms* and *He: Aphorisms from the 1920 Diary*.

The Guide   R. K. Narayan

'There is something almost Irish in the humour, buzz and blarney of Narayan's world which seems continents removed from the anguished ...dia of most fiction, and the rope trick of irony, fun and feeling is ...eautifully adroit' – *Observer*

The Fight   Norman Mailer

In 1975, at the World Heavyweight Boxing Championship in Kinshasa, Zaïre, an ageing Muhammad Ali met George Foreman in the ring. Mesmeric and profound, *The Fight* covers the tense weeks of preparation and the fight itself.

READ MORE IN PENGUIN

A CHOICE OF TWENTIETH - CENTURY CLASSICS

Blame Me on History Bloke Modisane

In this searing autobiographical work Bloke Modisane gives us the noise, the zest, the violent communality that was Sophiatown – the centre of black cultural life in Johannesburg until its destruction in 1958. His anguish as he recreates the town from the rubble of the bulldozers, rips off the page to rebuild it in our imagination.

A Portrait of the Artist as a Young Man James Joyce

'The *Portrait*, with its exalted Stephen, its impressionist background, its shadowy cast behind the brilliantly lit central figure and its succession of dramatic monologues, is written in a mood of enraptured fervour' – *The Times Literary Supplement*

The Quiet American Graham Greene

The Quiet American is a terrifying portrait of innocence at large. While the French Army in Indo-China is grappling with the Vietminh, back at Saigon a young and high-minded American begins to channel economic aid to a 'Third Force'. 'There has been no novel of any political scope about Vietnam since Graham Greene wrote *The Quiet American*' – *Harper's*

Good Morning, Midnight Jean Rhys

Jean Rhys wrote about women in an innovative and often controversial way, with perception and sensitivity. In *Good Morning, Midnight* she created an unforgettable portrait of a woman forced to confront her own inevitable loneliness and despair.

A Life Italo Svevo

Alfonso Nitti feels his country roots have been lost in the prosperous a enterprising world of banking. After a brittle and insincere affair with the daughter of his boss, Nitti dwindles to passive listlessness and, lacking the will to resist or defy his fate, stumbles towards oblivion.

READ MORE IN PENGUIN

A CHOICE OF TWENTIETH - CENTURY CLASSICS

Darkness at Noon Arthur Koestler

'A remarkable book, a grimly fascinating interpretation of the logic of the Russian Revolution, indeed of all revolutionary dictatorships, and at the same time a tense and subtly intellectualized drama of prison psychology'– *The Times Literary Supplement*

Les Enfants Terribles Jean Cocteau

Two children must die in following the rules of the 'Game' – which they invented as their own bizarre version of life itself. Paul and Elisabeth, brother and sister, sleep in the same room, and it is the room which is significant. For – wherever they go and whatever they do – it is the Room that contains them and the Game that controls them.

Selected Poems Osip Mandelstam

'One of the century's greatest lyric poets ... we can perceive a glittering poetry at once allusive, hard-edged and uncompromising. We see Leningrad black and shining, sitting like a hunched wild cat or transformed into "transparent Petropolis/where Proserpina rules over us"' – Elaine Feinstein in the *Sunday Times*

Delta of Venus Anaïs Nin

Anaïs Nin conjures up a glittering cascade of sexual encounters. Creating her own 'language of the senses', she explores an area that was previously the domain of male writers and brings to it her own unique perceptions. Her vibrant and impassioned prose magically evokes the essence of female sexuality in a world where only love has meaning.

Locos Felipe Alfau

First published in 1928, *Locos* enthralled and puzzled its contemporary critics. Through interlocking stories and narratives, it glimpses the lives of a group of café-dwellers and explores the nature of identity and reality. 'Makes thought-provoking as well as entertaining reading, curiously timeless like the world in which it unfolds' – *The Times Literary Supplement*

READ MORE IN PENGUIN

A CHOICE OF TWENTIETH - CENTURY CLASSICS

The Age of Reason Jean-Paul Sartre

The first part of Sartre's classic trilogy, set in the volatile Paris summer of 1938, is in itself 'a dynamic, deeply disturbing novel' (Elizabeth Bowen) which tackles some of the major issues of our time.

Lady Chatterley's Lover D. H. Lawrence

The story of the relationship between Constance Chatterley and Mellors, her crippled husband's gamekeeper, is Lawrence's most controversial novel – and perhaps his most complete and beautiful study of mutual love.

The Sword of Honour Trilogy Evelyn Waugh

A glorious fusion of comedy, satire and farcical despair, *The Sword of Honour Trilogy – Men at Arms, Officers and Gentlemen* and *Unconditional Surrender* – is also Evelyn Waugh's bitter attack on a world where chivalry and nobility were betrayed on every hand.

Kolyma Tales Varlam Shalamov

'Shalamov's experience in the camps was longer and more bitter than my own, and I respectfully confess that to him and not me was it given to touch these depths of bestiality and despair toward which life in the camps dragged us all' – Aleksandr Solzhenitsyn

The Amen Corner James Baldwin

Sister Margaret presides over a thriving gospel-singing community in New York's Harlem. Proud and silent, for the last ten years she has successfully turned her heart to the Lord and her back on the past. But then her husband Luke unexpectedly reappears. He is a burnt-out jazz musician, a scandal of a man who none the less is seeking love and redemption.